# The Disabled Tyrant's Beloved Pet Fish

Canji Baojun De Zhangxin Yu Chong

# The Disabled Tyrant's Beloved Pet Fish

Canji Baojun De Zhangxin Yu Chong

WRITTEN BY
## Xue Shan Fei Hu

TRANSLATED BY
## Mimi, Yuka

ILLUSTRATED BY
## Ryoplica

BONUS ILLUSTRATION BY
## Kura

COVER ILLUSTRATION BY
## Changle

Seven Seas

*Seven Seas Entertainment*

The Disabled Tyrant's Beloved Pet Fish:
Canji Baojun De Zhangxin Yu Chong (Novel) Vol. 1

Published originally under the title of 残疾暴君的掌心鱼宠[穿书]
(Canji Baojun De Zhangxin Yu Chong [Chuan Shu])
Author©雪山肥狐 (Xue Shan Fei Hu)
US English edition rights under license granted by 北京晋江原创网络科技有限公司
(Beijing Jinjiang Original Network Technology Co., Ltd.)
US English edition copyright © 2024 Seven Seas Entertainment, Inc
Arranged through JS Agency Co., Ltd
All rights reserved

Cover artwork made by 長樂 (Changle)
Arranged and license through JS Agency Co., Ltd., Taiwan
Interior illustrations: Ryoplica
Bonus color illustration: Kura

Seven Seas press and purchase enquiries can be sent
to Marketing Manager Lauren Hill at press@gomanga.com.
Information regarding the distribution and purchase of digital editions is available
from Digital Manager CK Russell at digital@gomanga.com.

Seven Seas and the Seven Seas logo are trademarks of
Seven Seas Entertainment. All rights reserved.

Follow Seven Seas Entertainment online at
sevenseasentertainment.com.

TRANSLATION: Mimi, Yuka
ADAPTATION: Acro
COVER DESIGN: M. A. Lewife
INTERIOR DESIGN & LAYOUT: Clay Gardner
COPY EDITOR: Leighanna DeRouen
PROOFREADER: Jade Gardner, Kate Kishi
EDITOR: Harry Catlin
PREPRESS TECHNICIAN: Melanie Ujimori, Jules Valera
MANAGING EDITOR: Alyssa Scavetta
EDITOR-IN-CHIEF: Julie Davis
PUBLISHER: Lianne Sentar
VICE PRESIDENT: Adam Arnold
PRESIDENT: Jason DeAngelis

ISBN: 979-8-88843-261-7
Printed in Canada
First Printing: April 2024
10 9 8 7 6 5 4 3 2 1

# TABLE OF CONTENTS

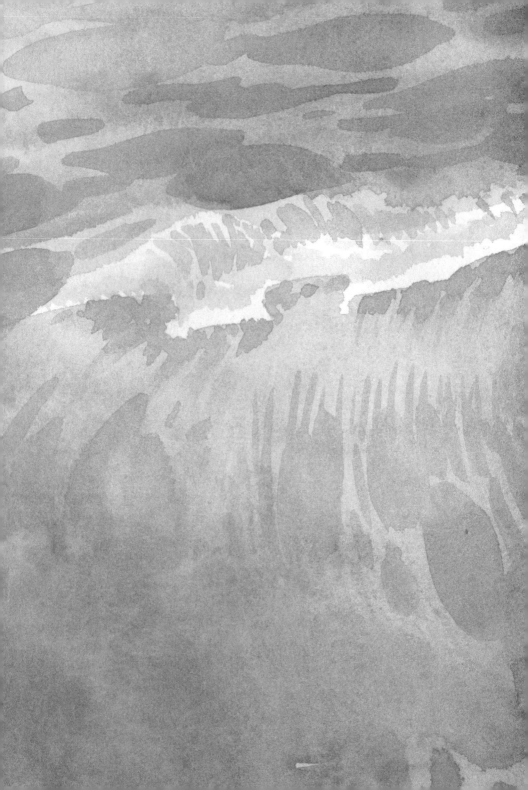

# The Fish in the Soup

L I YU FLOATED on the surface of the freezing cold water, utterly motionless.

He could vaguely hear the muffled noises of people moving about from somewhere above his head, but it was difficult to make out anything clearly. It was a little noisy, though, so he flipped over and opened his eyes. His entire body felt wet.

After the initial shock, his mind gradually began to clear. With dawning terror, he realized he was surrounded by water.

That was impossible. Hadn't he fallen asleep after staying up late reading webnovels? When did he fall into water?

More importantly, he couldn't even swim!

Li Yu flailed his limbs wildly. As he struggled, he felt something on his back move.

In the past, whenever he fell into water, the only fate that awaited him was sinking to the bottom. But to his surprise, this time, he found he didn't plunge straight down. Instead, he was staying afloat, as if an invisible hand were holding him up.

And the surreal, impossible-to-ignore rhythm behind him... What was that?

Li Yu peeked back at himself and startled. He'd always been proud of his long, slender legs—but now they were gone. In their place, a silvery, glistening fish tail appeared, swishing vigorously through the water, from side to side, up and down.

Well, that must be why he hadn't sunk.

Li Yu was speechless. What was going on? How did his legs turn into a fish tail? Was he...dreaming? Dreaming about turning into a mermaid?

As girly as it sounded, a mermaid was the only possibility Li Yu could think of where a human had a fish tail. No, he wasn't talking about the ugly-yet-cute dugong from the animal world—it was the ethereal, half-human, half-fish mermaid with long, flowing hair, a beautiful complexion, and a heavenly voice.

Everyone knew mermaids didn't exist in real life, so the only logical conclusion was that this was all a dream. And since it was a dream, he saw no problem with admiring his own beauty as a mermaid.

Li Yu glanced around, searching for a mirror, or anything with a reflection that could show his appearance. As he moved, he kept swishing his tail back and forth vigorously. It was actually kind of nice to have a tail to wave around as he pleased...

Unfortunately, this dream wasn't really going exactly as planned. There was no mirror in the water. Li Yu flipped over and, from force of habit, reached for his forehead to flick his bangs... Except this led to another problem. Li Yu quickly realized that no matter how hard he tried, he couldn't reach his own forehead. What...was wrong with his hand? Had his arm become shorter somehow?

Li Yu looked down in confusion. That was when he realized his hands, with their distinct joints, had been replaced with a pair of constantly paddling fish fins that were...well, the exact shape and texture of a fish's fins.

If his legs had turned into a tail and his hands had turned into fins, then...

Li Yu hurried to look at himself. Wait, wait. When did his stomach turn flat and slim, like...like you'd normally only see on a fish?

Not only did he have a long, slender belly, but he was also covered in silvery black fish scales.

Holy shit!

Li Yu took a deep breath, and a few bubbles actually came floating out. There, reflected on the bubbles' surface, he could see it clearly: his entire body had turned into a fish! Fish head, fish belly, fish scales... He was no mermaid, he was a proper carp![1]

Fear slammed into Li Yu so hard he froze, momentarily forgetting to swish his tail. Immediately, he began to sink.

Ahhhhh! He was going to drown! He was going to drown!

Just as he was about to crash into a black rock at the bottom, Li Yu used both his tail and fins to paddle frantically, managing to stop himself before he collided with the rock. Unfortunately, his tail wasn't so lucky.

Li Yu winced. That really hurt.

The fish tail wasn't just some decoration. He'd only hit it once, but Li Yu was in so much pain, he spat out a long trail of variously sized bubbles.

What was up with that? That hurt more than cutting into his leg with a knife... How could the pain be so real in a dream?

Li Yu's eyes widened slightly. No way! Was this...not actually a dream?! He had really turned into a fish—and not just any fish, but the most basic kind of carp?

Where exactly was he? How did he transform? There was no way he was turned into a carp just because his name was Li Yu, right? And most importantly—was there a way for him to change back?!

An entire herd of "WTF"s stampeded through Li Yu's mind. Before he had the chance to fully grasp the situation at hand, he heard someone speak.

---

1    Carp (鲤鱼) is pronounced liyu, the same as Li Yu's name.

A high, reedy voice rang out: "Xiaolinzi, we're still missing a live fish for the noble consort's[2] thousand carp soup!"

Another voice immediately responded, "Gao-gonggong,[3] this fish flipped over just now. The birthday banquet is an important matter, and this servant doesn't dare present it to the noble consort, so I was about to throw it away. Should I go get another..."

Li Yu was alarmed. He had been secretly celebrating the discovery that there were other people around him, but what was with all the "noble consort" and "gonggong" stuff? Did he transmigrate into a historical palace fish?

And what the hell was th-th-th-th-thousand carp soup??

Before he could figure it out, a light shone right into the water above Li Yu's head, splitting the dark in two. From that beam of light, a terrifyingly sized hand reached in! Li Yu almost passed out on the spot. This hand was way too big!

But after some careful consideration, he realized—of course it was. He was an ordinary little fish now. Obviously, a human hand would be colossal to a fish.

Every instinct inside Li Yu screamed that he was in danger. He couldn't help swimming all over the place. Without a moment's hesitation, the hand reached into the water, fingers outstretched, and clasped around Li Yu, who was bumbling around like a headless fly.

Now that he was a fish, Li Yu had no neck, so the hand covered most of his body. Li Yu yelped and struggled fiercely, his tail flapping violently. It was even more painful than hitting his tail just now. How could you grab a fish's chest and stomach?! It hurts!

But the person couldn't hear the fish's cries and just chuckled.

---

2   In Ancient China, the emperor's consorts were ranked. Noble consort (贵妃) was the second highest ranking after empress.
3   A polite way to address eunuchs.

"This fish is certainly lively. What do you mean it flipped over? Xiaolinzi, you didn't say that just so you could take this fish for yourself, did you?"

With all the ruckus around him, Li Yu's world was spinning, but he managed to catch a glimpse of the place he had been in before: a fish basket. Ensnared in the person's hand, he was lifted to meet their gaze.

Li Yu's fish eyes took in two people dressed like palace servants from ancient times. The one holding him was Gao-gonggong. He wasn't very tall, and he looked like a round, white dough ball. Next to him, Xiaolinzi looked a little like a flax stem.

Xiaolinzi hurried to kiss up to Gao-gonggong. He smiled and said, "Gao-gonggong, this servant would never dare take advantage with you overseeing everything. My eyes must've been playing tricks on me before—it's simply a misunderstanding. Since this fish is still alive, this servant will go and prepare the fish soup immediately..."

Li Yu, who was being held by Gao-gonggong, immediately became agitated. What? What?! Fish soup?!

"Thousand carp soup" might have been a complete mystery to him just a moment ago, but the concept of fish soup was definitely something he understood deep within his bones. He was a fish right now, and they were about to turn him into soup!

*Squeezing me is one thing, but turning me into soup is where I draw the line!*

Originally, Gao-gonggong had only visited the imperial kitchen to scold Xiaolinzi a little. Now that that was done, he was planning on leaving the fish for Xiaolinzi to deal with. Li Yu had lain quiet and still in Gao-gonggong's grip for some time, but now that soup was on the menu, he mustered all his strength to struggle free. The fish was slippery; in the split second that Gao-gonggong loosened his grip, Li Yu managed to get free and fling himself into the air.

Li Yu, still thrashing around as he flew through the air, leaving a long trail of water behind him, was terrified.

What was he going to do?! He was going to die! He was going to die! Was he still going to be made into soup if he died?!

Sob sob sob, he still hadn't figured out how exactly he had transmigrated into a fish in the first place. He didn't want to die! What if it stuck this time?!

Li Yu soared toward Xiaolinzi, completely out of control. Xiaolinzi reached out to grab him, but the fish was too slippery, and he couldn't get a firm hold of him. Li Yu was seconds away from splatting onto the floor when a long "meow" came from outside and a streak of snowy white fur bounded in. Just before Li Yu's tail hit the ground, the white figure caught him firmly in its mouth. Li Yu didn't even have time to celebrate his close call before his scales were standing straight up all over his body.

Holy crap. This shape, this sound—was this a fucking large white *cat*?! He'd managed to escape from the hand of a human, only to land directly in the mouth of a cat?!

How was he supposed to survive a cat's mouth?!

Li Yu had never been afraid of cats before, but now that he was a fish, he was scared to death. Cat's tongues were covered in spikes; if it licked him, would it take a chunk of him with it? He was completely paralyzed by fear. The cat was going to eat him! He'd be just a pile of fish bones! Being turned into soup wasn't sounding so bad anymore!

The large white cat that had appeared out of nowhere ignored Gao-gonggong and Xiaolinzi and sprinted out with the fish in its mouth. It all happened way too fast. It took Xiaolinzi a moment to react.

"Gao-gonggong, th-the cat has taken the fish!"

This sturdy, fat white cat looked a little familiar... With a start, Gao-gonggong realized who it was and kicked Xiaolinzi.

"What are you dawdling for?! Can't you see that's the noble consort's cat? Xiaolinzi, hurry and follow it! Don't let the precious Master Cat choke on a fish bone, otherwise the noble consort will never forgive us! After all, the cat of our master is also half a master..."

"Yessir!" There was a tinge of bitterness in Xiaolinzi's voice. You couldn't afford to offend even a cat master these days.

Li Yu was clamped between the white cat's jaws, and Xiaolinzi chased after them. Originally, he had hoped Gao-gonggong and Xiaolinzi would pull him out of the cat's mouth, since he was, after all, an ingredient for the fish soup. That made him more or less useful. But hearing what they were saying now, it turned out they didn't care about the fish at all and had no plans to save him. They were more concerned the cat might choke on his bones?

How fickle! These guys sure knew how to wait and see which way the wind blew!

As infuriated as Li Yu was, there was nothing he could do about his situation. All he could do was use every ounce of energy he had left to try and slip out of the cat's mouth.

But the white cat was not the ambitious yet incompetent Gao-gonggong, nor did it have the habit of eating and running at the same time. It held Li Yu delicately in its sharp teeth. Li Yu wiggled around, but its jaws didn't even loosen. On the contrary, they tightened around him.

Li Yu didn't dare move any more. He lay quietly in the cat's mouth, the tip of his tail quivering uncontrollably. This was way too scary. Li Yu couldn't help screaming, *"Help, someone save me!"*

It didn't matter who! Whoever it was, he'd do anything they wanted in his next life as long as they freed him from this cat's mouth!

But no human heard the fish, and neither did the cat.

The large white cat trotted on, unencumbered. Countless people saw it pass, but not a single one of them stopped it. It was exactly like Gao-gonggong had said: the cat of our master is also half a master.

While Li Yu's screams were going unheard, the white cat dug its claws into the floor tiles, skidding to an abrupt stop. Li Yu flinched as he felt the cat's teeth tighten around him.

The white cat's shining eyes glared at whatever was in front of it, a warning growl rumbling from its throat as if it were facing a formidable enemy. Detecting this shift in the white cat's attitude, Li Yu quickly looked to see why.

A young man with a tall, upright figure, draped in resplendent, luxurious robes, appeared in his field of vision. Like a god descending upon the earth, he blocked the great white cat's path.

# The Fish in the Cat's Mouth

LI YU WAS DELIGHTED. So there *was* someone who didn't kiss up to Master Cat!

If a cat's intellect could be compared to that of a two-year-old, then this large white cat was a spoiled child. No one had ever denied it anything. It had always gotten anything and everything it wanted. How dare this person presume to stand in the cat's way when it had a fish in its mouth! The white cat spun on the spot a couple of times, deciding it would demonstrate just who the real master was here. With the fish held firmly in its jaws, it pounced on the young man's shins.

THWACK!!!

The white cat pounced so hard that, even trapped inside its mouth, Li Yu could feel its muscles tense up. But its target didn't even flinch. Yowling, the cat bounced off the young man's firm legs. Li Yu felt its jaws loosen around him with a rush of elation, and rolled out of its mouth and onto the floor. Luckily, Master Cat wasn't very far from the ground, so the impact wasn't too harsh.

The white cat froze. Letting out a "meow," it readied itself to recapture its prey. Li Yu had only just managed to escape the cat's mouth—how could he let it snatch him up again? Desperate, he flapped his tail wildly and leaped into the air...only to leap so far that his tail slapped the cat right in the mouth with a resounding smack!

Li Yu was speechless. So was the white cat.

No way! All he wanted was to escape! How did he manage to accidentally slap the cat instead?! If fish could sweat, Li Yu would have been sweating bullets. As a fish that dared to slap a cat in the face, wasn't he asking to be eaten immediately?

With its fur standing on end from the sudden slap, the white cat raised one heavy paw and pressed it down on Li Yu's body. To the little fish, the cat's sharp claws might as well have been made of steel. Li Yu continued to struggle. *Ow, don't press on my head! It hurts, it hurts, it hurts!*

As a fish that dared make such a scene in front of a cat, it was a wonder he hadn't been swallowed already. Was his illustrious life really about to come to an end in a cat's mouth? Under the cat's paw, Li Yu's body hurt all over. He went limp from the pain, but unwilling to accept his fate, the tip of his tail still trembled.

It was then that he saw a pair of pitch-black, cloud-patterned boots slowly approaching. When the white cat caught him the second time, the youth in the luxurious robes noticed the commotion too.

Li Yu wasn't sure if he was imagining things now that his death was imminent, but he thought the young man had glanced over in his direction, just briefly.

But how was that possible? Neither Gao-gonggong nor Xiaolinzi deigned to spare him an extra glance. Just the briefest look at his opulent robes was enough for Li Yu to see that this youth was someone of status. Was it really possible someone like that would notice a little fish like him?

Li Yu's reserves of energy were almost depleted, and he could hardly lift his tail anymore. He laid there quietly, channeling the last of his strength into just taking breath after difficult breath.

Fish couldn't stay out of water for too long. Nor could they bear being bitten or clawed at by a cat. Poor Li Yu had managed to check both boxes.

With a swish of his robes, the youth crouched down. Li Yu watched his handsome face grow larger and larger as it drew closer and closer...

This face was handsome in the extreme, but as cold and beautiful as icy frost. The hair at his temples was so neatly arranged that it could have been cut by a knife, and he had eyes like cold stars, skin as pale as jade, red lips, and snowy white teeth. If Song Yu or Pan An[4] were still alive, he probably could have given them a run for their money.

Li Yu's vocabulary was quite limited when it came to compliments, so his brain very quickly ran out of words. Back when he was still human, he had been very confident in his own appearance and thought he was rather good-looking. Did the heavens know he was close to death and deliberately arrange for him to meet a more beautiful, ethereal man just so he could die with jealousy in his heart?

Whether you were a fish or a person, being close to death really brought out your honesty. Okay, fine. It was true, he was a little jealous.

Experiencing the phenomenon known as terminal lucidity, Li Yu's brain started to spiral into nonsense. Next to his ear, the large white cat meowed extremely unhappily—and all of a sudden, the pressure on his body disappeared, and the sharp claws that had held him down so tightly were gone!

Li Yu couldn't believe his luck. He tried moving his fish body. The pain was still intense, but...he really could move. What happened?

---

4    *Two of the four most handsome men of ancient China.*

Why would the white cat let him go for no reason? Li Yu looked up slightly and saw the cat rising up into the air! The youth in the opulent robes had picked it up roughly by the scruff of its neck.

Although this was a rather burly cat, it was obviously an expensive breed, with its pure snow-white fur and eyes like clear blue sapphires. Most people would at least pity this soft white fluffball and treat it tenderly, even if they didn't care for the noble consort. But this youth's expression was indifferent, with absolutely no regard for the cat at all.

Li Yu didn't understand what was happening. But what was most important here was that there was a sliver of hope for his life as a fish.

Thank the heavens, and thank this beautiful man!!

Having been dragged away from both the fish and the floor by force, the cat let out a furious, shrill yowl, its claws slashing wildly in the air. Perhaps this would have been enough to intimidate anyone else—but the tall young man was unimpressed.

Xiaolinzi, who had belatedly rushed to the scene, immediately fell to his knees upon witnessing all this. Li Yu couldn't help feeling shocked through his haze of pain. What was Xiaolinzi doing? There was no way he was kneeling because he wanted to save an ingredient, right?

Reality soon proved him wrong: Xiaolinzi was kneeling before the finely dressed youth. Kowtowing, he stumbled over his words. "Prince Jing, th-this is the noble consort's precious Master Cat, please have mercy…"

Li Yu was stunned. *This youth was a prince? Prince Jing?*

Hearing "noble consort" or "gonggong" had been one thing, but why did "Prince Jing" sound so familiar? But the thought only crossed his mind for a second. Li Yu had more important things to worry about; his fish life was still in danger.

The extravagantly dressed youth, Prince Jing, scoffed. His dark eyes swept across Xiaolinzi, but he made no move to release the cat.

The white cat had been yowling vigorously, but it seemed to have exhausted itself, its cries getting quieter and quieter. Prince Jing, exuding a commanding air, ignored it. Xiaolinzi remained kneeling on the ground, more and more sweat collecting on his forehead.

Li Yu was still lying on the ground. He was extremely grateful that this Prince Jing saved him from the large white feline bully, but could someone pay attention to him and put him back in the water? He was about to turn into a dead fish!

*What to do...* Li Yu wearily curled his tail, but no one could hear his thoughts.

"Your Highness, Your Highness... Wait for this old servant, I'm coming!" Another unfamiliar figure came running from the distance, hollering and yelling. It was an older eunuch. He came to a stop in between Prince Jing and Xiaolinzi, then took a huge gulp of air. This was Prince Jing's personal servant, Wang Xi.

"Wang Xi-gonggong, you're here!" Xiaolinzi's eyes brightened, thinking his savior had arrived. He hurried to bow as he said, "Please, please help me ask Prince Jing for forgiveness..."

"Forgiveness?" Wang Xi had finally caught his breath. He glanced carefully at Prince Jing's expression before shooting a fierce glare at Xiaolinzi. "This cat was the one that jumped at His Highness. Are you saying His Highness can't punish it?"

Xiaolinzi felt the world spin. He whimpered, "That's the noble consort's prized Master Cat..."

Wang Xi had already recognized the white cat, but as soon as Xiaolinzi brought it up, his rage shot through the roof. "It's just a cat! How dare it try to act like a master in front of His Highness!" he spat.

"W-Wang-gonggong..." Xiaolinzi had a sinking feeling he had misspoken and hurriedly slapped a hand over his mouth. While the noble consort's cat was essentially half a master compared to servants like him, it was nothing in front of descendants of the dragon!

Indignant with fury, Wang Xi spat on Xiaolinzi and cursed him out. Xiaolinzi trembled all over, head lowered, and was even more afraid to speak than before. After he was done with his tirade, Wang Xi turned back to look at Prince Jing. The prince's icy eyes moved slightly, and Wang Xi immediately understood.

Holding his hands up daintily, he turned around and loudly yelled, "This cat has offended His Highness, and His Highness is disciplining it a little. Why are you getting so worked up?"

Since the cat in Prince Jing's hand had failed in its attempts to intimidate him, its temper had more or less subsided. It seemed to realize it had hit a brick wall and settled on sticking out its pink tongue and mewling pitifully.

Most people's hearts would've softened at this point. But Prince Jing was not most people. He waited until the white cat stopped meowing and demurely lowered its head and then casually tossed it at Xiaolinzi.

Cats didn't fear heights. It soared from Prince Jing's hands and eagerly threw itself straight into Xiaolinzi's arms. Xiaolinzi barely had any meat on his bones, and he nearly coughed up blood when the cat collided with his chest.

Wang Xi coughed lightly. "His Highness is evidently in a good mood today, as he only reprimanded it a little. You'd better keep an eye on it, though. Should there be a next time... Hmph, I've lived to this age, and I have never seen anyone dare to anger His Highness twice."

"This servant understands!" Xiaolinzi kowtowed several times in a row.

Prince Jing waved a hand carelessly. Wang Xi spat at Xiaolinzi again and followed behind the prince.

Wait, they were going to leave? Just like that?

Li Yu had waited so eagerly for so long, but this Prince Jing, who had saved him and even spared him an extra glance, didn't seem to have any intention of helping him further.

Escaping from the jaws of the cat had already taken everything Li Yu had. Since no one could understand him, all he could do was muster up the last of his strength to curl his tail. His fish tail struck the floor lightly. Once, twice. His plea for help was so weak and pitiful, it was practically inaudible. It was enough to make anyone lose hope. But each time Li Yu wanted to give up, he pushed himself to keep going. Perhaps if he persevered, there would be a miracle.

There wasn't.

He kept swishing his tail until he couldn't lift it anymore. The boots that had once saved him didn't stop for him again. Li Yu gradually lost consciousness, his tail falling still. The air settled around him.

Prince Jing was already several meters away when he suddenly paused and turned around. A hint of confusion flashed across his cold eyes.

"Your Highness, wh-what's wrong?" Wang Xi also looked around, perplexed. Xiaolinzi had already run off with the white cat. There was no one else here.

Brow furrowed, Prince Jing made a shushing motion and walked back, Wang Xi following a few steps behind. The prince's attention was focused on the ground below his feet—he seemed to be looking for something. He soon arrived back at the spot where he had stopped before.

Suddenly, he paused and crouched down.

"Your Highness, please don't trouble yourself. What do you need? Let this servant do it instead!" Wang Xi clamored to stop Prince Jing, but the prince took no notice. He stubbornly pulled Wang Xi aside and picked something up from the ground with his own hands...

A palm-sized fish, to be exact. A fish that had been clamped between the jaws of a cat and was now covered with wounds.

"Your Highness, this..." Wang Xi trailed off uncertainly. *Isn't this a very ordinary carp? Why did Your Highness come back for this fish?*

This was the first time he'd ever been unsure he could understand His Highness.

Prince Jing hesitated for a moment. He reached out and touched the limp fish tail with his finger. The tail flopped against the floor lightly, weakly. Prince Jing's expression darkened. But the way he held the fish was exceedingly gentle.

"Your Highness! Your Highness, please let me!" Wang Xi spread his arms.

Prince Jing shook his head, holding the fish himself, and headed straight for the nearest garden. A dazed and uncomfortable Li Yu felt a long-awaited warmth. He could have sworn it was blankets and a pillow.

Sob sob sob, life as a fish was much too hard. But if he was going to die and turn back into a human, perhaps all this suffering would be worth it.

Li Yu was already celebrating on the inside when he heard the sound of the system: *‹Congratulations, user, the first part of the 'Moe Pet System' main quest, 'Tyrant's Priceless Pet Fish—First Meeting with the Tyrant,' has been completed.›*

# Priceless Pet Fish

FOR A MOMENT, Li Yu thought he was imagining things. But some time had passed, and it didn't seem like he was turning back into a human. Not only did he not change, some random "system" had popped up. It seemed to be called... Moe Pet System?

No sooner than he'd thought that, two rows of large golden words appeared before his eyes.

The system that had spoken up moments ago chimed in again, without his prompting: *<User, please select main quest or side quest.>*

Li Yu blinked. It seemed he had accidentally entered a system.

The system called him "user," so this was his personal golden finger, a cheat code for his transmigration. At least this meant his transformation into a fish hadn't been for nothing. Although he was still a fish and hadn't transformed back into a human, as long as he had this golden finger, perhaps he could find a way to get back to normal if he followed the system's instructions?

The previous prompt had said he had completed the first step of the main quest...

Out of habit, Li Yu tried to tap the words "main quest" as he would on a touch screen, but what was a routine action for a human was quite a challenge for a fish. His fins were too short to reach. He flapped his fins rather desperately, thinking, if only he could tap it...

when suddenly, the main quest flashed of its own accord, expanding into several lines of text.

*Got it. I don't need to touch anything with this system. I can control it using my thoughts.*

All the text under the main quest was dark, except for the very top line, which was lit up. Each line probably corresponded to a different main quest. With the desperate desire to turn back into a human thrumming through his veins, Li Yu skimmed through each main quest. They were all about fish. There was nothing about humans.

Other than "Tyrant's Priceless Pet Fish," which he had seen already, there was also "Tyrant's Pet Fish for Revitalizing the Family," "Postpartum Care for Fish," etc. It got more and more ridiculous as he read on. But the only one he could access was the topmost one, which glowed: "Tyrant's Priceless Pet Fish."

Li Yu had no other choice but to tap on it, albeit reluctantly. The progress bar and description for "Tyrant's Priceless Pet Fish" immediately popped up.

First, he looked through the description. It was super simple. All he needed to do was become the tyrant's beloved pet fish. Although it was a little clickbaity, it at least matched the name of the system: Moe Pet System.

Wait, wasn't he forgetting something? This "tyrant" kept coming up, but he still had no idea who that was supposed to be.

The system seemed to sense his confusion, and a transparent window popped out, surrounded by swirling rose petals. The window displayed Prince Jing's frustratingly handsome face.

The tyrant was Prince Jing.

Li Yu cracked a smile. So he'd completed "First Meeting with the Tyrant" when he encountered Prince Jing? Sure, this Prince Jing looked pretty cold and didn't speak much, but why did the system have to call him a tyrant?

The system had no response this time. Prince Jing's handsome face remained unchanged in the pop-up.

D-did this mean he had to continue tapping?

After some pondering, he poked Prince Jing's face with his tail. The system popped up with another prompt. The fluttering rose petals automatically reconfigured into a blurb about Prince Jing. He was the fifth son of the emperor of Great Chu, Mu Tianchi, and was born with a speech impediment. He couldn't talk.

Prince Jing was...Mu...Tian...Chi???

Li Yu felt like he had been struck by lightning. No wonder Prince Jing's name seemed so familiar. No wonder Prince Jing was way too quiet compared to Wang Xi or Xiaolinzi. Li Yu had been so preoccupied with running for his life that he didn't realize it at the time, but now he finally knew which book he had fallen into!

He knew the name Mu Tianchi very well indeed. He was the male lead from a webnovel Li Yu had stayed up all night to read when he was bored: *The Tyrant and His Delicate Concubine*. Mu Tianchi was a cold, ruthless tyrant who wouldn't hesitate to slaughter someone's entire family if he was displeased. But because he was mute, he still inspired a little pity.

Li Yu had transmigrated into a novel, with a system!

Never mind that this was a book about a tyrant, why did he transmigrate into a fish? Let's not worry about tyrants for now; why did he get paired up with the "Moe Pet System," and why were all his quests about fish...?

The system cut in with a voice message, speaking slowly. ‹*You've already transmigrated, so you might as well accept your fate. The purpose of your existence is to help improve the tyrannical male lead's personality. Apparently, having a pet can help cultivate one's tender, caring side.>*

Li Yu was dumbfounded. He knew this system had ulterior motives! He didn't want to do these weird tasks at all! Was the system going to force him to do them even if he didn't want to?

The system answered immediately: *<The Moe Pet System will not force its user, but if the user does not complete the quests, then you will never turn back into a human.>*

*<What?! I can't go back even if I die?>*

*<You can't.>* The system's voice held a note of finality. *<Failing to regain human form means retaining the life span of a fish. In the end, a fish will turn into fish bones and fish ash.>*

*<...What if I choose not to do these quests at all?>* asked Li Yu.

*<You will turn into fish bones and fish ash. Immediately.>*

Li Yu wanted to curse. Wasn't this the definition of forcing him?

The system piped up again to emphasize, *<The Moe Pet System will not force its user...>*

*<Can you please not repeat yourself!>*

Li Yu didn't want to turn into fish bones or fish ash, but he had no interest in turning the tyrant's personality around either. All he wanted to know was how he could become human again.

The system spoke: *<Once the main quest has progressed to a certain point, one of the steps will involve becoming human again.>*

*<That's more like it... Okay, it's just a main quest. Fine, I'll do it.>*

He was acting nonchalant, but Li Yu was hyperaware that he could not risk playing around with his own life. The Moe Pet System had one thing right: he had already transmigrated. He'd already seen for himself that the system was his golden finger and could appear in his consciousness, so he had to believe it.

Now that he'd resolved to do the quests, Li Yu started to calm down. He took a good look at his current quest, "Priceless Pet Fish." There were a number of steps to this quest. The first step, "First Meeting with the Tyrant," was already completed. The second step, "Interact with the Tyrant," was glowing. There was nothing else beyond that. It looked like he'd have to complete step two before he unlocked any more instructions for the next step.

...What a stingy system. It couldn't even be bothered to give him a more detailed prompt. "Interact with the Tyrant"? Interact how?

Li Yu was a little frustrated. What connection did the two of them even have? Prince Jing was a prince; Li Yu was merely a fish from the imperial kitchen. Did he have to turn himself into fish soup or braised fish so that Prince Jing could eat him?

The system chimed in: *<Use your brain. Think harder.>*

*What the fuck, system?* Why did it feel like it was taunting him?!

Li Yu couldn't figure anything out from the main quest. Then an idea came to mind—he went to check on the side quests.

Side quests were optional, and anyone who'd ever played a game knew that side quests usually weren't too hard and could come with generous rewards. The main quest was way too weird, but maybe Li Yu could pull some clues from the side quest.

His investigation proved to be fruitless, however, when he found the side quests were all grayed out, meaning it wasn't time for them yet. For example, one of the side quests was "Turn into a Koi." That one looked quite nice. If he had to be a fish for the time being, a koi fish would at least be better than the kind of carp that was a regular feature on the menu, right?

Even an idiot knew koi fish were lucky. Why wasn't this task available?

*‹Side quests have prerequisites,›* the system informed him. *‹You can only accept the quest once the prerequisites have been met.›*

*‹What prerequisites does the koi quest have?›*

The system replied, *‹Complete the main quest—'Priceless Pet Fish.'›*

*‹Fuck! I can't skip being a pet fish?!›*

*‹That's right.›*

Li Yu was clearly a man, but now he had to be another man's pet fish. And not just any man, a man with a bad temper who couldn't talk. Wasn't this way too hard? Did completing this quest even come with rewards? If the rewards weren't all that great, what was even the point?

Li Yu asked, *‹What kind of rewards do I get for completing 'Priceless Pet Fish'? There will be rewards, right?›*

*‹Yes,›* the system said. *‹You've already completed the first step, so the strength of your fish tail has increased. Please use it carefully. The reward for completing the second step is an inventory that you can take around with you. The rest of the rewards will be revealed as you continue to unlock new tasks.›*

Li Yu's eyes lit up. He didn't know how useful a stronger tail would be, but an inventory would be great! He could put stuff in it. Being a fish was so inconvenient. He needed to get over his embarrassment fast so he could complete these tasks!

While he was wrapped up in his thoughts, the system alerted him he was about to exit.

...

Li Yu woke up. As he opened his fish eyes, he came to the realization that he was lying in a blue and white porcelain tank, filled with water.

So his conversation with the system had all happened inside his own head. There was no way to tell what had been going on from the outside. Back in reality, he had passed out from everything he'd gone through at the claws of the white cat, and from being out of the water for too long. He'd already been unconscious for two hours.

Pain crashed down on his body in waves. He had yet to fully recover from his cat-induced injuries. A little dazed, Li Yu looked around at his surroundings.

Before he'd lost consciousness, he remembered thumping his tail on the ground until it nearly broke, yet no one had come to his rescue. Shouldn't he still be lying on the floor tiles right now? How did this change of scenery happen?

It didn't matter. He was injured, and he needed to rest, recover, and figure out where he was. He also had to find Prince Jing as soon as possible so he could complete this task. With that figured out, Li Yu set about carefully examining the world inside the tank.

This blue and white porcelain tank was a massive upgrade from the dark fish basket he found himself in when he first transmigrated. It didn't have the oily, smoky smell of the imperial kitchen, and it was bright and well ventilated, although the top of the tank was a bit on the tall side. When he looked up, he could only see a portion of the ceiling. Although the opening was small, he could see he was in a room with carved beams and painted rafters. This was clearly a place of wealth.

The water in the tank was very clear. Aside from a few aquatic plants swaying gently in the ripples, he was the tank's only occupant. Snow white stones lay beneath him. Li Yu observed the stones for a while. Each one was round, with any harsh edges smoothed away. When he lay on them, it felt rather comfortable. It made for a good place to heal from his injuries.

Li Yu wanted to rip off a piece of the plant, but after several minutes of struggle, he knew he could forget about using his fins as hands to tear it off—he could barely even use them to grab hold of the plant. No matter how hard he tried, he just couldn't get it to work.

He remembered what the system had said. It had boosted his tail's power. Perhaps he could try that? Li Yu swished his tail at the plant, not hoping for much.

*Ow! Ow ow ow!!*

That simple action tore at his injury. Li Yu grimaced in pain, regretting his impulsiveness slightly.

His tail didn't seem to have made any difference... But just as Li Yu was thinking the system had a habit of lying to fish, a glossy, green leaf drifted down gently and landed on top of his head.

Li Yu glanced at his tail excitedly. He pulled the leaf down with his mouth and used it to cover up most of his body, then he lay back down on his bed of white rocks. After all, the best way to heal from an injury was by lying down with a blanket. He'd rest some and recover his energy. Once he felt a little better, he'd look for Prince Jing.

He slept for a while before he was woken by a soft creaking sound. It was the sound of a door opening, he realized—someone had entered the room he was in. It must be the person who'd saved him and put him in this tank.

This tank contained water, plants, and even smooth stones—there was no way it wasn't supposed to be a fish tank. If someone had gone to the trouble of arranging all this, it must mean they wanted to keep him, not eat him.

Who could this person be?

The footsteps came closer, unhurried. With an unexpected feeling of anticipation, Li Yu raised his head a little and waited. Before long, a matchlessly handsome face appeared above the tank.

Oh my god, wasn't...wasn't that the target of his quests? Prince Jing? Mu Tianchi? Did that mean...Prince Jing was the one who saved him?

Li Yu was both surprised and delighted. This was too easy! To be honest, he still rejected the thought of being someone's pet fish—but now that he knew his savior was the target of his quests, he could suck it up!

So, what exactly should a good pet fish do...? Please his owner and make him happy, of course!

Li Yu tossed his leaf-covered head about and eagerly blew a little bubble toward Prince Jing.

*I'm such a cute fish! Please don't cut my head off!*

# Fish-Flavored
# Shredded Pork

L I YU WAS KEEN TO WIN Prince Jing over, and for good reason.

Having read the original book, Li Yu knew that, despite Mu Tianchi's tyrannical character archetype, he didn't start off as an oppressive dictator who killed people without batting an eye.

When Mu Tianchi was still just Prince Jing, he was at most a little cold and indifferent. His muteness meant he had long since lost the right to the throne. But in the end, it was he, the most unlikely heir, who had climbed, step by step, up to the throne. With a cold, ruthless decisiveness, he had bathed both his court and back palace with blood, completing his transformation from a silent, cold prince to a cruel tyrant whom the world feared.

This change didn't happen overnight; Mu Tianchi underwent a huge emotional journey before he reached his full tyrannical potential, but it would be impossible to explain the trials and tribulations he experienced in just a few sentences. In any case, since Mu Tianchi was still a prince right now, that meant his personality hadn't changed yet. In other words, this tyrant hadn't reached the point where he'd chop off someone's head as soon as look at them. That much was clear just from the fact that Mu Tianchi had not called for the white cat's execution when he first caught it.

Prince Jing may have punished the white cat for running into him, giving off a cold and heartless impression all the while, but he did let the cat go afterward. Not a single drop of cat blood was spilled. If this had happened after his ascension to the throne, that cat wouldn't have stood a chance.

But right now, Prince Jing's mindset was simple: "an eye for an eye," not "an eye for your whole family." Plus, Prince Jing had saved a fish like Li Yu. Wasn't that an example in and of itself?

So it wasn't hard to understand why the system wanted him to complete these tasks and improve the tyrant's personality. Better to start now, while Mu Tianchi was still Prince Jing and had yet to evolve into a true tyrant.

Li Yu deliberately adopted a humbler demeanor for the purpose of this task. If he was going to be Prince Jing's pet fish, he had to try to get into his owner's good graces.

But it was a tall order to ask Prince Jing to recognize devotion just from the movements of a fish. Li Yu blew bubbles until his mouth was sore. Prince Jing's eyes flicked over, but his gaze remained impassive, like an ice-capped mountain that was impossible to melt.

Li Yu very quickly exhausted himself. After everything he did to try to get into the prince's good graces, he couldn't even get him to crack the ghost of a smile. Wang Xi-gonggong, however, snorted and chuckled.

"Look, Your Highness, the fish you saved has come back to life. It's even sneezing." Wang Xi grinned widely from behind Prince Jing, cheerily watching the little carp blow bubbles.

How intriguing. Wang Xi didn't think the fish would survive, after seeing how limp and motionless it had been earlier. But in only a short amount of time, it was brimming with energy again.

*Hello? Can't you get it right? I'm not sneezing, I'm saying hi!*
Li Yu blew an annoyed bubble at Wang Xi. Oh well, it was pointless.
It wasn't like he could make humans understand fish. Swishing his
tail hurt too much, so he could only continue blowing bubbles.

But this only served to deepen Wang Xi's misunderstanding.
Concerned about the fish's excessive amount of bubble blowing, he
asked Prince Jing carefully, "Your Highness, is the fish sick? Why
does it keep sneezing?"

*You're the one sneezing! Your whole family's sneezing!*
Before Prince Jing could react, poor misunderstood Li Yu blew
a long string of angry bubbles. Wang Xi immediately grew nervous.
"Your Highness, is this fish choking on water?"

Prince Jing listened silently. He might not be able to speak, but
he wasn't deaf or blind. His mind was as sharp as a knife. How could
a fish sneeze or choke on water? Wang Xi was clearly just trying to
coax a smile out of him.

That being said, this fish... It was a little *too* lively.

Mu Tianchi had never seen a fish this animated before. As he
gazed down at the fish that kept blowing bubbles in the porcelain
tank and the leaf blanketed over its body, his lips involuntarily
twitched upwards into a smile.

"Master! Prince Jing, look over here! Over here!" Lying under
the blanket made moving a little cumbersome. Li Yu hesitated for a
brief moment before abandoning the leaf blanket he had acquired
not long ago to swim happily toward Prince Jing.

The second task in the main quest was to interact with the tyrant.
Despite all the bubbles he'd blown just now, no prompts had popped
up, so the system must not count that as "interaction."

This fish-scamming system never told him what constituted
"interacting." Li Yu had to just keep throwing things at the wall and

hope one of them would stick. He'd barely come face-to-face with Prince Jing before now, so he really had to take advantage of this opportunity and complete the second task in one go.

It was strange, though. Prince Jing was born mute and couldn't talk; Li Yu was a fish, and no one could understand him, effectively making him mute as well. In a way, he and Prince Jing had the same struggle. But since neither of them could speak, there was no way for them to communicate with each other. How were they supposed to interact?

Li Yu went through his mental catalog of tricks. As his eyes landed on the underwater plant, the cursed seaweed dance came to mind... Maybe he should do a bit of the seaweed dance for Prince Jing. The more he thought about it, the more he warmed up to the idea. If he couldn't find a chance to interact with the prince, he'd just have to create one himself.

But with his injuries this severe, he couldn't just sway his tail however he liked. He'd just have to keep his lower half still and focus on moving his upper half, which had seen the least amount of harm.

Imagining himself as a cute underwater plant, Li Yu just went for it, wriggling the top half of his body up and down in an exaggerated wave.

Mu Tianchi and Wang Xi were at a loss for words.

Prince Jing stared at the little carp. He was starting to think this fish was a little abnormal...but Prince Jing's face didn't betray any of his thoughts. He wasn't someone who let his emotions show easily, no matter how surprised he was.

Wang Xi, who was standing off to the side, felt like his eyes were playing tricks on him. He swallowed hard and said, "Your Highness, did this fish...pull a muscle?"

Wang Xi's first thought was that the fish, with all its swaying, was trying to please Prince Jing, but Wang-gonggong had only ever heard of cats and dogs who were intelligent enough to connect with humans. Could fish be that clever too?

Logically, they couldn't; therefore, Wang-gonggong was more inclined to believe the fish must have pulled a muscle.

Li Yu gaped.

*You've pulled a muscle! Your whole family has pulled a muscle!*

Wang Xi was such a mood killer. Li Yu didn't want to dance anymore.

The system didn't say a thing, even though Li Yu had danced for so long. He stopped dancing out of spite and drifted down to rest on the bed of white rocks. Swimming was the first ability he'd unlocked after his transmigration. Now that he could float and sink as he wished, he felt incredibly comfortable.

Prince Jing's eyes never left Li Yu. Seeing that the fish had stopped moving, he seemed to be contemplating something.

Wang Xi immediately latched on to a new topic of conversation. "Your Highness, why did the fish stop moving?"

Li Yu bristled. It was so hard being a pet! Why was there always a hater?!

Exercising great restraint, Li Yu turned around. As much as he wanted to sulk, he had a task to complete.

*‹Hey, system. What counts as 'interacting'?›* Li Yu tried to call out to the system. If the seaweed dance wasn't enough, this was going to be way too hard!

Perhaps the system was getting impatient too, because it decided to offer him a hint. *‹Interacting involves a back-and-forth.›*

Li Yu finally understood why, despite all his efforts, he wasn't able to complete step two. This whole time, he was the only one moving vigorously, while Prince Jing remained unmoved. That couldn't be considered a "back-and-forth" at all. But how could he get Prince Jing to reciprocate?

Li Yu sank deep into his thoughts. Not even the seaweed dance was enough to sway his tyrant master. Sob sob sob, it was much too hard being a fish.

While Li Yu was preoccupied with his dilemma, Wang Xi stared at the fish, pondering.

Wang Xi had served Prince Jing for many years, so he knew well that His Highness's countenance was cold, and his heart colder. It was rare for him to care about anything or anyone. But Prince Jing had not only found and saved this little carp, he'd even brought it here with his own two hands. So, what did this unusual act of saving the fish mean?

It meant the fish had caught His Highness's interest; His Highness had taken a liking to this fish. Prince Jing had even ordered him to prepare the fish tank to put the fish into. Didn't all these signs point to him wanting to keep it as a pet?!

Wang Xi was so happy he couldn't help smiling. Who cared what kind of pet he wanted to keep? There was finally a hint of warmth in this ice-cold prince.

Wang Xi made a few subtle comments but didn't dare to say anything too pointed. He was afraid that if he overstepped, Prince Jing's temper would flare up and he wouldn't want the fish anymore. That was why Wang Xi kept beating around the bush.

He noticed the prince's eyes hadn't left the little carp, steadily following its movements. While Prince Jing didn't react in any obvious way when the little carp wriggled around, he also didn't immediately turn around and leave. When the little carp stopped swimming, the prince's expression remained inscrutable, but the corner of his mouth that had lifted just a little fell back down. He was slightly unhappy.

Wang Xi fretted on the inside as he watched the scene unfolding before him. *This isn't how you take care of a fish! You can't just look!*

Wang Xi guessed that Prince Jing had never kept a fish before, nor any other kind of pet, and was probably at a bit of a loss. He suggested, "Your Highness...this fish...might it be hungry?"

Mu Tianchi shot a fleeting glance at him.

Correctly interpreting his silence as a command for him to continue, Wang Xi explained with a smile, "Humans lose energy when they're hungry. This lowly servant is thinking perhaps fish are the same. Perhaps it'll have more strength when it's full. I already prepared some fish feed. Shall I feed some to it?"

Mu Tianchi mulled it over before giving a small nod.

Wang Xi bowed, then quickly produced two bamboo boxes from his sleeves. One was filled with red fish feed, the other with green fish feed. Each piece was the size of a grain of rice.

As Prince Jing watched quietly, Wang Xi sprinkled a few pieces into the porcelain tank. Li Yu, who had been deeply engrossed in his thoughts, suddenly smelled food. His stomach immediately growled, reminding him that he hadn't had anything to eat in all the time he'd spent as a fish.

Was there delicious food here?

Li Yu glanced around at his surroundings, his attention soon catching on the flecks of red and green floating in the water. Whatever it was, it smelled amazing, somehow even more tantalizing than the delicacies he had eaten as a human.

He couldn't complete his quests on an empty stomach, Li Yu reasoned, and immediately dashed toward the source of the scent, circling one of the red pieces. This seemed to be...fish food.

He'd heard fish food was made from either flour or bugs. He didn't know which kind this was, but it smelled so good, he really wanted to eat it. Li Yu cursed himself for acclimating to fish tastes so quickly, but he was practically drooling. In the end, his hunger triumphed over his dignity.

Uh...how exactly did fish eat, again?

Li Yu approached cautiously, batting at the fish feed lightly with his fin. Suddenly, he felt an unyielding gaze on him. Li Yu looked up directly into Prince Jing's ink-black eyes staring down at him without blinking.

Li Yu froze.

He had originally wanted to use his fin to "hold" the fish feed and eat like a civilized person. But if Prince Jing noticed something was off...

Prince Jing was mute, sure, but his mind was still sharp as a dagger!

Li Yu hurriedly chomped down on the fish feed, then dove under the safety of his leaf, too embarrassed to eat like a fish in front of Prince Jing. Better to hide somewhere while he ate, then get back to working on his quest.

Li Yu gulped down a few bites, the fragrant food melting in his mouth. Thank god, it was made from flour and not bugs! But...why did it smell like fish-flavored shredded pork?[5]

...Who cared as long as he had food! Fish-flavored shredded pork was good, so what was there to complain about? He couldn't eat human food anymore, so this was actually a balm to his soul. Li Yu scarfed down the entire piece of red fish food, but his stomach was still rumbling. He decided to sneak out and grab a few more pieces.

---

5   Fish-flavored shredded pork (鱼香肉丝) is a famous Sichuan dish.

Hyperaware that Prince Jing was scrutinizing his every move, and petrified that he might notice something unusual, Li Yu made sure to take only one piece per excursion. He would seize one, take it away, and only sneak out for another once he finished the one he already had.

As he ate, he soon realized the red pieces tasted much better than the green pieces. The green pieces were a little bland.

Prince Jing watched, his gaze deep, as the little carp ate. For just a moment, he thought the way the little carp batted at the fish food looked almost human. But it happened so quickly, he couldn't be sure.

# The Fish Was Petted

**P**RINCE JING WAS STILL watching the fish intently when Wang Xi handed him both boxes of fish food. Wang Xi's eyes were filled with anticipation.

Having served Prince Jing for many years, Wang Xi knew exactly what his master wanted without the prince having to say a single word. Smiling, he said sincerely, "Your Highness, this old servant has a few things to take care of, but the fish still seems to be hungry. Could you help me feed the fish?"

Mu Tianchi paused for a second, surprised.

Wang Xi pushed the boxes toward him and continued very seriously, "There are two kinds of feed. The red one tastes like fish-flavored shredded pork, and the green one is mushroom and greens. This servant thinks the little carp seems to prefer the red one."

Mu Tianchi couldn't help but agree. The little carp did seem to have a little more life when it ate the red feed.

Mu Tianchi silently accepted the red-feed box. Wang Xi smiled until his eyes looked like two crescent moons. After reminding Prince Jing not to overfeed the fish, he made up some excuse and left the two of them alone.

Mu Tianchi hesitated, holding the box of fish feed. After all, he was treading in unfamiliar waters here. Down below, Li Yu waited and waited, but when it didn't seem like Wang Xi was going to feed him anymore, the hungry little carp swam up to the water's surface, waiting expectantly.

Li Yu and Prince Jing, fish and human, stared into each other's eyes.

Li Yu was startled—he hadn't expected to see Prince Jing. Then he remembered he was merely a fish. It didn't matter how long he stared at Prince Jing; the prince probably wouldn't notice.

What...was Prince Jing about to do?

Li Yu couldn't figure it out. The tall, imposing youth couldn't speak, always keeping his thoughts hidden behind those dark, fathomless eyes.

Mu Tianchi stood in front of the tank for a full ten minutes before he threw a handful of red pellets into the water with a little too much force, nearly pelting Li Yu with the torrential downpour of fish food. Li Yu gaped at Prince Jing in shock. He almost couldn't believe it.

By the time he realized what had happened, his body had already instinctively launched itself at the fish food Prince Jing had tossed in. Turning in a beautiful curve in the water, the little carp carefully held the food in his mouth. In his chest, his heart went *pit-a-pat*.

Not only had the tyrant saved him—he had even personally fed him!!

As soon as he swallowed the fish food, the system, which had been silent up until now, suddenly came to life. *<Congratulations, user. You have completed the second part of the Moe Pet System main quest: 'Tyrant's Priceless Pet Fish—Interact with the Tyrant.' Congratulations! You will now receive the corresponding reward!>*

Li Yu could have burst into tears. So this was what "interacting" meant!

In one big gulp, he devoured the last of the food that Prince Jing had tossed in. Belly full and fit to bursting, Li Yu drifted down to lie on the bed of snowy white rocks to take a quick nap. Anyone, human or fish, would feel sleepy after eating a full meal.

Now that the second task was taken care of, Li Yu didn't think it would be too late if he waited to collect his reward and took a little nap first. Thankfully, although the experience had been frightening, nothing dangerous had happened.

Li Yu couldn't fall asleep wherever he wanted when he had been human, but he had no such problem now. As a fish, he could sleep however he wanted, upright or lying down. Very soon, Li Yu fell into the embrace of a dream.

Recalling what Wang Xi had said, Prince Jing glanced at the little carp, then tapped on the tank with two fingers. Li Yu, who had been teetering on the precipice of sleep, was jolted awake by the sound.

*What is it? I want to sleep. Some people still have injuries to recover from...*

If it hadn't been for the quests, Li Yu wouldn't want to have anything to do with the tyrant at all.

Having noticed that the fish was still lying limply on the rock, Prince Jing extended a hand. Li Yu, who was still attempting to fall back asleep, felt the water move.

*What's happening??*

Li Yu was immediately wide awake, his terror chasing away any notions of sleep. As soon as he opened his eyes, he saw Prince Jing's hand reaching into the tank.

Li Yu flinched, fighting the urge to swish his tail. He was still injured, for one thing, so moving his tail hurt. And secondly, daring to swish his tail in Prince Jing's face would only mean one thing: a dead fish! Li Yu felt like his heart was strapped into a roller coaster—but, to his surprise, Prince Jing did not immediately grab him. Instead, he nudged him lightly off the bed of snowy white rock.

Did Prince Jing not want him to go to sleep?

Li Yu was utterly confused as Prince Jing's finger pushed him forward. Prodded by the prince's finger, Li Yu swam around nearly the entirety of the tank. He didn't know what Prince Jing wanted. Fear slowly crept over his heart. But after a while, he realized the prince seemed perfectly content with nudging him around and didn't seem to want to do anything else. Li Yu's pulse gradually calmed down. Occasionally, he'd give a few lazy swipes of his fins as a show of cooperation. Inevitably, his soft, tender fin would brush against Prince Jing's finger.

Mu Tianchi froze. His stare drilled holes into the insolent fish, who was completely unaware of what it had just done. If a person had dared to be so impudent, Prince Jing would have them torn limb from limb without question.

But this was a fish, not a person. There was no need to be so harsh.

Prince Jing's defenses were lowered, and he smirked, the corner of his lips lifting mischievously.

Li Yu was splashing around in the water with his fins when the tip of his tail felt hot. Immediately, he felt an unnerving sensation emanating from back there. He turned his head to look. The tyrant's expression was impassive as always, but his hand, the same hand that would kill without hesitation...what was it doing?!

*Ow, d-don't curl my tail around your finger! My private area is right there! It tickles! Don't just touch wherever you want... Hey!!*

The little carp's tail trembled violently. Help! He didn't think the tyrant would pet a fish!

With Prince Jing pushing him along, Li Yu made several laps around the tank and steadily felt more and more energetic. At last, the prince finally stopped and let him go. Li Yu swam by himself for a while and soon realized his stomach no longer felt bloated.

Was Prince Jing forcing him to swim to give him a chance to digest the enormous meal he had just eaten? *There's no way, right?* he thought, amused. He was pretty sure Prince Jing wasn't the kind of person who'd look out for a little animal. Li Yu added this incident to his collection of other unsolved mysteries, where it joined Prince Jing in saving his injured and unconscious self.

Prince Jing raised his eyebrows slightly as he realized his sleeve had gotten wet.

Li Yu thought Prince Jing would change immediately. After all, he was a prince, accustomed to a life of luxuries and riches. There was no way he'd allow himself to wear dirtied clothes, even if it was just a wet sleeve.

Prince Jing left shortly after, just as Li Yu expected. Li Yu could no longer see his face peering at him from above the tank.

But, oddly enough, Li Yu didn't hear the sound of a door opening and closing. What kind of master would change by himself? Servants were always at their beck and call to help with things like that. Although Prince Jing couldn't speak, he could still open the door and order for someone outside to wait on him.

Li Yu waited and waited, but he didn't hear anything. After the nap he'd taken, his tail didn't throb as much, and he felt a lot better. It seemed like fish recovered faster than humans. Either that, or it was because he had the system. Li Yu decided to try using his tail again.

Unless Prince Jing walked over himself, it was practically impossible to see the prince from Li Yu's position inside the fish tank. Li Yu wanted to confirm that the prince wasn't in the room anymore before collecting his reward from the Moe Pet System, just in case the prince wanted to play with him again, only to find an unconscious fish.

Li Yu tested his tail, swishing it back and forth a few times. It really didn't hurt anymore. He summoned every bit of power he had and, with a swoosh, managed to launch himself high into the air. Before his leap of faith, Li Yu had already mentally prepared himself to take a good look at the world outside of his tank. The room was just as he imagined: ornate and magnificent, befitting a prince.

*There's Prince Jing! He's still in the room!*

The moment he leapt into the air, he spotted Prince Jing's figure, standing only a few meters away. His black robes had yet to be fastened completely, so Li Yu had an unobstructed view of the smooth lines of his muscles. Dark eyes gazed toward the little carp, shocked and stunned.

For a moment, man and fish stared at each other.

...Oh no! How did he manage to catch Prince Jing in such a state of undress? H-he thought he would've finished changing by now...

In addition to overestimating how quickly Prince Jing would get changed, Li Yu must have been confused and underestimated the complexity of historical clothing. Now it looked like he was some pervert spying on a beautiful man!

Li Yu quickly took it all in—everything he was supposed to see, as well as everything he wasn't. His face burning, he twisted his body and dove back into the fish tank with a little splash.

Why didn't this Prince Jing hide behind something if he was going to change?!

...All right, fine, there was only a fish in the room with him, there was no need for him to hide anything.

Li Yu darted under his leaf blanket as soon as he heard Prince Jing's footsteps approaching. Prince Jing may not have realized Li Yu had been looking at him, but he wasn't blind: he definitely would've noticed a fish jumping straight out of the tank, right?

The prince definitely noticed!

Li Yu lay there, heart in his throat, trying his best to pretend he was a normal fish. By now, Prince Jing had already arrived at the tank. Once again, he felt the uneasy sensation of the prince's piercing gaze on him. It felt like there was someone pointing a blade at his back. Li Yu discreetly turned around so that his tail was facing Prince Jing, in an effort to cover up what he just did.

"Your Highness, Your Highness!" Before Prince Jing could do anything, Wang Xi's anxious call came from outside. Li Yu let out a sigh of relief.

Prince Jing fastened his jade buttons and took one last, long look at the suspicious little fish. Then he strolled to the door and pulled it open.

Wang Xi greeted him respectfully, "Your Highness. The emperor has sent someone."

The emperor was Prince Jing's father. The prince's expression turned serious as he followed Wang Xi out to accept the imperial edict.

Prince Jing was finally gone!

Li Yu was delighted, but he stayed as still as a statue, pretending he didn't understand anything that was happening outside his fish tank. After the sound of footsteps faded into the distance, he swam to a quiet corner of the tank and quickly entered the system.

The second part of the "Priceless Pet Fish" quest was complete, which meant he could finally collect his reward of inventory space. And while he was at it, he also had to take a look at what the third step was. At this rate, he'd surely be turning back into a human any day now! Li Yu was very pleased with himself.

He had just entered the system when a prompt popped up, asking him if he would like to check out his inventory. Li Yu selected "yes," overjoyed, and his inventory immediately opened up before his eyes, giving him a clear view of the inside.

All Li Yu's praises caught in his throat as soon as he laid eyes on it. He thought his inventory would at least be the size of a storage room, but this was about the size of an adult's palm.

*No way! What's the point of having such a tiny space? So stingy!*

The system replied: *<Since the user thinks the space is too small, would you like to give up your reward?>*

Li Yu had almost forgotten the system could read his thoughts and shook his head hurriedly. *<No, no! It's better than nothing.>*

*<There is currently only one inventory slot,>* the system informed him. *<Side quests can increase inventory slots.>*

*<That's more like it. As long as I can get more...>*

But this was all the space he had for now. What could he put in it? At most, he could probably fit one or two things in there.

Despite having only been a fish for a few hours, Li Yu had been entertaining a lot of secret daydreams about this space. He had envisioned being able to store an enormous pile of fish feed, a bunch of medicine for his injuries, or even a large tank of fresh water for emergencies. That way he could be a rich and carefree fish. But there were two problems. First, he hadn't managed to acquire any of those things, and second, it turned out he only had a tiny amount of space. For a moment, he was at a loss for what he could even do with the little resources he had. Meanwhile, Prince Jing had stepped out to receive an imperial edict, but who knew when he'd be back? He didn't have much time, so he just had to accept the space now and figure it out later.

A ray of light shot out from the inventory, landing somewhere near Li Yu's left fin. When he took a look after the light had faded, he realized one of the scales beneath his fin had changed into the color of jade.

# 6

# The Fish Swimming at the Bottom of the Bowl

THE SYSTEM GAVE Li Yu a tip: <*You don't need to enter the system first if you want to use the inventory. To use the shortcut, you can tap the jade scale three times. You can put anything within your field of vision inside, so long as it fits, using just your thoughts...*>

The system continued talking. Li Yu smiled. As limited as the inventory space was, its method of usage was pretty cool. Not too shabby.

He went to check on the main quest in the system. Just as he thought, the second task, "Priceless Pet Fish," was now completed. The third task, which had previously been hidden away, was now revealed.

The third task: "Get Along with the Tyrant." Time limit: three days.

Li Yu was speechless. Getting along with the tyrant, interacting with the tyrant—didn't this system know anything else? Not to mention, the bar for "interacting" had already been so high—he hadn't been able to do it alone, and he needed Prince Jing to participate as well. So what on earth did "getting along with" entail? And there was a fucking time limit too??

What was going to happen if he didn't complete it before time ran out?

*<Exceeding the time limit counts as a failure, and the user will become fish bones and fish...>*

*<All right, enough! I got it! I just have to complete the task within three days, right? Can I at least rest today and start tomorrow?>*

*<Sorry, the timer started from the moment you completed the second task.>*

*What???*

Li Yu took a closer look and realized it was right. Right next to the task was a small countdown, seconds ticking slowly down. This fucking system! Why didn't it let him know the timer had already started?! What if he had slept for three days?!

So time still passed while he was in the system. Li Yu couldn't waste any more of it; he quickly exited and came back to the real world, arriving just in time to hear Wang Xi's voice. It turned out that while he was accepting his reward, Prince Jing and Wang Xi had already returned, and Wang Xi had spoken for a while.

Luckily, the prince hadn't come over to visit Li Yu. He hurriedly swam around a little, shaking himself out of his dazed stupor to prove he was still very much alive. Pressing up against one side of the tank to listen, he could faintly hear Wang Xi's muffled voice.

"Why did the emperor call Your Highness to Qianqing Palace so suddenly?" the eunuch asked. "This old servant heard the emperor had visited Zhongcui Palace, so I thought the noble consort must have said something to him. After all, that white cat...is the noble consort's beloved pet."

Something seemed to occur to Prince Jing; a mocking smile curled his lips.

"This servant didn't mean anything else by that," said Wang Xi hastily. "Of course, Your Highness wouldn't care for such things, but you do, at the very least, have to show some respect to the emperor.

I'll accompany you and explain things clearly to him. I refuse to believe the noble consort can conceal the truth!"

When Prince Jing showed no reaction, Wang Xi continued, "Then I'll follow Your Highness..."

Mu Tianchi thought about it for a while before reaching over and blocking Wang Xi's way. He shook his head.

Wang Xi froze. "Your Highness...doesn't want this servant to come this time?"

As Prince Jing's personal servant, Wang Xi had taken care of the prince since he was a child. He could tell what the prince wanted just from a single glance. If the prince wanted to speak, Wang Xi was almost always able to say exactly what the prince wanted. The sudden summons of Prince Jing to Qianqing Palace led Wang Xi to guess the noble consort had probably hinted something to the emperor. Without Wang Xi there by his side, wasn't the prince doomed to take the fall?

Prince Jing's dark eyes flicked to the top of his head expressionlessly.

Wang Xi understood at once. "The emperor ordered Your Highness to go alone? You're not allowed to bring anyone with you?"

Prince Jing nodded.

Wang Xi was speechless. The emperor summoned Prince Jing and yet wouldn't allow him to "speak." What was the meaning of this?

The worst-case scenario would be if, after years of Zhongcui Palace exerting its influence, the emperor turned his affections away from His Highness and onto the second prince. Wang Xi's eyes immediately burned red. "No... This old servant will follow Your Highness even if it means my death!"

Prince Jing looked at his sorrowful face and hesitated a moment before tapping his shoulder lightly. Deliberately going against the emperor's wishes would only give the other side an advantage.

Besides, Prince Jing didn't think a mere noble consort could do anything to him.

"Then...what does Your Highness plan to do?" Wang Xi sniffled.

Prince Jing's distant gaze landed on the porcelain fish tank that stood behind Wang Xi.

"Y-Your Highness wants to..." Wang Xi was shocked. He couldn't mean...?

The way Prince Jing held himself was calm and relaxed, an easy grace about him. The very picture of confidence.

Wang Xi gritted his teeth. "Since Your Highness has already made his decision, this servant will obey and go prepare."

Li Yu heard everything. The noble consort wanted to make things difficult for Prince Jing, and Wang Xi was discussing a plan of action with the prince. But Li Yu wasn't worried about Prince Jing at all.

In the book, even though the noble consort seemed to have the emperor's favor, she didn't end up living very long. Li Yu figured this wasn't a big deal since there wasn't a detailed passage about this particular situation in the book. Nothing major was going to happen; otherwise, how would Prince Jing ascend to the throne?

Prince Jing was the kind of person who held grudges—an eye for an eye. If the noble consort really dared to try something, she wouldn't be reaping the rewards; she would be suffering the consequences!

Anyway, as far as Li Yu was concerned, Prince Jing seeing the emperor was none of his business. He was a fish. All he had to do was wait quietly in his tank for the prince to come back before continuing with his task. While the three-day time limit wasn't very long, it wasn't too bad either. He had completed his first two tasks entirely by chance, so perhaps it would be the same for this one...

To his surprise, though, he watched Wang Xi rummage through the prince's chests and shelves, where he procured a little jade bowl.

He approached the fish tank with an ominous look on his face. Li Yu tensed.

*Wait. Stop! What are you doing!!*

Li Yu screamed. Wang Xi, sleeves rolled up, quickly snatched up Li Yu and deposited him in the jade bowl.

The jade bowl was much too cramped, and the water it held was very shallow. There was barely space for Li Yu, who was forced to curl up into a circle to fit inside. He couldn't even swim normally, let alone roll around. If he exerted even just a tiny bit of force, he would surface from the water.

It wasn't very safe. Li Yu curled around himself pitifully.

Wang Xi murmured to him, "Little thing, you'll have to bear with this for a while, since His Highness has decided to take you with him. Be good and don't embarrass him."

Holy fucking shit, what was Wang Xi saying? Was Prince Jing okay?? A man who couldn't speak bringing a fish that also couldn't speak? Li Yu didn't want to see any emperors or noble consorts!

Knowing that Prince Jing was a noble prince and that he had the rest of the plotline ahead of him, Li Yu didn't think the emperor would do anything to his son. But Li Yu, on the other hand, was an entirely different matter. He was just a fish. If the emperor didn't like him, he could easily throw him away or roast him...

*Wake up!* It wasn't up to Li Yu to decide where he went. With this trip, the fate of his fish life was up in the air. He had to come up with a contingency plan, and fast.

There was still one spot in his inventory!

Li Yu took a deep breath. While Wang Xi was distracted, he

frantically tapped on his scale, thinking, *Let me save some clean water, I want water...*

He could survive as long as he had enough water—unless the emperor decided to cut off his fish head. Although there was water inside the jade bowl he was in right now, it was much too shallow to feel safe. If the person holding the bowl had shaky hands, he was fucked. He wasn't going to leave his life in some stranger's hands; he was going to save himself by saving some water!

Li Yu hadn't put anything in his inventory yet. He definitely didn't expect it to come into use so quickly. He had only heard the system explain its application once, so he was purely relying on luck.

Good thing he had a pretty good memory and remembered most of what the system had said. Instantly, the water in the porcelain tank became shallower, while Li Yu's inventory filled with water.

*I have water!* Satisfied, Li Yu put away his inventory.

Wang Xi called a group of servants into the room. They were all busy with their own tasks, so no one noticed the volume of the water changing inside the porcelain fish tank. Since Prince Jing had decided to take the little carp to see the emperor, Wang Xi had to make sure everything was taken care of. He prepared several small jade bowls of around the same size and various changes of clothing— all of which had to be taken along with the prince, as a precaution. Wang Xi may not have been able to go with the prince to see the emperor, but the least he could do was take care of Prince Jing on the way there.

Prince Jing gestured, indicating that he would hold the little carp who was about to meet the emperor. Wang Xi handed the bowl over respectfully, and Prince Jing glanced inside.

The bowl was quite small, so the fish couldn't even fully stretch out inside. Wang Xi said there was nothing they could do about that—it wasn't like they could take a large bowl to see the emperor; that would stick out like a sore thumb. The little carp might have been more comfortable, but what would the emperor think?

Prince Jing didn't care what the emperor would think; the bowl was too cramped. He shot Wang Xi a judgmental glare.

Wang Xi thought his eyes were playing tricks on him and rubbed his eyes hard. "Your Highness, y-you're going to see the emperor. It's best if you take this jade bowl…"

Prince Jing sidestepped around him and pointed at a different bowl that had been taken out during Wang Xi's search for the jade bowl. This bowl was huge, with delicate ripples of water painted on the side. It was fully large enough to hold a pot of soup.

Wang Xi's jaw dropped.

Prince Jing was a stubborn man: whatever he wanted he was going to get. The large bowl was quickly brought over. Glancing briefly at Wang Xi, Prince Jing poured the little carp, along with the water, into the large bowl himself. Then he filled it up with more water.

Li Yu was suddenly freed from the confines of the jade bowl. What happened? Why did it change again? But this new bowl was so much cooler! He liked it!

Li Yu demonstrated his fishiness to the extreme, swimming and jumping around in his new domain. Since Prince Jing had moved him into a larger bowl, he had to amend his impression of the prince. Perhaps tyrants were, on occasion, good at taking care of their pets!

Seeing how delighted the fish was, Prince Jing's lips twitched a little. After a second's thought, he brought out the box of red fish feed. He carefully shook out a few pieces into the bowl, in case this fish became hungry in its overexcitement as they made their way to the palace.

Li Yu couldn't be more grateful, completely unaware that from afar, between the large bowl and the floating red pellets, he looked like a large bowl of goji fish soup.

With one hand supporting the bowl on the bottom, Prince Jing covered the top with the other, in case the fish got too lively and jumped out. Even though he wasn't touching him directly, Li Yu could still feel the heat from his palm.

It was warm and unexpectedly cozy.

Li Yu had originally had doubts about whether this person was reliable, but if the prince protected him like this, it should...be safe, right?

The little carp's anxious heart gradually calmed until it settled down to the rhythm of Prince Jing's footsteps.

# The Fish Meets
# the Emperor

**P**RINCE JING BROUGHT Li Yu to Qianqing Palace. As they made their way over, the system, which had been silent this whole time, suddenly spoke to Li Yu.

*‹The prerequisites have been met for the side quest 'Clear, Bright Pearl.' Would the user like to begin the quest?›*

What was going on? He hadn't "gotten along" with Prince Jing yet, but now there was another quest. And a side quest too? He couldn't glean anything from just its name, though. Li Yu didn't want to overcomplicate things by having to worry about a side quest and the main quest at the same time; he'd be overworking his poor fish brain. But out of curiosity, he still asked about the reward.

The system replied: *‹The reward for the quest is a temporary transformation medicine, allowing the user to return to human form for a short period of time. The effects will last two hours. There will not be any penalty for failing the side quest.›*

A medicine that could turn him back into a human? Why wasn't this brought up before? Even if it only lasted two hours, couldn't he just do the quest a couple more times, receive the reward over and over, and use them one after the other? Then he could stay human forever!

*‹The reward can only be claimed once.›* The system mercilessly reminded him as it witnessed his naive stupidity.

*‹Fine. I already knew you were a fish-scamming system.›*

He absolutely had to do this side quest. He had nothing to lose if he failed. If he had the medicine to transform, he could pick a suitable day to eat a ton of human food, talk a lot, and go anywhere he wanted to—

Li Yu was originally human, but it wasn't until he became a fish that he appreciated how freeing and delightful it was to be a human. It would only be a short couple of hours, but getting to re-experience being human for even that amount of time was simply too alluring!

*It's just one more task. I'll do it.*

This quest called "Clear, Bright Pearl" consisted of only a single line: obtain one luminous pearl.

The stupid system's quests had always been vague in its instructions, but Li Yu was already used to it. He had no idea what a luminous pearl could possibly have to do with him, a fish. The system had previously explained that side quests could only be activated after the corresponding prerequisites had been fulfilled. Seeing how this side quest became active while Prince Jing was taking him to Qianqing Palace, it must have something to do with seeing the emperor... So it didn't seem like he'd need to make any detours.

Despite being royalty, Prince Jing didn't like to ride in a palanquin. Holding the little carp, with Wang Xi trailing behind, he made his way to Qianqing Palace at a leisurely stroll. The head eunuch, Luo Ruisheng, had already been waiting in front of the doors to Qianqing Palace for some time, and as soon as he saw Prince Jing, he rushed forward to greet him, bowed, and escorted him inside. Wang Xi couldn't go in, so all he could do was wait anxiously outside the palace.

They had finally arrived. Li Yu swam to the water's surface, taking in the view of Qianqing Palace. As expected of the emperor's quarters, it was a majestic and extravagant structure filled with all sorts of rare and precious furnishings. The scent of sandalwood wafted by. Li Yu was utterly mesmerized.

As magnificent as the room was, though, there was no fish tank in sight. Li Yu much preferred the quarters with the porcelain fish tank.

It was only because of this excursion that he discovered Prince Jing was keeping him in Jingtai Hall. Even after the title of "prince" was bestowed on him and he left the palace, Jingtai Hall, where Prince Jing had grown up, was still reserved for him. It truly was Prince Jing's territory. Li Yu was quietly proud of himself for managing to get into the tyrant's lair without much effort.

He scanned his surroundings, but, to his dismay, he didn't spot any luminous pearls. Li Yu had hoped the system would give him some hints, especially since the side quest had come out of nowhere, but there hadn't been another peep from the stupid system since it announced the side quest.

Li Yu had to set both the main and side quests aside for the time being. Without any leads, all he could do was leave it up to fate. Seeing the emperor was more important right now.

In the book, the emperor had quite a backstory with Prince Jing. In the original story, Prince Jing's mother, Empress Xiaohui, had already been in ill health before she gave birth to the prince. After he was born, she couldn't bear the fact that her son was mute, and she passed away shortly afterward. The emperor deeply loved and respected Empress Xiaohui, so his feelings for his son had always been complicated, and he never grew very close to him. This was especially clear after Prince Jing turned sixteen, when the emperor ordered him to move out of the palace and into his own manor. All the other princes had only received their respective manors after they were married, but it didn't seem to matter to the emperor that

Prince Jing remained unmarried to this day. As such, many people believed Prince Jing was unwanted and unloved.

Li Yu was not one of those many people.

The reason the emperor was so distant from Prince Jing wasn't because he didn't care for him, but because he sought to protect him. As Empress Xiaohui's son, Prince Jing had a much higher status than most. But no matter how noble he was, his muteness prevented him from inheriting the throne. Although the emperor had no desire to foster a close relationship with Prince Jing due to his wife's death, this was still his cherished wife's flesh and blood. Ordering him to move into his own manor early was the emperor's way of protecting his son. Ultimately, the emperor hoped this son would be able to live a peaceful life.

All else aside, Prince Jing wasn't really the tolerant type. When he was a child and the other young princes taunted him for being mute, Prince Jing would just roll up his sleeves and beat them up. After the emperor found out, everyone was punished, but he also privately warned the other princes to be kinder to Prince Jing.

With Prince Jing's inability to speak, his education was a challenge too, but the emperor specially appointed a strict teacher who had experience teaching mute and deaf students. The emperor never voiced his love for Prince Jing, but his actions spoke for him. Li Yu, therefore, was not at all worried about this trip.

In the main hall of Qianqing Palace, the emperor sat on a throne carved with intricate flying dragons, draped in bright yellow imperial robes. He nodded slightly when Prince Jing entered. "Tianchi, you've arrived."

Prince Jing set the large bowl that held the little carp on a small table off to the side and bowed seriously. The emperor beckoned him to stand back up, smiling. As he looked at his son from a distance,

he noted that Prince Jing was just as cold and quiet as always. Naturally, the emperor's gaze fell on the large bowl Prince Jing had brought.

In the emperor's experience, bowls generally held soup. If someone came into Qianqing Palace with a bowl, they were usually there to present the soup to him. Assuming that Prince Jing knew what he had done wrong and had brought an offering of soup to apologize, the emperor chuckled. "How considerate of you."

The misunderstood Prince Jing wasn't sure how to respond.

Of his sons, the emperor rarely tried to get closer to this one. He felt his heart warming at the sight of the prince trying to please him. He immediately ordered Luo Ruisheng to bring forward the prince's "soup."

Prince Jing couldn't speak; there was nothing he could do to stop Luo-gonggong in time, and the head eunuch nimbly picked up the large bowl before he could make his objection clear. Another eunuch waiting on the side handed over a silver needle.

At first glance, the soup looked like goji fish soup. Needle in hand, Luo-gonggong was about to test it for poison like usual when he made eye contact with the lively little carp that had poked its head out of the water to watch all the commotion.

Luo-gonggong was so alarmed that he nearly dropped the bowl. "Aiyou, Prince Jing, what did you bring?"

Equally startled by Luo-gonggong's sudden appearance, Li Yu immediately sank to the bottom of the bowl.

*It's alive!* Luo-gonggong realized with a start. This wasn't fish soup!

"What exactly did Prince Jing bring?" The emperor was too far away to see, but Luo-gonggong's exclamation had made him curious.

While Luo-gonggong struggled to think of how to answer, Prince Jing got up, approached Luo-gonggong, and took the bowl back, all without saying a single word. The emperor looked on in befuddlement. Prince Jing proceeded to bring the large bowl before the emperor himself, but he didn't look like he had any intention of handing it over. His hands remained clamped around the bowl.

The large bowl, with its water-ripple patterns, held a large volume of water. Swimming inside it was a small, palm-sized carp.

The emperor paused. "Prince Jing, what is the meaning of this?"

Mu Tianchi smiled as he reached a finger into the water, swirling it gently.

Li Yu had managed to steal a glance at the emperor from within the water and saw a middle-aged man with a square face and a short mustache. It was fortunate that Prince Jing's other features were more like Empress Xiaohui's, Li Yu thought, and that he only shared his eyes with his father. If he looked more like the emperor, it would have been a blow to his good looks.

Perhaps because he'd sensed Li Yu's criticism, the prince suddenly dipped his hand into the water. Li Yu was at a loss for what to do. He realized after a few seconds that the prince was playing with him. But they were standing before the emperor right now. What was the prince trying to do?

Ever since Prince Jing had switched out his bowl, Li Yu knew the prince wasn't planning on giving him to the emperor. When it came to presenting gifts to the emperor, looks were paramount. Of course, a small, dainty jade bowl would be more suited to the ruler's tastes, but since the prince had passed on the jade bowl, it was clear he had no plans on using him to try to please the emperor.

In that case, why did the prince bring him to see the emperor? Why play with him in front of the emperor?

Oh well, who cared. If the master wanted to play with his pet, it was the pet's duty to...respond.

Li Yu shoved down his embarrassment. This wasn't the first or second time he had to act cute for Prince Jing. He swam, stopping in between the prince's fingers. After hesitating for a moment, Li Yu nuzzled his fish mouth against Prince Jing's finger affectionately.

Whoa... There was the smell of fish food. The mouthwatering red kind.

His movements were initially a little stiff, but as time went on, he began willingly chasing after the other man's finger.

As Prince Jing looked down at the little carp swimming happily in the bowl, a light shone faintly in his eyes. The emperor almost thought he was seeing things. Prince Jing had always been cold and harsh, keeping his emotions under tight lock and key. And yet here he was, playing with a fish in a way that could only be described as gentle...

In the past, concerned that Prince Jing was too unsociable, the emperor had tried sending many cats and dogs to his son in the hope of providing him with a companion. But the prince never even spared them a single glance, never mind accepting one of them. At the time, the emperor thought the prince perhaps simply disliked pets. But now, for some reason, the Prince Jing who didn't like pets was making an exception for a fish, of all things?

Dazed, the emperor considered the different possibilities. After a while, and with great difficulty, he opened his mouth. "Do you mean to say that you've started taking care of this fish?"

Mu Tianchi nodded slightly.

Prince Jing had actually decided to raise a pet fish. The emperor was flabbergasted. It wasn't a bad thing, since this son of his seemed to be finally demonstrating some human feelings, but...this fish...

It wasn't even a precious, auspicious koi. It was just a little run-of-the-mill carp. It looked like the kind that was usually made into soup. Prince Jing's tastes sure were...something.

At this point, the emperor had already forgotten why he had summoned the prince. "A pet fish," he said with a twitch of his lips, sounding a little forced. "Not bad."

Li Yu watched Prince Jing nod and felt like a little pony had trotted proudly across his heart. Although Wang-gonggong, and even Li Yu himself, had long since accepted that he was Prince Jing's pet, this was the first time the prince was acknowledging it himself. Did the prince bring him here for the sole purpose of announcing Li Yu as his pet in front of the emperor? What a high-profile and distinguished pet he was!

Li Yu was floating on cloud nine. The point of the main quest, "Priceless Pet Fish," was for him to become Prince Jing's pet fish, after all—and now the prince had straight up announced he was his pet in front of the emperor! Didn't that mean the main quest was complete?

But there was no prompt congratulating him on completing a task. Apparently a concession from Prince Jing wasn't enough for this stupid system. He still had to press on until he succeeded at "getting along" with the prince.

A eunuch rushed in announcing that the noble consort and the second prince were outside, requesting an audience.

That was when the emperor remembered why he had summoned Prince Jing. He gave the prince a meaningful look, but he was so busy playing with his fish that he didn't react. The emperor sighed lightly. "Let them in."

# The Fish Is Angry

LI YU WAS RIGHT NEXT to Prince Jing. When he heard that the noble consort was coming, he wanted to take a look at her. Having already seen the emperor, who looked roughly the same as the description in the book, Li Yu also wanted to see what the woman who dared provoke a tyrant looked like. Except his current position was a little off to the side, and his view was blocked...

Li Yu kept swimming back and forth, straining to peek, but to no avail. Just when he was about to give up and resort to eavesdropping, Prince Jing, who had been observing him for a while, moved the bowl so that it faced the entrance to the palace perfectly.

Li Yu was startled. A coincidence? Did the prince somehow notice him trying to look at the noble consort?

Prince Jing had demonstrated a considerable aptitude for pet fish care so far. But there was no way he could be this attentive, right? Perhaps he just felt like moving the bowl, no big deal. Li Yu quickly convinced himself not to get caught up in pointless speculation. Since he had a clear view now, he was going to look his fill.

Before long, a graceful woman draped in imperial robes walked into view, surrounded by attendants and servants and leading a tall youth.

Noble Consort Qiu's hair was heavy with pearls and jade. Crab apple blossoms in full bloom were embroidered around the hem of her light purple robes. With skin brighter than snow, she was beautiful beyond compare, and it was obvious the noble consort knew how to take care of herself. If it wasn't for the tall second prince trailing behind her, with eyes that looked rather like hers, it would have been very difficult to discern that she was already at least thirty.

Li Yu sighed dreamily. It was no wonder such a beauty was the most favored concubine in recent years.

According to the book, Noble Consort Qiu was at the peak of her life at this point in the story. The emperor had already privately let her know that he planned on making *her* son, the second prince Mu Tianzhao, the crown prince.

The emperor, like many emperors of the past, wished for his di son[6] to inherit the throne. Years ago, he had made his first son, Empress Xiaohui's son, the crown prince, only for the boy to tragically pass away at age seven. The emperor and empress grieved for years until Empress Xiaohui gave birth to the fourth prince. The emperor once again had thoughts of making him the crown prince, but unfortunately, the fourth prince was not blessed. He suffered a cold at two years old and unexpectedly passed away at an even younger age.

One after another, Empress Xiaohui suffered the loss of her sons. Despite how fragile her health had become, she was determined to give birth to the fifth prince, Prince Jing, regardless of how reckless it might be. But the heavens decided to play a cruel joke on the emperor and empress, and both of them received a great shock when they realized the youngest di son was born mute.

---

6    The di son (嫡子) is a son born from the di wife (嫡妻). The di wife is considered the "official" wife of the man, even if he has multiple wives. Sons born to the di wife have higher status in the family than the shu sons (庶子) born to other wives. In nonroyal families, the eldest di son is usually the one who inherits the father's title. In the royal family, the eldest di son is usually the first one to be considered for the throne.

After Empress Xiaohui passed away, the emperor felt his fate must not be aligned with his di sons, so he never mentioned making anyone the crown prince again. But now, after twenty years, there was finally some movement from the emperor, and Noble Consort Qiu could not be more ecstatic.

Although the emperor's favor toward her was as clear as day, he never showed any hint of granting her the title of empress. But so what? As long as her son, the second prince, was named crown prince and ascended the throne, it made no difference if she was empress or not!

The noble consort thought her suffering had finally come to an end; she even seemed to walk with a spring in her step!

Once Lady Qiu had greeted the emperor along with the second prince, the emperor asked her to approach. As he intended to pronounce the second prince as the crown prince, he had to afford her this respect.

The noble consort smiled daintily and sat down next to the emperor. She glanced down at Prince Jing, her expression victorious. So what if he was the son of the empress? So what if he was born more noble than her son, the second prince? Prince Jing would still need to bow his head to the crown prince, the future emperor.

She and the second prince shared a knowing smile, but Prince Jing didn't make any indication that he noticed.

Prince Jing's gaze never strayed from the little carp. His finger was still submerged in the water, playing with the fish's smooth back every now and then. Li Yu was getting a little pissed off from all the touching. *Hey, you're being too rough! A fish can't take it!*

Li Yu evaded his hand, glaring fiercely at Prince Jing. When Prince Jing found his fingers fishless, his dark, unblinking stare lingered pointedly on the little carp.

The temperature in the air around them suddenly plummeted.

Was the tyrant angry because Li Yu wouldn't let him squeeze him? Fine, whatever. Good fish didn't fight with humans, especially not their owners. He knew Prince Jing was probably upset at the sight of Noble Consort Qiu sitting next to the emperor. What child would be happy seeing another woman take his mother's place? Lady Qiu was full of smiles, but her smile held an edge of provocation; she was clearly showing off.

Prince Jing was obviously in a bad mood, Li Yu decided. He had a good reason for using him as a stress ball. He leaned back in, nuzzling against Prince Jing's finger, hoping to make him feel better.

*I'll let you squish me, but don't be so rough, okay?*

Prince Jing pursed his lips at the way his fish was clearly trying to please him and continued to squeeze the fish's back.

Li Yu endured it in silence. If he felt that Prince Jing was truly being too rough and he couldn't take it anymore, he would dart to the side with a swing of his tail. But, a little while later, he would always swim back, allowing Prince Jing to use him as an outlet for his anger.

The little carp didn't seem to hate his touch, Prince Jing noted, but why did it keep shying away and then coming back?

...Was he handling the fish too harshly, he wondered...?

The prince's touch became gentler.

Li Yu instantly felt better. Who knew having his back squeezed like this could feel this nice? It was even a little ticklish. Li Yu curled his tail around the prince's finger to show that he liked it.

Prince Jing realized this little carp wasn't that hard to understand after all.

Fish and human were absorbed in their own little world. They didn't care how they might look to anyone else.

Having already seen Prince Jing like this, the emperor watched the prince with the little carp with rapt attention. He never knew his coldhearted and distant son could play with a fish.

Meanwhile, Noble Consort Qiu's smile was frozen on her face. Prince Jing had managed to humiliate her without saying a single word. "What's the matter with Prince Jing?" she asked, trying to get the emperor to notice the prince's rudeness.

There was a smile warming the emperor's face as he said, "Noble Consort, Prince Jing has started caring for a fish recently. What do you think?"

Of course, Lady Qiu didn't think it was any good at all. She had come here with a goal, and she wasn't going to sit back and watch a drab, gray fish disrupt her plans. If the emperor was acting like this, he must have forgotten what she'd told him earlier and was feeling soft toward Prince Jing.

But the noble consort had come prepared. She tossed a glance to one of her trusted servants waiting on the side. The servant immediately left, then quickly returned with a snowy white ball in her arms.

Lady Qiu delightedly hugged the snowy white ball to her chest and smoothed its fur. She said gently, "Has the emperor forgotten about my Piaoxue after seeing Prince Jing's fish?"

By now, the emperor had also remembered why he had summoned Prince Jing. He chuckled, rubbing his nose.

The snowy white cat slowly raised its head and let out a meow. It was clearly conspiring with its owner. Li Yu, who had been playing with Prince Jing, heard the meow and was so alarmed that all his fins stood on end. Did Qianqing Palace also have a cat?

Carefully, Li Yu swam to the surface of the water to see what was going on—and there it was, nestled in the noble consort's arms. The snow-white cat's sapphire eyes homed in on him immediately.

That shape, that sound...w-w-wasn't that his greatest enemy?!

With a shudder, Li Yu immediately dove down to the bottom of the water. But it was too late. As soon as the large white cat laid eyes on him, it let out an excited yowl, scrambled out of the noble consort's arms, and shot toward him like an arrow.

*Ahh, save me! The cat wants to eat fish!!*

He had thought that if he ever came face-to-face with his arch-nemesis again, he'd be able to find some escape route—or if worse came to worst, he'd slap the cat in the face with his tail. It wasn't until he was in front of the cat for real that he realized its teeth had left a serious mark on his instincts. Just the memory of that bite was enough to make him tremble.

Trapped in the bowl, Li Yu had nowhere to escape to, leaving him with no choice but to curl into a ball beneath Prince Jing's hand. He prayed the large white cat wouldn't see him, but he knew he was fooling himself.

The cat wasted no time in pouncing, and it showed no fear of water as it opened its mouth to snap up the fish. Just as it seemed as though Li Yu was going to end up in the cat's mouth, Prince Jing held the curled-up little carp in his hand closer to him. The cat bit down on empty water.

"Meow?" Confused, the white cat looked up and saw a face that it would never forget. "Meow!!!" Suddenly, the cat felt like all hope was lost.

Prince Jing's face was as icy as frost. With a flick of his fingers, the white cat was flung off, barreling into the legs of the servant who had brought it.

The servant let out a scream of pain. The impact left the white cat dizzy, but it managed to stand back up, shaking its head fiercely. It abandoned any thought of catching the fish and rushed straight back into the noble consort's arms.

From his hiding place under Prince Jing's hand, Li Yu peeked out from the gaps between the prince's fingers. Prince Jing was rolling with laughter. As expected of his tyrant master! The white cat got what it had coming again!

Noble Consort Qiu was secretly delighted at seeing Prince Jing raise a hand right in front of the emperor. She bent down to pick up her white cat, which was still howling pitifully and made a show of examining it. She pretended to be distressed as she scolded, "Piaoxue, you terrible thing! Haven't you learned from last time? Why did you have to provoke Prince Jing? Do you not take me seriously?"

All of Li Yu's happiness evaporated at her words. He was so furious that if he'd had a foot, he would have stamped it. While the noble consort *seemed* to be reprimanding her cat, in reality, she was playing one of her little games. She was reminding the emperor that this wasn't the first time Prince Jing had taught her beloved pet a lesson and that he didn't treat her with the respect she deserved, as the noble consort and as his shu mother.

After Lady Qiu spoke, of course the second prince, Mu Tianzhao, piped up in support. "My brother, the fifth prince, is just being a little mischievous. He didn't mean any harm. Royal Father, Mother, please don't blame him."

Li Yu's eyes rolled back in his head. He blew out a huge bubble with a "pop," and turned his tail disdainfully toward the second prince.

The second prince's voice was mild, but underneath that gentle veneer was a ruthless countenance, even more so than the noble consort. While the noble consort played her little games, the second prince was practically accepting Prince Jing's guilt for him by saying he had no ill intentions, as though afraid the emperor couldn't reach that conclusion on his own.

This evil cannon fodder!

Despite knowing Prince Jing would eventually inherit the throne, and Mu Tianzhao and the noble consort would both meet grisly ends, Li Yu couldn't help but feel a little anxious. This mother-son duo was teaming up and taking advantage of the fact that Prince Jing couldn't speak, especially since Prince Jing didn't even have Wang Xi-gonggong with him this time. Prince Jing had saved him so many times now, Li Yu couldn't sit idly by and watch them bully him.

But what could he, a fish stuck in a bowl, do to the noble consort and her son, who were like the sun, shining brightly in the middle of the sky? Li Yu was so indignant, his cheeks puffed up. He started to swim in frustrated circles in his bowl.

The noble consort and her son's actions had the desired effect. The emperor's expression darkened as he remembered the noble consort's tearful complaint from earlier. "Prince Jing, I heard you threw her cat on her birthday. Is this true?"

On the day of her birthday, the noble consort had gone crying to the emperor that Prince Jing had hurled her precious pet, Piaoxue. Now that he had witnessed Prince Jing's treatment of Piaoxue with his own two eyes, he was starting to believe Noble Consort Qiu.

Not that the emperor had any affection for the cat; it was merely a pet. Who cared if Prince Jing wanted to hit or kill it? Privately, the emperor didn't think it was much of a concern. But this situation involved the noble consort, who was, after all, Prince Jing's shu mother. Behind her was the second prince, who was also the emperor's choice for crown prince. The emperor didn't want there to be any bad blood between Prince Jing and the future crown prince, which was why he had summoned Prince Jing in the first place. He wanted to get to the bottom of the situation and give the noble consort an explanation appropriate enough to appease her.

But Prince Jing gave the noble consort a fleeting, cold glance and made no move to explain. He continued to play with his little carp, eyes lowered.

For some reason, though, this little fish's cheeks were puffed out. It was especially obvious when Noble Consort Qiu spoke, almost as if he was angry. Prince Jing was rather amused; could this fish see through the noble consort and her son's trickery too?

# The Fish Is Belly-Up

I N THE FACE OF Prince Jing's clear indifference, the emperor
felt a little awkward.

"Fifth brother, our Royal Father is asking you a question."
Mu Tianzhao reminded him, with what might have been a smile.
The second prince had always been a little wary around Prince Jing
because of the difference in their statuses. Now that he was about
to become the crown prince, though, he was going to take that
all back.

Prince Jing looked up, but not to acknowledge the second prince.
Instead, he looked at the head eunuch, Luo Ruisheng. Luo Ruisheng
had been prepared ever since the emperor had ordered Prince Jing to
enter Qianqing Palace alone. At Prince Jing's glance, Luo-gonggong
ordered a few servants to bring the necessary ink and paper before
him. It might be a bit inconvenient, but even if he couldn't speak,
he could still write.

Prince Jing accepted the brush with his right hand, his left still
playing with the fish. He didn't even look at what he was doing; he
just wrote a couple of strokes and tossed the brush away.

Not daring to look at what the prince had written, Luo Ruisheng
brought the prince's writing up to the emperor, his head lowered.

When the emperor's gaze fell on the strong, powerful strokes that
made up the vigorous characters, he couldn't help feeling a pang of

sadness in his heart. But this was not the time to admire the prince's calligraphy.

The only thing the prince had written was, "It deserved it."

For as long as the emperor could remember, the prince had never once lied. This was the reason the emperor had decided to summon him, to question him directly. Back when Prince Jing had punched the other princes, he never tried to hide what he'd done, so the emperor didn't think he would deceive him in this instance. Since the prince said the cat had deserved it, then something must've happened that he didn't know about. He couldn't be too hasty.

The emperor's expression darkened, and he looked toward Head Eunuch Luo. "Luo Ruisheng, go find out who else saw what happened that day."

Noble Consort Qiu's face twisted, betraying her panic. She had spent so much time preparing for this moment, but now the emperor was doubting her just because of a couple of random words from Prince Jing?

But as the noble consort dabbed at the corners of her mouth with a silk handkerchief embroidered with crab apple blossoms, her somewhat ferocious expression settled back into its beautiful facade. So what if the emperor investigated? There wasn't a shadow of a doubt that Prince Jing abused the cat. Not to mention, she even had an eyewitness... It would be good if Prince Jing admitted it, but it would be even better if he made a fuss and refused to confess.

Xiaolinzi was quickly brought over from the imperial kitchen. The emperor decided to carry out the questioning himself, since the matter involved his son, Prince Jing.

Xiaolinzi knelt there, his voice quavering as he recounted everything he saw that day. "...This servant saw...as soon as Prince Jing saw the noble consort's cat, h-he grabbed it," he finished.

Of course, Noble Consort Qiu was at least two steps ahead, having ordered her trusted servants to bribe Xiaolinzi before she even came to stand before the emperor. She knew the witness would be on her side.

"Your Imperial Majesty, it seems I didn't misunderstand the situation. Shouldn't Prince Jing give me an explanation?" She smiled.

"Prince Jing, do you have anything to say?" Was this what all his questioning had come to? The emperor rubbed his brow. He was getting a little tired.

A ruthless light flashed in Prince Jing's eyes. Noble Consort Qiu must have gotten her claws into Xiaolinzi, distorting the truth. He originally wanted to request that the emperor should summon a guard who had been working at the time for questioning; he doubted Xiaolinzi was the only eyewitness in such a large palace. But after considering the matter further, he quickly lost all desire to do so.

It didn't matter if there were eyewitnesses present that day or not; each side would have their own version of what had happened. The situation wouldn't change; why go through all that hassle? No, he'd be better off going straight for Xiaolinzi's throat. It was unlikely this person would stick to his story under threat of having his throat sliced open. It would be the quickest and most effective way to force him to tell the truth.

*Don't do it!*

Li Yu was extremely worried. He had a pretty good guess as to what Prince Jing's next move would be, having read the original book. Prince Jing would be walking straight into the noble consort's trap if he got violent in front of the emperor, further souring his relationship with his royal father.

But if he didn't resort to violence, what else could Prince Jing do?

The noble consort had clearly come prepared. First, she had managed to convince the emperor to prevent Wang Xi from accompanying Prince Jing, effectively taking away the prince's voice. Now, she'd provided an eyewitness who was extremely unfavorable toward Prince Jing. The prince was out of options.

Aside from Xiaolinzi, the only ones who were present at the time were the cat and Li Yu. With Xiaolinzi deep in Noble Consort Qiu's pocket, there was no way he'd speak the truth. Who was left to be Prince Jing's witness? That cat?!

Was there perhaps other evidence?

Without realizing it, Li Yu had drifted to the bottom of the bowl—he'd forgotten to even keep swimming, trying his hardest to remember how the white cat had run into Prince Jing.

An image came to him. When he'd peeked at Prince Jing changing, he had caught sight of what looked like a bruise on his leg.

He had been so embarrassed at the time that he didn't take a good look, and what he did see had been too brief. Besides, it wasn't out of the ordinary for a man to have some bumps and bruises on his body, so Li Yu didn't think much of it. But he remembered the bruise had been right on his shin, around the same height as the cat. Was that Piaoxue's doing?

It was possible. If it were true, then it would prove the cat had attacked Prince Jing, and he had just cause for punishing it!

Li Yu felt a rush of excitement at the thought of being able to clear Prince Jing's name. But now came the hard part—how could he let the prince know about his epiphany?

He couldn't speak, so he had to get inventive! Desperately, he concentrated all his energy on his tail and mustered up all the strength he had to swing it.

His fish tail came smacking down, and with a splash, almost half the water in the bowl sloshed out. In the silent Qianqing Palace, so quiet you could hear a pin drop, the sound of the water splashing onto the golden tiles was downright cacophonic. The emperor's eyes darted to the fish.

"Prince Jing, what is wrong with your fish?" he asked, baffled.

Prince Jing had been staring daggers at Xiaolinzi. His glower was enough to convey his thoughts: *You're a dead man.* But at the little carp's sudden movement, he turned to look at the fish, where it waited expectantly for him.

*Closer...closer... Now!!*

A quick and accurate swish of his tail, and Li Yu splashed all the remaining water in the bowl at Prince Jing.

Prince Jing had rolled up his sleeves to keep himself dry while he played with the fish. But in just a split second, his face, chest, and robes were completely soaked, with his pants as the biggest casualty. Prince Jing said nothing, but his expression was like a dark storm cloud as he wiped at the water dripping down his face.

Li Yu zipped to the bottom of the bowl to hide, too terrified to look at Prince Jing. Sob sob sob, the tyrant looked ready to explode! But he had no other choice. Plus, he didn't know it would get *this* wet.

Would the tyrant deal with him first, then Xiaolinzi, before going to change his clothes?

Ah! Prince Jing...was reaching toward him!!

Li Yu squeezed his eyes shut. Was this tyrant about to kill a fish?!

But after waiting with bated breath, all Li Yu felt was a light tap on his head, followed by a touch on his back. He was dumbfounded.

Prince Jing glared at the troublemaking little carp, before getting up and bowing to the emperor.

The emperor understood and said, "You may change quickly. We'll continue this once you return."

Wang Xi had been standing just outside, waiting anxiously. As soon as he saw this window of opportunity, he rushed in with a set of dry clothes for Prince Jing and slipped into the side hall to help him change.

Li Yu let out a sigh of relief. Thank goodness Prince Jing didn't lose his temper. He had intentionally splashed water on Prince Jing's pants in the hopes that the prince would see the bruise on his leg when he changed and think to use it as proof. But it was fine even if the prince never saw it, because Li Yu had still managed to buy the prince some time to cool down. In addition, now that Wang Xi was here, there was someone who could protect and speak for Prince Jing. Together, the prince and Wang-gonggong should be able to come up with a strategy to deal with the noble consort.

If worse came to worst and they were forced to concede this particular conflict to the noble consort, the emperor would, at most, ask Prince Jing to apologize to her—he wouldn't actually punish the prince. It would leave the noble consort and her son feeling smug for a while, but Prince Jing could always get his revenge later. As he waited for Prince Jing to finish changing, Li Yu swished his tail happily at how well everything had played out.

Lady Qiu eyed the fish Prince Jing had brought. For years, she'd held a mix of hatred and envy for Prince Jing in her heart. Prince Jing might not be present in the room right now, but she wasn't going to let him go unscathed.

She stood up, sauntered over, and peered down with interest at the fish in the bowl. Something seemed to occur to her as she let out a light peal of laughter.

Mu Tianzhao had followed her over. He chuckled. "Mother, what is this fish? I've never seen the likes of it before."

He and his mother both had that kind of attitude to things they considered beneath them, so this really was the first time Mu Tianzhao had ever seen a live carp.

The noble consort pursed her lips, then laughed daintily. "My son is of royal blood; how could you be expected to recognize such a crude thing? It's nothing but the most ordinary fish used for cooking."

His lips twitched up into a smile. "My brother's taste is certainly quite unique. Perhaps I should ask our royal father to gift him some fish with a little more value."

Their words of admiration were thinly veiled barbs aimed right at Prince Jing. Li Yu halted directly underneath the two of them, not even bothering to hide the fact that he was openly listening to them, utterly disgusted by their words. How dare they insult his owner and say he had no taste—that was the same as insulting *him*! They even had the audacity to say he was crude. Not even the emperor had gone that far.

Li Yu flicked the water angrily. He had to do something.

All of Lady Qiu's attention was on the little carp as she came closer. She had never seen such a lively fish before—but of course, she could never have guessed that, when it had splashed water all over Prince Jing just now, it had done it on purpose. After all, it was just an ordinary fish.

But this fish had more guts than the noble consort could ever imagine! As she peered down at him, Li Yu was preparing himself to give her a face full of water. He had already drenched Prince Jing; there was no way he was going to show any mercy to cannon fodder.

But as the noble consort approached, a flash of light caught Li Yu's eyes, and he noticed a golden phoenix hairpin by her forehead. Held delicately within the beak of the phoenix was a large sparkling pearl about the size of a person's thumbnail.

Li Yu felt his stomach drop. He had a bad feeling about this.

That couldn't be...the eponymous pearl from his side quest, "Clear, Bright Pearl," right?

The system, which had been silent for a long time, replied lightly: *<User, you got it right.>*

Li Yu was stunned.

*Stupid system! Can you get any more annoying?!* How was a fish supposed to retrieve a pearl from the forehead of the emperor's beloved concubine?!

Splashing her was out of the question for now. The noble consort was still a little too far away. He had to get her to come a little closer first. Li Yu readied his fish tail. He was going to strike back! For the pearl! For Prince Jing!

As for how...

The noble consort was very calculating in the book, which meant she was also very suspicious. An idea started to take form inside Li Yu's head. If you wanted to deal with these kinds of dirty tricks, you had to fight dirty too.

How did a fish flip over again?

Li Yu rolled over playfully, trying to rotate his belly up slowly. He floated in the water in that position without moving a muscle. It wasn't a comfortable position for a fish. But if he endured it for a little bit, he would definitely get results.

The second prince was looking straight at the bowl while he spoke to Noble Consort Qiu. He saw it clearly when, suddenly, Prince Jing's fish twitched strangely, then flipped over.

"Mother, what's wrong with the fish?" he blurted out.

Noble Consort Qiu, who was still basking in her smugness, glanced over, and her heart nearly stopped. Didn't fish flip over when they died? But this fish had been so lively just a second ago...

Lady Qiu hardly cared whether a fish lived or died, of course, but this was the fish Prince Jing had brought before the emperor. The emperor himself had been acquainted with it! But now the prince had left to change his clothes, and the two of them were the closest to the fish when it suddenly died—who'd be able to explain that??

Was this all part of Prince Jing's plan? She'd used Piaoxue to cause problems for him, so he was using this fish to turn the tables on her? It was very possible. Otherwise, why would Prince Jing bring a fish to see the emperor? He had been waiting for this exact moment!

This conspiracy theory was growing more and more likely to Noble Consort Qiu, who was well-versed in back palace drama. As the fish floated belly-up in front of her, she began to panic.

# Fish-Style Slap

HAVING BEEN the favored concubine for several years, Noble Consort Qiu knew the emperor still had a soft spot for Prince Jing, which was why she harbored such great resentment for the prince. What if this incident brought the emperor's anger down on her—and in turn on the second prince, just when he was on the verge of becoming the crown prince!

Noble Consort Qiu refused to let herself and her son suffer through such a disaster, so she came up with what she felt was an ingenious idea.

"Zhao-er, come. Don't make a sound. Let's...let's hide the fish, quickly."

Mu Tianzhao was bewildered.

Lady Qiu didn't want other people to get involved. Qianqing Palace was not her territory, and the emperor was right there, on the throne—if she asked her trusted servants to deal with this, it would only serve to attract his attention. The fewer people who knew that Prince Jing's fish had died, the better.

Noble Consort Qiu and the second prince neatly blocked the bowl from onlookers' curious eyes, quietly devising a plan.

First, Lady Qiu would hide the fish, then pretend to notice that the fish had vanished, triggering a search party ordered by the emperor. While everyone was distracted, she'd have time to furtively acquire another live fish. She would then have someone find it at just the right time and place. It would be a flawless switcheroo.

"Won't someone be able to tell?" Mu Tianzhao was a little hesitant. His ascension to crown prince was tantalizingly close and he didn't want anything to endanger it.

"What are you afraid of?" Noble Consort Qiu laughed coldly. "A fish like this, it's just a soup ingredient. They all look the same. Prince Jing probably won't even be able to tell the difference." Noble Consort Qiu was brimming with confidence, convinced her plan was foolproof—otherwise, she wouldn't have dared to come up with something like this. What else was she supposed to do? Just wait around for Prince Jing to make her life difficult?

She took another glance at the flipped-over fish floating on the water. They had to hide the fish well so that no one would be able to find it. The best place would be inside her sleeves. No one would dare search the noble consort!

Suppressing the urge to hurl, Lady Qiu reached for the fish using her handkerchief. Just as she was about to touch the fish though, the very tip of its tail, which had originally been motionless, started to shake. Then it started struggling.

Noble Consort Qiu and the second prince jumped. Stunned, Mu Tianzhao asked, "Mother, wasn't that fish supposed to be dead?!"

How could a fish come back to life? This was way too bizarre!

Noble Consort Qiu didn't have time to speculate any further, nor did she have time to respond to the second prince. She'd wrapped the fish up in her handkerchief, but it was still very slippery—and now it was squirming around quite hard. If she let it slip out of her hand and fall onto the floor, here in Qianqing Palace, right in front of the emperor...

She had already taken the first step; there was no turning back now!

Sweat continued to bead on the noble consort's forehead. This woman had lived in the lap of luxury for a long time now, so she didn't have much grip strength. Furthermore, she was dealing with Li Yu, an expert at struggling. This time, he went all out. With his newly stronger tail, it didn't take much for him to escape from her grasp.

This was the closest the little carp was ever going to get to Lady Qiu!

By now, Li Yu had a lot of experience swinging his tail around. He calculated the distance and made a clean swing. His original plan was to jump onto the noble consort and give her a good scare—then, in the ensuing chaos, he'd snatch the pearl. If that didn't work and he ended up on the floor, he could just swing his tail a couple more times to try to get back into the bowl. The bowl was very close by. Being away from the water for such a short amount of time shouldn't be a problem... And besides, he had all that fresh water stored in his inventory.

But unfortunately, he used too much force. With one flip, he managed to set a whole new record, landing smack dab in the middle of the noble consort's face. *Uh oh*—

Noble Consort Qiu's vision was suddenly obstructed by something cold and slippery. Prince Jing's fish had thrown itself onto her face! She screeched in terror. "Ahh—!"

Her scream instantly lit a fire under Li Yu. This was, after all, the first time he had ended up on someone's body—er, face—as a fish. His tail flapped furiously in alarm, slapping the noble consort's face over and over again!

The second prince didn't even know how to react. The flurry of slapping noises finally jolted him out of it, though, and he yelled in a panic, "Mother, Mother! Someone, come quickly! Save my mother!"

"Zhao-er, get it off! It's on my face, it's on my face!!" All that the shocked and terrified Lady Qiu could see were wet gray scales. She couldn't stop screaming. Mu Tianzhao wanted to help, but his hand froze midair, too afraid this fish would fly onto him next. Who knew what might happen?!

In the chaos, Li Yu found a suitable position on the noble consort's face and swished his tail once again, aiming for the glistening white pearl. This time, he took careful command of his strength to slap the golden hairpin with pinpoint accuracy. Bingo! The pearl fell from the hairpin onto the floor, just like he planned.

Noble Consort Qiu had put a bit of thought into choosing her hairpin, hoping to entice the emperor even when night fell with this priceless luminous pearl—but now she was panicking too hard to fret about her hair accessories.

Li Yu flapped his fins a few times, straining to reach the fallen pearl, but it was no use. That pearl was standing between him and turning back into a human, and it was about to fall onto the golden bricks.

It was all or nothing! Li Yu flung himself toward the jewel.

Meanwhile, the emperor had been enjoying his tea while he waited for Prince Jing when he suddenly heard the noble consort and the second prince shouting and yelling. The emperor rushed over along with Head Eunuch Luo to see what had happened, only to find the noble consort with her hair in disarray, face paper white. Her hands were flailing about, clawing at nothing, while the second prince stood off to the side in uncertainty.

The emperor didn't see Li Yu. Of course he wouldn't notice a little carp on the ground, chasing after the pearl, when the consort and her son were making such a fuss.

"What is going on?!" demanded the emperor, furious.

Li Yu couldn't reach the luminous pearl. As it hit the floor and rolled away, he made a lunge for it, but it was too late. Just as he was about to reach the pearl, a pair of hands materialized from above and pressed down on his little fish body.

Who was getting in the way of completing his quest?!

Incensed and indignant, Li Yu glared up—and straight at Prince Jing's face. Li Yu could see anger simmering beneath the surface.

F-fuck. Here he was flopping around, high off adrenaline at the prospect of completing his quest, only to get caught red-handed by the tyrant. Li Yu blew a listless bubble. He wanted to hide and flat-out deny everything. But he was in Prince Jing's palm—there was nowhere to hide!

Had Prince Jing seen him slap Noble Consort Qiu and steal the pearl? He had to be in big trouble with the prince! But he wasn't playing around for no reason.

Noble Consort Qiu was definitely going to report Li Yu to the emperor for what he just did, but so long as he returned to the bowl before the emperor noticed him, there was no way the emperor would believe her. After all, how could a fish jump out of the bowl, humiliate Lady Qiu, and then jump back in?

Right, he needed to get back. It felt awful to be out of the water. He had to figure out a way to return to the bowl without Prince Jing noticing...but that was way harder than tricking Lady Qiu had been. Prince Jing was no fool—Li Yu had to be careful.

While Li Yu was still racking his fish brain for ideas, Prince Jing slipped him gently back into the water.

Li Yu was shocked and relieved to find himself surrounded by water in his bowl again. Wow, the tyrant actually put him back! He wiggled a bit to demonstrate his affection, but Prince Jing glared at him again. The little carp could clearly read the threat in the tyrant's eyes: *I'll deal with you later.*

Li Yu shrunk back.

*Wait, is that why he didn't get mad earlier? He was saving it for later?*

He didn't want to be fish soup, and he didn't want to die either, so Li Yu decided he might as well let the tyrant pinch him a few more times. He arched his back into Prince Jing's hand in an effort to wiggle his way back into the prince's good graces. Surely letting Prince Jing get a few squeezes in would get him out of trouble?

Prince Jing stared, unimpressed.

"Your Imperial Majesty, please believe me. I don't know why Prince Jing's fish just leaped onto my face..."

Lady Qiu was still in shock as she knelt in front of the emperor, weeping. She loathed Prince Jing with all her heart, so much that she wished for his death. Did she fall into his trap? Had Prince Jing acquired a fish with the ability to resurrect itself for the sole purpose of embarrassing her in front of the emperor?

This terrifying ordeal had Noble Consort Qiu shocked out of her wits. She felt like everyone and everything was out to get her.

The emperor rubbed his temples and looked over at Prince Jing, faintly confused. Prince Jing scoffed and gestured at the bowl, placed not too far away, with his chin. He'd made sure no one was paying attention when he put the little carp back in. Since Noble Consort Qiu had bribed people to slander him, he'd give her a taste of her own medicine. Let her have a turn at being unable to explain herself.

Prince Jing took another glance at the intriguing little carp that had managed to create this situation for him. What divine fortune.

The emperor ordered Luo Ruisheng to investigate the scene, only to be informed that Prince Jing's fish was swimming happily in its bowl. This time, the emperor was irate. "The noble consort is telling a bald-faced lie! Prince Jing's fish is clearly still in its bowl!"

Lady Qiu felt all the blood rush to her head. Fury and anxiety saturated her voice. "Your Imperial Majesty, it's true! That fish flew out just now!"

The emperor's brows furrowed. "So you're saying a fish can fly. And not only can it fly, but it flew out, harassed you, and then somehow flew back?"

At this point, the fish was like a trigger for Noble Consort Qiu. She nodded furiously. "That's exactly it. Zhao-er saw it too."

"Noble Consort, have you gone mad?" The emperor sighed, disbelief written all over his face. Lady Qiu had seemed fine before, but all of a sudden, she was kicking up a fuss, spewing all sorts of foolishness. A fish that could fly? How was that possible? If she hadn't gone mad, why else would she talk such nonsense? And even mess up her own hair?

"If you want to make up ridiculous stories, then so be it. But do you have to try to drag Zhao-er down with you?"

Mu Tianzhao had opened his mouth to corroborate his mother's account, but on hearing the emperor's words, he shut it again. Noble Consort Qiu kept shooting him pointed looks, but...since the emperor didn't believe her, the emperor would only become more upset if he insisted on backing her up. What was the point of playing the hero for a fleeting moment?

Mu Tianzhao would give up anything for the position of crown prince. In a sensible tone, he said, "Royal Father, you're right. I...I did not see it clearly."

Mu Tianzhao guiltily avoided his mother's look of disbelief. He was about to become the crown prince—was it wrong to have some self-preservation?

The emperor said unhappily, "Noble Consort, even Tianzhao agrees. What do you have to say for yourself?"

Lady Qiu bit her cherry lips. "Your Imperial Majesty, I...I forgot myself and misspoke. Please forgive me."

Even her own son had turned his back on her, so what else could she say? She'd had a momentary lapse in judgment? It didn't matter how much she complained, it was useless if the emperor didn't believe her. The best thing for her to do now was to keep her head down and wait for the emperor's anger to dissipate. There was no need to fight with a stupid fish.

Right at the moment that Lady Qiu admitted her folly, Prince Jing's boot stepped on an embroidered handkerchief. Wang Xi, who had been following behind Prince Jing, rushed forward and picked the handkerchief up.

Wang Xi shook the handkerchief out to check who it belonged to and let out a shocked exclamation.

"Wang Xi, what is *your* issue?" groaned the emperor, whose head was beginning to hurt from all these things happening one after another.

Wang Xi said, "Your Imperial Majesty, this servant just picked up the noble consort's handkerchief...but why does it have fish scales on it?"

As he spoke, Wang Xi raised the handkerchief so that everyone could see. A handkerchief embroidered with crab apple flowers. Even the emperor knew it belonged to the noble consort. And just as Wang Xi said, there were a few fish scales still stuck to it.

Why would the noble consort's handkerchief have fish scales on it? There was only one fish in all of Qianqing Palace!

Prince Jing's fierce eyes flashed over to the noble consort, his gaze as sharp as a knife. Wang Xi immediately spoke for the prince. "Fish scales are part of the fish. They don't fall off for no reason. Did the noble consort do something to our Master Fish while our prince wasn't here?"

As expected of Prince Jing's spokesperson! A powerful attack from Wang-gonggong. Li Yu was delighted. But when did he become a master? He was just a fish!

*Master?* The emperor was speechless.

Wang Xi beamed as he explained, "Your Imperial Majesty, this servant heard this from Xiaolinzi first. Xiaolinzi called the noble consort's cat Master Cat. It's only logical for His Highness's fish to be Master Fish."

As the master of the world, the emperor was everyone's master. Was the noble consort trying to put the cat and the emperor on the same level by calling it "master"?

"Nonsense. Do not call them that in the future." The emperor glared at Lady Qiu. "Noble Consort Qiu, what did you do to Prince Jing's fish? Why are there fish scales on your handkerchief?"

There was no way the noble consort was going to admit she had used the handkerchief to pick the fish up. She hadn't realized it at first, but the moment she walked over to look at the fish, the tables had been turning against her. This fish definitely had it in for her. She'd barely even had time to do anything to it—the fish was clearly the one who was tormenting her!

Noble Consort Qiu sobbed. "Your Imperial Majesty, why don't you ask Prince Jing? He was the one who bullied my Piaoxue first..."

"Your Imperial Majesty!"

Throwing everything to the wind, Wang Xi fell to his knees and declared loudly, "People are always taking advantage of His Highness's inability to speak in order to frame him. As you know, his injuries take a long time to heal; it's been true since he was young, all the imperial physicians know this. When His Highness was changing just now, this servant noticed a large bruise on his leg. Its position matches the body shape of that cat. That day, the noble consort's cat ran into His Highness first—that's why His Highness taught it a lesson. This servant implores Your Imperial Majesty to believe His Highness!"

A bruise from the cat? Noble Consort Qiu's pupils constricted. Why hadn't she thought of such a flaw in her plan?

The emperor was very upset to hear that Prince Jing had been "injured," and he immediately called for an imperial physician to "treat his injury." Once the doctor confirmed that there really was a bruise, the emperor was no longer able to contain his ire. "It's just a cat—how dare it injure a prince?! It seems he was right—it really did deserve it.'"

If the cat was the one who ran into Prince Jing, Xiaolinzi must have lied. A quick investigation uncovered the truth: he had been bribed by the noble consort. Qianqing Palace was a bloodbath.

The flames of the emperor's temper surged to a fierce blaze. He hadn't announced the crown prince yet, and Noble Consort Qiu was already out for Prince Jing's blood. When she became empress dowager in the future, would Prince Jing make it out alive?

The emperor confined Lady Qiu to her palace, where she was banned from coming out without a summons. Originally, he'd been planning to promote her to imperial noble consort[7] soon after her birthday, but he really didn't feel like it anymore. Even looking at the future crown prince, the second prince, put him in a foul mood.

Lady Qiu could have never predicted that her carefully planned scheme would be thwarted in the end by a mere fish.

Li Yu had really gone above and beyond this time. It was rowdy out there in the palace, and listening to the kerfuffle was making

---

7   Imperial noble consort (皇贵妃) is only one rank below the empress, and as a sign of respect, when there is an empress, there usually isn't an imperial noble consort. When the position of empress is empty, and someone gets promoted to imperial noble consort, it is a signal that they hold the same authority as that of empress and may be promoted to empress soon.

him sleepy. Thinking there were still a couple pieces of food left at the bottom of the bowl, Li Yu managed to pull himself together enough to swim over and eat the fish food. Just as he was about to doze off, he was hit with a feeling that he had forgotten something.

...Wait, the clear, bright pearl! He'd almost forgotten! Li Yu immediately flew up to the surface, scanning his surroundings. There it was! The pearl was sitting all by its lonesome in a corner of the palace. No one had realized the noble consort's hair ornament was missing a luminous pearl.

Li Yu was itching to go for it. All he had to do was sneak out and grab the pearl. Even a touch would be good! Perhaps that would be enough for a "quest complete."

But just then, Wang Xi strolled over, all smiles, grabbed his bowl, and headed outside.

*What???*

It turned out the emperor was still reprimanding Lady Qiu. Prince Jing didn't have the patience to listen any longer, so he got up to leave. The little carp that had accompanied him to meet the emperor obviously had to leave with him too.

"Hey, are you kidding me? I haven't grabbed the pearl..."

Wang Xi was only a few steps away from leaving the palace, bowl in hand, when he saw the little carp leaning against the rim of the bowl. It seemed to be staring longingly in a particular direction.

Wang Xi nearly laughed out loud. He shook his head. He must be imagining things.

As he watched the pearl get farther and farther away from him, his chances of completing the mission dwindling, Li Yu felt himself deflate. Right next to him, Prince Jing noted that the little carp looked listless. He considered for a moment, and then ordered a servant to go and take a look. Before long, the servant came back holding a pearl.

Prince Jing recognized the luminous pearl; it was the same one the noble consort wore on her head. He was very sure this was what the little carp had been looking at, because when he emerged from the side hall after changing, he saw the little carp flopping after it. It wanted the jewel that badly?

"Master, Master, please give me the pearl!" An invigorated Li Yu swam over. He shimmied cutely, trying to cozy up to the prince by swimming in circles around his hand. It was obvious Li Yu was trying to kiss up to him.

Did the fish think wiggling cutely a few times would get him the pearl? It wouldn't be that easy. Prince Jing still had a bone to pick with him.

With a faint smile, Prince Jing slipped the pearl into his sleeve.

# The Fish Made
# a Mistake

L I YU FOLLOWED PRINCE JING and his servants back to
Jingtai Hall.

He made countless attempts to endear himself to the
prince on the way there, but Prince Jing, who had been tapping him
on the head back in Qianqing Palace, didn't react at all. He even
tucked away the luminous pearl. Li Yu was a little frustrated.

Didn't he at least deserve some credit for inconveniencing Noble
Consort Qiu? Was it *that* hard to let him hold the pearl for a bit? It
wasn't like he was going to monopolize it; he only needed it to complete his quest. After the quest was finished, he'd be done with it!

But there was no need to get himself too worked up. Perhaps it
was just a coincidence that Prince Jing had taken the pearl. Com-
munication between a fish and a mute prince was too difficult.

Li Yu switched tactics and started swimming in circles around
the bowl. Perhaps by mimicking the shape of a pearl, he could give
Prince Jing a hint... But the prince kept on acting like he couldn't
see him.

"Little thing, what are you trying to do?" Wang Xi chuckled.

Wang-gonggong had resolved to take good care of this fish from
now on. Although it was just an ordinary, edible carp, this little
creature had brought Prince Jing a substantial amount of good luck.
It had splashed the prince with water, but that had allowed them to

discover the bruise from Piaoxue, which in turn was what helped them get one over on the noble consort. Wang Xi had looked down on Xiaolinzi for calling Piaoxue "Master Cat," but now he was all too eager to eat his words and call the fish "master" too.

Li Yu stiffened at Wang Xi's question. How could he make these people understand that all he wanted was the pearl? He didn't want anything else!

Should he swim in the shape of the word "pearl"?!

No, probably not. If he really did manage to write something, he might scare Wang Xi witless. Worse yet, what if Wang Xi mistook him for a fish spirit? Cultivation had been banned ever since the founding of the PRC. May the heavens have mercy—he was just an innocent transmigrated fish!

He'd better come up with something else.

Wang Xi carried the large bowl to the room that the little carp had been in before. Li Yu watched as the prince moved farther and farther away. Hey!! Wasn't he supposed to live with the tyrant? But after thinking about it some more, Li Yu realized he hadn't actually seen a bed or anything to sleep on... The prince had only entered that room to change. It obviously wasn't his bedroom.

In ancient times, a concubine's favor with the emperor could apparently be determined by how far away she lived from him. It was probably the same for pets...

But a pet that didn't live with its owner practically wasn't a pet at all! Li Yu could see it now, he was going to fail all his quests, and there was only one way that led—fish bones and fish ash!

He couldn't be separated from Prince Jing!

Li Yu had been looking kind of wilted, but now he was full of energy again. Living was way more important than some bright, shiny pearl. He still had to "get along" with Prince Jing.

Since Wang Xi had asked him what he wanted, Li Yu was going to show him. He bravely poked his head out of the water to look in Prince Jing's direction, his gaze bright and gleaming—

Wang Xi was so happy he couldn't close his mouth. "Oh, this little thing can't bear to part from His Highness, it wants to stay with him."

Li Yu was incredibly flustered at being called "little thing" again, but desperate times called for desperate measures. He blew a bubble.

"That's somewhat difficult, little thing." Wang Xi must have been in a surprisingly good mood, because he actually gave the fish an explanation. "His Highness doesn't like others in his room."

Li Yu was baffled. This was the first time Li Yu had heard of his tyrant owner having a pet peeve like that. This bit of characterization probably wasn't in the book...

The prince in the book was just made up of rows of cold and lifeless text, but the Prince Jing before him was an actual, living, breathing person. And Li Yu knew that people were multifaceted and much more complicated than words on a page could describe.

Li Yu could accept this new information. Prince Jing didn't like others entering his room, fair enough. But he wasn't just anyone— he was his pet fish. Li Yu continued wagging his tail at Wang Xi. He *really* wanted to go.

Wang Xi couldn't help smiling. Sometimes he felt like this little carp was very intelligent and a bit clingy. Who didn't like a clingy pet?

He wanted to help the little carp. He liked fish. Fish were quiet. They didn't get in the way, no matter where you put them; they were more or less a decorative piece. But it turned out he didn't need to convince Prince Jing, for the prince had already taken the bowl from him, a dark expression on his face.

Wang-gonggong was getting the sense that the prince wasn't in the greatest of moods. Not for the first time, he found himself thinking that he really couldn't understand Prince Jing.

Prince Jing carried the little carp to the forbidden bedroom where no outsiders were permitted to enter. He had given the fish the cold shoulder all the way back from Qianqing Palace, but now it dared to wag its tail at Wang Xi?

Prince Jing hadn't been standing too far away when the fish was playing with Wang Xi. His gaze as he watched them could have frozen the entire room. It was a very peculiar feeling—like when he was young and Mu Tianzhao had stolen something that belonged to him. It had made him very unhappy, and only seizing it back made him feel a little better.

He had already said so in front of the emperor: the fish was now his. He should be the one to decide where it lived. He didn't need anyone else to intervene. Accordingly, he took the fish away to his room and told nobody to bother him.

Wang Xi would never be able to imagine the inner workings of Prince Jing's mind. In order to please his master, Wang-gonggong hastily ordered some servants to bring over the porcelain fish tank from the first room. He was worried about Prince Jing's lack of pet fish knowledge too, so he also summoned a few servants who had experience taking care of fish, cats, and dogs. Just in case.

After everything was settled and he had been moved back into his porcelain fish tank, Li Yu did a lap around the tank. Someone had already changed the water, and the leaf blanket and bed of white rocks were still waiting for him, untouched. This was truly the best place; it was much nicer to swim in here than in the bowl.

...Somehow, he realized, he had gotten used to thinking about things from a fish's perspective. He didn't know whether to laugh or cry; was it a good or bad thing that he had adapted to all this so quickly?

After dawdling for a while and making sure nobody was paying attention to him, he ducked under the leaf blanket, pretending to rest, and entered the system.

The last time Li Yu had done this, he had been bursting with joy, excited to receive his prize. It was a very different story this time around; he was deflated and gloomy. He had made little to no progress in either the main or side quests. The fish-scamming system greeted him as usual but didn't provide him with any extra hints.

Half of the allotted time for the "getting along" step in the "Priceless Pet Fish" quest had already slipped by. Seeing the emperor hadn't helped him make any progress either. It was obvious he had to work a little harder.

It was a shame he couldn't complete "Clear, Bright Pearl." Maybe he should give it another try? It was just within reach...

Either way, Li Yu thought, he was already in Prince Jing's room. He was supposed to be his pet—he needed to have a little less shame about it. It wouldn't be all that weird for him to wiggle his way into his owner's clothes and *just* so happen to accidentally pull out a pearl or something, right?

Time was of the essence. Resolving to leave his shame behind, Li Yu exited the system.

While he was inside the system, he couldn't tell what was happening in the outside world. Now that he was out again, he shook himself and came to the abrupt realization that he was lying...lying in the tyrant's hand!

Li Yu nearly jumped out of his skin.

Prince Jing cupped his hands, holding the fish so that it was still surrounded by water. He had never observed the fish up close before.

As soon as the little carp settled down, he couldn't resist taking a look.

It was a strange fish, he thought, but it was also intriguing.

When he'd first picked the fish up, he noticed it was completely stiff. Unmoving. His brow twitched, and he immediately called over a servant who had raised fish before. After examining the fish for a few minutes, they concluded it was likely asleep. Prince Jing then called over another servant for a second opinion, and this one said the exact same thing.

After roughly ten minutes, Prince Jing dismissed all of them and continued staring at the fish alone. If it was asleep, then it would eventually wake up. He wanted to see what other tricks this fish had up its sleeve.

The little carp didn't "sleep" for long. Prince Jing was so close that he saw the fish tail twitch a little. Then, without warning, the fish jolted forward, nearly falling over in the water...

...Not for the first time, Prince Jing thought that the fish had the same dazed kind of look as a person who'd just woken up. But as soon as the fish saw him, it seemed sluggish. Prince Jing was slightly annoyed and tapped on the little carp's head. Why had it been so lively in front of Wang Xi, but seemed wooden and slow with him?

The tap made Li Yu shake his head, remembering the task at hand. He started to wiggle his tail in his attempt to wheedle his way into the prince's favor. Ever since he had become a pet fish, swishing his tail and begging for pity was the only other survival skill he had outside of swimming.

Except his owner didn't appreciate it. Prince Jing scoffed, his expression cold. Trying to kiss up to him now? Too late.

His palm was only so big, and it was impossible for the fish to keep wiggling like this without touching his hand. The feeling of the fish tail against his palm was a little odd, but Prince Jing refused to let it show.

Li Yu took no notice. He was still trying to act cute, but his eyes kept trailing over to Prince Jing's clothing. The prince had put the luminous pearl in his sleeve, he remembered. If he could sneak into the prince's sleeve...

Wait, he was in Prince Jing's hand right now! He could pretend that fish were very slippery!

Li Yu swam to the edge of the prince's palm, deliberately slowly. He just needed to turn his body and flip over. But...while he managed to do exactly that, as soon as his body left the confines of his palm, Prince Jing caught him with his other hand and put him back.

Li Yu was stunned.

*I'll flip again! Again!*

He tried twisting from the other side, but Prince Jing was faster. With his hands carefully cupped, he was able to hold him completely.

Li Yu was *pissed*.

Prince Jing peered down at him. He almost looked like he was smiling—he was doing it on purpose! Did he hide the pearl just to toy with him?

Li Yu's mind spun. He thought smugly, *Then how about this?!*

He didn't fight against the prince. Instead, following the line down Prince Jing's palm and arm, Li Yu slid down.

Prince Jing froze. At first, he thought the fish had been making a break for it, but he absolutely did not expect it to try to wriggle into his sleeve. Aided by the water in Prince Jing's hand, the little fish slid down his arm, managing to slip right into his sleeve in the blink of an eye.

Prince Jing, normally as sturdy as an ice-capped mountain, felt goosebumps erupting all over his skin. He furrowed his brows tightly.

Meanwhile, Li Yu, who had successfully managed to infiltrate enemy territory, found himself stuck to a large patch of mu...mu...muscle.

Wh-what was this feeling? Did Prince Jing not wear an inner robe?

Li Yu lay against this unknown muscle, his face blazing. In his original world, he was but an innocent boy who had been single his entire life. Now that he had transmigrated into a book, he was suddenly touching skin to skin...with another man!

He was so embarrassed!

Li Yu was so flustered he wanted to cover his face with his fins, but they were too short. With no other way to unleash his emotions, he resorted to fiercely flapping his tail instead. Prince Jing, who had been bearing with all of these bizarre sensations, felt something scratching at him nonstop.

How could anyone put up with that? Prince Jing was about to break out in a cold sweat. He quickly untied his clothes, wanting to pull the troublesome fish out.

Inside his sleeve, Li Yu was getting more and more annoyed. The sleeve was narrow and dark; if he moved around, he would slide further down, unable to stop. If he opened his eyes, the fabric would stab into them. Filled with regret over his impulsive decision, Li Yu was desperate to leave. In a fit of distress, he thrashed around even more wildly. But his struggling only increased Prince Jing's discomfort.

As he flailed about, though, Li Yu spotted a faint glow. Dizzily, he wondered why there would be light in Prince Jing's clothes. Could it be—

The clear, bright pearl?

How sneaky! Prince Jing may have stuffed the pearl deep into his sleeve, but he couldn't fool Li Yu! Victory was just one step away; he could do it!

Li Yu fought hard to move toward the light. He'd come this far already. Nothing could stop him now! No matter what, he had to touch it first!

As he shuffled closer to the light, he thought he could see a hazy, round thing. Oh, pearls were round!

Li Yu opened his mouth wide and went for it. The moment his fish jaws closed around the round thing, Li Yu was overcome with emotion. Terrified the pearl might roll away from him, he clamped down hard.

Li Yu felt Prince Jing flinch violently. The next moment, his dark surroundings brightened. All the clothing that had been in the way was now gone, and he could see Prince Jing, his upper half completely bare, with a rare hint of pink on his cheeks. He scowled down at Li Yu, irate.

With the luminous pearl in his mouth, the little carp couldn't blow bubbles, so he opted to wave his tail happily at his owner instead. Which was when he realized he was lying entirely on the prince's chest.

Hold on.

How did he get from the sleeve to here? Keeping his death grip on the pearl, Li Yu scoured his surroundings. All he could see was a landscape of pale skin. Especially here, where the pearl was, he could feel the prince's pulse within his chest.

Wait. Li Yu finally noticed something was wrong. Did Prince Jing hang the pearl around his neck? It was the noble consort's pearl—did he have to go so far? The make and model of the pearl was not quite right either. The texture felt...a little soft.

Li Yu arrived at a horrifying conclusion. Trembling, he opened his mouth and reluctantly looked at the "luminous pearl" he had just held within his mouth.

That wasn't a pearl. Not at all. That was...the thing used to differentiate between the front and back of a man!

The fish suffered a devastating blow. The little carp collapsed, dropping down from Prince Jing's chest, but Prince Jing, with his lightning-fast reflexes, managed to catch him.

Just then, Wang Xi pushed open the door. He had wanted to ask Prince Jing a question, but he had waited some time, and the prince never came out of his room. Left without another choice, Wang Xi came in to take a look...only to be faced with Prince Jing in a state of undress, face flushed pink, and fish in hand.

Wang Xi was shocked!

Who knew what Wang-gonggong, experienced and knowledgeable in all his worldly wisdom, was thinking about when he came upon this scene. He was so aghast, his voice even changed. "Your Highness, you can't! The fish is too small! It won't be able to take it!"

This entire day had just been a never-ending stream of embarrassments. God, please just let this fish die!

# The Fish Wants
# to Apologize

LI YU KNEW he had screwed up big time.

There was no question about it: Prince Jing must be furious. Not only had Li Yu splashed water on him and caused a huge ruckus in Qianqing Palace when Prince Jing wasn't there, now Li Yu had gone and felt him up too. Li Yu's ancestors must be protecting him—it was the only way he could explain why the prince hadn't killed him then and there.

He couldn't remember how he went from Prince Jing's hand back to his fish tank, nor could he recall swimming back to his bed of white rocks. Normally, fish fell asleep in the blink of an eye, but Li Yu had spent half the night tossing and turning and hadn't slept a wink.

But the moonlight outside the window shone into the porcelain fish tank, making the bottom of the water sparkle and shine. Li Yu felt his mood lift a little at the sight.

Thinking about what he had gone through, he felt even more humiliated. No matter how shameless he was, that was it for him. There was no way he was going to attempt to complete "Clear, Bright Pearl" again. He should just give up on the side quest and focus on the main quest. He was sure there would be other opportunities for him to transform back into a human in the future.

Having finally convinced himself, he decided to put all his energy into figuring out how to "get along" with Prince Jing. But this whole mess had scared him pretty badly. Whenever he saw Prince Jing, he felt uncomfortable all over, as though he could still feel the softness in his mouth. His fish tail felt like it was being roasted over an open fire, the heat spreading quickly through his entire body.

How could he be so foolish as to confuse a pearl with...*that*?

Li Yu buried his head under his leaf blanket in a huff. If he was this miserable, Prince Jing probably wasn't much better. Li Yu knew that if he was in Prince Jing's royal shoes and he had been bitten *there* by a fish, he'd never hear the end of it as long as he lived.

And he just had to do this to himself right after he insisted on staying in Prince Jing's room! They couldn't get away from each other anymore. There was nowhere for him to find an antidote for his regret.

Without really meaning to, Li Yu started avoiding Prince Jing. When the prince passed by, Li Yu either had his tail turned to him, or he was hiding motionlessly under his blanket, pretending to be asleep. He only acted cute for food when Wang Xi came to see him.

Wang Xi would feed him a plethora of red-colored food, but for some reason, his gaze would always be tinged with pity. He would whisper, "Little thing, you've suffered a lot. Eat more and grow fat."

But it was dangerous for a fish to fatten up. The little carp started to grow wary. Did Prince Jing want to turn him into fish soup?

Thank goodness Wang Xi still used a ruyi[8] to nudge him into swimming a few laps after each meal. At first, Li Yu didn't understand why he did it. But he soon learned, from Wang-gonggong's chatter, that fish weren't supposed to eat too much, and he was pushing Li Yu to swim around so he could digest better.

---

8    A ruyi (如意) is a decorative Chinese scepter. Its name means "as you desire," and is a symbol of good fortune.

Perhaps it was because he had followed the taciturn Prince Jing for many years, but Wang Xi never seemed to run out of things to say. When he stood before his master, Wang Xi had to carefully consider his words before he spoke, but he had no such qualms when it came to the little carp.

The image of a hand came to mind, making Li Yu pause. The fingers were pinched together, gently pushing him to swim around. He'd gorged himself back then too... So Prince Jing had been helping him digest that time. But because he couldn't speak, and because of his personality, Prince Jing didn't reveal it to anyone.

As grateful as Li Yu felt, his guilt just continued to grow. He knew Prince Jing was good to him, and yet he had...taken advantage of him...

It had been a misunderstanding, an accident, but he knew he was still at fault.

A bit wrung out, the little carp wondered if he and Prince Jing would be able to go back to how they were before. Was he going to have to continue avoiding the prince, never complete his quests, and eventually turn into fish bones and fish ash?

Li Yu couldn't accept his life ending for such an outrageous reason. He needed to pull himself together. He wanted to complete his tasks happily with Prince Jing and not have to hide whenever he heard the prince's footsteps.

He...should try to apologize. Misunderstanding or not, he was still the one in the wrong. As long as he apologized, even if an apology from a fish meant nothing to the prince, he could at least turn over a new page and face Prince Jing like normal.

But the problem was, how was he going to do it?

He had already spun in circles and danced the seaweed dance plenty of times, so those wouldn't be worth anything. He couldn't write, leaving him no way for him to communicate in a human language. He couldn't even prepare a proper gift. The porcelain fish tank he lived in, the bed, and the blanket—none of those belonged to him.

How could he show he was truly sorry?

Li Yu swam a lap in the tank, troubled. Then his gaze fell upon a lone piece of fish food.

It was a chunk of fish food Wang Xi had thrown to him not too long ago, but Li Yu hadn't touched it because he didn't have much of an appetite. But since it was given to him, it now belonged to him. He could give *this* to Prince Jing to demonstrate his sincerity.

Li Yu picked up the food and hid it. Worried it might not be enough, he hid a couple more, until he had six pieces—an auspicious number.

Prince Jing was rarely in his room during the day. He usually only came by at night. Once night fell and the lamps had been lit, Li Yu figured it was about time. He picked out the pieces of fish food and laid them out carefully. Happiness expanding his chest, he waited for Prince Jing to return.

*So what if I bit my owner there? I'm just a fish, you can forgive me, right?*

Tonight, however, unbeknownst to Li Yu, Prince Jing had something to take care of and had returned to his manor outside of the palace. Li Yu waited until he couldn't stay up any longer. But Prince Jing never came back that night.

Prince Jing hurried back to Jingtai Hall bright and early the next day, the morning dew clinging to the bottom of his boots. Wang Xi led a group of servants to help him change. At the first opportunity, Prince Jing shot a glance at the porcelain fish tank.

Ever since the little carp bit him, Prince Jing felt like the fish had been a little listless. Moreover, this listlessness was directed at him, personally, and no one else. The fish would swish its tail when Wang Xi was over there, but as soon as Prince Jing walked over, the only thing he'd see was a clump of water plants.

Prince Jing was a little irritated. Wasn't he the one who had been bitten? How dare this fish ignore him when he hadn't even done anything yet?

Prince Jing wasn't a very laid-back person. He couldn't stop thinking about it—he needed to set things straight between him and the fish and establish some rules. While he wouldn't be so cruel as to deprive his own fish of food and water, Prince Jing still wanted the fish to suffer a little hardship, so it'd think twice about getting too rowdy and making more trouble for him.

He had already written the rules down one by one, and all that was left to do was have Wang Xi implement them. One of them was that he was going to seal the pearl from Qianqing Palace in a clear jar, then put the jar in the fish tank. Prince Jing knew how badly the little carp wanted the pearl, but he wasn't going to just hand it over. Making it look at what it couldn't touch would build character. That way, it would come to understand that one couldn't have everything one wanted in life.

"Your Highness, do...do you think the little thing will understand what you mean by this?"

Wang Xi really wanted to tell the prince that this little thing was just a fish; a fish definitely wouldn't be able to understand such profound principles. Unfortunately, he didn't have any power to talk Prince Jing out of it.

Prince Jing was adamant. He nodded solemnly: it must be done.

Wang Xi sighed. He couldn't go against his master's wishes. He went to prepare.

After changing, Prince Jing strolled to the fish tank. The little carp wasn't hiding anymore, nor was it on its white stone bed. Instead, it had fallen asleep in front of a neat line of fish food.

For a moment, he thought someone was abusing the fish to the point that it was starting to store food.

The little carp woke up soon after. He peered around and noticed the fish food had remained untouched. He looked up, and when he met Prince Jing's eyes, he started to spin happily in circles.

No, no. Li Yu shook his head. He almost forgot himself and started to dance the seaweed dance!

Li Yu tried his best to lower his head in the water. His fins were too short for him to clasp his hands in front of him to bow, so he gave up on the gesture and instead brought each piece of fish food before Prince Jing, lowering his head again each time.

Prince Jing wasn't quite sure how to react.

Wang Xi was shocked. "Your Highness, what is this little thing doing?"

Prince Jing looked from the row of food to the little carp's constantly bobbing head. He watched it for a while, thinking. Was the little carp asking for forgiveness, trying to kiss up to him, or something else? Regardless of the reason, the fish seemed to...want him to eat.

But humans couldn't eat fish food, obviously. The corner of Prince Jing's lips twitched at the fish's absurd ideas.

Seeing that the prince was deep in thought, Wang Xi didn't dare make a sound. But the servant Wang Xi had sent off before to carry out the prince's orders had returned, so Wang Xi timidly interrupted, "Y-Your Highness... The luminous pearl has been put into the bottle at your request."

Wang Xi had to call out to Prince Jing several times before the prince pulled himself out of his reverie.

In Wang Xi's hand was the little bottle with the luminous pearl. Originally, Prince Jing had signaled to Wang Xi that he would punish the little carp by placing the pearl, trapped inside the bottle, into the fish tank himself. The bottle was very secure, and the opening had been sealed with wax. There was no way a fish would be able to open it.

But at the sight of the fish blowing bubbles at him, Prince Jing hesitated. He stopped Wang Xi. Wang Xi didn't understand what was happening, but Prince Jing had already grabbed the little bottle from him. The bottle, clutched in his hand, hovered just above the fish tank.

The luminous pearl's glow was dazzling, even from inside the bottle. Its glimmer filled up the whole fish tank, and Li Yu's attention was drawn to it instantly. There was no doubt that was the clear, bright pearl he had been yearning for. Was he dreaming? What was going on? He'd completely given up on this side quest, but now the prince was bringing out the pearl?

Li Yu was haunted by the memory of what had happened the last time he was too impulsive, and he didn't dare make any sudden movements. He sat obediently in his tank, his tail quivering in anticipation. What was the prince doing? It couldn't be what he was thinking of, right?

The youth standing before the fish tank silently opened the bottle and dumped the pearl straight into the tank.

One couldn't have everything they wanted in life...but as long as someone held him sincerely in their heart, he would take care of them, even if it was just a fish.

Li Yu watched the luminous pearl fall in slow motion, like a dazzling meteor shooting by.

He let out a cheer, his tail flinging him high into the air, and caught the pearl.

# The Fish Wants to Fight for Love

"CLEAR, BRIGHT PEARL"—success!

The long-awaited sound of the system's chime was like the heavens singing down to him. Li Yu was so happy he could float, but since he was right in front of Prince Jing, he had to restrain himself. He couldn't just enter the system and abandon Prince Jing.

As soon as the quest was complete, Li Yu had no further use for the luminous pearl. He was struggling to hold on to it and wanted to put it down, but Prince Jing and Wang Xi were both gathered at the porcelain tank, gazes burning as they stared down at him...

He felt like if he dared to abandon the pearl now, the tyrant might stab him to death with his eyeballs.

Prince Jing must've given Li Yu the pearl because he thought he really liked it, right? Li Yu couldn't just get rid of the pearl after he had made such an effort to apologize. He had to make it seem like he adored it, but his mouth was really sore from holding it.

He thought it over some more, and then he set the pearl down at the bottom of the tank and nudged it shyly with his mouth. The round pearl rolled forward a bit before coming to a stop. Li Yu continued to use his mouth to prod at it, pushing the pearl quite a long way around the tank. *Might as well pretend it's a soccer ball,* Li Yu thought to himself as he played gleefully.

"Your Highness, look, the little thing loves the pearl you gave it. It's rolling it around."

Just moments ago, the little carp had been jumping around happily and even caught the shining pearl from its owner's hand. Wang Xi couldn't be more excited.

Hm...except this pearl that was being rolled around the tank could fetch quite the price. Wang Xi couldn't help feeling a little sorry for the noble consort.

As the little carp chased and played around with the luminous pearl, the cool, clear light made the silvery gray of the fish gleam. It was a rare and breathtaking sight.

Prince Jing smiled lightly. The little fish really did want the pearl.

Li Yu rolled the pearl until he had pushed it into a corner. Pretending he was tired, he lay down on the white rock bed and entered the system. Sure enough, he was immediately met with the reward prompt for finishing the side quest.

Suppressing his excitement, Li Yu carefully read through the instructions for the transformation medicine. He was just about to confirm and accept when a light bulb went off in his head and he realized something.

The bottle that held the medicine looked rustic and was carved with images he had never seen before. It might not look very big, but where was he, a fish, supposed to store it if he accepted it right now? Was he supposed to let it float in the water in his inventory?

...What a cursed image.

After considering his options, Li Yu asked the system, *‹Will the medicine disappear if I don't accept it right away?›*

The system replied: *‹No. Rewards from completed quests will be held indefinitely.›*

Li Yu nodded, satisfied. *<Very good. Then I'll just leave the prize for now and use it when the time comes!>*

The system said nothing.

Li Yu felt like he had just discovered a whole new world. The inadequate size of his inventory wasn't going to stop him from using such a clever method to store the things he didn't need right now. He was always being tricked by the system—it felt good to outsmart it once in a while!

When he first heard about the transformation medicine, he'd been ecstatic. But having spent more time thinking on it, he couldn't just use it willy-nilly. Li Yu didn't exist in the original book, and if he suddenly appeared in his human form, it might create additional chaos that he didn't need or want. Plus, there was also the issue of being able to maintain his human form for only two hours. Everything had to be planned out in advance: it was important he think about the timing and purpose of his transformation. He also had to find a suitable getaway plan on the off chance he turned back into a fish in front of everyone. That would be no good either.

He could worry later; the medicine was in his hands now.

Li Yu cheerfully closed the quest "Clear, Bright Pearl." He checked the main quest again and immediately deflated.

The time left for "getting along" was still counting down, reminding him that he had less than a day before the time was up. If he couldn't complete this main quest, it didn't matter if he had the medicine; he wouldn't ever get a chance to use it.

*<We're already at this point, and the fish-scamming system still won't give me a single hint. Don't you have a conscience?>*

*<The system has no conscience,>* the system agreed. *<Please have some patience when completing your quest.>*

...He always knew this thing was heartless.

Li Yu exited. Night had fallen, dark and quiet, but the luminous pearl was still emitting its soft, faint glow, lighting up the porcelain tank as if it were daytime. Li Yu covered the luminous pearl with the leaf blanket to block out its light, and then he yawned and fell asleep leaning against the pearl.

Li Yu awoke to the smell of ink. The row of fish food he had saved to give to Prince Jing was close by. Prince Jing hadn't touched his gift. It'd be such a waste if his gift was left sitting so long it went bad. Looked like it was up to Li Yu to take care of it himself.

After eating, he thought of the main quest that was now doomed to fail. Was he just supposed to float there and watch the time trickle away?

No way. He was going to check on what Prince Jing was doing, then take matters into his own hands and force them to have some sort of interaction. Throwing something against the wall and hoping it stuck was better than not throwing anything at all.

Li Yu could hear Prince Jing moving around in the room, but the porcelain tank was a little too tall. If the prince didn't walk over, it was very difficult to see him.

Li Yu quietly gathered his strength in his tail. Now very familiar with his tail, and practically an expert at jumping out of the tank, he wanted to take it to the next level and try a new, never-before-attempted trick. Instead of only stealing a brief glance before inevitably falling back down to the bottom, Li Yu would grab on to the side of the tank and lean against it. Holding on to the edge required body-fin coordination. He wasn't sure he'd be able to do it.

Prince Jing, who was writing at his desk, heard a noise and saw the little carp come leaping out with a swish of its tail.

Prince Jing had seen the carp wave its tail a few times, so he wasn't surprised. Although the emperor hadn't believed Noble Consort

Qiu when she insisted the carp was able to fly, Prince Jing didn't doubt it. He knew his fish could "fly" in its own way, but he wasn't about to speak up for the noble consort.

Seeing the fish prepare to jump again, Prince Jing relaxed. It would fall down soon enough.

But Prince Jing waited for a while, and the fish didn't fall. Instead, it smacked into the edge of the tank. It flapped its tail and fins furiously but slowly started to slide down.

And then, splash.

Undeterred, the little carp jumped up again without hesitation.

Prince Jing watched, bemused. At this point, he had a pretty good guess as to what the fish was trying to do. The second time the little carp fell back into the tank after another bout of flailing, he reached over and lifted the fish up at just the right moment.

This time it was Li Yu's turn to be confused.

The little carp had been absorbed in waging a great battle against the fish tank when he suddenly felt weightless and was picked up. He looked up—who else could it be but Prince Jing?

Li Yu curled his tail happily around Prince Jing's finger: *Master, you've come to help me!*

Prince Jing coughed lightly while holding the fish. His finger felt a bit ticklish. He had moved without thinking and didn't think to find something to put the fish into beforehand. Concerned about the little fish being out of water for too long, Prince Jing gently put the fish in a clean tea bowl.

Made out of white jade and wrapped in a hint of green, the tea bowl was shaped like flower petals and was just big enough for a fish. Prince Jing poured some fresh water into the tea bowl. It was very shallow, so as soon as the little carp was in the tea bowl, it could look up with ease to see its surroundings.

Although he was now living in Prince Jing's room, a fish's field of vision from the inside of a tank was very limited. He could hear the sounds of people coming and going every day, but he had never seen what the room looked like. In this new position, he was suddenly able to.

Li Yu was a little disappointed.

Compared to the exquisite luxury of Qianqing Palace, Prince Jing's room looked rather shabby. After surveying his surroundings, though, his conclusion was that the room suited the tyrant's cold disposition: reserved, simple, and mature. Prince Jing evidently only kept the essentials, as there was a pitiful lack of interior decor. It was almost like a snow cave.

No matter, Li Yu thought. The entire reason he was here was to turn the tyrant's personality around. Perhaps he could bring some warmth to the snow cave.

Next to the tea bowl was a brush and ink. After Prince Jing set Li Yu down, he sat down and picked up the brush.

So he was going to write or draw! Li Yu remembered the ink he had smelled earlier and swished his tail excitedly. He knew quite a lot about this subject; he could give the prince some ideas.

Whenever the little carp felt joyful, its tail would lift high up in the air. Prince Jing shot him a warning look, and Li Yu immediately put his tail down. He was definitely going to be sent back to his tank if he accidentally got the prince's calligraphy or painting wet. The little carp settled on staring quietly but ardently.

Prince Jing considered, then smoothed out the paper. With a few quick strokes, he outlined a vivid, lifelike fish.

Li Yu peered over. That head, that body, that tail... Wow, Prince Jing was drawing him! Li Yu was so thrilled someone was willing to draw a portrait of him that every time he looked at Prince Jing, he felt delighted all over again. Maybe Li Yu should put in a little effort too. Perhaps he should try modeling for Prince Jing, since he was the prince's muse?

After some solemn deliberation, the little carp twisted in the tea bowl in what he thought was a truly majestic pose. In reality, it was just a very curvy "S."

Prince Jing smiled. The little fish was quite sharp. Keeping his eyes on the fish, he added a few more strokes. Although neither of them spoke, there was an air of amicability as the human and fish enjoyed each other's company.

"Your Highness, Your Highness!" Wang Xi came in to report, drenched in sweat. "His Imperial Majesty's gifts have arrived."

Prince Jing set down his brush and moved the painting to the side to dry. Just before he headed out to accept the gifts, he glanced back and saw that the little carp was swaying its tail, its face turned to the painting, as though it wanted to try.

Prince Jing's eyelid twitched. He turned around and grabbed the tea bowl with the fish in it; he didn't want to find a few new tail imprints on the painting when he returned.

Li Yu was bewildered to find himself suddenly whisked away.

The news of Noble Consort Qiu trying to frame Prince Jing had already traveled to every corner of the palace. If this had happened a couple of years ago, the emperor would have never allowed the matter to pass so easily, but since he already had plans for the second prince to be the crown prince, he had to consider the second prince's reputation. In the end, the emperor treated Mu Tianzhao coldly for a few days, but his choice for crown prince remained the same.

While the emperor had, indeed, punished the noble consort, he had to put in some effort to comfort Prince Jing as well, as was evidenced by the long list of gifts. Without batting an eye, he shoved all sorts of priceless treasures at the prince as though they cost nothing.

One of them was especially unique: a pair of koi that had been gifted to the emperor by a foreign country. There were only a few pairs of these fish in the world.

The emperor had given gifts to Prince Jing before too, but the prince had always been a difficult person to please. He had no need for gold or silver, and no interest in beauties. Every time he had to decide on a gift for Prince Jing, it gave him a headache. Now that he'd discovered Prince Jing actually had interests, the emperor waved his brush so enthusiastically it was like he'd been injected with steroids. If the prince liked fish, then he would give him more fish.

A huge smile split Head Eunuch Luo's face as he directed servants to deliver a three or four-foot-long fish tank into Jingtai Hall. This tank was truly rare, as it was carved from completely transparent crystal. Inside the tank were two koi: one red and one gold, both handpicked by the emperor himself. They had clearly been taken care of extremely well, because both of them were huge. When they swam together, their colors flowed like rays of light. It was quite a sight to behold.

Li Yu was currently in Wang-gonggong's hands, munching on the food that Wang-gonggong had sprinkled into his bowl, but upon seeing that the emperor had shoved a few more fish at Prince Jing, Li Yu's jaw dropped in shock. A piece of food floated away.

In this day and age, did even fish have to compete for love?

With his intelligence, how could he stoop so low as to fight with other fish? But...he had quests he had to complete. If the prince no longer cared for him, who was Li Yu going to complete his tasks with?

No. He had to fight.

Li Yu observed carefully, resolving to guard Prince Jing the way a hen looked after her eggs. If any other fish tried to seduce Prince Jing, he would chase them away. The little carp secretly began readying himself for battle. But after Prince Jing took his time to admire the crystal fish tank with the rare koi inside, he ultimately didn't accept them.

Prince Jing was not swayed. To Li Yu's relief and delight, the pretty koi had failed to tempt him.

And of course, when Wang-gonggong brought him back to his room and saw that his porcelain fish tank had been replaced with the huge, crystal fish tank that originally held the koi, Li Yu was even happier.

# The Fish Wants
# Revenge on Society

L I YU HAD SWITCHED to a completely new dwelling. The new fish tank was several times larger than the old one, and it was sculpted from a solid piece of crystal. Such a large piece of crystal was a rare find in ancient times, and these kinds of treasures were reserved for the royal family. But to Li Yu, who was from modern times, crystal like this wasn't particularly uncommon. He was used to seeing large transparent fish tanks everywhere, so Li Yu had no concept of the price of his new residence. And no one would ever think to point this out to a fish.

All the little carp knew was Prince Jing had moved his familiar white rock bed into the new tank, using the exact same kind of stone to expand his sleeping area. The water plants were moved in as well; not a single leaf was missing. Prince Jing had also added an ornamental mountain for him to play in, with part of the mountainside made to resemble a lounge chair. When Li Yu lay on it, there was room for him to move around, and he wiggled a few times to express his enjoyment. Lady Qiu's luminous pearl had been placed in the corner of his new tank. Perhaps Prince Jing was worried he'd get bored with just the one pearl, because the prince gave him plenty of other jewels in different colors and sizes.

Li Yu didn't know how expensive the crystal was, so of course he wouldn't be able to tell that all these other balls were made from precious gems. The craftsmanship in ancient times wasn't sophisticated enough to cut the gems perfectly; most of the time, gems were only carved for the purpose of being inlaid into decorations, and so the gem's natural beauty and shine wasn't as prominent. Li Yu could only recognize something as a gemstone when it sparkled and shone, so he assumed all these rounded jewels in the fish tank were just regular rocks—just unusually colorful regular rocks.

Wang Xi-gonggong, who often came to look after the little carp, saw it build a pile out of the jewels that had been scattered in the tank and pick out a pigeon blood ruby. The little carp swung its tail vigorously, sending the pigeon blood ruby into the stack of jewels and knocking them all over.

The corner of Wang-gonggong's lip twitched, watching this scene. These were the premium gemstones the emperor had given the prince some time ago. His Highness had ordered the jewels to be made into spherical shapes, because he assumed the little thing had taken a liking to round things. It appeared as though the little fish did indeed enjoy them—he even started playing with the noble consort's luminous pearl less once he received the jewels that His Highness gave him.

Li Yu spent a long time just getting used to his new tank. By the time he realized it, there was less than half a day left in the "getting along" quest.

Holy shit, why did he start playing for real?

Li Yu hurriedly chucked away the jewel he was playing with and looked around for Prince Jing. The crystal fish tank was transparent enough that he no longer needed to jump up high in the air to see him: the prince was currently reading a book at his desk. The sunlight scattered through the window lattice, enveloping the beautiful youth in a gentle, golden glow.

Li Yu stared, dumbstruck. Before, whether he was in the porcelain fish tank or the tea bowl, he always had to look up to see Prince Jing, and by now Li Yu was used to his cold expression. He had no idea that the same face could look so gentle and soft.

Li Yu stared at Prince Jing blankly, feeling an inexplicable ache in his heart.

In this world, the person he spent the most time with was Prince Jing, and the time they'd spent together had been filled with happiness. In another few hours, his fish life was going to come to an end; Prince Jing would never know that his pet fish had been a person from another world.

An absurd idea suddenly popped up in Li Yu's mind. Maybe he should just forget everything and use the transformation medicine. So what if he caused a little bit of chaos? He was human. It was so unfair that he had randomly transmigrated into a fish. It wasn't so unreasonable for him to want to say goodbye to this world as a human.

Li Yu was about to enter the system as a fish who had nothing to lose, when Prince Jing put down his book and approached the tank. Li Yu had probably stopped by the walls of the tank for too long, long enough that Prince Jing had taken notice while he was reading.

Li Yu wagged his tail listlessly at the prince, waving goodbye to him for the last time. But Prince Jing misunderstood and thought the fish wanted to play again. Although it was easy to see the fish through the crystal tank, the tank was larger and taller, which made it much more difficult to put his hand in the water and play with the little carp the way he did before.

A bit of a shame, Prince Jing thought. His hand itched to play with the fish but had to settle for pressing against the walls of the crystal tank.

Li Yu paused, then swam over slowly. He was currently a fish who was in a dangerously volatile mood—it wouldn't be easy to make him happy.

He instinctively blew a bubble toward Prince Jing's fingertip.

A corner of Prince Jing's lips quirked up as he slid his hand a little further. The little carp hurried to follow.

Li Yu had already forgotten about his revenge on society as Prince Jing played with him.

*Ahhhh, there's really not much time left.*

Fine. The prince was treating him so well, he...he shouldn't cause trouble for him.

Separated by the crystal wall, the little carp could only rub longingly against the spot where Prince Jing's finger was. He spent his final two hours with the prince like this.

*<User, time is up,>* the system interrupted.

Li Yu realized in a daze that he had already entered the fish-scamming system. He wasn't quite sure what had happened to make him suddenly enter the system. He didn't turn into fish bone and fish ash before Prince Jing's very eyes, right?

*<Please don't be nervous, user. You're still alive,>* the system assured him.

Still alive? That was good.

Li Yu didn't get to relax for long before realizing something wasn't right: shouldn't he have failed, since he ran out of time?

The system explained: *<The time limit for the task meant you had to use the entire duration of the countdown.>*

*<...Why didn't you say that earlier! You're messing with a poor fish again!!>*

*<I've already reminded the user to be patient,>* the system told him. *<You needed to wait until the allotted amount of time had passed, at*

*which point the system will determine whether or not you've failed the quest.>*

Li Yu thought back. The system did prompt him to be patient before, but who on earth would get such a vague hint?!

*<So did I succeed?>* Li Yu asked unhappily.

The system answered: *<Please look at the main quest.>*

Following the system's prompt, Li Yu went to check the "getting along" step of the "Priceless Pet Fish" main quest. The countdown had been replaced with a little square that was flashing different colors.

The system continued: *<This time, the criterion for success is how satisfied the tyrant was over the last few days. Green means success, red means failure.>*

*<Can you talk normally? Enough bullshit! What exactly is my result?>*

The system suddenly stopped. The little square that kept continuously changing colors also stopped.

If he failed, he would turn into fish bones and fish ash!

Gathering his courage, Li Yu went to look at the final result. To be honest, he was quite confident. Although he'd caused a lot of trouble for the tyrant and taken advantage of him, the tyrant had grown quite fond of Li Yu. He probably wouldn't get red.

Li Yu quickly glanced at it, only to see that the result the system had given him was—multicolored.

Li Yu's heart was shaking from top to bottom. *<What does multicolored mean?>*

The system spoke: *<Congratulations, user, for completing 'getting along.' The reward is heightened healing powers.>*

Li Yu brushed aside the reward. His mind was fixated on one thing: wondering if the splendid colors meant a splendid job.

*<It means he was very satisfied,>* the system said.

Li Yu beamed. Was the prince very pleased with him? Ha ha ha ha ha, thank the heavens. Thank Prince Jing!

The little carp trembled and exhaled loudly, relieved, before jumping high into the air.

Li Yu exited the system and realized he was lying in Prince Jing's hand. It turned out that he had been in the middle of playing with Prince Jing when he entered the system. The stupid system hadn't taken care of anything for him, so he sank to the bottom without any warning. Right in front of the prince.

It had been a shocking sight, leaving Prince Jing to assume the fish must have fallen sick again.

The servants waiting outside Prince Jing's room already had experience with this, since a similar thing had happened before. The fish had already gone stiff, but other than that, there didn't seem to be anything wrong with it. The servants just had to vaguely tell him that his fish was asleep.

Prince Jing's face remained grim as he waited for the fish to wake up.

As soon as Li Yu saw Prince Jing, he felt the corners of his eyes prickling. Prince Jing didn't know that the fish in his hand was actually a human, nor did he know that Li Yu had just gone through a life-or-death situation—and yet it was his love for him that had saved Li Yu.

The little carp stared at Prince Jing's handsome face, emotions welling up inside his chest.

Fish couldn't cry, and they couldn't speak. No matter whether Li Yu was happy or sad, as a fish all he could do was swish his tail and blow bubbles. But Li Yu wasn't just any fish. If he felt excited, he had to show it in some way, and right now, he wanted to show Prince Jing just how grateful he was.

Li Yu thought about how animals like cats and dogs expressed their affection. There wouldn't be anything wrong with him nuzzling Prince Jing's face like that too. Plus, Prince Jing was holding him in his hand right now. He wouldn't get a better opportunity than this!

Li Yu did his best to straighten out his body, but fish were not the same as cats and dogs. Cats and dogs could stand up and lay their paws on their owner's shoulder, but no matter how tall Li Yu stood, his fins were still nowhere near long enough, and he couldn't reach anything. He just struggled uselessly for a while and then toppled back into Prince Jing's hand.

Li Yu wasn't discouraged. He still had a powerful tail in his arsenal. As long as he aimed for Prince Jing's face, he was going to make it. He just had to remember not to use too much force; he wanted to nuzzle up to Prince Jing's cheek, not slap him in the face. He had to be gentle.

This time, Li Yu didn't miscalculate the force required. But his sense of direction wasn't very good; he missed the mark and jumped too far to the side.

Unfortunately, the little carp didn't notice at all. As he sprang forward, Prince Jing's face grew larger and larger. The little carp was secretly filled with joy. Without any regard for everything else, he leaned in with his mouth and randomly wiggled around.

His sharp little fish mouth rubbed against something incredibly soft.

*Prince Jing's face feels so nice,* he thought. *But shouldn't cheeks be flat? Why does this feel kind of wavy and a little hot?*

Li Yu paused. No way. What was he rubbing against?

Li Yu's eyes widened in shock as he realized his fish lips were pressed against Prince Jing's man lips. Prince Jing's dark, pitch-black pupils stared back at him unblinkingly.

Once again, once again, *once again*, he made a mistake!

Shuddering, the little carp slid down from the prince's lips. He never wanted to see the prince again.

Prince Jing held the fish in one hand, then rubbed his lips, his mouth a little sore thanks to the fish bumping into it. Was this little fish up to no good again? He could already picture the fish slipping into a deflated state again for the next few days.

Li Yu, who had finally completed a small step in the main quest, entered an even deeper state of self-reflection than before. He was just in the middle of preparing a second round of apology fish food to the prince when the fish-scamming system dropped another bomb on him out of the blue.

<*Hello, user. The fourth step of the main quest 'Tyrant's Priceless Pet Fish—Share a Bed with the Tyrant' has already begun. Please complete the quest carefully.*>

Were his gifts for Prince Jing not enough for the system? Now he had to share a bed with the tyrant? Fish couldn't even leave the water! How on earth was he supposed to sleep with a human?!

But the system never answered him; that was what made it a fish-scamming system.

# The Fish Wants to Get in the Bed

L I YU ANALYZED all the quests he'd done so far. The fish-scamming system's titles had all been a little clickbaity. The quests weren't hard to do—so long as he was able to dispel the clouds and see what the quest was really asking.

"Interacting" and "getting along" just meant daily interactions with Prince Jing. "Clear, Bright Pearl" might have looked challenging at first glance, but there were no specific requirements on how it needed to be completed. Touching the luminous pearl was all he needed to succeed. He just got unlucky and ran into a string of stupid accidents in the process.

By that logic, he shouldn't have to think too hard about sharing a bed. As long as he was in the same bed as Prince Jing, using the same pillow, it would probably be all right. The system didn't even say they had to share a blanket, nor did it mention actually sleeping. There was plenty of wiggle room there.

Li Yu thought about it for a moment and concluded perhaps it was only the title of this quest that was a little insane. It should be doable.

His confidence received an enormous boost when he repeated his analysis to the system and all it said was: *‹The user just has to complete the quest.›*

*Very good. It didn't deny me outright, so it must be okay.*

Now all he had to figure out was how to get into the same bed as Prince Jing and share a pillow. Obviously he would have to do it when Prince Jing was sleeping!

Fish couldn't leave the water. Even if they could stay out of water for a short while, a fish had to stay wet. Could a sopping wet fish share a bed with Prince Jing? Of course not. Even if he somehow managed it, Prince Jing would never forgive him. Dirtying his owner's bed was probably a much more reprehensible crime than taking advantage of his owner.

This left Li Yu with no other choice but to complete the task while Prince Jing was sleeping, so he wouldn't know. And so, the task had now changed into a plan to sneak into Prince Jing's bed while he was asleep and wriggle around on his pillow.

The crystal fish tank was quite a distance away from Prince Jing's bed. He would have to aim carefully for this jump. And he'd still have to find some way to return to the tank once he'd touched the pillow. This wasn't a normal level of difficulty.

Last time, the countdown kept him in a state of fear, but there was no time limit this time. He could practice a few times in preparation.

When no one was around, Li Yu secretly started practicing his jumping from the crystal fish tank to the bed.

The first time, as expected, he fell onto the floor. He was still several feet away from Prince Jing's bed. He had braced himself for it to hurt, but no pain came. The award for "getting along" came to mind; perhaps his physical fitness had also gone up.

Since falling didn't hurt him, he could give it a couple more tries... Wait, he didn't have to jump over in one leap. He could attempt a triple...jump...

Li Yu jumped toward his destination once more, each hop getting him one step closer to Prince Jing's bed. Jumping several times wasn't hard. The little carp was a little exhilarated. But he didn't manage to get to Prince Jing's bed before he wasn't able to take it anymore and was forced to scamper back.

Once he was back in the fish tank, Li Yu realized there were a bunch of puddles on the cloud-patterned floor tiles. He didn't know what to do about that.

It seemed like jumping back and forth posed a problem. There was also the noisy issue of his tail slapping against the floor. If he thought that was loud, wouldn't it be much more frightening to hear it in the middle of the night? What if he woke up Prince Jing?

*It's too difficult to complete this mission as a fish,* Li Yu lamented. If he were human, none of this would have to be so difficult.

...Did this mean he had to change back into a human to complete the task?

Li Yu was a little hesitant. He did have the transformation medicine...and this task, which was so difficult for a fish, would be a piece of cake to a human. But he had wanted to spend those two hours doing something meaningful, not just forced to complete another quest on a time limit.

The fish-scamming system had said there was only one transformation elixir. Completing the main quest would turn him back into a human too, but there was no knowing how long that would take. Did he really have to use the medicine now? What if there was a quest later that required him to be human?

Making this decision was even harder than jumping around. Li Yu decided to try a few more times as a fish. He hadn't tried any other tactics yet, after all.

Perhaps the heavens decided to help him out this time. Wang Xi noticed the puddles the little carp had left all over the floor and thought it was funny. Chuckling, he told Prince Jing, "Your Highness, it seems like the little thing likes to take walks."

This was how Prince Jing found out the fish had left its tank.

Prince Jing had already seen the little carp chasing after the luminous pearl on Qianqing Palace's golden floor tiles; taking a walk was nothing in comparison. But even such a large fish tank couldn't contain him... Prince Jing's gaze on the little carp was somewhat complicated.

Li Yu feigned innocence, blowing bubbles: *Master, it's not that I like taking walks; I just want to jump into your bed.*

Prince Jing's response to this development delighted Li Yu. He really indulged his pet fish: he ordered Wang Xi to arrange a few tea bowls filled with clear water on the floor, in case the fish jumped out and needed water halfway. Prince Jing had no problem with the fish taking walks; he just didn't want to return home to a fish corpse.

As soon as the master's order came down, the servants had to go out of their way to figure out where to put the tea bowls. There had to be some strategic thought behind the bowls' placement, so the little carp could use them, but also so Prince Jing wouldn't step in them. Wang Xi studied it for quite some time and consulted Prince Jing as well. The tea bowls were placed in areas that the prince didn't frequent, with most of them gathered around the fish tank. One of them just so happened to be on the way to Prince Jing's bed.

The little carp wiggled gleefully. He didn't expect happiness to arrive this soon. His tyrant owner just opened up a cheat for him!

Wang Xi even switched out the carpet in the room for a water-absorbent one, in case the little carp got the floor wet from jumping around.

This really was a godsend. Li Yu had been worried that he'd leave a wet mark on the pillow, but he had nothing to fear with this new carpet. The day the carpet was laid out, Li Yu returned the water in his inventory back to the fish tank for the time being and surreptitiously stole a piece of carpet to put in his inventory instead. This way, he could use the carpet as a cushion whenever he wanted, so he didn't have to worry about dirtying the pillow anymore.

All the preparations were complete. Now Li Yu just needed to wait until the prince was sound asleep to make his move, so that he wouldn't be woken by all the tail slapping.

Prince Jing returned very late that night. Li Yu heard the door, but the prince didn't order anyone to light the lanterns after he entered. Instead, he felt his way to the bed and slipped under the covers, knocking over a few of the tea bowls on the ground in the process.

Li Yu chuckled. Did Prince Jing get drunk somewhere? Drunk was good; it'd be easier for him to complete his task.

Li Yu waited a while, long after the bed had gone quiet. He was already familiar with the route, and with a few hops, he arrived at the head of the bed. He whipped out the water-absorbing cushion, put it to the bed, and, with a light bounce, landed on the cushion.

Prince Jing had his back turned to him, his head shrouded by the blanket. He was very still, with half of his jade pillow peeking out.

Li Yu couldn't have asked for a better scenario. As an extra precaution, he touched the jade pillow with his fin, being careful to not get it wet so Prince Jing wouldn't notice the next day. "Sharing a Bed" should be complete.

With all that taken care of, he waited for the system's prompt. But nothing happened. Li Yu was a little flustered and very confused. What had gone wrong?

Li Yu was on the verge of climbing completely on top of the jade pillow—or, if that didn't work, burrow into the blanket. He was already very close to the person on the bed when he suddenly smelled a light fragrance.

Li Yu froze. Since when did Prince Jing start using women's perfumes? Last time, when he pecked Prince Jing on the lips, Li Yu was sure he hadn't smelled such a cloyingly sweet scent.

At the same time, the person on the bed flipped over and stared at Li Yu with dazzlingly lustrous eyes. Li Yu got a good look at this person's appearance in the moonlight filtering through the window lattice. It wasn't Prince Jing—it was a beautiful woman.

No wonder the main quest didn't update. It wasn't Prince Jing on the bed at all!

Startled, Li Yu fell backward and slid off the jade pillow.

The unfamiliar woman was shocked as well. She raised her hand, tucked under the blanket, as if she was about to retrieve something. But when she realized it was just a fish, she scoffed lightly, then lay back down under the blanket with one pale shoulder sticking out.

Li Yu froze. The moment the woman had lifted her hand, Li Yu saw what she wanted to grab. It was a blade, and one so shiny that Li Yu was almost blinded!

This was...

At first, when he realized it was a woman in a state of undress in Prince Jing's bed, he thought it was just some servant who wanted to seduce Prince Jing to climb the social ladder. But this woman had hidden a knife underneath the blanket. That complicated matters. She wasn't here to climb any ladders; she was likely a female assassin trying to take Prince Jing's life!

No wonder this person knocked over a few tea bowls. Prince Jing would never have done that!!

Li Yu curled up in the blanket, doing his best to make himself inconspicuous to the assassin. At the same time, he was confused.

In the book, Jingtai Hall was described as being like a fortress, so how did this woman skirt around its guards and break into Prince Jing's bedroom?

Before he could rack his brains further, Wang Xi's voice could be heard faintly from outside the door, calling out, "Your Highness." Prince Jing was about to come in.

Li Yu panicked. How could he let Prince Jing know that there was an assassin in the bed?

Oh right, this woman wasn't dressed properly—she likely wouldn't kill him right off the bat. Prince Jing also knew martial arts, and he had servants too, so she'd definitely wait until his guard was down.

As long as she didn't go for the kill immediately!

The door was pushed open lightly. Li Yu and the assassin both held their breaths.

Wang Xi lit the candles. Prince Jing glanced inside the room and immediately caught sight of the shape lying on his bed.

"How dare you!"

As soon as Wang-gonggong saw there was someone else here, he was livid. Who dared crawl into His Highness's bed?

The woman on the bed acted as though she was deaf. She sat up, still wrapped up in the blanket, and revealed her beautiful visage. She let out a seductive laugh, her voice ringing like silver bells. The sweeter her laughter sounded, the colder Li Yu felt. He desperately prayed in his heart for Prince Jing not to be bewitched by this woman.

Wang Xi was about to rush forward and drag the woman away when Prince Jing stopped Wang Xi mid-step, ordering him to stand to the side.

The woman laughed smugly. "Your Highness likes me."

Prince Jing approached, face completely devoid of expression. He glanced at the woman, while Li Yu watched nervously, desperately hoping he would throw the woman out. But to his horror, Prince Jing raised a hand to caress the woman's face!

The woman smiled as she leaned into his touch. Although the prince's fingers were so cold they made her shiver, she knew he had fallen for her, hook, line, and sinker.

Stupid Prince Jing! There was obviously something wrong with this woman!

Li Yu was so furious that he was about to jump up to reveal himself to Prince Jing, when things suddenly took a turn. A cold light flashed through Prince Jing's eyes, and quick as lightning, he wrapped his hand around the woman's throat.

Prince Jing might not have been able to speak, but he didn't need to. Anyone who dared enter his room always had an ulterior motive. There was only one way this would end for them: death!

The woman didn't expect him to strike so swiftly when everything had been fine just a moment ago. Ignoring the burning pain in her throat, she reached into the blanket, scrabbling for the knife that she had hidden in a desperate bid to save herself. But something inside the blanket bit her harshly.

Startled, she lost her focus, and before she could scream, Prince Jing pierced through her chest with a sword.

She stared down at the hole in her chest in shock and then looked back up at Prince Jing's impassive face. She didn't even get a chance to say what her owner sent her to say—she'd thought the prince would at least spare her life so he could question her. But the prince didn't care at all! He just wanted her dead!

Prince Jing twisted his sword viciously, and the assassin slowly fell over. He pulled out his sword and glanced at the blood on it

in disgust. Wang Xi heard the commotion and ran in, with a group of people following closely behind, only to see the woman on the floor. He sneered, "She must have had a death wish."

Prince Jing recalled seeing the woman searching for something in the blanket, but she had let go for some reason. Figuring she had hidden something in the blanket, he flipped over the blanket and found his fish curled up, trembling.

What was going on?

Prince Jing reached out to pick up the fish, but the little carp, who normally loved to curl its tail around his finger, flinched away in fear.

# Don't Be Afraid, Fish

PRINCE JING TRIED to extend a hand to the little carp again. Li Yu still flinched away.

Li Yu was terrified. This was a completely different feeling from his fear of being turned into fish bones and fish ash. He had just witnessed Prince Jing kill that woman right in front of him. The bloodshed was terrifying.

He knew Prince Jing had killed the assassin out of self-preservation. He was also well aware that even if Prince Jing hadn't killed her, there was no way for her to escape execution after attempting to murder a prince. But Li Yu was born and raised in an era of peace. He had never seen such bloody violence, and this shocking scene of slaughter had come out of nowhere. He was not mentally prepared for it at all. This was all too much for him.

When Prince Jing was with him, he was usually quiet and peaceful; he could even be called a little warm at times. Although Li Yu always called him "tyrant," he had never really understood the meaning behind that word as deeply as he did today. With just a glance, Prince Jing had passed judgment on whether the other person should live or die. His brow didn't even twitch when he took her life.

The thought process of the rulers of the past was completely different from what Li Yu was taught in school. It felt as if Prince Jing, with his cruel aura suddenly revealed, was a stranger to him.

Li Yu feared this Prince Jing. What would happen when he finished his quest and became human again? he thought in terror. Would the prince also cut him down with a single strike of his sword?

...Definitely. To Prince Jing, what would the difference be between him and the assassin? They were both ants that dared to trespass on his territory.

His thoughts inevitably trickled back to the dead woman next to him, and he couldn't stop trembling.

Prince Jing saw the little carp shaking uncontrollably and moved to touch his head instead. Li Yu knew he was Prince Jing's pet fish and shouldn't avoid his touch, but no matter how he tried to convince himself, every instinct was screaming at him to fear Prince Jing. He kept thinking Prince Jing reeked of blood. It was too much for him to take, which only made it harder to forget.

After a few failed attempts, Prince Jing could see the fish was rejecting him. What was wrong with the fish? Prince Jing couldn't figure it out, but he knew that fish couldn't be out of the water for too long. Its fins were already starting to dry out.

Prince Jing shot Wang Xi a look, then turned back to the little carp. The ever-attentive Wang-gonggong immediately said, "Please don't worry, Your Highness. This old servant will take care of the little thing."

Wang Xi hurried to the edge of the bed. Li Yu released the breath he had been holding. He didn't feel any aversion to Wang Xi, and he allowed the servant to pick him up gently and put him back in the crystal fish tank.

Li Yu felt much better back in the water. He turned around to look at Prince Jing. The prince's frigid eyes bored holes in him. It scared the little carp so badly that he dove inside the ornamental mountain to hide.

By now, Prince Jing had noticed that the little carp tolerated Wang Xi's touch, but not his own. His gaze darkened a little. This wasn't the first time the little carp had avoided him. But the other times, it had been after the fish had done things like bite him or bump into him. He knew his fish was special, with some unusually human reactions to things. So what had happened this time to cause this?

Prince Jing felt annoyed for some inscrutable reason. He reflected on what he had done that was different from Wang Xi...and he figured it out pretty quickly.

Prince Jing looked down at his sword. He had taken care of the assassin just now. Could it be...the fish was afraid because it could smell blood on him?

The blood had never actually touched Prince Jing, but he still laid down his sword and went to wash up. He purposely changed into a set of clean, white robes, ordering a servant to burn the sullied ones. After he cleaned up, Prince Jing went to visit the little carp, but to no avail: Li Yu still shied away from him.

As he watched from the side, Li Yu was a little touched to see the tyrant's willingness to change his clothes for his sake. He felt he was overreacting, but it wasn't easy getting over the fear of someone or something. Even though he could see Prince Jing's obvious displeasure, Li Yu couldn't control his reaction.

Prince Jing pursed his lips, pacing before the crystal fish tank. He finally stopped, reached in with one long arm, and scooped out the fish that had been put into the tank just minutes ago.

Li Yu thought the prince must have completely lost his patience and struggled frantically. Gazing at the fish calmly, Prince Jing brought over a flower petal-shaped tea bowl and put the fish inside.

...Oh god, was he going to dispose of him now?

All of Li Yu's hope evaporated. But Prince Jing surprised him by doing something unthinkable: he placed the fish by his pillow.

Li Yu didn't have a single idea what was going on.

The mess on the bed and the blood on the floor had already been cleaned up, leaving no trace of what had just happened. But Li Yu knew that even though there was nothing left to see, it didn't mean it never happened. The murderous intent that had instantly appeared on Prince Jing's face, the decisive way he stabbed his sword into the assassin's chest... It was all still burned into his memory.

But more than that, he was afraid Prince Jing would treat him like that one day.

Prince Jing observed him for a while, brushing his head with his finger. Li Yu lowered his head fearfully, his body trembling. Prince Jing gently knocked on his head, then lay down next to his tea bowl.

Li Yu was stunned. Prince Jing wanted Li Yu next to him even while he slept? *Wait, i-i-isn't this...sharing a bed?*

Li Yu felt a rush of excitement at the revelation. His main quest could still be salvaged at a time like this... But Li Yu's heart was a mess. Of course he wanted to complete the quest, but there was still his terror of Prince Jing...

These two emotions were locked in fierce combat with each other, but in the end, the thought of completing the quest was much too tempting and helped to dilute some of his fear.

Li Yu stretched out his tail, the tip creeping carefully along the edge of the jade pillow. Sharing a bed was only half the quest; the other half was to share a pillow. Armed with his experience with the previous quests, he was sure he would succeed as long as he touched the jade pillow.

This time, the Prince Jing next to him was the real deal. As soon as his tail brushed against the jade pillow, the system very clearly notified him that he had completed the step "Share a Bed." But Li Yu felt no joy from completing the mission.

He was right next to Prince Jing, and when he looked up, his eyes met Prince Jing's. It seemed like his gaze could see through everything. The little carp's breathing stuttered, his tail shook, and he shrank back, hiding his face in the water.

If he was discovered, would the tyrant kill him?

Li Yu couldn't help thinking back to the female assassin covered in blood. He felt so restless he wanted to bite. He opened his mouth randomly, and suddenly bit down on—Prince Jing's finger.

He screwed up again! Li Yu felt his eyes filling up with imaginary tears that cascaded down his face. How was he supposed to know Prince Jing had reached over again?!

Prince Jing's finger was still in Li Yu's mouth. Li Yu tearfully looked at Prince Jing. Prince Jing observed him quietly, letting him bite.

Li Yu spat the finger out. Sob sob sob, not like this! All he wanted to do was get closer to the tyrant who doted on him!

Prince Jing saw Li Yu let go and didn't even get mad at him. On the contrary, he rubbed Li Yu's head, pushed the jade pillow toward him, then closed his eyes and went to sleep.

What was Prince Jing doing?

Li Yu was exhausted as well, but he was still too scared to sleep, and even more afraid to enter the system right next to the prince. The tea bowl was too small, making him feel like he was trapped on the bed. He was so frustrated.

Before tonight, it would have been laughable for a mere tea bowl to contain him, and he would've jumped out without a second thought. But that was back when he'd been too naive to realize he was tickling the head of a tiger.

Li Yu lay there quietly, feeling Prince Jing's breathing slowly even out. For more than an hour, the prince did not move. He was probably fast asleep.

Li Yu was just about to enter the system to check on his quest when Prince Jing suddenly shifted to face him. Li Yu immediately scrambled back in case Prince Jing flattened him into a fish cake.

It was a good thing that Prince Jing had good sleeping etiquette and always slept very properly on one side of the pillow. Seeing that the prince was truly asleep, Li Yu mustered up his courage to approach.

Prince Jing's sleeping face was close enough for Li Yu to touch. The thick lashes that fanned over his frosty eyes made him seem harmless like this. The little carp's racing heart didn't feel so panicked anymore. Prince Jing wasn't too scary when he was asleep.

But, of course, who would look vicious in their sleep? Besides, he couldn't forget how quickly Prince Jing could change gears, going from calm to murderous at the drop of a hat.

Li Yu suddenly froze. That was right; they were both Prince Jing. The Prince Jing who killed the assassin mercilessly and the Prince Jing who was gentle and kind to him were one and the same before him.

Li Yu had always said people were multifaceted. Well, this was Prince Jing being multifaceted. Although he'd never gotten to know Prince Jing's murderous side before, his ruthlessness didn't vanish just because Li Yu didn't see it. The prince's gentleness toward him and his heartlessness toward others existed simultaneously.

Whether Li Yu feared him or lived in ignorance, Prince Jing was Prince Jing; he had never changed. Li Yu couldn't start doubting the prince's kindness to him just because he had killed an assassin. If he really wanted to lay it all out, he had offended Prince Jing countless times. If the prince had any desire to hurt him, he would've done it ages ago, right?

After thinking all of this through and reaching this epiphany, Li Yu felt a lot better. Looking back at Prince Jing, who was sleeping quietly on the other side of the jade pillow, Li Yu's perspective did a 180. He awkwardly wondered if Prince Jing had pushed the pillow toward him before he fell asleep because he thought Li Yu wanted it?

It was very possible! Didn't he also place tea bowls all over the floor for him and change his clothes just to get rid of all the evidence of the murder? He hadn't even been angry when the little carp bit him.

Prince Jing really was very good to his fish. Li Yu shouldn't fear and distrust him over a little shock... Perhaps he should make up with Prince Jing tomorrow.

Having suffered such a big shock, and having thought until his brain was smoking, the little carp picked a spot closest to Prince Jing in his tea bowl, yawned, and quickly slipped into dreamland. Quests? Those could wait until after he woke up!

When he woke up the next morning, Prince Jing noticed the little carp huddled up next to him. The tea bowl was flipped over on its side and had left a huge wet patch on his clothes. Prince Jing moved his hand closer, and the fish, half-asleep, scooted over to nuzzle into it.

Fireworks exploded in Prince Jing's heart. He didn't know why this fish's attitude toward him had gone from high to low and then back to high. All he knew was that putting the fish closer to him was quite effective.

The emperor was beside himself with fury when he learned that an assassin had managed to infiltrate Jingtai Hall. After confirming that the prince was fine, every strand of hair on his head intact, he commanded the palace guards to conduct a thorough investigation. They had to give Prince Jing an explanation one way or another.

The emperor felt guilty that Prince Jing had almost gotten killed. Prince Jing originally lived outside the palace, and the only reason he had come to live at the palace for a while was because the emperor summoned him for the noble consort's birthday. But this had only led to more suffering for Prince Jing. Alongside his awards, the emperor also ordered the prince to return to his manor to rest.

At long last, Prince Jing could finally leave the palace.

After receiving the royal edict, the prince made no delay. He immediately ordered Wang Xi to pack everything up. In theory, both Prince Jing Manor and Jingtai Hall were Prince Jing's dwellings, so both places had servants. Prince Jing had come and gone from the palace many times now, so there wasn't much for him to pack. This time, however, there was the addition of a ridiculously pretentious fish tank.

Half of the palace came to watch the commotion. People had heard the ill-tempered Prince Jing had gotten a new pet fish, and it seemed as though the fish had an even higher status than the noble consort's cat. This fish had even been approved by the emperor, who had gifted the tank himself. This must be a precious breed of fish indeed!

The crowd saw eight people carrying a crystal fish tank, the bottom laden with jewels. At the top, a small, grayish carp was blowing (dream...) bubbles (...ing).

The crowd of servants was stunned.

# The Fish Wants to Rebel

WHEN HE WOKE UP, Li Yu was already at Prince Jing Manor, completely oblivious to the fact that a bunch of people at the palace had already judged him from head to tail. But even if he did know, he wouldn't care. By now, he was well aware of his identity as a fish. In short, he just had to blow his own bubbles and let those boring people talk all they wanted.

It didn't really matter to him if his tank was in the palace or at the manor; he lived in a fish tank either way. What put him in high spirits was Wang-gonggong placing him in Prince Jing's bedroom, so he was still living with the prince. His fear of Prince Jing had left just as quickly as it came. He felt more trusting and sincere toward Prince Jing now and was more shameless than ever about acting cute.

Ever since he transmigrated into this book, he had been preoccupied with two things: diligently performing his duties as a pet fish and worrying about his quests. The original storyline of the book was a long way removed from his fishy life. He slept well and ate well next to Prince Jing without ever needing to worry about the plot. After all, he was a fish—what could he do?

But Prince Jing's attempted assassination had brought the plotline back into focus for him.

Once the second prince, Mu Tianzhao, learned that Prince Jing had left the palace, he sent a trusted servant over with a letter.

The servant very earnestly asked after Prince Jing's health, then relayed that in three days' time, the second prince would host a banquet in Prince Jing's honor, asking him to please attend.

Wang Xi brought the letter to Prince Jing with a disdainful expression. Prince Jing gave a cold laugh and tossed the letter aside without opening it.

From inside his tank, Li Yu stared at the letter, deep in thought.

The second prince might be destined to live the life of cannon fodder, but he was still the emperor's current pick for crown prince. He was probably doing this to save some face after being humiliated at Qianqing Palace.

No one on Prince Jing's side really respected the second prince. Despite being the oldest of the emperor's sons, Mu Tianzhao often hid his true motivations behind a false smile and grand gestures. In front of the emperor, he pretended to care for his younger brothers, and around the younger princes, he pretended to be a good older brother. In reality, this older brother had sabotaged many of his younger brothers.

As someone with the cheat code to the book, Li Yu had a pretty good idea of what the second prince was thinking. Amongst the other princes, Mu Tianzhao feared the third prince the most because he was the closest to him in age and fought with him on everything. But the one Mu Tianzhao *hated* the most was Prince Jing.

Although Mu Tianzhao was the eldest, the line of succession didn't follow the order of birth. The di son always came first. As Prince Jing's mother was Empress Xiaohui, his status was much higher. If Prince Jing had been able to speak, there was no way the emperor would have given the throne to the second prince instead. Because of that, Prince Jing had always been a thorn poking at Mu Tianzhao's side. But he couldn't let that show in front of the emperor.

The emperor had high hopes for the future crown prince's morals and conduct, and the second prince knew that. No matter how much he disliked Prince Jing, he had to treat him kindly. Ever since Lady Qiu's fish fiasco, the emperor had been rather displeased with him, and Mu Tianzhao had realized that nothing was guaranteed until the position of crown prince was officially his. He couldn't celebrate his victory yet. Fortunately, Prince Jing's near assassination gave him an excuse to feign concern for his brother's well-being, in order to make up for last time. To the emperor, it would look like he had learned from his mistake and was making amends.

The second prince had thought all of this through meticulously—except that Prince Jing didn't care at all and made it clear he wasn't going to attend.

But the second prince refused to give up. He ran to the palace and begged the emperor for his help in convincing Prince Jing. Deep down, the emperor wanted Prince Jing to get along with the future crown prince, and since the second prince was willing to extend the olive branch, the emperor gave him his full support. To encourage Prince Jing to cooperate, and also to make things easier on the second prince, the emperor decided to act as the middleman, ordering the banquet to be held at Prince Jing's manor instead. He also ordered all the princes to attend and appointed Prince Jing as the host. This way, the second prince and Prince Jing could easily reconcile at the banquet.

Thanks to the emperor's assistance, the second prince had achieved his goals. When Prince Jing received the edict, his expression darkened.

The emperor knew that Prince Jing was naturally cold and withdrawn. Never mind entertaining the other princes, just having a few more guests than usual at his manor would sour his mood.

The emperor especially sent Head Eunuch Luo to explain that the servants and chefs would be sent over at the time of the banquet, taking away any burden of preparation off Prince Jing's shoulders; all he had to do was show up as the host.

The emperor had gone to all this trouble just so his sons could form a bit of a brotherly bond. Prince Jing sat by himself in his room for a while, staring at all the arrangements. He no longer had any objections.

As soon as Wang Xi caught wind of anything happening in Prince Jing's manor, Li Yu pretty much knew as well. Prince Jing had rejected the second prince, and now that the emperor wanted Prince Jing to host a banquet out of the blue? Even if he was thinking with his fish tail instead of his head, it was obvious that the second prince must've hit a roadblock and gone through the emperor to make this happen. Li Yu was speechless.

But a banquet was a banquet—it had nothing to do with a fish like him. In any event, the second prince wasn't going to get what he wanted; they were all just passengers on Prince Jing's journey.

But that reminded Li Yu—there'd been a banquet Prince Jing had held at the beginning of the book. That was where he'd run into the other male lead of the book, *this* book, *The Tyrant and His Delicate Concubine*—in other words, the delicate concubine. To directly quote the nauseating words the book had used: "Their fates were then forever entangled."

Li Yu had been a transmigrated fish for a while, but the quests the system gave him had all been weird ones; it had never tried to involve him in the plot of the book. With such a limited area of movement, and only being able to interact with a limited amount of people or things, even if he wanted to do something, it wouldn't be easy. It was just like the fish-scamming system had said: the purpose of his existence was to change the tyrant's personality. If he was able to do that, it didn't really matter how the plot progressed.

Li Yu truly didn't care about the plot. But the second prince's actions made him wonder: was this banquet the same as the one in the book?

With Prince Jing's temper, there was no way he'd willingly host a banquet like this. The book never mentioned the reason behind Prince Jing's banquet, which meant there were no inconsistencies between the current reality and the book—everything matched up.

All of Li Yu's scales were standing on end. Was Prince Jing about to meet the love of his life—the delicate little concubine?

That had to be it. After all, in the world of the book, one main character was the top, the other was the bottom. They were fated to meet. No matter how convoluted the process was, they were always meant to be together. Hadn't he always known this book was a story about Prince Jing and his little concubine?

He was just a pet fish. Why hurt his fish brain by thinking so much?

Li Yu shook his head, doing his best not to care about it, and went to play with the jewels in his tank instead. But he just wasn't interested in them... Maybe he had played with them too much.

The emperor's edict went out.

The younger ones, the seventh and eighth princes, were only children, and they still lived in the palace. When they heard that Prince Jing was holding a banquet, they were eager to come out and play.

The other two older princes were much more mature. The third and sixth princes both politely responded that it was a rare opportunity for all the brothers to gather in one place, and that they would prepare elaborate gifts. The third prince, Mu Tianming, even suggested bringing some servants who were adept at singing and dancing to liven things up further.

Pleased to see his sons getting along, the emperor accepted all these suggestions on Prince Jing's behalf.

Although Prince Jing didn't need to worry about planning the banquet, Wang Xi still kept an eye on things for his master. Li Yu listened as Wang Xi-gonggong rambled on and on. After a while, he sank to the bottom of the tank, unwilling to resurface.

The third prince's suggestion basically confirmed the plot— because one of the "servants who were adept at singing and dancing" was the delicate little concubine in the original book. His appearance stood out amongst the crowd, and the moment Prince Jing laid eyes on him during a performance, it was love at first sight.

Unfortunately, the little concubine was the third prince's servant, and for about half the book, he didn't even like Prince Jing. But this was the first and only time Prince Jing had fallen in love. The high and mighty tyrant suffered setbacks at every turn, and nearly lost his life, but he couldn't even have the one thing he yearned for.

How clichéd. It was the typical "I love you, but you don't love me, and yet I still love you." A lot of readers were into this kind of thing, though. Apparently, it was relatable for them.

How could they do that? How could they torment Prince Jing?

When Li Yu read the book, it didn't bother him in the least. Back then, Prince Jing had just been a character in a book. But now Prince Jing was a real person to him. Li Yu was pretty close to him and had seen many sides of the prince that nobody else had. He considered Prince Jing to be his master. Li Yu was furious, angrier than if he himself had been the one going through the torment.

The dejected little carp took his anger out on the jewels in the tank for a while, until the sullen thought came to him: so what if he was mad? The person who liked the little concubine was Prince Jing, and Li Yu was just a pet fish...

Perhaps one day, the little concubine would become his second owner, and he would have to earn favor with him the same way he had to earn favor with Prince Jing. Eventually, he would have to live together with this second owner.

Even...even just the thought of it was unbearable. He suddenly understood the lost feeling other pets had when their owners abruptly got into a relationship.

A formerly doting pet owner could end up eventually losing interest in their pet. If the second owner got along with the pet it would be fine, but if they didn't, would the original owner do anything to the second owner?

No, if it came down to it, the owner would definitely get rid of the pet.

Li Yu laughed bitterly. He would never allow himself to land in such a situation. If Prince Jing wanted to go through the motions of the plot, he could go right ahead. It wasn't like Li Yu could stop it from moving forward; he was just a fish. But he had to at least do whatever he could, right?

Since Prince Jing was holding a banquet, numerous visitors would be coming and going. Prince Jing would be too busy meeting the little concubine to worry about Li Yu. That meant he could turn into a human without any reservations and do whatever he wanted!

He just didn't want to meet the second owner!

# The Fish Wants to Transform

LI YU DECIDED he would use the transformation medicine on the day of the banquet.

When he completed the "Share a Bed" quest not too long ago, he had received a bizarre reward: a lifelike, life-sized fish plushie that was nearly a perfect replica of his own fish body. All the prizes before had been inventory space or enhancement to his abilities, so he had really been looking forward to it—except it turned out he had busted his ass just to get an apparently useless object. Li Yu immediately thought the system was scamming him once again and didn't collect the reward. Now that he was planning on turning human, though, the toy didn't seem so worthless after all.

If he turned human and the fish tank was empty, it would only be a matter of time before a passing servant noticed—he'd be found out immediately. It was almost as if this fish plushie was there to help him sneak out. It lay completely motionless in the water. But from a distance, it really did look like him!

The next step after "Sharing A Bed with the Tyrant" was "Gain a Deep Understanding of the Tyrant." Li Yu was used to weird quests by now, and these clickbait titles no longer fazed him. As usual, when he asked for clarification, the fish-scamming system pretended it was dead.

"Gain a deep understanding" was even more vague than "interact" or "get along." Li Yu wasn't sure where to begin; he'd tried out a bunch of different things so far, but he still hadn't made any progress. He decided to set it aside for the time being.

With only two hours to be human, Li Yu meticulously planned everything out. Most people would be at Ninghui Hall in Prince Jing's manor, where the banquet was due to be held. Between the servants and chefs from the palace and the entourage accompanying each of the princes, the manor would be bustling and lively. With so many people coming and going, Li Yu didn't need to worry that he'd draw any attention by showing up as a completely new face.

First things first, he wanted to make his way to the kitchen and eat human food. Since becoming a fish, all he'd been able to eat was fish food. The red fish food he was given was made from flour, which only served to heighten his craving for ordinary human food. He wanted to stuff himself with normal, homestyle stir-fry. The manor's kitchen definitely wouldn't be short on food, since they had so many guests to serve. From what he'd heard from Wang Xi, the chefs would usually make several plates of each dish at banquets like this because they were afraid of running out of food. If Li Yu just tasted a bit of each dish, he wouldn't even come close to finishing any of them.

After eating, he planned to take a stroll through Prince Jing's manor. He hadn't gotten the chance to do that yet. Apparently the emperor had arranged for an opera troupe to perform, so he could watch people from ancient times perform opera and snack on some sunflower seeds. Originally, he also wanted to take a gander outside the manor, but he was afraid he wouldn't be able to get back in. There were guards stationed in front of the manor, and he didn't have enough time...

He had a contingency plan, though. His inventory was already filled with clear water and fish food, so if he brought a tea bowl along, he was set. If something did happen and he couldn't make it back to the bedroom before time ran out and he turned back, all he'd need to do was jump into the tea bowl. There was nothing to fear.

He had thought of everything there was to think of. His plan seemed foolproof.

In order to prevent people from figuring out that the fish plushie wasn't the same as the real him, Li Yu made sure to act less lively in the days leading up to the banquet. Most of the time, he just laid on the white rock bed. Prince Jing came to see him a few times, and Li Yu swam toward him out of habit to nuzzle into his finger. When he got close, though, he remembered he had to keep his distance, so with a swish of his tail, he swam off coldly.

Prince Jing didn't know what to make of it.

On the day of the banquet, Wang Xi went to Ninghui Hall with Prince Jing early in the day. Although the emperor had everything taken care of, as the host, Prince Jing still had to greet the guests. Wang Xi also tried to help with some things on the side. As per Prince Jing's wishes, several servants were ordered to guard the bedroom Li Yu was in. They didn't have to be there for the entire time, lest the little carp get a scare when it came out for a stroll, but they still had to come by and check on the fish every now and then.

Prince Jing sure knew how to make things harder for other people.

As soon as Prince Jing left, Li Yu accepted the fish plushie reward and positioned it on the white rock bed. He looked at it for a while and still felt a bit worried, so he covered it with the leaf blanket. From far away, it really did look like he was sleeping. With the plush arranged to his satisfaction, Li Yu leaped into the nearest tea bowl.

It was time to accept the transformation medicine.

He took a deep breath. When the system asked him again, this time, he chose "accept." In the blink of an eye, the transformation medicine bottle fell into his fins.

At first, he'd been worried that he might not be able to open the bottle as a fish, but the bottle seemed to be able to read his thoughts. As soon as he wanted to use it, the seal just disappeared.

...Could it be another trap?

Now that the transformation medicine was in his grasp, Li Yu faltered. He could hear music playing faintly in the distance, and he knew the dancing and singing that had been specially prepared for this banquet was starting. The little concubine was about to show up, if he hadn't already.

The fateful meeting was about to take place, right...?

Well, fateful meeting or not, he only had two hours. He was just going to be eating next door; no big deal.

Li Yu stopped hesitating. Feeling a little complicated about it, he downed the medicine in one gulp.

The medicine...didn't taste like anything. After drinking it, he smacked his lips a few times. In the next second, his vision blurred.

Fuck. He didn't know the medicine would have side effects!

The little carp gradually lost consciousness.

...

*Ninghui Hall.*

The third prince, Mu Tianming, rose many times to toast Prince Jing.

Mu Tianzhao beat him in almost every aspect. Mu Tianming, unlike Mu Tianzhao, had a mother who was of lower status than Lady Qiu, and he was also a few years younger. Ever since he made the decision to compete with the second prince, Mu Tianming had been opposing Mu Tianzhao in everything.

Since Prince Jing was born with a disability and had no hope of ever ascending to the throne, he posed no threat to Mu Tianming. If Mu Tianzhao didn't like Prince Jing, then Mu Tianming obviously had to be on Prince Jing's side. If Mu Tianzhao wanted to suck up to Prince Jing, then he would have to get in the way! As long as the second prince was unhappy, the third prince was happy!

Although Prince Jing wasn't particularly useful and the emperor had never granted him any real power, he nevertheless had Empress Xiaohui's family, the House of Cheng'en, behind him. That was a huge advantage.

Over the years, Mu Tianming had given Prince Jing plenty of gifts, but they had all been rejected. He had been trying to come up with a reason to approach Prince Jing when Mu Tianzhao's mother, Noble Consort Qiu, did something stupid. The third prince immediately jumped at the chance.

But Prince Jing was not the kind of person who could be swayed by gifts. He was very difficult to kiss up to. None of the previous gifts had worked, so Mu Tianming and his trusted subordinates came up with numerous other ideas. They'd realized...while Prince Jing didn't lack anything, the one thing that was missing from his manor was wives. And so Mu Tianming had decided to try gifting a few bed partners to Prince Jing. Not only could they entertain Prince Jing, he could also have someone around to speak on his behalf. It would kill two birds with one stone.

All the dancers he'd brought to Prince Jing's manor were unrivaled in beauty. The lead dancer was a young man with an elegant and refined appearance, gleaming red lips, and white teeth. With makeup, he was more beautiful than the female dancers. Mu Tianming had no idea what Prince Jing's tastes might be, so he'd prepared both men and women. What if, as they danced, one of them just so happened to catch Prince Jing's eye?

Once the banquet began, Mu Tianming was the first to toast Prince Jing, but Prince Jing didn't like to drink, so he didn't accept. Then, Mu Tianming offered to bring out his dancers to perform for Prince Jing, but Prince Jing also didn't like to watch dance, so he declined this as well.

Mu Tianming was suddenly put in an awkward position.

The sixth prince, Mu Tianxiao, who was the third prince's lackey, hurried to smooth the situation over for Mu Tianming. He glanced at the seventh and eighth princes, who, after so long, were finally able to leave the palace. Having heard there was a fresh new dance to watch, the two children couldn't be any more excited. Although Prince Jing didn't mingle with the adult princes much, he usually wouldn't oppose the younger ones. With Wang Xi's gentle encouragement, Prince Jing at last relented and permitted the dance to take place.

At Mu Tianming's orders, the dancers finally emerged.

The third prince had put in a lot of effort to plan this. After finding out that Prince Jing had acquired a pet fish recently, he specially choreographed a dance of fish and lotus. Most of the dancers wore green, playing the part of lotus leaves, while the lead dancer was dressed in white, transforming into an elegant lotus blossom. The third prince thought he had outdone himself.

Prince Jing forced himself to watch. The third prince had said this was a dance of fish and lotus, but he didn't see a single fish from beginning to end. There was a dancer in white with a striking appearance, but his eyes held sorrow and resentment and seemed to glimmer with unshed tears. Rather than enjoyment, Prince Jing felt anger. Had this dancer been mistreated?

Mu Tianzhao watched as Prince Jing stared fixedly at the lead dancer, and his heart nearly fell out of his chest out of fear that Mu Tianming was about to get Prince Jing over to his side. He rose as well and said sincerely, "Fifth brother, I'd like to personally apologize, as your brother, for the offense that my mother caused a few days ago. I hope you can find it in yourself to forgive her."

As soon as the second prince spoke, servants took the chance to push the third prince's dancers to the side. The third prince was furious, but his hands were tied: he wouldn't dare fight with the second prince in front of a crowd, leaving him no choice but to swallow his irritation and observe the situation quietly.

At Mu Tianzhao's mention of Noble Consort Qiu, Prince Jing scoffed, and Wang Xi immediately spoke up on his behalf. "All will be fine if Lady Qiu self-reflects properly, as the emperor ordered. His Highness obviously won't ignore the emperor's will and pursue the situation further."

Mu Tianzhao's mouth was dry. He had originally planned to ask for Prince Jing's forgiveness and then request for him to shorten the noble consort's house arrest. Why did he feel like Prince Jing had blocked any room for further discussion?

"Your older brother has another request." Having failed once, Mu Tianzhao continued shamelessly, "My mother lost a luminous pearl. I heard one of fifth brother's servants picked it up. Thank you for keeping it safe, but if it's convenient for you, I ask that you please return it."

The luminous pearl that Lady Qiu had lost had been precious, but the way she had lost it was humiliating; in actuality, Noble Consort Qiu never wanted to see the pearl ever again. Mu Tianzhao was just making up an excuse—if Prince Jing returned the pearl, it would give off the impression that he and Prince Jing were on decent terms.

The emperor loved seeing the two of them get along—even if it was fabricated.

The second prince wanted the luminous pearl? Prince Jing exchanged looks with Wang Xi. The two of them instantly thought of the pearl lying at the bottom of the fish tank.

Prince Jing didn't really care for Noble Consort Qiu's pearl. He had given the little carp many jewels since then, and it hadn't touched the pearl in ages. He had been meaning to secretly get rid of it, but if the second prince wanted it, he might as well return it.

Prince Jing nodded at Wang Xi. Mu Tianzhao was privately pleased. As long as Prince Jing handed over the luminous pearl, this would all be over. But Wang-gonggong chirped, "Second prince, please come with this old servant to retrieve the pearl."

Mu Tianzhao didn't know how to react. He had been the one to ask, and Prince Jing didn't oppose it, so the second prince couldn't very well back down, especially with all the other princes watching. He followed Wang Xi through the winding hallways to the interior of the manor. He was a little hesitant, afraid one of Prince Jing's henchmen would launch an attack from the dark, but thankfully he made it out in one piece.

Wang Xi let Mu Tianzhao into a room, pointed to a huge crystal fish tank, and said with a chuckle, "There was an accident with the luminous pearl, and it sank to the bottom. Second prince, you may go ahead and retrieve it."

Mu Tianzhao was horrified.

Wang Xi was clearly making his life difficult on purpose. The second prince was appalled. What was Prince Jing doing? How did the luminous pearl end up in the fish tank? It was a colossal fish tank—he could barely see the end of it—and it was packed with jewels. How was he supposed to find it?

Mu Tianzhao gritted his teeth and peered in. He wanted to locate the pearl first, then call for someone to retrieve it for him. He spotted a fish lying on a bed of white rocks. There was even a leaf covering the fish. How unusual.

This fish seemed like the one Prince Jing had brought, his beloved pet fish.

Mu Tianzhao and Lady Qiu had both suffered at the hands—no, fins—of this fish. Immediately, the second prince was on high alert. He wanted to stay far away from this accursed fish.

That was when he realized there was something strange about the way the fish was lying there. It was stiff all over. Not the slightest movement.

Prince Jing's fish seemed to have died again.

The second prince's stomach dropped.

# The Fish Disappeared

BEFORE ALL THIS, the second prince would've never spared a second thought for a fish, but this fish was different. He had to tread carefully. This fish had made serious trouble for him before. The wretched thing seemed to be dead, but it was all too possible that it was just playing a trick on him.

After the emperor put Noble Consort Qiu on house arrest, she had screamed herself hoarse that the fish was all part of Prince Jing's scheme. The second prince had similar suspicions, but if he wanted to save his image in front of the emperor—if he wanted to make sure the crown prince position was firmly his—then he couldn't ignore Prince Jing. He certainly couldn't show him any outward disrespect.

Prince Jing's position was unique; he could be considered a test for whoever was next in line. The crown prince had to make the emperor think he was benevolent and treated all his brothers well, especially Prince Jing, who was of nobler birth than he. So even if the second prince and Noble Consort Qiu had to suffer a little bit now, it would be worth it.

After what had happened with Lady Qiu, he knew that no matter what this fish did, he couldn't take it lightly. In the face of sudden change, he himself must remain unchanged. Since Wang Xi had come here with him, as long as he pretended he hadn't noticed anything, Prince Jing couldn't pin the blame on him.

So that was exactly what he did. But he couldn't help it—his eyes kept being drawn back to the cursed fish. It had been a while now, and the fish still didn't so much as move...

The second prince's eyelid twitched. That fish might really be dead.

He had to get out of here as soon as possible.

The second prince turned to Wang Xi. "I still have something to take care of at home, so I'll be taking my leave now. If the luminous pearl is found, please have someone bring it back to me."

Wang Xi smiled and shook his head. "Since Your Highness asked for it personally, you must, of course, take a look yourself first..."

Wang Xi had been with Prince Jing for many years and frequently came in contact with Mu Tianzhao, but this was the first time Mu Tianzhao had thought this old geezer was hard to get rid of. The more he wanted to leave, the harder it was for him to do so. Right at that moment, a servant who had been designated to take care of the fish, walked in. He immediately sensed something was wrong and pointed at the fish in the tank. He hurried to say, "Wang-gonggong, look. His Highness's fish isn't moving."

Mu Tianzhao let out a barrage of curses in his head.

Wang Xi quickly ran over and examined the fish from several angles. He knew this little carp had a "problem" of constantly "falling asleep." And it hadn't been moving around much, recently. Wang Xi hadn't thought much of it when he saw the fish lying there quietly, but now that the servant had mentioned it, it was a little *too* quiet. Had something happened to the fish?

Wang Xi carefully scrutinized the fish for a little while more, before saying uncertainly, "Don't take your eyes off of the fish. I'm going to go get His Highness." His expression was grim as he turned to Mu Tianzhao. "Second Prince, His Highness will be here shortly. Please wait a moment."

Mu Tianzhao had suffered at the fins of this fish before, and the fear still lingered. And now Wang Xi was trapping him here, which made him rather angry. "What do you mean by this? What does Prince Jing's fish have to do with me? I didn't even touch it!"

"Oh? Second Prince, this old servant didn't say anything—why are you getting so flustered?" Wang Xi chuckled insincerely. "Perhaps you weren't aware, but this fish is our Highness's precious pet. Even the emperor knows about it. It's nothing personal; anyone who enters this room must wait for His Highness to make a decision."

He really was relying on his master's authority, and even had the audacity to bring up the emperor! Mu Tianzhao's gaze went cold. If even one of Prince Jing's servants dared to treat him like this, then what kind of attitude would Prince Jing have toward him?

Not for the first time, his mind strayed to the crown prince position... Fine, he'd let this mute have his moment of smugness. Once he was on the throne, he'd make sure he wouldn't even be able to cry.

Mu Tianzhao forced his expression to relax. He said, "Let's just wait for my fifth brother, then."

*Ninghui Hall.*

After the second prince left, Mu Tianming suggested the dancers continue. The third prince refused to let the second prince disrupt his hard work.

Prince Jing didn't care either way; there was no harm in the performance continuing. The first few notes of the music had only just filled the air when a familiar little servant sprinted in. Despite how far away he was, it was still clear the servant was in a hurry, and anxious. Prince Jing vaguely recognized this servant; he always followed Wang Xi around. He waved the servant over.

The servant immediately approached and whispered into the prince's ear.

The servant wasn't clear on the details either; he had just been sent over in a hurry by Wang Xi. Following Wang-gonggong's instructions, he relayed that something had happened to Master Fish and that they had to consult Prince Jing, but the servant couldn't elaborate on the specifics. Prince Jing remembered that the second prince had gone to retrieve the luminous pearl. It was more than likely the second prince was involved, which explained Wang Xi's ambiguous instructions.

Did the second prince harm his fish?

Prince Jing's expression hardened. With a swish of his sleeves, he sent the singers and dancers away. The third prince made to protest, but Prince Jing just waved him off and headed into the inner chambers.

He quickly arrived at his room. Wang Xi and all the servants were waiting there, along with the second prince, who had a somewhat ugly look on his face. Prince Jing completely ignored the second prince and, before Wang Xi could say anything, made a beeline for the crystal fish tank.

His fish lay there quietly on the white rock bed.

Prince Jing studied it for a while, then reached into the water and touched the fish's back. As soon as his fingers brushed its scales, his expression changed. He immediately scooped the little carp out.

Wang Xi inched closer, and out of the corner of his eye, he saw Prince Jing...squeeze the fish flat???

Wang Xi realized quickly, "Your Highness, this...this isn't a real fish!"

Prince Jing threw the fake fish at Wang Xi. Wang Xi held it in his hand, turning it around and around. From a distance, this fake fish really did look like the real thing...but it felt soft and had no bones. How was it made?!

The little carp wasn't in the fish tank, and a fake fish had taken its place. Now this was a disaster.

"Your Highness, who would do such a thing?"

Placing a fake fish in the fish tank was clearly a tactic to fool them. Who had the nerve? And more importantly, where was the real fish?

Mu Tianzhao had planned to clarify the situation, to tell them that this time, the fish dying had nothing to do with him, but now it turned out the fish was fake? He was utterly speechless. And worst of all, he was the only outsider to have stepped foot in Prince Jing's room.

Prince Jing's gaze landed on him, pinning him in place. The second prince felt like he had fallen into a trap again, this time by a fake fish! He wanted to defend himself, say he had absolutely nothing to do with the fake fish or the real one, but would Prince Jing believe him?

The second prince was about to protest when something flashed before his eyes. The next thing he knew, Prince Jing's sword was held against his neck.

"Fifth brother, wh-what are you doing? I had nothing to do with this..."

The second prince was scared out of his wits. It felt like Prince Jing's sword was about to slice through his throat. He never thought Prince Jing would threaten him over a fish!

Prince Jing's sharp gaze flickered over to Wang Xi, and Wang Xi spoke for him. "Second prince, please tell the truth."

"I really am! I only came to retrieve the luminous pearl. I...I may not like this fish, but if I had really done something, why would I put a fake fish in? Wouldn't it make more sense for me to just throw it away?" The second prince was desperate to live.

Prince Jing studied the second prince for a while, eyes narrowed, considering the veracity of his words. Cold sweat poured down the second prince's face in rivulets.

Finally, Prince Jing lowered his sword and ordered people to escort the second prince out. Considering that his life was on the line, Mu Tianzhao was probably speaking the truth. There was no need for him to do something in such a roundabout way. Besides, if anything like this happened, the second prince would be the first suspect. There really was no reason for him to do something so stupid.

It probably wasn't Mu Tianzhao.

But the fake fish was clearly there as a distraction to keep him from discovering the fish had vanished. Who would go to such lengths? And to what end?

Prince Jing had acted out of anger just now, using violence to try to force Mu Tianzhao to tell the truth. Now that he had calmed down a little, he started ordering people to investigate whether anything was amiss with the room.

After a round of inspecting, the servants discovered the window to the south was ajar. Prince Jing didn't usually open his windows. That specific window faced his garden.

There had been quite a few tea bowls on the ground so that the little carp could come out of its tank and roam around. Prince Jing had a good memory and could recall the exact location of each tea bowl. After counting, he realized one was missing. The simplest inference was that someone had used the tea bowl to steal the fish, then escaped through the window.

Prince Jing contemplated the situation some more. Then he ordered the servants to search through the room and see if anything else was missing or had been moved. After a while, Wang Xi came back to report, "Your Highness, someone has gone through your closet. A set of inner robes a-and underwear are gone. Nothing else is missing or has been touched."

Prince Jing didn't know how to react.

Wang Xi was confused too. Someone had stolen both His Highness's fish and his underwear? There was clearly something wrong with this thief.

On Prince Jing's orders, Wang Xi commanded the servants to investigate anyone suspicious in the direction of the gardens, especially anyone holding a tea bowl. Prince Jing would stop at nothing, even if it meant having to dig into the ground, to find his little carp.

While Prince Jing was busy trying to find his fish, a youth was making his way down the ornamental mountain.

An hour ago, after drinking the transformation medicine, Li Yu had lost consciousness. When he came to, he realized he had returned to his human form. Li Yu was absolutely elated. He was even more ecstatic upon looking at his reflection in the bronze mirror: he had returned to his own original appearance. But immediately after that, he was faced with a fresh new danger—now that he'd turned back into a human, he wasn't wearing any fucking clothes!

Li Yu hadn't thought about the issue of clothing, because when he was a fish, he was covered in scales that were part of his body. As soon as he turned human, though, his clothes were nowhere to be seen! The fish-scamming system hadn't mentioned such an important detail!

...Fine. It *was* the fish-scamming system, after all.

The most pressing thing right now was to find some clothes.

Li Yu had transformed in Prince Jing's room. When he was a fish, he saw Prince Jing every day, so he obviously knew where the prince kept his clothes. There were only Prince Jing's clothes here anyway. Li Yu went to look in the closet.

There were all kinds of clothes in Prince Jing's closet, but he was much taller than Li Yu. In addition, long robes and wide sleeves were more common in ancient times. He was going to look ridiculous in Prince Jing's outer robes, and without the proper robes inside, when he walked, it would be easy to...accidentally reveal something...

But that wasn't his biggest concern right now. Most of the servants would be able to recognize their master's clothes. Li Yu was afraid of having his cover blown or rousing suspicion, but he couldn't just walk around in the nude. After some careful thought, he picked out a set of Prince Jing's inner robes and underwear.

Robes worn against the skin were always slightly smaller than outer robes. Inner robes also didn't have any embroidery or patterns, so they ought to be less conspicuous. Plus, he had taken the clothes from a closet Prince Jing barely touched. It was probably either new or a spare. He wouldn't feel too weird wearing it.

Anyway, he needed to look at the big picture here. Even if Prince Jing *had* worn it, he just had to grit his teeth and bear it. An innocent boy like him couldn't just run around buck naked!

There was nothing he could do about the shoes. Prince Jing's feet were larger than his. He might as well go barefoot if he had to wear such ill-fitting shoes. Besides, it was easier to move around without them.

Back in his own world, he had short hair, but in a rare display of benevolence, the system had changed it up for him. He now had medium-length hair down to his shoulders, which wouldn't stand out too much in the ancient world.

Li Yu casually gathered his hair at the back of his neck and changed into the robes. He then filled a tea bowl with clear water and put some fish food in it, successfully combining the three objects into one, and stored it in his inventory.

He glanced one last time at the life-sized fish plushie lying perfectly in his place in the fish tank. As long as no one went to touch it, they wouldn't suspect a thing. Everything was ready.

Li Yu deliberately opened the window closest to the garden. He, of course, wouldn't leave through this window; there were probably loads of guests wandering in the garden. This was just to divert attention.

Then, he opened a different window: one facing an ornamental mountain with no guards in sight. After clambering onto the windowsill, Li Yu carefully wiped away his footprints and ducked inside a hole in the ornamental mountain.

# A Fleeting Glance

PERHAPS LI YU had been a fish for too long and was too used to the swishing motions of swimming, but it was a little harder than he expected to control his legs. At first, it felt like he was floating rather than walking, and he kept stumbling. But this feeling didn't persist for very long, and he soon got used to it.

Because he didn't have suitable shoes, his feet were bare. Luckily the weather was warm, so he didn't feel cold. Prince Jing's manor was kept very clean, and by paying attention to the ground beneath his feet, he managed to avoid getting into any accidents after he made his way out of the ornamental mountain.

But with bare feet and only inner robes, he was a terrible eyesore. That was also why the servants who ran into the unfamiliar Li Yu didn't dare approach and question him.

Prince Jing was hosting a banquet today. The manor was filled with guests, all of whom were nobility or aristocracy and would need an invitation to enter. There were guards keeping watch outside the manor too, so there wouldn't be strangers wandering within the manor walls. Someone bold enough to dress like this was probably some lord's son acting out.

But it also wasn't appropriate to just let this little lord wander around like this. Someone had already dashed off to retrieve

Wang-gonggong so he could take care of it. Other people followed Li Yu from a distance.

A kind auntie servant saw Li Yu walking barefoot and couldn't bear to watch any longer. She came up to him and asked in a gentle voice, "Which family are you from? Why are you dressed like this?"

Having heard Wang Xi talk quite a lot, Li Yu didn't have any problems speaking to other people in ancient times. He replied vaguely, "Ma'am, I...I'm here as a guest. I got lost."

He thought he had everything down pat when he had been planning this all out, but complications kept cropping up. First, he had neither clothes nor shoes, then after he figured that out, he thought the kitchens would be easy to find, except Prince Jing's manor was way too big. He was too afraid to ask for directions and was starting to get frustrated and anxious. It had already been hard enough to find his way out of the ornamental mountain.

The auntie could see that this young man's face was clean, delicate, and likable. His dark eyes were exceptionally spirited, looking like a pair of black beads submerged in mercury. She couldn't help the fondness flooding her heart.

"If the little lord is lost, how about I take you to see Wang-gonggong?" said the auntie.

There was no way he could come face-to-face with Wang Xi. "No need!" he said hurriedly. "Wang-gonggong must be at Ninghui Hall right now. I'll be able to find my way back... But, Auntie, do you know where the kitchens are?" He rubbed his stomach, red-faced.

The auntie immediately understood and chuckled. "Is the little lord hungry? If you think me trustworthy, please follow me."

The auntie was wearing what the servants at the prince's manor wore, and she had an apron on. Li Yu implicitly trusted Prince Jing's servants, so he followed the auntie into the kitchens.

Li Yu talked with her the whole way there and found out the auntie was a cook in Prince Jing's kitchens. Li Yu felt like he had hit the jackpot. There was no way he was going to go hungry with a cook leading the way.

This auntie's last name was Xu. When the two arrived at the kitchens, Li Yu's eyes nearly fell out of their sockets—here at last were the dishes that he had been dreaming about day in and day out!

Auntie Xu brought out a plate with a smile and asked Li Yu what he liked to eat. Li Yu stared at the food, drooling, and listed out a whole bunch of dishes shamelessly.

Auntie Xu picked out a few based on his preferences and carried over two whole plates, along with a wooden bowl packed full of steaming white rice on a tray. "These dishes have already been brought out to the masters, so they won't need them anymore. These are all extras, and no one's touched them yet. Please eat as much as you want."

This was the first time anyone had been so kind to him since he'd turned back into a human. The thick steam rising from the food made his eyes water. He thanked Auntie Xu, accepted the bowl, and began wolfing it down. The unique taste of human food bloomed on the tip of his tongue, making him feel like his time as a fish had been nothing but a dream, and yet—

Staring down at his bare feet, he remembered the medicine was just a temporary fix. Very soon, he would turn back into a fish.

Auntie Xu saw he was inhaling the food as though he hadn't been fed in several days and urged him to slow down in case he choked. Li Yu smiled but didn't explain.

"Little lord, why are you alone?" Auntie Xu asked hesitantly. The youth before her was about the same age as her younger son, and she couldn't help but feel concerned.

Her words brought his worries back to mind, but he couldn't mention Prince Jing outright, so he replied, "My...my master is about to get married. He won't have time for me anymore, so I came out for a stroll."

Auntie Xu paused. Master? Married? Was this youth the male concubine of some noble? No wonder he had run out in such a rumpled state. He had probably been tossed out by the future wife and gone hungry for some time.

Auntie Xu's imagination conjured up a whole scene of the di wife dealing with the side wife. Li Yu made it sound pitiful, but she didn't look down on him. On the contrary, she patted his hand kindly and comforted him, "Don't worry. Stay here for a little longer and eat some more."

But he couldn't continue walking around in just his inner robes. After taking a quick glance at Li Yu's size, Auntie Xu pulled out a set of her younger son's clean robes and a pair of cloth shoes. The robes were a jade green, the same color as the seaweed that Li Yu liked. Li Yu had just been worrying about what to do about his clothes and shoes, and he was delighted by this turn of events. He briefly considered discarding what he wore already as he changed, but in the end, he decided to continue wearing Prince Jing's inner robes and underwear.

Auntie Xu probably thought Li Yu would feel awkward if she probed any further, so she didn't continue asking.

Finally getting the chance to indulge in human food, Li Yu only very reluctantly put down his chopsticks when there was a slight bulge rounding his stomach. After he finished, he followed Auntie Xu around in the kitchens, using it as an opportunity to digest the food he just ate—a habit he'd picked up from being in Prince Jing's care and maintained even as a human.

The ancient kitchen was bustling with activity. The assortment of knives and cutting boards caught Li Yu's attention, but he knew to look only with his eyes and keep his hands to himself, so the cooks didn't get mad. He also noticed a fish basket and remembered the noble consort's thousand carp soup from when he first transmigrated. He asked curiously, "Auntie, are you going to make thousand carp soup too?"

Auntie Xu laughed. "That's a dish for birthday banquets in the palace. The prince's manor doesn't have such customs. His Highness did have fish soup often in the past, but he's stopped now."

As Auntie Xu spoke, it seemed more and more like she was just talking to herself. But Li Yu heard and thought, *Is that because of me?* After all, Prince Jing really did dote on him. As he thought about all the different ways Prince Jing was good to him, Li Yu couldn't help feeling a little sad.

Auntie Xu smiled as she asked him, "Did you ask about fish soup because you wanted some?"

Li Yu shook his head emphatically. Why would he, a fish, drink fish soup? Please, no. He changed the subject and asked Auntie Xu where the opera stage had been set up.

According to his plan, after eating and enjoying a little opera, he should be heading back. He had already lost a substantial amount of time due to the issue of the clothes and getting lost, and he didn't know how much longer he had.

Auntie Xu informed him that the stage was in the Yayin Garden near Ninghui Hall. Li Yu made to hurry there, but he caught a glimpse of a few bamboo boxes just before he left.

These bamboo boxes looked familiar to Li Yu. Auntie Xu generously opened a few to show him. "This is the fish food His Highness asked for specifically. There are many kinds, though it's not anything rare."

For some reason, Li Yu's nose started to sting, as if he was about to cry. He pointed at the box holding red fish food. "Could I take some?"

Auntie Xu said, "Of course. The kitchens have plenty, so we won't run out, but this is for fish. Are you sure you want some?"

Li Yu nodded. "Y-yes."

Auntie Xu packed up half a box for him, assuming he also had a fish.

Li Yu stuffed it into his sleeve, the way people in ancient times did. Then he thanked Auntie Xu and headed toward Yayin Garden.

As he passed Ninghui Hall, he definitely had to hold himself back from peeking in, Li Yu thought warily. At this time, the main characters, top and bottom, were meeting. It had nothing to do with him and there was no need for a fish to do anything.

He steadfastly avoided looking in the direction of Ninghui Hall. At Yayin Garden, he could hear the sounds of the opera in the distance. But the guards outside Yayin Garden stopped him and asked to see his identification.

*Oh no,* Li Yu thought. No one had checked him in the kitchens. Why did he need to be checked at the opera? Besides, where was he supposed to get such a thing?

It hadn't occurred to Li Yu that, because he was wearing Auntie Xu's son's old robes and cloth shoes, he looked like a servant. The manor's rules stated that ordinary servants were not permitted in Yayin Garden, which was why the guards stopped him.

Li Yu didn't dare argue with the guards. He didn't have much time left. He didn't need to watch the opera, and if he wasn't welcome here, then there were other places where he could visit. Li Yu decided to go somewhere else, but as soon as he turned around, he came face-to-face with a familiar figure.

...Wasn't that Wang Xi-gonggong!

Li Yu barely had time to open his mouth to greet him when Wang Xi waved his hand, and all the nearby guards surrounded Li Yu.

"Capture this person!"

Wang Xi was still panting; it was clear he had been running for a while. Just a few minutes ago, he had been scouring the garden with Prince Jing. He hadn't paid much mind to the news traveling around. That is, until he heard a servant say there was a young lord dressed in only inner robes wandering around the manor. The more Wang Xi thought about it, the more likely he thought that this was the thief who stole Prince Jing's clothes.

He pondered further. The clothes had gone missing together with the fish. That meant the person who stole the clothes was the thief who stole the fish. He immediately alerted Prince Jing, sending someone to fetch him so he could take a look.

Li Yu was shocked at seeing Wang Xi stop him. There was no way all of his arrangements in Prince Jing's room had been found out that quickly. Then he remembered he was now human. He had to be careful to not reveal anything and raise Wang Xi's suspicions.

Li Yu smiled as he asked, "Wang-gonggong, what is it?"

Wang Xi scoffed, "You thief, you dare ask when you stole His Highness's fish?!"

Li Yu did a double take. Wang-gonggong had always been cordial toward him. He wasn't used to being yelled at, sob sob sob! Wait, did they already discover the fish plushie and the window he had purposefully left open?

There wasn't much time left. If he was captured by Wang Xi and he transformed into a fish in front of all these guards...

Li Yu wanted to calm down, but this wasn't something that could be solved by calming down. He had to find a place to hide first. He couldn't turn into a fish in front of all these people!

An idea struck. He yanked something out from inside his sleeve and yelled, "Over there—!"

He hurled the object with all his might. With Wang Xi and the guards distracted, he turned on his heel and broke into a sprint!

Wang Xi originally hadn't been certain if this youth was the thief, so he had bluffed. But now, seeing him run away... That meant he really was guilty!

But the thief was too quick, and Wang Xi didn't get to see what he had flung before he made his escape. Wang Xi gritted his teeth, terrified the person might have thrown the fish out. He quickly ordered a few guards to take a look, while he and the rest of the guards gave chase.

Li Yu sprinted as fast as he could and found a room to hide in.

Meanwhile, Prince Jing had been searching with a few people in the gardens. After receiving Wang Xi's message, he rushed over to meet up with him. Together, they trapped Li Yu in the room where he was hiding.

It was quickly confirmed that what the youth had thrown was fish food. There was no doubt about it: this person had stolen the fish. Wang Xi couldn't have been more furious. Once he caught that person, righteous justice would be doled out. Not only had this person caused trouble during a banquet, they even dared to steal the prince's clothes and his cute, lively fish. They deserved to be sliced through thousands of times!

"Hurry up and come out. Hand over the prince's fish, otherwise you'll have to face the consequences!" Wang-gonggong yelled fiercely as he banged on the door.

Li Yu poked a hole in the window and peeked out. Prince Jing stood outside the room, grim-faced and holding his sword. But as soon as Li Yu laid eyes on Prince Jing, his fish instincts kicked in and he wanted to swish his tail.

Then he remembered he was human right now. Prince Jing didn't know him as a human. If they met, that sword in the prince's hand would stab him to death.

Wang Xi wanted him to hand over the fish. On the one hand, he was very moved; on the other hand, this wasn't what he wanted at all. The fish in question was right in front of them! What was Li Yu supposed to hand over!

At first, he was planning to wait until everyone had left before leaving the room, but with the situation as it was now, Prince Jing and Wang Xi were both waiting for him like predators outside the burrow of a rabbit. There was no way he was leaving anytime soon.

Li Yu's tears were practically flowing down his face. *All I did was go out to eat. How did I end up in this situation...*

Suddenly, the system beeped a warning! *‹User, you cannot maintain your human form for much longer...›*

Stupid system! It usually played dead, but now it was giving him a countdown! He was about to turn back!

It had taken so much work to transform just once, and now it was all going to be over. Li Yu only had time to eat one meal! But that wasn't the most important part. The important part was that right now, he was trapped in this room. If he turned back into a fish right here, how was he supposed to explain how a human "disappeared" at the same time the fish appeared?

Li Yu had an idea. Counting down the time, he yelled at the people outside the door, "I won't leave! Come and get me! If you catch me, I'll hand over the fish!"

Li Yu was trying to buy some time for himself as well as prepare for what was to come. When a cornered person made such a bold challenge, the reasonable assumption was that they'd laid some kind of trap, so the people outside usually wouldn't barge in right away.

He thought this would be enough to make Prince Jing falter for a bit, but—

He barely finished shouting before Prince Jing broke through the door.

Li Yu yelped in alarm.

A youth Mu Tianchi had never seen before was standing stock-still in a jade green robe. The young man glanced back at him before hastily escaping out a window.

Mu Tianchi wasn't going to fall for the same trick twice. He had previously been fooled by the open window, mistakenly believing that the thief had left that way. The thief's deception had led him to look in the wrong place, and he failed to catch the thief.

This time, he made sure the person had absolutely no escape out of the room. He had several guards stationed at each of the windows before ordering Wang Xi to yell at the thief within.

Mu Tianchi chased after the youth, his long legs carrying him across the room in just a few strides, but the youth had already leapt onto the windowsill. He looked over his shoulder and flashed Prince Jing a mischievous smile.

Mu Tianchi froze. Was it just him, or did this youth…

He was a delicate, clean young man, his eyes as bright as colored glaze. There was something unbelievably familiar in the way his lips quirked up.

Mu Tianchi hesitated for a moment, but that moment cost him: all he managed to catch was a single corner of the suspicious youth's robe. In the blink of an eye, the youth jumped out of the window.

Mu Tianchi wasn't concerned, though. He waited quietly for the guards lying in wait to capture the youth. But after a while, he still heard nothing.

He made his way outside to look for himself. The hidden guards reported that they hadn't seen anyone. Mu Tianchi furrowed his brows and spotted a heap of clothes piled up beneath the window. And on the ground was a tea bowl, with his fish inside, swimming happily.

# Fish Selling Himself

**L**I YU'S HEAD was swimming at first, but he very quickly realized he had turned back into a fish.

His plan should've been foolproof. He was going to act like he had escaped out the window, "disappeared," and left only the fish behind. But first of all, he wasn't expecting Prince Jing to break in so fast! Okay, yes, he was touched at how deeply Prince Jing cared about a fish, but now he had no time for his plan! Not only had the prince seen his true appearance, but he had also almost transformed right in front of him.

He had nearly tripped in his haste to escape out the window. It was a good thing he'd turned back into a fish the moment he jumped, because it turned out Prince Jing had stationed people outside as well. Even if he had "escaped from the window," so what? There were all these guards out here, and not one of them had seen so much as a glimpse of him.

How could anyone explain the fact that a person had just disappeared and left behind a pile of clothes?

Li Yu thought that, at this moment, Prince Jing was even more of a cheater than the system. At least when the system tricked him, he could find a way to get around it. But when it was Prince Jing tricking him...there was nothing he could do about it.

The guards who had been lying in wait all agreed that they hadn't seen any youth. As he watched Prince Jing come closer to examine his clothes, Li Yu waved his tail hard, hoping to divert Prince Jing's attention. There shouldn't be anything incriminating about the clothes he had left behind, but he was afraid Prince Jing would somehow connect the dots.

Although the reason he was swishing his tail was to distract Prince Jing, it looked a bit like he was "selling himself."

*Ah! Selling myself a little bit is ok, but I absolutely cannot be mistaken for a fish spirit!*

As soon as Prince Jing heard his tail move, he stooped down to pick up the tea bowl. Li Yu swished his tail even more vigorously. Prince Jing was still a little angry. He glared at the fish, sparking some guilt in Li Yu. Knowing how much the prince liked it, he curled his tail around Prince Jing's finger, hoping to appease him. Every time his tail touched the prince's finger, Prince Jing seemed to relax a little.

As expected, faced with Li Yu acting cute on purpose, Prince Jing temporarily forgot about the pile of clothes. Lips pursed, the prince pinched the little carp's back gently. Li Yu knew that meant he was willing to play with him.

Pushing his embarrassment aside, Li Yu continued to "sell" himself by acting cute.

A guard walked over to give his report. "Your Highness, there's a pond nearby. Perhaps the thief caught the guards before they were ready and swam off." The guards had come to this conclusion because of the clothes; after all, a person couldn't just disappear into thin air. They'd already given themselves headaches trying to figure this out, but this was the only possibility they could come up with.

Li Yu was shocked. They could even find a rational explanation for something like this?

It made sense, though: a normal person would never consider the prospect of a human turning into a fish or a fish turning into a human. Their first deduction would, of course, be that the suspicious youth managed to get away.

The guards' explanation wasn't outside the realm of plausibility. Prince Jing nodded, wanting to take a look at the pond himself, in case there were any suspicious footprints or anything like that.

Li Yu desperately threw himself onto his palm. There was nothing at the pond! He couldn't let Prince Jing go look!

Prince Jing's brow was relaxed, despite Li Yu's frequent interruptions. He knocked on the fish's head lightly. Li Yu had been wondering for a while now why Prince Jing kept doing that, but no one could tell him.

Seeing that Prince Jing was no longer so wary, though, Li Yu let out a sigh of relief. He'd finally managed to escape unscathed! It wasn't a terrible outcome that they'd all concluded he must have escaped through the pond.

After the guards finished examining his clothing, Wang Xi also confirmed that the inner robes and underwear on the ground belonged to Prince Jing. The rest of the clothing consisted of an ordinary, old robe, and a pair of old cloth shoes.

Auntie Xu was brought over in a matter of minutes. She identified the robe she had given to the youth. Auntie Xu felt terrible. Never did she expect that harmless, innocent youth to be a Master-Fish-stealing thief! As she recalled giving the youth fish food, she felt so immensely regretful she wanted to kick herself. She told them everything she knew: that the fish thief was a male concubine who had been chased out by his master's di wife.

Wang-gonggong didn't know how to process that information. What kind of ridiculous reason was that? This person stole His Highness's fish because he was being bullied by the di wife? What did that have to do with anything?

Li Yu was also listening in Prince Jing's hand, but he could barely understand what they were talking about. He was just someone who'd gotten lost; how did the auntie manage to come up with this scenario where he was someone's side wife?

Auntie Xu kept kowtowing. Li Yu couldn't bear to watch. He peeked at Prince Jing, afraid he was going to punish her out of anger.

After observing Prince Jing's expression, Wang Xi intoned severely, "For hiding a thief, she should be thrown out of the manor."

Li Yu's heart nearly stopped.

No! He wasn't even a thief. Auntie Xu just felt sorry for him and gave him some food to eat. Why did she have to be chased out? He didn't want to get Auntie Xu in trouble all because she had been kind enough to help him.

Li Yu hurriedly curled his tail around Prince Jing's finger, then rubbed back and forth pitifully.

Prince Jing looked down. He *did* find the fish in the end, and his pet fish seemed unharmed. Prince Jing was in a pretty good mood. He glanced at Wang Xi.

Wang Xi immediately understood. "Since the fish master has returned unharmed, and in consideration of the fact that you weren't aware of the situation, we won't throw you out this time. Thirty strikes of the board. Let this be a lesson learned."

Tears of gratitude poured down her face. She had been too careless; she couldn't afford to lose this job at the prince's manor. Her skin was thick, and a beating was nothing compared to expulsion.

Li Yu still wasn't happy with this outcome, but as he watched

Auntie Xu bow in thanks, sincerity written all over her face, he hoped he had at least helped a little. The guilt in his heart eased somewhat.

If he overused his charms, the effects would eventually wear off; Li Yu stopped before it was too late. Prince Jing, who had been enjoying the fish's attention, was suddenly bereft.

Wang Xi waved away Auntie Xu and said to the prince, "Your Highness, servant Xu has been dealt with, but this old servant still thinks something is off. Why did the thief steal the fish?"

Remembering the sleeve he had torn off earlier, Prince Jing indicated to Wang Xi to bring it over. Aside from a few wet patches, there was a silver scale caught on the cloth.

Holy shit, how could he leave behind such an obvious clue?

"Your Highness!" Wang Xi said, shocked. "How could a fish scale be stuck to the thief's sleeve?"

A shadow passed over Prince Jing's face.

There had been a fish scale on Noble Consort Qiu's handkerchief after she had touched the fish. Since there was one on the thief's sleeve, that could only mean one thing: the thief had also touched the fish.

How dare he!

Wang Xi spoke for Prince Jing, "Your Highness, the fish master has truly suffered a lot."

Prince Jing patted the fish's head to comfort him.

*Uh...?*

Should he celebrate the fact that he had tricked the noble consort before?

Now that Prince Jing had found the fish, Wang Xi reminded him that there were still guests at Ninghui Hall. The guests all had to wait for him to return to bid their goodbyes if they wanted to leave.

This was, after all, a banquet planned by the emperor. It was normal enough for the host to leave temporarily to deal with some things, and that was just what Prince Jing was like, but he couldn't just come and go as he pleased.

Since Prince Jing was too lazy to go back to his rooms, he headed straight for Ninghui Hall, holding the fish in the tea bowl in his hands.

Li Yu, who had been planning to use the time to secretly take care of a few loose ends, silently protested. No! He didn't want to go meet the second master!

But a fish had no say in its master's decisions. Prince Jing carried him into Ninghui Hall and placed him down on the main table. Every single guest in the hall stopped in their tracks. They had all heard that Prince Jing had started taking care of a fish and that he treasured it like nothing else. This must have been it!

It wasn't clear who started it, but the guests all started to shower praise upon the little carp.

Li Yu swished his tail happily, feeling a bit giddy. Aiya, he wasn't as good as they said he was. Yes, he was indeed cute and intelligent, but anyone who said he was prettier than a koi had to be blind.

Suddenly, Li Yu's dark eyes landed on a young man in white dance robes. This youth was exceptionally pretty, his features so fine they could have been painted on. Amidst the chaos, he stood quietly, standing out in the boisterous crowd. This main character aura... This "I don't need to seduce anyone, everyone automatically falls for me" aura...

Li Yu startled. Could this be the other protagonist, the bottom?

The bottom's name was Chu Yanyu. Li Yu leaned against the ledge of the tea bowl and observed him. Although he didn't like the second master, Chu Yanyu's delicate features were far too alluring, drawing Li Yu's eyes to him.

Prince Jing's brows knit together. What was the fish staring at? With a flick of his long fingers, Prince Jing pushed the little carp back into the tea bowl. Falling down unexpectedly, Li Yu playfully splashed some water right at Prince Jing. Except he avoided it!

Prince Jing laughed silently. Li Yu shook his tail, happily thinking that his master was also pretty. He was happy with just looking at the prince; no more looking at Chu Yanyu!

Second Prince Mu Tianzhao watched as Prince Jing brought the fish in. His lips twitched, but he didn't say a word. He *knew* that fish wouldn't die so easily. This was probably another one of Prince Jing's schemes.

He seethed silently. How dare Prince Jing threaten him over a fish? When he ascended to the throne, he would make that mute pay.

As soon as the third prince, Mu Tianming, saw Prince Jing return, he steeled himself and, for the third time that night, offered to present his dance. Prince Jing allowed it.

Despite having been ignored twice so far, Chu Yanyu didn't let it bother him. He shook out his sleeves and glanced behind him. The sixth prince met his gaze from where he sat, not too far away. At the slight dip of the sixth prince's head, Chu Yanyu bit his lip and turned to bow graciously.

This time, Li Yu was hanging entirely off the side of the tea bowl. While everyone was gasping at Chu Yanyu's appearance, Li Yu was focused on the moment Chu Yanyu's eyes flickered to meet the sixth prince's.

In the book, Prince Jing had fallen in love with Chu Yanyu as soon as he laid eyes on him, but Chu Yanyu didn't like Prince Jing back; his affections lay with the sixth prince. On the surface, he was a dancer given to Prince Jing by the third prince, but in reality, he was loyal to the sixth prince over either the third prince or Prince Jing.

The sixth prince had never been shown any favor by the emperor, and so he had become the third prince's lackey in the hopes that he could live a better life. The third prince needed someone who could sing and dance, so the sixth prince offered up the boy he had loved since they were children—Chu Yanyu, who loved him in return.

The sixth prince's ambition was hidden deeply inside his heart, but there was only one person he could trust. Chu Yanyu was more than happy to sacrifice himself for the sake of the sixth prince's future.

The dance began. Chu Yanyu had arranged the music and choreographed the routine. Despite all the interruptions so far, the guests were quickly immersed in the exquisite dance. After the group dance came the duet between Chu Yanyu and another dancer, a stunning woman.

Skirts whirling about, the dancers were like white lotuses in full bloom amongst the lotus leaves. Li Yu had absolutely no interest in the dance. In fact, he wanted to sink to the bottom of the water, but the tea bowl was too shallow, so he couldn't get very far. He had to settle for lying in the tea bowl, glancing at Prince Jing from the corner of his eye. Prince Jing...was enjoying Chu Yanyu's dance.

Li Yu blew a little bubble and turned away. He didn't want to look at him anymore.

In the original book, Prince Jing asked Chu Yanyu for his name once the dance was over... But after the last note of the dance dissipated into the air, Prince Jing didn't say anything.

The second prince couldn't help but gloat. He might not have been able to put on a show of brotherly love with Prince Jing, but at least the third prince didn't achieve anything either.

The third prince couldn't hold it in anymore and asked Prince Jing for his thoughts. Resting his cheek on his hand, Prince Jing gave Wang Xi a slight glance.

Wang Xi immediately replied, "It's fine."

And that was it.

The third and sixth princes, who had worked so hard to present Chu Yanyu to him, were both silent.

Li Yu was even more perplexed. What happened to the love at first sight that he couldn't resist? *Master, have you fallen asleep? Wake up, your wife's about to disappear!*

# The Fish Is Wanted

PRINCE JING HADN'T TAKEN a fancy to any of the dancers. The third prince had been so confident in Chu Yanyu, but all Prince Jing did was watch the dance. He didn't even give the dancer a second glance. All the praises Mu Tianming had been ready to sing were suddenly stuck in his throat.

Chu Yanyu was hardly perturbed. With his eyes lowered to the ground, it was impossible to tell what he was thinking. The sixth prince nudged Mu Tianming. "Third brother?"

Mu Tianming had already embarrassed himself enough today, what was once more? He swallowed his pride and squeezed out a smile. "I'm glad fifth brother thought it was fine. I myself thought it was quite lovely. In fact, I personally selected the lead male and female dancers. Why don't I gift them to fifth brother to pass the time?"

With him speaking so plainly, everyone knew what the third prince meant. Mu Tianming refused to believe Prince Jing would remain indifferent when faced with a direct gift.

Prince Jing switched hands, resting his cheek on his left. He pushed the little carp, who had popped out of the water again to look around, back in. Prince Jing's gaze swept toward Wang Xi once more.

Wang Xi, who seemed connected to Prince Jing on an intuitive level, said, "His Highness said...no."

"No." Not "no need," or "no thanks." "No" meant he wasn't even interested.

Mu Tianming was at a loss for words.

"Prince Jing, are you unhappy with me in some way?" Chu Yanyu's thin back was ramrod straight, fingers curled tightly into fists. His eyes flickered with fury. He already had someone in his heart, but for Prince Jing to treat him in such a way was downright humiliating. An extremely prideful man, Chu Yanyu wasn't going to let such an indignity pass without questioning it.

Li Yu was shocked. He didn't expect this. Was this still the delicate little concubine from the book who treated Prince Jing coldly? How did it get flipped around?

As soon as he'd finished speaking, though, Chu Yanyu regretted his thoughtlessness.

Prince Jing smiled mockingly, shook his head, and rose, tea bowl in hand. He ordered Wang Xi to send their guests off. Chu Yanyu didn't know how to react. Did Prince Jing shake his head because he was dissatisfied with him?

Wang Xi suddenly spoke, "Chu-gongzi, don't misunderstand. His Highness doesn't mean anything by it. Only...what concern would it be of His Highness's whether you were good enough or not?"

The third prince, Chu Yanyu, and the sixth prince were all shocked into silence.

Mu Tianming's head started to hurt. Prince Jing wouldn't even accept a gift that was hand-delivered to him. What was he supposed to do now?

Prince Jing kept Li Yu in the tea bowl, preventing the little carp from jumping out. Glee secretly shot through Li Yu at seeing Prince Jing's indifference toward Chu Yanyu. In the book, Prince Jing had constantly chased after Chu Yanyu, doing too much for his sake and getting injured too many times. If Prince Jing hadn't fallen in love with him, did that mean the prince's heart was safe?

But would changing the plot have some impact on Prince Jing in the future, due to the butterfly effect? After some internal struggle, Li Yu stopped worrying about it. He was here to change Prince Jing's personality, after all, and wasn't that already a change to the original plot of the book?

Li Yu finally returned to Prince Jing's room. The prince poured him back into the crystal fish tank, where Li Yu noticed the plush had disappeared. The prince had probably already figured out the secret...

Li Yu smiled derisively. There was no way Prince Jing had figured out that *he* was the one who placed the decoy, right? No, there was almost no chance. If Prince Jing couldn't even conceive of the possibility of him transforming into a human, how could he come to the conclusion that a fish had placed the plush?

No, there was nothing to worry about. He was going to keep on following Prince Jing and kissing up to him. As Prince Jing paced before the fish tank, Li Yu chased after him.

Suddenly, the prince stopped. He pulled something out of his sleeve and dropped it into the tank. Bemused, Li Yu looked up and saw a blackish blob floating down slowly to land next to him. It was a fish that looked exactly like him.

Li Yu did a double take. Wasn't this the plushie?

He snuck a glance at Prince Jing. What did he mean by this? Acting as though he was an ordinary fish who didn't have a single thought in his brain, he snatched the plush up. He didn't dare drag the plushie onto the bed of white rocks and cover it with the leaf blanket like before. That would just be outright exposing himself!

He swam a few laps in the water, nudging the plush like it was a toy. Prince Jing saw how much the little carp seemed to enjoy playing with the toy. From far away, it looked like he had a pair of inseparable pet fish.

The prince paused, suddenly annoyed with the fake fish. He'd have Wang Xi get rid of it later. But he had other things to take care of, so he walked over and sat down at his desk.

Li Yu had thought of a new way of playing with the plush, by laying it across his back like he was carrying it. The plush was very light, so he didn't feel tired at all. After playing for a while, he realized Prince Jing was preoccupied with work, so the little carp pressed himself up against the walls of the crystal tank to peek at him.

Prince Jing was drawing again.

He had painted the little carp once before in Jingtai Hall and even asked Wang Xi to hang it up afterward. Prince Jing had brought the painting with him when he returned to the manor, where it was currently hanging on the wall diagonally opposite the crystal fish tank. *Was Prince Jing drawing him again?* Li Yu thought delightedly.

He was going to go pose!

Li Yu abandoned the fish plush and jumped into a tea bowl on the floor. His agility had been compromised slightly after devouring basically an entire feast as a human, and it took him a few jumps to reach Prince Jing's desk.

There was a flower petal-shaped tea bowl on the desk that he visited quite often. Prince Jing seemed to have expected that the fish would come watch him paint, as he didn't seem the slightest bit surprised at the carp's sudden appearance.

Prince Jing's painting was a little larger this time. Li Yu held his breath. Although it wasn't done yet, and he couldn't see the entire thing right now, he could make out a hand and a foot. They seemed to be wearing clothes. Prince Jing wasn't drawing a fish this time; he was drawing a person.

Li Yu's heart sank. Was this Chu Yanyu? Despite rejecting the third prince, Prince Jing's heart was still with Chu Yanyu?

But that didn't seem like Prince Jing's style at all. In the book, Prince Jing was the kind of man who would stop at nothing to keep the person he loved by his side. There was no chance that Prince Jing was still thinking about Chu Yanyu after he'd rejected him outright. It was more likely this was a portrait of Wang Xi than it was of Chu Yanyu.

Li Yu waited quietly for Prince Jing to finish drawing and then coloring. This painting was a little complicated, and it took him a full hour to complete.

Prince Jing picked up the painting and shook it. That was when Li Yu finally got a good look at the entire thing. Prince Jing was a talented painter, and the colors came together with a vivid and lifelike impression. Captured in the strokes of the painting was a youth in green robes. His hands rested on the windowsill as he turned back, a smile lighting up his face.

Holy crap, why did this person look kind of familiar? Wasn't this his human form? Did Prince Jing recreate the moment he almost got caught?

Prince Jing painting a fish was understandable, but a person he'd barely met? The little carp couldn't figure it out.

Prince Jing set the painting to the side and rang a jade bell to call for his servants. Wang Xi quickly entered from outside.

Prince Jing handed the painting over to Wang Xi solemnly. Wang Xi then leaned in and whispered something in his ear for the prince's confirmation. After his affirmative, Wang Xi's expression looked rather serious.

Was Prince Jing going to ask Wang Xi to hang it up so that his human portrait and fish portrait were side by side? They were both him, but it was a little weird...

"Rest assured, Your Highness," Wang Xi said, "this old servant will order the guards to look for the person in this portrait immediately."

...*What?*

Prince Jing drew a circle on the paper. Wang Xi nodded. "I'll make sure they search along the pond's edge. We'll definitely find this person."

He'd spent so long distracting Prince Jing with his body and the prince was *still* determined to capture him?

Well, whatever, even if they had the portrait, they wouldn't be able to find him. They wouldn't find anything in the pond, because the person they were searching for was currently in Prince Jing's fish tank.

After the banquet in Prince Jing's manor, a dejected third prince left with Chu Yanyu and the others.

Mu Tianming refused to believe that all his careful preparations had gone down the drain. After a round of discussions with his trusted advisors, he decided to deliver Chu Yanyu and the other female lead dancer to Prince Jing's manor anyway. As soon as he left them there, Mu Tianming dashed off faster than a thief, thus forcing Prince Jing to accept them.

The news of the third prince gifting Prince Jing some people circulated quickly, soon reaching the emperor's ears. The emperor was amused, but ultimately, he was quite pleased to see the third prince's efforts to get on Prince Jing's good side.

The banquet had been held on behalf of Prince Jing and the second prince, but according to his scouts, Prince Jing's fish had vanished after the second prince visited Prince Jing's rooms. Was the second prince causing trouble for the fish again?

The emperor was still alive now, but if the second prince couldn't even let a fish go, what would happen later? Would he try to get rid of Prince Jing?

The emperor wondered if he had revealed his choice of crown prince to Noble Consort Qiu too early. This wasn't the first time Mu Tianzhao had disappointed him, after all. As a warning to the second prince, a few days after the banquet, the emperor awarded only the third prince with a tea set.

It wasn't anything precious, but no one else received this honor, not even the second prince. Because the emperor had rewarded him specifically right after he had sent people to Prince Jing's manor, Mu Tianming thought he had hit on the right way to get closer to Prince Jing. This could only mean that the emperor hoped he and Prince Jing could get along.

The sixth prince had also correctly guessed the emperor's intentions. The emperor rewarding only the third prince and not the second prince signaled the beginning of the second prince's downfall.

"This is all thanks to your recommendation." Mu Tianming smiled as he patted Mu Tianxiao's shoulder. "It was a good idea to send Chu Yanyu into Prince Jing's manor."

The sixth prince smiled back gently, not letting even a sliver of resentment show on his face, even though his lover had gone to Prince Jing's manor. "Yanyu's clever. He won't let you down, Brother."

When Prince Jing heard the news from Wang Xi, his expression was mild. Wang Xi-gonggong already had a wealth of experience with outsiders trying to cram people in the manor. The emperor himself had sent many people, over the years—men and women, fat and skinny. Prince Jing didn't like any of them, so they were all sequestered in a courtyard in the manor. No one was allowed to come out without permission. After they'd stayed for a year, those who wanted to leave the manor could leave. Those who wanted to stay all became servants.

Now the third prince had sent over Chu-gongzi and his female counterpart. His Highness had already made it very clear he didn't want them, but the third prince had gone and left them there anyway. Looking at Prince Jing's expression, Wang Xi knew that the courtyard was about to get two new additions.

# Bathing with the Fish

LI YU WAS COMPLETELY OBLIVIOUS to the roundabout way Chu Yanyu was entering the manor. He assumed a direct rejection by Prince Jing would be enough to put him off. A grand total of zero sparks had flown between the main top and bottom. Li Yu was a bit worried that it'd affect Prince Jing's future.

*<System,>* he called out, *<what'll happen if the plot completely changes?>*

Prince Jing hadn't taken to Chu Yanyu at all. It felt off to him.

The system rose from the dead to reply: *<Everything will be fine as long as the user completes his Moe Pet Fish mission.>*

...Did that mean the plot was allowed to become totally unrecognizable, then, as long as he completed his fish(y) missions? Li Yu was kind of excited. At first, he'd been worried that the fish-scamming system would give him some kind of mission to get Prince Jing and Chu Yanyu together, but apparently the plot progression was none of his business. It'd be pretty nice if Prince Jing could dodge the angsty relationship he had with Chu Yanyu altogether, he thought. Besides, if Prince Jing didn't like Chu Yanyu, Chu Yanyu probably didn't like Prince Jing either—how could a fish like him press their heads together and order them to kiss? It'd be impossible.

For the first time, Li Yu felt like it wasn't all that bad to have a system. Sure, it scammed him all the time, but it wasn't totally useless.

Just as he was celebrating, the system reminded him: *‹The altered plot will affect the course of future events. Plot points unrelated to the altered plot will still progress, and plot points related to the altered plot will change accordingly. Please be prepared, as the user will not be familiar with the modified plot.›*

It was rare for the fish-scamming system to be so talkative, but what it was saying made sense to Li Yu. The original book did have a lot of plotlines that revolved around the relationship angst between Prince Jing and Chu Yanyu, so those plotlines would obviously be influenced if Prince Jing wasn't pursuing Chu Yanyu. That was the butterfly effect.

Li Yu the fish was very generous. *‹It's all right. I'll be prepared.›*

But would it affect Prince Jing's path to the throne? What if the butterfly was too strong and ended up slapping his throne away with its unnaturally muscular wings?

Prince Jing was the di son, and he didn't get along with the other princes, so if he couldn't become the emperor, he was practically guaranteed a miserable fate—so Li Yu still wanted him to become the emperor.

System: *‹No matter how it happens, the tyrant's "protagonist" status guarantees he will become the emperor. This is an unavoidable canon event.›*

With that sentence, Li Yu was reassured. Next, he planned to slowly and leisurely study how he was going to "attain a deep understanding" of the tyrant.

*‹Oh, right. Since you answered me, then help me with this too. I think I understand Prince Jing pretty well already, so what exactly does a "deep" understanding mean?›*

...Sure enough, the fish-scamming system promptly played dead as soon as he brought up one of his missions. Typical.

No matter. Li Yu still politely bade the system good day.

When he regained his senses, he found that Prince Jing had lifted him out from the fish tank again. From time to time the little fish would simply fall asleep like this, and whenever that happened, Prince Jing would watch over him. They were both used to it by now.

Li Yu flapped his tail to show that he was alive and kicking, but Prince Jing frowned. Perhaps he'd happened to touch Li Yu's belly when he lifted him out of the tank and felt that something was off, because he was currently rubbing Li Yu's fish belly.

...Ah. Prince Jing's actions reminded Li Yu that his normally flat fish belly was a little swollen. Right, he remembered: when he turned into a human he'd absolutely gorged himself, but his bulging stomach was the same after he turned back into a fish. Perhaps the system didn't notice this problem either.

*I just ate too much. I'm fine.* Li Yu wanted to explain, but he couldn't. Prince Jing kept rubbing his belly with that strange expression on his face for a bit, until he came to the conclusion that the fish was sick again and called for someone to come.

The servants who'd examined the fish for "sickness" before now examined his belly for a bit. One of them wiped the sweat from his forehead and said, "Your Highness, the fish seems to have eaten too much."

"It'll go away after a little more swimming around," another servant added. "It's not because...the fish is, um...pregnant."

The other servants present wanted to poke their eyes out. This fish was male! Why did His Highness ask such a question?!

*What?!* Li Yu was scared shitless by what the servant had said. Pregnant?! Did Prince Jing think he had little fish inside him?! How would that be possible? Men couldn't get pregnant, and male fish couldn't give birth to little fish!

Did Prince Jing get his gender wrong even though he'd been taking care of him for so long? Li Yu puffed up in anger. After the fish had been "examined" to his satisfaction, Prince Jing tried pushing him around with his finger so he could digest his food, but Li Yu had no desire to move. He just lay there on the prince's hand.

Luckily, the food he'd eaten when he was a human was still easily digested when he turned back into a fish, so Li Yu was back to normal in no time, full of vim and vigor. The recovered Li Yu soon forgot his anger and started trying to think of things he could do that might help him get a "deeper understanding."

He had a breakthrough when he remembered a saying he'd often heard in modern times: As a man, to obtain a deeper understanding of another man, one must take a bath with him.

He might as well try and take a bath with Prince Jing, he thought. He managed to complete the bed-sharing task, after all, so how hard could it be to take a bath with him? If Prince Jing was willing to put him on his jade pillow, he probably wouldn't be against bringing him into the bathtub. Provided, of course, that he didn't fall into hot water and turn the whole tub into fish stew. But the hot water problem was easy to solve—there were definitely ladles in the bathroom, or other tools for scooping up hot water.

Li Yu couldn't help but think that it would have been nice to have a mission where his job was to become a little hot spring fish... But the system ignored him. It probably thought he wasn't worth talking to.

When it was time for Prince Jing to take a bath, Li Yu jumped around more excitedly than he ever had before.

Wang Xi was outside holding a portrait of human Li Yu, stopping at nothing to try to capture his likeness, but when he turned around and caught sight of the little carp, his wrinkles bloomed into a smile.

"Little thing, do you want to get into the bath with His Highness?"

Li Yu leaped toward the side of the fish tank. He went all out this time, becoming completely shameless, blowing bubbles at Wang Xi and acting cute.

Wang Xi consulted Prince Jing. Prince Jing found Li Yu's actions a little strange too, and after a bit of thought he agreed and had someone make the proper arrangements.

Wang Xi fetched a large wooden ladle meant to hold water, which he used to scoop out the little carp from the tank, along with some of the water. In the bathroom, Prince Jing had already finished making preparations.

There were quite a lot of charcoal braziers in the bathroom, making the room warm and cozy. Behind the screen placed in the middle of the room was a bathtub almost as tall as a person, where Prince Jing sat in his inner robes, motioning Wang Xi to come over and put the wooden ladle in the water.

The wooden ladle holding the little carp floated in the bathtub, making it look like Prince Jing was bathing in the bathtub while the fish was bathing in the ladle.

Li Yu wiggled eagerly in the ladle, trying to move it toward Prince Jing. But the ladle was much lighter than the small tea bowls he was used to, and since it was both floating in water and filled with water, he found it hard to control his strength. Li Yu couldn't move the ladle forward, and instead started spinning in circles—he was pretty dizzy after just a couple of spins.

Prince Jing smiled a little and lifted his hand to stop the spinning ladle. When Li Yu fully came back to his senses, he was met with the sight of Prince Jing's handsome face, a face that seemed even more pristine in the bath. He even saw a water droplet slide down Prince Jing's cheek to his Adam's apple; his Adam's apple rolled, and the water droplet fell.

...Li Yu hadn't inadvertently bitten or chewed anything this time, but just like last time, he felt like he was getting cooked over a fire. It was definitely the hot water's fault. He buried his head in the wooden ladle's water, feeling a bit embarrassed. *Calm down a little!* he told himself firmly. He was a fish who would do anything to complete his quests; he must not be tempted by the beauty of his owner!

He lifted his head, wanting to swim closer—but he used too much strength, and instead of spinning in place, the ladle abruptly tilted to the side and fell over!

Seriously. He was about to win a Darwin Award here.

Hot water surged into the ladle, and Li Yu lamented that there were more ways for a little fish to die than just turning into fish bones and fish ashes—after everything he'd gone through, he still had to contend with being boiled into soup.

The water—

*Huh? The water's not hot?*

A stunned Li Yu floated in the "hot" water for a bit before it sank in that he could still swim. The water pouring in from the tub was cold too!

What was going on?

Li Yu carefully swam out of the upended wooden ladle, now in the same bathtub as Prince Jing. It didn't take too long for him to understand what was going on: Prince Jing had replaced the hot water in the tub with cold water, since he wanted to "play" in the bathtub.

*Ue, ue, ue... Owner, how could you treat me so well?*

Li Yu flapped his tail twice, trying to swim closer to his owner. It was rare for a fish and a human to be so close, with nothing in between them. Prince Jing smiled slightly as he scooped up a handful of water and poured it onto Li Yu's head, as if he was getting revenge on the little fish for all the times he'd splashed him in the past.

*You bully! You dare tease a fish?!* Li Yu shook off the water on his head while Prince Jing smirked smugly. Li Yu had never seen such an expression on him, and without pausing to think, he leaped over, opening his mouth and biting chaotically.

A human and a fish were tussling in the water.

At first, Wang Xi was worried that Prince Jing wouldn't be able to physically tolerate being soaked in the cold water, but the water he was bathing in had been left in a warmed room with charcoal braziers for a while by now, so it shouldn't be freezing cold anymore. Plus, Prince Jing would sometimes practice his martial arts in cold water during winter, so it should be fine.

But just in case, Wang Xi still prepared some ginger soup for when Prince Jing got out of the bath, to drive away the cold.

His Highness seemed in much better spirits after the little thing—Master Fish—joined him in the tub. Wang Xi was sincerely happy for Prince Jing as he listened to them splashing around from outside.

After the bath, Li Yu was scooped back into the wooden spoon and brought out by Prince Jing himself. Li Yu tittered happily— there'd been a mission update during his water fight with Prince Jing. It looked like taking a bath together to understand a man deeply was the correct line of thinking.

Li Yu waited until the middle of the night to check out the reward. He'd been in a bad mood back when the quest first popped up, so he hadn't been paying too much attention to it, but he told himself to keep his expectations low—the fish-scamming system had given him a lousy fish plushie last time, after all.

When he collected the reward, a bright light briefly flashed under his fin before disappearing, much like what had happened when he received the inventory reward.

Li Yu lowered his head to take a glance. Next to the jade scale that he used to access his inventory, there was another, very similar scale.

*<What is this for?>*

What if he tapped the wrong one in the future, since they looked so similar and were so close to one another?

Li Yu tried to poke the new scale but didn't feel anything in particular. The next moment, though, he found that his body...had grown bigger. He looked toward his fins in surprise, only to find that his fins had turned into hands!

Delighted, Li Yu asked, "System, what's going on?"

He touched his face happily. His face was smooth, free of fish scales—he didn't understand why, but he had turned into a human. Was this what the system was talking about when it said he could turn back into a human if he kept completing the missions? Was he fully back now?

*<Apologies, user. This is just a skill,>* the system began to explain, late as always.

*<...Skill?>*

*<The main mission will become increasingly complicated from here onward and will be harder to complete if you can't turn into a human,>* the system said. *<The reward this time is a skill that allows you to maintain your human form for an hour, once per day.>*

*<...What kind of skill is this?>*

It didn't even last as long as the transformation medicine! But if he could use it once per day... Wait, didn't the system say there was only one bottle of the transformation medicine?

The system was lying again. If he'd known he was going to get a skill that would let him turn human for an hour a day, he wouldn't have been so stingy and calculating when he used the transformation medicine!

*<There is only one bottle of the transformation medicine. The reward this time is a skill, but if you dislike it, user, you can give it up.>*

Li Yu panicked. *<Who said I wanted to give it up? I earned this by working hard on my quest!>* He hunched over his jade scales protectively. Now that he'd turned back into a human, the jade scales had turned into two scale-like markings under his arm.

*<Then please use it well,>* the system replied. *<The next mission is the final quest in the 'Priceless Pet Fish' mission. Once it's completed, all your stats will be doubled, your inventory slots will increase by one, and you can begin the side mission 'Turn into a Koi'...>*

Was he finally about to finish a main quest? The rewards sounded quite lavish, and he would be able to start the long-awaited koi mission soon. But what exactly *was* the last mission?

In the mindscape where the system resided, the words "Tyrant's Priceless Pet Fish" started glowing golden. Li Yu examined the last step of the quest.

The last step: "Intimate Contact with the Tyrant."

There were no more details.

Li Yu suddenly had a bad feeling. *<Wait. 'Intimate contact'... Is that the kind of 'intimate contact' I'm thinking of?>*

*<Please come to your own conclusion, user.>*

...Okay. When it really mattered, the system had started bullshitting again.

Li Yu puttered around the system for a while. His time as a human ran out quickly, and he changed back into a fish; since this transformation was the result of a skill instead of medicine, Li Yu didn't feel any unpleasant side effects. Now that the transformation was finished, the jade scale lost its luster, indicating that it could not be used until the next day.

With this skill, he could turn into a human once in a while, but he had to be careful. He couldn't show himself whenever he wanted, since Prince Jing was still looking for him everywhere—

Mind fully occupied, he exited the system. Luckily, even though he'd been in his human form in the system, in the waking world, he was still a fish. Perhaps the system had helped him. The image of a human man fainting in a fish tank was pretty alarming.

He'd already progressed to the last stage of "Priceless Pet Fish." Just one more step, and he'd be done with a main quest. He was getting closer and closer to turning back into a human...and to do that, he had to work hard at achieving "intimate contact."

Yet the only intimate contact he could think of was...mouth-to-mouth.

With the help of the tea bowls laid out across the floor, Li Yu jumped lightly from the fish tank to the foot of the bed. It was late now, so Prince Jing was asleep; Li Yu stared at his luscious lips, remembering how he'd bitten them before and had to apologize for it with fish food, and now...he had to do something so shameless.

No need to think so much; it was just a mission. He and Prince Jing were already good friends who understood one another deeply, Li Yu kept telling himself, so he had to strike while the iron was hot and get this over with now. It'd only get more embarrassing as time went on.

Having managed to convince himself, the little carp jumped onto the jade pillow, closed his eyes, and inched his fish lips forward.

But...it was so much easier to do something like this accidentally. Doing it on purpose was hard.

Li Yu felt like he'd been inching forward for a while, but the softness he remembered still seemed out of reach...

He opened his eyes, only to find that Prince Jing had turned around. Li Yu stared at the back of his head.

*...Then I'll jump again!*

He leaped to the other side, doing his best to stretch his fish lips out. But he still didn't make contact. He opened his eyes.

Prince Jing opened his eyes too.

Li Yu all but forgot where he was. With a guilty conscience, he immediately started flapping his tail, revealing his impure intentions. Except his thumping on the jade pillow was way too loud.

*Sob sob sob! What should I do?!*

Prince Jing, who had probably been woken up by the fish jumping around, found his pet lying on his pillow and flapping its tail as soon as he woke up. Still sleepy, Prince Jing dragged the nearest bowl over and put the fish in; he patted Li Yu's head lightly and lay down to sleep again.

*What the hell!* Could someone tell Li Yu what the head patting meant?!

Li Yu didn't dare make another attempt to inch his mouth forward. He didn't want to wake up the sleeping figure in front of him again. Forget it. Next time... Well, he wasn't in a hurry anyway.

Li Yu hunkered down next to Prince Jing and fell asleep too.

An unexpected visitor came to Prince Jing's manor.

Prince Jing was cold toward most people, so he hardly ever invited any guests. There were usually only two types of people who came to the manor. The first type was people from the palace who were there to sort out business and announce royal edicts. The second type was Ye Qinghuan, the heir of the House of Cheng'en.

This young lord liked a good crowd, the opposite of Prince Jing's preferred solitude, but he just wasn't afraid of Prince Jing's frosty disposition and often came to the manor just to hang out. Ye-shizi didn't care that every time he visited, Prince Jing's face was as dark as the bottom of a wok. It made him happy, even. Prince Jing could tell everyone else who came to scram, but not him—because Ye-shizi was his cousin. At most, he could only order the guards to grab Ye Qinghuan by the collar and throw him out.

Ye-shizi hadn't been able to attend the banquet that was recently held at Prince Jing's manor, because he had official matters to attend to, and he quite regretted missing out on the fun. He rushed over to Prince Jing's manor as soon as he had time—just a couple of days later.

He'd also heard that Prince Jing had started taking care of a pet—a pet fish, at that. Ye Qinghuan had actually made this trip to show off his own pet, a dog. He thought that he had a little more in common with Prince Jing now, and they'd be able to chat with each other about their pets.

Wang Xi led Ye Qinghuan, with his dog in tow, to meet Prince Jing.

When he saw his cousin, Ye Qinghuan grabbed a chair, sat down excitedly, and immediately started asking after the fish without having Wang Xi announce him.

"Tianchi, are you really keeping a fish as a pet?"

Prince Jing glanced at the large black dog behind Ye Qinghuan, decked out in a heavy collar of pure gold. Instead of throwing his cousin out immediately like he usually did, Prince Jing signaled Wang Xi to bring the fish tank out.

The crystal fish tank from the emperor hadn't been moved since it was brought to Prince Jing's residence, as it was extremely inconvenient to move something so heavy and large. But since Ye-shizi was visiting, Prince Jing wanted to move the fish tank. Wang Xi felt both helpless and amused as he thought, *Who asked Ye-shizi to show off in front of His Highness? Of course he's going to show off in return!*

Honestly, there would have been nothing wrong with just letting Ye-shizi enter the room to see the fish, but Prince Jing clearly didn't care for the dog. Besides, the fish tank would also be much easier to view outside the room than inside it.

Ye Qinghuan didn't have to wait too long before the fish tank, half the height of a person, was escorted in. Ye Qinghuan's mouth dropped to the floor and was left there, forgotten. It wasn't that Ye-shizi had never seen crystal—but the jewels piled in the fish tank were almost enough to blind him. Yet the fish inside was clearly just a normal, small, gray carp!

"You didn't throw your entire money pouch into that fish tank, did you?" Ye Qinghuan muttered. He didn't actually care about a pet's value, but someone like Prince Jing, who was willing to spoil a fish, was a far greater rarity than his fish.

He'd intentionally tried to show off the pure gold collar on his dog's neck, but it was nothing compared to Prince Jing's fish tank. The gold collar was expensive, yes, but even money might not be able to buy Prince Jing's fish tank and everything inside it.

Prince Jing glanced at him with an *Are you an idiot?* expression on his face.

Ye Qinghuan gulped. He suddenly remembered that Prince Jing was rich, but he never really showed it, so what had happened for him to show it off now?

Ye Qinghuan didn't want to be embarrassed, so he snapped his fingers. His large black dog bounded over, wagging its tail and pawing at his legs. The young lord immediately regained some of his lost confidence and hugged his dog, who in turn nibbled on his face. Ye Qinghuan smirked at Prince Jing.

Prince Jing knew that Ye-shizi was provoking him, but he'd never snapped at his fish or trained him before. He thought the young lord was being childish and wasn't quite expecting anything.

Li Yu, in his fish tank, was watching Ye Qinghuan and his dog as well. He could tell what was going on from a single glance—were the pets going to compete? Li Yu's tail flapped in excitement, and he rushed to the front of the crystal tank. It was time to help his owner earn some more respect! What could a dog do? He'd beat ten of them in a row!

Prince Jing noticed his fish looked...quite eager. Why not give it a try, then? He hesitantly stretched out his hand, palm up.

Li Yu knew that Ye Qinghuan was trustworthy, so he flicked his tail and effortlessly jumped out of the water, landing directly on Prince Jing's palm.

Vindicated, Prince Jing held up his fish and softly squeezed his back. Li Yu wanted to use this opportunity for some intimate contact, but Prince Jing moved faster than him and placed him in a petal-shaped tea bowl that Wang Xi had prepared ahead of time.

Ah, he'd failed to steal a kiss... Li Yu flopped unhappily in his teacup. *Sob sob sob, let me out! I have to finish my mission!*

Ye Qinghuan gaped in disbelief. Prince Jing was playing with the fish and the unappealing fish actually jumped—not only did he jump, he also jumped into Prince Jing's palm with deadly accuracy. His own dog wouldn't lick the center of his palm if there wasn't food on it, but Prince Jing didn't feed his fish anything!

...He lost, he lost. Ye Qinghuan felt like he'd lost the meaning of life.

Wait. He rubbed his face as he remembered something, and asked, "Tianchi, what's your fish's name?"

Prince Jing stared at him.

"My dog's name is Xiongfeng."

Ye Qinghuan grinned, feeling like he'd won this round. He was sure that someone as boring as Prince Jing wouldn't think of giving his pet a name. Even if Xiongfeng wasn't as smart as the little carp, he still had Prince Jing beat when it came to names.

Li Yu didn't really understand what was going on and wanted to laugh, but before he could giggle, his gaze met Prince Jing's. He instantly had a bad feeling. If Ye-shizi was going to brag about his dog's name... He suddenly remembered how Wang Xi called him "little thing." Did Prince Jing want to...

No! "Little thing" was much less dignified than "Xiongfeng"!

Li Yu immediately shook his head and wagged his tail, trying to demonstrate his disapproval.

Prince Jing was indeed thinking about how he really hadn't named his fish yet. There were actually a couple of ways to address him—most servants called him "His Highness's fish," or "Master Fish." Wang Xi had called him "Master Fish" once or twice, but he called him "little thing" most often...

Then why not just decide on "little thing"?

But Wang Xi was the one who'd come up with that name, and Prince Jing didn't know how he felt about that. He'd always called him "this fish" in his thoughts.

It was about time to give him a proper name.

Prince Jing pressed his lips together, asked for some ink and paper, gave it some thought, and wrote the word "xiao."

He turned his head to find the fish's burning gaze fixed on him.

Prince Jing smiled, added the word "fish," and tossed the paper to Ye Qinghuan.

"Why'd you give me this?" Ye Qinghuan was holding the calligraphy but hadn't realized what it was yet.

Wang Xi, who had faded into the background, leaped out and confidently explained, "Ye-shizi, His Highness wants you to remember that Master Fish's name is 'Xiaoyu.'"

Ye Qinghuan was speechless. What an unbelievably dull and unimaginative name!

*Xiaoyu?* Li Yu's eyes lit up. This was an excellent name; he used to have the exact same nickname in the modern world. He quickly spit out a bunch of bubbles, trying to show how much he liked his new name.

Ye Qinghuan's arrival had refreshed Li Yu's impression of Ye-shizi from the book. Ye Qinghuan was Prince Jing's cousin, and one of the few royal children who was still upright and open-minded. He was sometimes prone to saying annoying things, but that was really his only flaw.

And Li Yu never knew that the real Ye Qinghuan had a dog. It was probably a small detail in the original book, just like the noble consort's Master Cat.

Unfortunately, this detail almost cost Li Yu his life, especially when Ye Qinghuan had someone untie Xiongfeng's chain.

Xiongfeng started running around wildly, kicking up a cloud of dust; Li Yu could've heard the ruckus from a mile away. This dog had never seen a fish before, so he ran over excitedly to give him a sniff.

When he was human, Li Yu wasn't afraid of cats or dogs, but as a fish, he was afraid of both. Dogs might not like to eat fish, but they loved grabbing things in their mouths. Xiongfeng's glistening white teeth were much larger and sharper than Piaoxue's. What's more, Ye-shizi's dog was quite persistent when it came to things that interested him and insisted on poking his nose into things and smelling them before he stopped.

Right when the dog was about to poke him with his nose, Li Yu shrieked, "HELP!!!" The little carp flopped around wildly in a panic, forgetting he was in a tea bowl and splashing water everywhere.

As Xiongfeng dashed forward, Prince Jing moved in front of the teacup, so the dog ran into a human wall, just like Piaoxue did back then. Xiongfeng was an overly enthusiastic dog, so running into something didn't make him mad at all. Since it was his first time in Prince Jing's residence, he was also curious about Prince Jing, as he'd never met him before.

While Xiongfeng might not have been afraid of Prince Jing, however, Ye Qinghuan knew what Prince Jing was like when he was angry. Afraid that his dog would get a beating, he hurriedly said, "Tianchi, don't raise a hand against him. You still have to keep in mind who his owner is—my Xiongfeng is naturally friendly and doesn't bite humans."

He didn't bite humans, but could he guarantee that he didn't bite fish? Ye-shizi wasn't quite sure of that himself.

Very good. Prince Jing glanced at Ye Qinghuan and laughed coldly at him.

He didn't end up dealing with Xiongfeng; instead, he turned around and ordered Wang Xi to pick up Ye Qinghuan and his dog and throw them out together.

Xiongfeng frightened Li Yu so badly that the fish's secret plan to steal a kiss from Prince Jing when he didn't expect it had flown right out of the window. But Ye-shizi's arrival had helped him recall a plotline that this young lord was involved in. The system had told him that some plotlines would still happen and others would change. What was going to happen to this one?

In the original book, the third prince gained Prince Jing as an ally through Chu Yanyu. The House of Cheng'en, as the family of the former empress and Prince Jing's family, had no need to support any other prince but still indirectly helped the third prince for Prince Jing's sake.

After they found out that the House of Cheng'en had helped Mu Tianming, Mu Tianzhao's family held a grudge. At the same time, the country of Jinjue had sent their princess over to be married, and the emperor planned to have her marry Ye-shizi. However, as the second prince was afraid that the third prince would also receive support from the country of Jinjue through this marriage, he plotted to frame Ye Qinghuan: Ye Qinghuan would "accidentally" kill the princess.

With the princess dead, there would be no marriage. Mu Tianzhao didn't care if the country of Jinjue ended up becoming an enemy of the empire or not. What was important was that, according to his plan, the emperor would punish Ye-shizi to soothe diplomatic relations, and the Duke of Cheng'en would plead for mercy. Then Mu Tianzhao just needed to have the ministers on his side speak of justice and insist that Ye-shizi and the Duke of Cheng'en had brought shame on the memory of Empress Xiaohui. The emperor would at least take away their titles and dismiss them from their positions, and the rest of the family would be impacted as well.

The second prince had greater power in court than the third prince did; with the third prince's personality, Mu Tianzhao knew that he would choose to protect himself if pleading for mercy failed. He would then swoop in to win over the Duke of Cheng'en. If he could win him over, then the Duke of Cheng'en and his family would be loyal to him; if he couldn't win him over, then at least he would have put the third prince at a disadvantage.

The second prince was knee-deep in plots and schemes, but the most despicable thing of all was the sixth prince's behavior: when he discovered the scheme by chance, he kept his mouth shut, told the Duke of Cheng'en and the third prince nothing, and instead chose to wait and let the tragedy happen.

However, the Jinjue princess wasn't the one who ended up being killed. Instead, it was the emperor's most beloved youngest daughter.

The emperor was furious. Ye-shizi was executed, the Duke of Cheng'en was exiled, and Prince Jing, having been implicated as well, was confined to his residence. The sixth prince volunteered to take on some of the emperor's burden and married the awaiting Jinjue princess. Yet the third prince still believed the second prince was behind everything and assumed the sixth prince was helping him earn the trust of the country of Jinjue, and thus started trusting the sixth prince even more—when in truth, the sixth prince was secretly already winning over the third prince's people.

All of this happened because of the sixth prince's opportunism. The chance arose for him to drive the wedge between the two princes even deeper, so of course he took it—and managed to eradicate the power of the House of Cheng'en while he was at it.

The second and third princes were dangerous, but the sixth prince was even more malicious. He helped gain the backing of the House of Cheng'en through Prince Jing and Chu Yanyu, but then he found out that the House of Cheng'en was already stretched to its limits. Realizing they were even less likely to be of use to him than he'd thought, he decided to cut off the arm of support he'd personally brought in for the third prince, since he already trusted him completely. At the same time, he could turn the second and third princes against each other, thus giving himself an opportunity.

The princess had nothing to do with the princes' power struggle, but the sixth prince still sacrificed his own younger sister. He knew that the emperor would still show the Duke of Cheng'en some mercy over the death of a mere princess from another country—but if it was their own princess who died, the emperor would no longer need to hold back on account of Empress Xiaohui.

Clearly, the sixth prince had the darkest heart of all. He hid behind the third prince and plotted for both the second and third princes to defeat each other. Without these manipulations, he never would have gained the opportunity to fight Prince Jing for the throne and nearly win.

In the fight to become the heir, there were countless casualties—the most innocent of which, in the original book, would be the House of Cheng'en and Ye-shizi. But now, a turning point had presented itself. Since Prince Jing didn't like Chu Yanyu, it would be immensely difficult for the third prince to receive help from the House of Cheng'en. Would the second prince still plot to frame Ye-shizi?

If the second prince hadn't put that plan into motion, then the sixth prince's plan wouldn't have kicked off yet either.

Li Yu had very little contact with Ye-shizi. The young lord might be a bit irritating, but he was one of Prince Jing's few friends, and a direct relative. To die in the contest for power, as innocent as he was... In the original book, the sixth prince failed to win the position of heir, and even though Chu Yanyu begged for his mercy, Prince Jing still sacrificed the sixth prince to Ye Qinghuan's family—it was clear that he was incredibly regretful.

*If Ye-shizi's plotline still exists,* Li Yu thought, *I should help as much as I can.*

But he was just a fish. What could he do? Ye-shizi came to Prince Jing's residence more often than anyone else did, but it still wasn't very often. Li Yu could only turn into a human for an hour a day, so he might not be able to run into Ye-shizi, and even if he did, an hour wasn't enough time to persuade Ye-shizi to believe him...

Prince Jing was still the one Li Yu had the most contact with, so he had to go through Prince Jing.

Just as he was thinking about how he was going to go about it, the fish-scamming system suddenly interrupted. *‹User, you've met the prerequisites for the side quest 'Impenetrable Defense.' Would you like to begin?›*

*‹What side quest?›* said Li Yu. *‹How come I can activate it even though I haven't done anything?›*

*‹It activates when the user is willing to save cannon fodder characters from the book without anything in return.›*

Li Yu laughed. So Ye-shizi was also...ahem, cannon fodder. But with Ye-shizi's qualities...he was probably still the most eye-catching cannon fodder.

It would be best if the side quest was considered completed after people were saved. If it was anything like "Clear, Bright Pearl," he'd lose his mind.

Li Yu still had to worry over the intimate contact mission, though. He asked cautiously, *‹What's the mission, exactly? And the rewards? Let's hear it.›*

The system guided Li Yu to look at the "Impenetrable Defense" mission. The mission was quite detailed—as long as he protected the person he wanted to save in the given period of time and prevented their death, the side quest would be completed. It was right in line with what he wanted to do, and he liked the title "Impenetrable Defense." It meant that as long as he was able to protect and guard the person well, he was like a metal wall.

*‹And the rewards?›* Li Yu asked.

*‹The user can choose from these rewards once the mission is completed...›* The system started to list them off mechanically.

Li Yu didn't really want to listen. *<Fine, I'll see what they are when the mission is completed instead.>*

The fish-scamming system's rewards were getting more and more fantastical. Well, even if there was no mission, he would still help Ye-shizi. The reward wasn't really important.

Li Yu's plan was to deliver a letter to Ye-shizi that outlined the second prince's plan to frame him. Even if Ye Qinghuan didn't believe the letter, the House of Cheng'en might at least be alerted, and if they were somewhat already prepared, then it would be difficult for the second prince to harm him.

Since Li Yu already had the skill that let him change into a human, he didn't have to worry about how he was going to write. But it wasn't until he was actually faced with writing the letter that he suddenly realized...in ancient times, people wrote in traditional characters. Li Yu could guess and read some traditional characters, but he wouldn't be able to write an entire letter with them.

He'd suddenly become illiterate...

Still, it wouldn't stop him. Since he could mostly read traditional characters, he just had to find a book with lots of words and copy it.

There weren't many books in Prince Jing's bedroom, but there was a large study room that Li Yu hadn't been to yet.

When Prince Jing planned to go to the study, Li Yu jumped into his palm and grabbed onto his fingers, refusing to get off.

Prince Jing glanced at him fondly. *What in the world should I do with you?* he thought. This fish had been getting bolder and bolder ever since it was given a name. Oh well. Prince Jing might grumble, but he didn't hesitate at all to grab the flower petal tea bowl that the little carp often stayed in.

When he got to the study, Prince Jing placed the fish on the side as usual and brought over a set of books to read at the desk.

The little carp was always very quiet when Prince Jing read in his own room, but this time, instead of being obediently silent as usual, Xiaoyu kept trying to stretch his head toward the book he was reading and flapped his tail vigorously.

*The angle's off! I can't see!*

...Did Xiaoyu want to play again?

Prince Jing was pretty easygoing with his fish, so he smiled and moved the tea bowl closer to him. Wang Xi had been informed that the fish was coming to the study, so he'd laid a couple of thick, water-absorbent blankets on the table in advance.

Li Yu could finally see the book. As he watched, he took note of as many characters as he could that he might use while writing the letter. He planned to practice writing the characters when no one else was around.

Prince Jing noticed while reading that Xiaoyu's head was moving up and down consistently.

...Hmm. He suddenly had the feeling that the fish could read.

No, he definitely saw it wrong, right?

Prince Jing put his book down and rubbed the spot between his eyebrows. He noticed that as he put the book down, the little carp slowly tipped forward in his tea bowl...until he fell onto the page with a soft poof.

*...Ah,* thought Prince Jing. *So he fell asleep.*

Li Yu despaired. *How come I fell asleep?!*

# Even the Best-Laid Plans

WHILE PRINCE JING WAS OUT, Li Yu took the opportunity to transform into a young man.

This was the first time he'd used the transformation skill outside of the system interface, and it was kind of overwhelming. But he had urgent matters to attend to. He suppressed his excitement as much as possible.

After he transformed back into a human, he still didn't have any clothes to wear, but it wasn't a big deal. Li Yu nonchalantly took out a new set of underclothes and underwear from the closet, as if he'd done this a thousand times before. He didn't have long as a human, so he didn't have time to do anything else. For now, until he was able to properly write the letter to Ye Qinghuan, this was fine.

Once he finished getting dressed, he found the cuffs of the robes were too long; he rolled them up, exposing his pale forearms. He carefully examined the things on the table; Prince Jing's brush and ink were all there, but he couldn't use them recklessly. If he left any traces for Prince Jing to find, all his efforts up to now would be for nothing.

Li Yu thought back to how he'd watched the servants organize the room when he was bored. Based on those memories, he walked to the shelves and opened the drawer in the middle to find spare brushes and ink. He took out a brush, a stack of rice paper, and a half-used inkstick.

In ancient times, the ink first had to be ground from an inkstick. Li Yu had seen Prince Jing grind ink before, and it would be easy to replicate his motions... But the only inkstone he could find was the Duan inkstone on the desk, which belonged to Prince Jing. There was no way he could use that. Besides, it was currently clean... It'd be too obvious if he used it.

Li Yu pursed his lips and chose one of the tea bowls on the ground to use as an inkstone for the time being. Now, everything was ready. Li Yu positioned his Four Treasures of the Study on a corner of the desk, poured some clear water into the bowl, and started to grind the ink.

He'd never done this before, and he wasn't sure when to stop grinding, so he just decided to stop when the water turned black and dipped his brush in the ink.

Li Yu set his cheek on his palm, held the brush, and thought about how to phrase his message. He'd memorized a lot of characters from Prince Jing's book, but there were still some characters he didn't know how to write. Prince Jing's book wasn't a dictionary, and it was hard for a fish to sneak around and find the exact characters he wanted.

...Whatever. Even if he couldn't write a few characters clearly, or got them wrong, it was fine as long as Ye-shizi got his message.

Mind made up, Li Yu picked up his brush and started to write his letter. He wrote several drafts, one after another, revising the letter again and again. Once he had read it to himself and thought it looked all right, he copied that version. He waited for the ink to dry, then he folded it, made a simple envelope from another sheet of paper, and crammed it in.

Now that the letter was done, all he had to do was give it to Ye Qinghuan.

Li Yu stored the finished letter in his inventory to keep it safe. Then he wiped the brush clean and put it back where he originally found it, along with the ink and paper. He wiped down the desk he'd touched too.

He couldn't just throw away the rough drafts, though—they had to be destroyed. Li Yu wavered between burning and eating the paper, but since paper tasted awful and he was afraid Prince Jing would notice something strange about his belly again, he lifted the lid of an incense burner in the room.

By the time he'd disposed of everything, the fish-scamming system started counting down his remaining time in human form. Li Yu took off all his clothes and hid them in the pile of clothes that Prince Jing had already worn. A servant would take them all away for cleaning later, so there would be no traces left.

...He was so smart and resourceful, he thought, that he could become a spy.

When Prince Jing returned, Li Yu was sleeping soundly on his white stone bed. Prince Jing felt something was off the moment he stepped over the threshold, though everything looked just like how he'd left it. Somehow, his subconscious just felt that there was something wrong.

He looked at his fish first. Xiaoyu was lying quietly on the white stone bed; right when Prince Jing was about to go over and check, the fish spit out a bubble.

...His fish was fine.

Prince Jing walked around the room once, slowly, and finally figured out what was wrong: something had been burned in his incense burner, but there wasn't the smell of incense. Prince Jing opened it up, but he didn't find anything strange except for the ash scattered around the outside of the incense burner.

Very peculiar.

Prince Jing forbade others from entering and leaving his room unless necessary, so the servants of his residence would not do something like this. It looked like someone had come in and burned something in the incense burner—and very possibly did other things as well.

Prince Jing called for Wang Xi and had him investigate thoroughly.

Wang Xi immediately checked everything in the room. He quickly found that one of the writing brushes stored in a drawer had frayed, and a stack of paper was missing, along with half an inkstick.

Prince Jing's face darkened. Had another thief appeared so soon, even though the last one hadn't been caught yet?

The servant in charge of laundry was just about to take away Prince Jing's clothes for washing when Wang Xi, careful as ever, stopped him. He flipped through the clothes, and his eyes lit up.

"Your Highness, look..." Wang Xi pulled out an inner robe from the pile of clothes. The sleeves of this garment were rolled up, and there were a number of ink stains on it.

Prince Jing thought back to the past couple of days. He knew that he hadn't gotten ink on his inner robes recently, and there was no need for him to roll up the sleeves, since the garment fit him well.

...Inner robes again. Did the thief have something against his clothes?

Probably not.

"Your Highness, this servant recalls the one that escaped by water last time," Wang Xi quietly reminded Prince Jing.

Prince Jing nodded. He agreed that this was too great a co-incidence—it was probably the same person. Since the thief wasn't caught last time, he came back again.

But what exactly was his goal?

A smile flashed in Prince Jing's thoughts. Secretly, he couldn't quite believe that the young man with such refreshing looks could be the thief who stole his clothes multiple times. And why did he steal his fish? Trying to express his anger over getting kicked out by the di wife was a bit of a reach.

Prince Jing felt sure there must be some huge secret behind this young man, he just hadn't figured out what it was yet.

But whatever the case, he wouldn't let the thief take away his fish anymore. Prince Jing secretly ordered Wang Xi to double the guards and increase the number of people looking for the thief.

All the while, the little carp was still sound asleep, unaware that his actions had set off a chain of disturbances in Prince Jing's residence. He was originally sleeping facing the inside of the fish tank—when he turned over, he was met with Prince Jing's face.

Right away, Prince Jing and Wang Xi noticed a long, black mark on his body that hadn't been washed away by the water yet. Wang Xi, shocked, asked Prince Jing for directions. When he fished out Xiaoyu and wiped him down, they realized the fish was covered in ink.

Prince Jing was deeply perplexed.

"Your Highness, look!" A servant hurried over with a tea bowl to ask for further instructions. For some reason, the cup was filled with ink instead of clear water.

*Ink again,* thought Prince Jing. *Why ink?*

The ink-stained garment Wang Xi found, the bowl filled with ink, a ruined brush, a used inkstick, the missing rice paper, and a disturbed incense burner... The mystery intruder had most likely used the cup as a grindstone in his room, used the brush and ink to write something, and burned something in the incense burner.

And Xiaoyu... How could ink have gotten on *him*, Prince Jing wondered?

Li Yu was still bleary-eyed when Wang Xi took him out of the fish tank, but when he realized that a servant had found the tea bowl with the ink and Prince Jing was examining the ink on his body, he jolted awake at once.

Fuck. He was too careless. He didn't notice he'd gotten ink on his hands and wiped it on his body, and he'd put the teacup down when he was done with it and forgotten to pour the ink out. The best-laid plans of fish and men often go awry!

Prince Jing might even start suspecting him now. He couldn't be mistaken for a fish spirit! Li Yu immediately broke away from Wang Xi and doggedly jumped into the inky tea bowl, pretending to be excited, like he really loved it, and dyed himself darker than a squid.

Prince Jing had been splashed by the fish a number of times now, so he knew what was going to happen as soon as the fish lifted his tail. He raised his arm to cover himself, intercepting most of the ink splashes with his sleeve. Of course, his sleeves had still been stained quite badly... Wang Xi, beside him, wasn't so quick, and gained a smattering of new ink spots on his face.

Wang Xi tried to smile to smooth things over. "...Master Fish is quite spirited," he said, wiping his face with his handkerchief.

Prince Jing, expressionless, figured it was obvious where the ink on the fish had come from. The fish clearly did it while he was playing around!

Li Yu continued to act like a cute little squid in the face of

Prince Jing's fish-targeted eye lasers. His fake image was hanging by a thread, but he'd managed to hold on!

With the letter finished, now he had to figure out how to send it. Li Yu thought about waiting until the holidays and smuggling it into one of the gifts that the two manors exchanged—but it was difficult for a normal person to get near those gifts, and he couldn't guarantee that Ye Qinghuan would actually see the letter himself. He decided to try to make his move when Ye Qinghuan came to Prince Jing's residence instead.

Luckily, since Ye-shizi's beloved dog couldn't measure up to a fish, Ye-shizi brought him over again soon. This time, Ye-shizi had brought a golden ball with him. He threw the golden ball as far away as possible, and Xiongfeng immediately ran after it and brought it back to him.

This would have to shut Prince Jing up, he thought. "No matter how smart a fish is, it's still not as good as a dog."

Prince Jing gave Ye Qinghuan a pitying glance, then gestured at him to look in the fish tank.

Ye-shizi took a look. At first, all he saw was a bunch of jewels, but soon he spotted Prince Jing's Xiaoyu swimming around casually, stacking the jewels sky-high, and then he picked up an aquamarine with his tail and tossed it to knock over the stack of jewels.

Prince Jing's fish could do tricks like that? Ye-shizi was so jealous that his eyeballs almost fell out of his head. He'd lost again.

Xiongfeng, on the other hand, was immensely excited by this sight. He wagged his tail around wildly as if he was cheering the fish on. Li Yu swam over. He wasn't so afraid of Xiongfeng with a crystal wall between them, and he started boldly flapping his tail toward Xiongfeng, as if teasing him. Xiongfeng became even more lively, trotting in front of the crystal fish tank as if he wanted to jump in and play with the fish.

Watching the two of them was making Ye Qinghuan a little dizzy. Help! Wang Xi escorted him away to rest.

But Xiongfeng stayed behind, looking at Xiaoyu expectantly. He reached his nose out several times, trying to sniff him, but was met with the cold crystal every time. He barked impatiently.

Li Yu's eyes lit up. If it was just him and Xiongfeng...he could use this as an opportunity.

*Xiongfeng! Become a messenger for your master!*

Ye-shizi had to rest a bit because of his dizziness. When he came back, his darling pet dog Xiongfeng's fur was half-soaked and he was holding a white envelope in his mouth, pawing at his legs.

*What's this?* Shocked, Ye-shizi pulled the letter out of Xiongfeng's mouth.

# Fish Eating Dessert

A T FIRST, Ye Qinghuan thought it was just a joke, and he read the letter with a smile on his face. The letter was only a couple of lines long, but by the time he finished reading it, Ye Qinghuan's expression had changed.

Prince Jing treated Ye-shizi flippantly, but Ye-shizi was still his younger cousin. Naturally, he wanted to know what had shocked him to this extent. He glanced at Wang Xi.

Wang Xi stepped forward and spoke for him, "Ye-shizi, what's the matter?"

Ye Qinghuan looked like his soul had left his body, and it took a while before he returned to his senses. He passed the letter over and asked, "Tianchi, do you know who wrote this letter?"

Wang Xi took the letter and handed it to Prince Jing without even reading it. But when Mu Tianchi skimmed through it, he was shocked.

The writing on this letter was probably the most disjointed thing he'd ever seen in his life. There were only a couple characters written correctly—most of them were missing strokes, as crooked as if they'd been blown over by the wind. A six- or seven-year-old child could do better than this.

Not only were the characters ugly, but the letter...spoke of an event that made one's blood run cold.

The second prince intended to harm Ye Qinghuan by framing him for killing the Princess of Jinjue. The letter warned Ye Qinghuan to keep an eye on the second prince's actions, and, more importantly, not to trust the sixth prince.

The emperor only had four princes who'd come of age. Everyone knew that the sixth prince was the third prince's follower and that the second and third princes were butting heads; meanwhile, Prince Jing didn't get along with any of them.

This thin piece of paper mentioned three of the four princes in addition to Ye Qinghuan, who was obviously related to Prince Jing. As Prince Jing realized this, his expression turned serious.

The House of Cheng'en was the former empress's family, so the emperor relied heavily on them, and their rich, stable future was pretty much guaranteed. The di princes born to the former Empress had all either died young or been disabled. The House of Cheng'en had no legitimate prince of their own, and with their current status, there was no need for them to align themselves with any of the princes. The duke rarely had any contact with the princes, as he wanted to avoid conflict as much as possible. But conflict would find them.

The letter had been delivered through Xiongfeng. It was written extremely strangely, and its contents were even more unbelievable. Ye Qinghuan couldn't tell if it was real or not, and he had other misgivings as well. Was it perhaps a trap to trick the House of Cheng'en?

Mu Tianchi gave it some thought and coughed lightly. Ye Qinghuan lifted his head at the sound to see Prince Jing pinch a mark on one of the names on the letter.

Ye Qinghuan could tell that Prince Jing was trying to bring his attention to the words "the Princess of Jinjue."

Ye Qinghuan paused. "Are you asking why the Princess of Jinjue?"

If it was anyone else, it might have been more believable, but the Princess of Jinjue? Neither Prince Jing nor Ye Qinghuan had heard any recent news about Jinjue, and it was quite far from their own capital. They'd never even seen the princess, so why would the second prince kill someone like that and frame Ye-shizi for it?

And there was the dilemma. If the letter was just a trap to trick the House of Cheng'en, there would be no need to involve a foreign princess; thus Prince Jing was more inclined to believe, or at least partially believe, the letter.

Prince Jing took a brush and paper and wrote, "Be prepared, just in case."

Ye Qinghuan fell silent for a while, fully understanding what Prince Jing meant.

"It's better to believe it than to disbelieve it," he said. "I'll have my people keep an eye on the second prince, and...the sixth prince. Let's see what they're going to do."

*And let's see what the person who wrote the letter wants.*

"Thank you for your quick reminder. I probably would have had a headache over this for a while." Ye Qinghuan smiled candidly and patted Prince Jing's shoulder. Outsiders all said Prince Jing was withdrawn and didn't care about anything, but in actuality, he was careful and perceptive.

Ye Qinghuan's overly familiar action made Prince Jing furrow his brow slightly.

"Oh, right," Ye Qinghuan said. "Who do you think sent this letter? They even used Xiongfeng, so they must be familiar with my habits. Perhaps it's...someone I'm close with?"

Ye Qinghuan's guess made sense. Prince Jing wanted to know who'd sent the letter too, but he had different thoughts.

It's true that the letter was delivered through Xiongfeng, but it was also given while Ye-shizi was visiting Prince Jing's residence. If it was simply someone who was familiar with Ye-shizi, why would they do it right under Prince Jing's nose?

Prince Jing was more inclined to believe that the person was already embedded in his residence somehow, and only used Ye-shizi's visit as an opportunity to give him the letter.

The people and connections mentioned in the letter were complex and entangled. Taking another glance at the wild writing, many strokes were forked, yet each stroke was still forceful. With this type of writing style, the brush would have...

A thought suddenly struck Prince Jing. He'd seen a frayed brush like that just a few days ago—in his own room! It must have been that young man. Prince Jing had guessed that he'd written something in his room, so was it...the letter that Ye Qinghuan was now holding?

"...Tianchi, what are you thinking about with such a serious expression?" Ye Qinghuan put up two fingers and waved them in front of Prince Jing's eyes.

Prince Jing mercilessly slapped away his troublemaking hand.

Ye Qinghuan laughed. "Are you thinking about who they are and where they are? I have my own ways of locating whoever it is, but—" Ye Qinghuan glanced at Prince Jing and stubbornly stopped right when it was getting juicy.

Prince Jing looked impatiently at him, signaling with his eyes: *Spit it out.*

"Pfft." Ye Qinghuan laughed and continued, "I have my own ways of locating this person. If you want to find out who sent the letter, then answer a question of mine first." Ye Qinghuan felt he couldn't be any more resourceful for using this opportunity to get something out of Prince Jing. He smugly said, "I heard you moved back here because you were attacked in the palace. I haven't been able to figure it out, but how did the assassin get into your room when Jingtai Palace, your own dwelling, is full of guards?"

Ye Qinghuan had been eager to gossip about this for a very long time. Everyone in the palace was trying to guess who sent that assassin, but Prince Jing had already killed her, and the imperial guards who searched the corpse found nothing useful either.

There were two main theories in the palace. One was that Noble Consort Qiu had a grudge against Prince Jing since the emperor punished her on his account. Even if the noble consort wasn't the one who ordered the assassination, people believed it had to do with her. The other theory was that someone else was framing Noble Consort Qiu—she was the first person anyone would think of when an attempt was made on Prince Jing's life, after all. This was also part of why the second prince was so desperate to "reconcile" with Prince Jing. Of course he wanted to help Noble Consort Qiu, but he was also afraid that the emperor would listen to the rumors flying about the palace.

As Prince Jing's younger cousin, Ye Qinghuan was naturally quite worried about him and wanted to know who was bold enough to make a move on him in the palace. The third prince was eager to try to compete with the second prince and had covertly allied himself with the sixth prince. The princes were in a state of mutual hostility.

"So—if you tell me who exactly sent the assassin, then I'll find the person who wrote the letter," he declared.

Why did Prince Jing kill the assassin instead of keeping her alive for questioning? Ye Qinghuan was sure he must know something and just didn't want to tell him.

Prince Jing snorted coldly and glanced at Wang Xi, who covered his mouth and privately laughed before ordering the guards to grab Ye Qinghuan's collar.

"Tianchi, what are you doing?!" Ye Qinghuan was shocked.

Wang Xi slowly said, "Ye-shizi, have you forgotten? His Highness hates it when others try to negotiate with him, so why did you try it?"

...Fine! He was the idiot for thinking he could get anything out of Prince Jing!

Wang Xi ordered someone to lift Ye-shizi up and was about to throw him out when Ye Qinghuan made a last-ditch effort. "Wait! If I'm chased out, who's going to find the person who sent the letter?"

"That's enough, Ye-shizi," Wang Xi said cheerfully. "His Highness wants me to ask you if you want to be kicked out, or if you'd rather tell us?"

"Come on!" Ye Qinghuan complained half-heartedly. He decided not to be stubborn about it, though, and went ahead and revealed his plan...

Which turned out to be Xiongfeng. Since the person who wrote the letter had Xiongfeng deliver it, Xiongfeng must have seen him. They would be able to find the person if Xiongfeng led the way.

This method...certainly had not occurred to Prince Jing.

Ye Qinghuan untied the leash and jabbered away at Xiongfeng, asking for his help. It wasn't clear if Xiongfeng understood him or not, but when Ye-shizi was done speaking, Xiongfeng licked the center of his palm and turned to trot away.

Ye Qinghuan said hurriedly, "Come on. He's going to find him."

Prince Jing and Ye Qinghuan glanced at each other and came to a mutual understanding, then trailed behind Xiongfeng.

Earlier, when Prince Jing and Ye Qinghuan were gone, Li Yu had turned into a human right away, frightening Xiongfeng into a barking frenzy. When he was in his human form, Li Yu wasn't afraid of Xiongfeng, but he had to feed the dog some red fish food to calm him down.

Unexpectedly, Xiongfeng liked the fish food a lot; he stopped barking and even licked Li Yu's hand. After getting Xiongfeng under control, Li Yu took the letter out of his inventory and had Xiongfeng carry it in his mouth to send it over.

At this point, the rescue mission was over half-finished; the rest was up to Ye-shizi.

It would have been better if he could have gone with Xiongfeng, but neither of the forms at his disposal would be any good for it—as a human, he would be chased out of the manor, and as a fish, he probably wouldn't be able to catch up with the dog. So Li Yu decided to stay where he was and wait for Xiongfeng after he'd delivered the letter.

The transformation went smoothly this time, and there was a lot of time left before he needed to turn back into a fish. Li Yu didn't dare run around, though, so he just got dressed and sat in the room, staring in a daze at the soft, pink, peach blossom-shaped desserts on the table.

Each one was shaped exactly like a peach blossom, and they were quite fragrant; Wang Xi said that it was a confection made by a chef from the palace, and Prince Jing would sometimes have some. Since Wang Xi had put the pastry there himself, there shouldn't be any problems with it. Li Yu sat for a while, bored, and then set his sights on the pastry.

The last time he transformed into a human, he was much too busy writing the letter to eat any human food. The time before that, he ate the food Auntie Xu gave him, but there were no desserts. Now that this plate of inviting pastries was right in front of him, Li Yu felt...a craving.

This was Prince Jing's dessert. It was normal for a pet to steal a little taste of his master's dessert, right?

The peach blossom pastries were neatly stacked into three layers, forming a tidy little mountain. There were three in the topmost layer. Li Yu picked a larger one and took a bite out of it.

The pink-colored pastry was crispy and sweet, and it really did taste like peach blossoms.

Li Yu was worried that his time was almost up, so he finished it quickly. But once he finished the first one, he wanted another, so he grabbed a second piece and shoved it in his mouth. He didn't plan on eating too much, but...now that he'd taken away two pieces, there was a gap, and the pastry mountain was imperfect. Li Yu gave it some thought, then took out two pastries from the bottom layer and re-arranged the rest of the pastries—now that layer was smaller, though, so he took another piece from the second layer and rearranged that one...

As a result, the entire mountain shrank.

Li Yu nodded, satisfied, and ate the excess peach flower pastries, stuffing his cheeks.

He was chomping enthusiastically on his dessert when there was loud barking outside. Li Yu was happy at first. Was Xiongfeng returning after a successfully completed mission?

Li Yu glanced out of the window to see Xiongfeng happily wagging his tail, running like the wind with Prince Jing and Ye-shizi in tow.

Crap!!!

Stupid Xiongfeng! He agreed to complete the mission alone! He promised not to betray him! Why did he lead these two over?

He was caught in a dead end! Again!

# Bringing the Fish Everywhere

L I YU COULD TURN INTO a human for an hour at a time now—he'd turn back into a fish when his time was up, but before that, he was stuck in human form. It was impossible to cancel the transformation halfway through. The fish-scamming system didn't give him a way to do it.

Prince Jing was about to unknowingly trap him in a room again. This room was quite large, but there was nowhere to hide—getting into the closet or hiding behind a curtain would be as good as asking for death.

Li Yu stood up and ran to open the window inside. He seriously had to jump out of the window again.

He remembered that he'd climbed through this window when he used the transformation medicine before, and that it was close to the ornamental mountain outside. The path was familiar!

Li Yu tried to open the window latch, but the same window that had opened so easily last time wouldn't budge! What was going on? He jiggled it twice, panicked, but the window didn't move. He suddenly realized that the window most likely couldn't be opened because it had been sealed.

There was no need to guess who did it, but when was it sealed, and why hadn't he known about it?

A cold sweat broke out on Li Yu's back. If this window didn't work, then he'd try the other ones.

But he tried each one and found to his despair that none of them would open. He knew there were guards outside the door too, so he wouldn't be able to get out that way.

Xiongfeng's barks were getting closer and closer. Li Yu raised his head. If Prince Jing caught him...

Prince Jing had been looking for him for such a long time. Would he kill him on the spot?

Should he say, *Stop, master! I'm your pet fish!*

It was hard to imagine how Prince Jing would react when he found out Li Yu was his pet fish. But if he just made up a random lie instead, it wouldn't be long before he was found out. If he ended up in Prince Jing's hands, they wouldn't need any special tricks to discover his secret—all they had to do was wait for him to turn back into a fish...

He still had one more step of the main quest to complete, but he'd been so focused on saving others that he didn't put much effort into getting "intimately close" with Prince Jing. If Prince Jing knew his real identity, it would be a miracle if he didn't kill him. He definitely wouldn't be allowed to do any more of his quests.

Was there really nothing he could do?

Sweat rolled down Li Yu's nose as his eyes frantically darted around, sweeping across every single object in the room.

Prince Jing and Ye Qinghuan followed closely behind the running Xiongfeng.

Xiongfeng, about to run into the inner portion of the manor, looked like he was going to run straight into Prince Jing's room. Prince Jing was a bit thrown off.

He already suspected that the young man who'd escaped before was the one who'd used Xiongfeng to deliver the letter. Could it be that the young man, even after his intense search, had not left the manor yet? Prince Jing recalled that the people he'd sent out had never returned with any useful information. At first, he'd thought this person was simply too crafty, but he'd left clues in his residence and his room over and over...

Perhaps he wasn't thinking in the right direction—perhaps the person never went far in the first place and had been hiding in the residence all this time, since the most dangerous place was also the safest!

If Xiongfeng was on the right track and the thief was really hiding in his room...Prince Jing would make sure he couldn't escape this time!

Xiongfeng was about to enter the room when he suddenly stopped and sniffed around.

Ye Qinghuan came up and petted his beloved dog's head. "Why aren't you chasing him anymore?"

Xiongfeng barked twice, then turned around to go toward the small bamboo forest outside the room, running to a person at the entrance.

...Wrong way?

Prince Jing glanced at him suspiciously, hesitated, then followed Xiongfeng to the bamboo forest.

Back in the room, Li Yu had been certain he was about to face a formidable opponent. *Sob sob sob, scared the fish half to death.*

He didn't know why Xiongfeng had decided not to come over, but one thing was clear—Xiongfeng swerving in another direction had helped him out immensely. His transformation time was almost up...

As long as he could turn back into a fish and get back in the fish tank, he wouldn't be found out!

Xionfeng ran up to the person in front of the bamboo forest and wagged his tail, expressing his friendliness. The person was dressed in white; he knelt down and affectionately patted Xiongfeng's head. Xiongfeng seemed to like him, as he circled around him several times.

Ye Qinghuan looked him up and down. He would have mistaken him for a woman at first glance, he thought, if he weren't wearing men's clothing. "Who are you?"

The man bowed, neither overbearing nor self-effacing, and said, "If it pleases my lord, I am Chu Yanyu. I reside in the Qingxi Garden. I was just passing by, but for some reason, your dog bounded over."

"So your name is Chu Yanyu... Xiongfeng seems to like you quite a bit." Ye Qinghuan smiled, but he didn't mean anything by it. He was normally kind to beautiful people. He wasn't attracted to men, but that didn't stop him from appreciating this great beauty's alluring face.

However, Ye Qinghuan didn't quite believe Chu Yanyu's explanation. Cheng'en manor was exceedingly large; what sorts of tricks hadn't he seen? Xiongfeng rarely ever ran up to strangers, so Chu Yanyu had almost certainly done it on purpose somehow.

Ye Qinghuan's frequent visits to Prince Jing's residence hadn't been for nothing either—he knew this courtyard was where Prince Jing put the prospective concubines that others had gifted him. It seemed like Chu Yanyu's origin was suspicious.

He didn't think he'd run into something like this at Prince Jing's residence.

Ye Qinghuan burst out laughing. This wasn't his residence, so he just had to watch the show. No need to overstep and intervene.

It hadn't been long since the banquet in his residence, so Prince Jing recognized Chu Yanyu. His cold gaze fell on Chu Yanyu's hands—Chu Yanyu claimed he didn't know why Xiongfeng came toward him, but Prince Jing's eyes were sharp, and he'd already noticed that Chu Yanyu had hurriedly kicked a green leaf aside. The green juice on his fingertips had yet to be wiped off completely.

Prince Jing's eyes darkened. There was no doubt that Chu Yanyu was lying; he'd deliberately used some trick to make Xiongfeng run over. Displeased, Prince Jing glanced toward Ye Qinghuan.

Since Prince Jing and Ye-shizi had left in such a hurry earlier, Wang Xi hadn't caught up yet, so Ye Qinghuan, who'd suddenly become a mouthpiece, gaped uselessly... In the end, he just coughed lightly, pretending to not understand.

Prince Jing glared at him again, and Ye-shizi relented. He unwillingly asked, "Chu Yanyu, why are you here?"

Chu Yanyu knelt in greeting, then raised his head and said, "I heard His Highness and Ye-shizi were looking for one skilled in calligraphy. Please let me have a try."

Ever since Chu Yanyu entered Prince Jing's manor, he had been staying in Qingxi Garden. Prince Jing's residence was heavily guarded, so it took the sixth prince great effort to deliver a letter to Chu Yanyu. In that letter, he'd asked him to captivate Prince Jing so he could enlist the help of the House of Cheng'en.

Chu Yanyu truly wanted to help Mu Tianxiao, but he hadn't so much as seen Prince Jing since he got here. Everyone in Prince Jing's manor treated the residents of Qingxi Garden like outsiders, him included, and had their guard up with them at all times. If he wanted to give Mu Tianxiao a helping hand, he had to get out of Qingxi Garden first and gain Prince Jing's attention again.

When Chu Yanyu entered the manor, the third prince had shoved a bunch of money on him to further secure his loyalty; Chu Yanyu had spent a lot of it to bribe a patrolling guard outside Qingxi Garden.

The servants in Prince Jing's residence were extremely difficult to bribe, so the guard only agreed to pass along bits and pieces he heard, most of which were quite useless.

This time, though, the guard told Chu Yanyu that Ye-shizi came to the residence with a dog, and that Prince Jing and Ye-shizi were looking for someone—it seemed to be someone good at calligraphy. The guard wasn't stationed where all this was happening, so he wasn't quite sure about the details, but after Chu Yanyu learned about this, he came up with a plan to run into Prince Jing using Ye-shizi's dog and recommend himself for the position.

He was an avid reader and remembered reading about how dogs loved a certain leaf that gave off a fragrant scent. Someone in Qingxi Garden grew such plants, and Chu Yanyu managed to pick some. He then asked the guards to let him out of Qingxi Garden; it was, in fact, possible for those living in Qingxi Garden to go out for a walk, but they were not allowed to go too far and had to be accompanied by guards.

The guard helped him for the sake of the money and asked to follow him in person. Having attained his goal of leaving Qingxi Garden, Chu Yanyu took advantage of the guard's carelessness and slipped away.

He'd heard the guard mention the general layout of Prince Jing's manor, so he tried his best to walk in a direction that would allow him to run into Prince Jing. From a distance, he could see Prince Jing and another young man chasing a black dog—the guard must not have been lying. The young man had to be the heir of the House of Cheng'en, and the dog his favorite pet.

Chu Yanyu suppressed his fear of dogs, crushed the leaf, and smeared the juice on his fingers. The dog was easily lured in, its nose as sensitive as ever.

Chu Yanyu had no role or name in Prince Jing's residence—he was just someone who had been sent in from the outside, so he wasn't even considered a servant and had no right to even call himself "this lowly one." He used to follow the sixth prince Mu Tianxiao, whom he was close to, and Mu Tianxiao knew he regarded himself highly, so he never asked Chu Yanyu to address himself with a lower title. Chu Yanyu did not consider himself of humble birth, so he awkwardly called himself "I." It seemed refined and courteous, but it was actually extremely rude.

If Wang Xi had heard him, he would have chewed him out, but Ye-shizi never cared much about these conceited customs. As for Prince Jing, he was on the cusp of rage, but not because of Chu Yanyu's form of address.

Prince Jing was very displeased with Chu Yanyu for daring to divert and disrupt Xiongfeng from his original route. Chu Yanyu might as well have said *I am the one you're looking for.* Prince Jing stared at him for a moment and scoffed coldly.

Chu Yanyu felt his confidence wavering under that gaze. Because the sixth prince had asked him to seduce Prince Jing, Chu Yanyu told himself he had to capture his heart. Since Prince Jing was mute, however, he had no idea how to read him—but he did know that the look in his eyes right now was not one of infatuation, and it frightened him a bit.

Wang-gonggong finally caught up to them. Prince Jing pointed with his chin and moved his fingers; after some thought, Wang Xi ordered someone to prepare a brush and ink. Prince Jing wrote down a few characters and tossed the paper to Chu Yanyu.

Chu Yanyu didn't understand what he meant, so Wang Xi said, "His Highness is ordering you to write each of these characters once."

Ye Qinghuan moved closer to glance at the paper and smiled. Chu Yanyu didn't know this, but those characters were ones that had been on the letter. Chu Yanyu said he was the one they were looking for, so obviously they had to check his handwriting.

Chu Yanyu thanked him and copied the characters after some deliberation. To impress Prince Jing, he wrote the characters beautifully in small, regular script lettering with one hand, then again in flowing, unrestrained cursive with the other.

He was always worrying about how he had never been able to show off his talents—everyone praised him for his looks, but it was his talent that he was truly proud of. And this was it.

Unfortunately, Prince Jing only glanced at his talent indifferently. Even the brush he had just set aside got a longer glance. Prince Jing flicked his sleeves in disgust, and Wang Xi immediately said, "His Highness says you're not who he's looking for. And to fuck off."

Chu Yanyu was struck dumb.

He still wanted to say something, but Wang Xi had already ordered the guards to take him away.

He heard Wang Xi cursing. Since he broke the rules by leaving Qingxi Garden without permission, both he and the guard he bribed were punished with two hundred strokes of the board. The guard was immediately thrown out from the manor, and Chu Yanyu, with all his talent, was dragged back to Qingxi Garden to stew in his own juices. Wang-gonggong said this was Prince Jing's order—if he died outside, they would have to inform the third prince, but if he died in Prince Jing's residence, they could just bury him.

Chu Yanyu was more than frightened enough, tears streaming down his face as he lay on his bed covered in injuries. Nobody had ever treated him like this before. How could this man be so cruel?

After Xiongfeng was distracted by Chu Yanyu, he didn't want to move anymore. No matter how much Ye Qinghuan tried to get him going, Xiongfeng would just lick his hand quietly. They probably wouldn't be able to find the person they were looking for.

Ye Qinghuan smiled apologetically at Prince Jing. He hadn't expected to encounter an obstacle like this.

Prince Jing dazedly looked at Xiongfeng for a bit. If Chu Yanyu hadn't appeared, then the original direction Xiongfeng was going in was...

His room.

It would probably be too late if they went now, but Prince Jing still ordered Wang Xi to keep an eye out and got ready to go himself.

"Tianchi, I'll go with you." Ye Qinghuan wanted to know who sent the letter too.

Prince Jing paused, glanced back at Ye Qinghuan, shook his head lightly, and left.

Ye Qinghuan was baffled.

Beside him, Wang Xi sighed. "Ye-shizi, His Highness has his guesses. Please leave it to us to handle it."

Ye Qinghuan's eyes widened. "Does he have other clues? Who is it?"

Wang Xi's expression became pained. "His Highness has had people investigating for a long while now, but we still haven't even found his name. It seems to be someone's male concubine."

Another person's male concubine sent Prince Jing a letter? Ye Qinghuan scratched his head, confused. Was he that charming?

Prince Jing stood in front of his room and threw the doors open, but there was nobody inside.

He knew that this young man was good at escaping, as well as cleaning up his traces. Occasionally he might even leave some misleading clues behind—but there would always be some traces of him left.

After the young man had escaped last time, Prince Jing secretly ordered Wang Xi to seal the window so it would be impossible to open. This time, at least, it would have been impossible for the young man to escape through the window.

As usual, Prince Jing gave his fish a glance—the fish was swimming casually in his tank.

Prince Jing decided to look for clues himself this time. He walked around the room once but didn't find anything. Since his underclothes and underwear had been taken every time—once strewn randomly on the ground, and once mixed in with the clothes he'd already worn—Prince Jing thought that he should start with his clothes, so he opened his closet.

He didn't notice that there was a gaze behind him that had followed him since he entered the room.

In the crystal fish tank, the little carp was practically glued to the tank wall, almost not daring to breathe, as he watched Prince Jing rummaging around his room.

Xiongfeng had bought him time by not coming directly into the room, so Li Yu had taken off all the clothes he was wearing. Ever since the increase in his inventory size, one slot held clean water, and the second slot held other things. After the letter was delivered, a slot became available that could definitely fit a set of clothes, but if he put it in there and Prince Jing wasn't able to find his clothing, he would still suspect that his clothes were stolen.

So Li Yu just folded them up and put them back in the closet.

It quickly became obvious that he'd made the right choice. Prince Jing simply curled his lips up after opening the closet, as if he didn't find anything suspicious...

But in the next moment, even though he shouldn't have noticed anything, Prince Jing effortlessly pulled out the clothes Li Yu had been wearing!

*What???* Li Yu was stupefied. He even forgot to swim. *How did he do it?*

He'd been way more careful than usual—the clothes weren't dirty, and they looked the same as all the other folded clothes in the closet. He didn't put them on the top either, so Prince Jing shouldn't have noticed.

Li Yu had no idea that Prince Jing had secretly ordered Wang Xi to embroider numbers on the inner lining of his clothes after the second time his clothes were taken. The clothes that were placed in the closet had to be ordered by number...

Since the thief had stolen from him twice, Prince Jing suspected the thief would do it again.

As long as he checked the order of the numbers, he would know whether someone had moved them—and someone did!

But that was all he found. The thief wasn't trapped in the room like he thought he'd be; he'd gotten away again. And with a method he couldn't figure out.

Prince Jing walked over to the tank, watching his fish swim and thinking about the young man's whereabouts.

The look of concentration on his face made Li Yu afraid. He was so handsome... No, it was because Prince Jing was too smart! He was always just about to figure out Li Yu's identity! Li Yu couldn't underestimate him.

Li Yu made up his mind and decided to sell himself again!

But Prince Jing was with him all the time, so it was probably hard to impress him anymore. Thanks to Xiongfeng, Li Yu was reminded that some dogs—Xiongfeng included—liked to run in circles and chase their tails. Li Yu planned to give it a try and chase his own tail!

Even if he looked silly, it was fine as long as he could distract Prince Jing!

Li Yu twisted his body, chasing the tip of his tail as he tried to resist the shame, repeating to himself silently, *As long as you don't treat your tail as a tail...*

As he chased it around, he was surprised to find that his head could touch his tail. Thanks to his fish nature, Li Yu couldn't resist playing with it. *I accidentally got carried away, aaaahhhh!*

Prince Jing quickly noticed his fish playing with his tail and watched him for a bit without realizing it. This was new to him. He'd never seen a fish playing with its tail before.

When the fish stopped, Prince Jing scooped him out and plopped him into a nearby tea bowl as always, petting him a little. Li Yu shamelessly wrapped his tail, which had just patted his own head, around Prince Jing's finger.

The coldness in Prince Jing's eyes slowly disappeared, and he smiled and shook his head.

Hmph! He said he didn't want it, but he definitely wanted it deep down! Li Yu saw right through his insincere master and wouldn't let go of his finger.

Suddenly, Prince Jing looked surprised, as if he'd seen something. He stopped playing with him and pushed the fish's head lightly to the side.

Li Yu was puzzled. But the reason quickly became clear, as Prince Jing carefully removed a piece of food stuck between a fin and his body.

...Ah.

Li Yu usually ate fish food, so it wasn't out of the ordinary for him to drop a few pieces of fish food here and there. Since he was

Prince Jing's fish, there was no need to worry about getting the water dirty, as the servants changed his water frequently enough.

But the piece of food was...pink...

*Fuck! A peach blossom pastry!*

He ate a couple pieces of peach blossom pastry while he was human, and when he turned back into a fish, his mouth was still stuffed full. He'd remembered to wipe his face, but it seemed like he hadn't wiped it clean—how could he have known it'd fall onto his fin after he transformed?

Li Yu felt guilty, and he was afraid that his identity was once again in danger of being found out.

Prince Jing was lost in thought for a bit. He looked around the room and seemed to guess that it was a peach blossom pastry from the table. In spite of himself, the corners of his mouth twitched a few times.

Since the little fish could jump around the room, he might have jumped onto the peach blossom pastry.

Did he perhaps want to eat one too, Prince Jing wondered? Well, why not? The pastry was vegetarian, so it was probably all right for the fish to eat.

He slowly walked over and brought the plate of peach blossom pastries to the tank, breaking a pastry into pieces and sprinkling it into the clear water.

Li Yu froze for a moment, shaking his body happily. Prince Jing hadn't even considered suspecting him, and instead, he was feeding him peach blossom pastries personally—this was the last thing he'd expected! Sob sob sob...he felt touched somehow.

The texture of the broken peach blossom pastry in the water was still quite nice to a fish.

Seeing how happily the fish was eating, Prince Jing picked up a piece for himself. But as he brought it to his mouth, he just so happened to glance over at the remaining pastries from the corner of his eye.

The pastries were arranged as they usually were, but it was obvious that the number was wrong.

The imperial family was very particular about things, so even snacks and fruits given to them had to be an auspicious number. But it was clear that, even counting the one in his hand and the one he fed the fish, this was not an auspicious number of pastries.

The peach blossom pastries had been touched...

As soon as he realized this, Prince Jing immediately put down the pastry in his hand. He knew the servants would never dare to touch the things in his room, so there was only one person it could have been.

Luckily, the pastries weren't poisoned, or his fish...

Prince Jing's gaze grew heavy as he watched the little fish, with a small piece of peach blossom pastry on his head, impatiently trying to push another piece into his mouth.

...The little fish's cuteness disrupted his train of thought.

Prince Jing shook the jade bell and summoned the guards outside his room.

All the guards reported the same thing: *Before Your Highness came, only Ye-shizi and Wang Xi-gonggong entered the room, and definitely nobody else. Ye-shizi visited with his dog, and when Ye-shizi left, the dog stayed in the room for a bit before running out on his own.*

As to whether or not Xiongfeng had a letter in his mouth when he ran out of the room, the guards weren't sure.

Prince Jing rubbed the spot between his brows. None of this made sense. If Ye Qinghuan and Wang Xi were the only ones who entered the room, then what in the world had caused the clothes to be moved and the incorrect number of peach blossom pastries? If the thief entered the room without the guards noticing, it would have been impossible for him to get out, since the windows were sealed...

The thief was still able to come and go as he liked, even though Prince Jing had already made several arrangements.

"Tianchi, Xiongfeng seems to have recovered."

Wang Xi led Ye Qinghuan and his pet dog into the room. Xiongfeng excitedly bounded to the fish tank, wagging his tail at the little carp to tell him he'd completed the task and begging to be praised.

Li Yu swam over quickly and flicked his tail twice too: *Stupid dog! Don't loiter around me!*

But dogs couldn't understand fish—when Xiongfeng saw the little carp swimming toward him, he tried nosing the fish. He just bumped into the crystal wall every time, but he still kept on trying.

Ye Qinghuan embarrassingly looked on as his dog continued to act stupidly.

This scene reminded Prince Jing of something. When Xiongfeng delivered the letter to Ye Qinghuan, he was mostly wet, and he was still slightly wet even now. But the fish tank in the room wasn't broken, and it was impossible for Xiongfeng to get into the fish tank. So how did he get wet?

Nothing made sense—from the unidentifiable, unlocatable young man who kept appearing in his room, to the clothes and peach blossom pastries that had been moved even though nobody had entered or left the room...

He felt like he almost had it. Just a little more and he could connect everything together and figure out the truth.

When Wang Xi finished recounting everything, Ye Qinghuan's eyes widened. He gulped. "Tianchi," he said, with a hesitant expression on his face, "your room wouldn't be haunted, would it?"

...Haunted?

Prince Jing paused and gave a cold laugh. Where would he get a ghost? Definitely not—at most just a thief. And even if there were ghosts, he wasn't afraid.

Xiongfeng barked excitedly a few times, still wanting to poke the fish with his nose. Prince Jing saw his little fish shrewdly hide among the rocks, only leaving his tail out. Prince Jing, who wasn't afraid of ghosts, was calmed even more by the sight of his fish.

Things couldn't continue like this. He wasn't afraid of thieves, but he was afraid that the thieves would do something to Xiaoyu—and increasing his defenses hadn't accomplished anything.

Prince Jing glanced at Wang Xi. Since increasing his defenses wasn't effective, there was only one other option.

Ye Qinghuan thought Prince Jing's fish and his own Xiongfeng were somehow fated, so he wanted to take the fish back to Cheng'en Manor and take care of him for a couple of days. That way, he could experience the joy of having a fish as well. But before he could bring this up to Prince Jing, he saw Wang Xi take out...a crystal bottle that was much larger than an ordinary tea bowl.

Well, it looked like a crystal bottle. It was adorned with a gold cap and had a handle to make it easier to carry.

Wang Xi opened the crystal bottle without delay, poured in some clean water, and carefully put the little fish, still hiding in the rocks, inside.

The little carp swam around in happy curiosity as soon as he was plopped into the crystal bottle.

Ye Qinghuan was stunned. "What are you guys doing?"

Wang Xi smiled and responded, "His Highness is worried about Master Fish, so he'll bring him wherever he goes. There are holes on the gold cap, so he won't suffocate; it's perfect for Master Fish."

Ye Qinghuan was bewildered beyond belief. "It's not enough for you to put him in the large fish tank that the emperor gifted you? You're going to take him everywhere with you?!"

To think he even considered asking Prince Jing for his fish—he was going to bring the fish with him everywhere, there was no damn point.

Prince Jing cast a derisive glance at Ye-shizi, picked up the crystal bottle, and left.

# Fish as Solitary as Snow

**P**RINCE JING DECIDING to keep him in a crystal bottle and take him everywhere was both lucky and unlucky for Li Yu.

The Tyrant Master worrying about his fish's safety was obviously a sign of affection. Li Yu was touched, but if he was spending all his time in a bottle with a lid, it would be impossible for him to turn into a human. By the time he realized this, though, he'd already been carried around for most of the day. The outside world was just so enticing! Li Yu had never thought he'd be able to spend a day looking around like this as a fish, so he kept his fish eyes open, swimming idly in his bottle and taking in the sights.

Everyone greeted him properly when they saw him, satisfying little Li Yu's modest ego—okay, sure, they were actually greeting Prince Jing, but it felt good to pretend once in a while.

Prince Jing liked to take his fish around with him too, since it was convenient. The fish tank was so heavy that a person had to be specifically assigned to carry it; tea bowls or regular bowls were too shallow, and the fish could fall out if he wasn't careful. The crystal bottle solved all these problems. He could even bring it into the palace with him.

Having experienced the benefits for himself, Prince Jing wanted to keep the fish in the crystal bottle.

At first, Li Yu was pretty happy with this, but a couple of days passed, and he realized Prince Jing had no intentions of putting him back into the fish tank at all. He was actually trapped in here! He was much less pleased with this development.

The bottle allowed him to stay with his master all the time, but he couldn't do any of his missions, or turn into a human. He could only watch as opportunities rushed past him—not to mention how uncomfortable it was.

A fish trapped in a bottle was as solitary as a flake of snow.

He had to get Prince Jing to understand that the bottle might be convenient, but it'd be better if he didn't stay in here too long, for the sake of his mental and physical health.

At first, he wanted to take extreme measures to demonstrate his dissatisfaction. He thought about trying to scare Prince Jing by flipping upside down and showing his underbelly... But then he saw Prince Jing order Wang Xi to affix a chain to the bottle's handle and wrap the chain around his hand a few times so that he wouldn't drop and break the crystal bottle.

Prince Jing's palm turned red from the strain. The little carp's heart felt a bit sore and tender—being uncomfortable because he was trapped in a bottle was one thing, but it was far more uncomfortable—heartbreaking, even—to see Prince Jing in such pain for his sake. Li Yu didn't want to scare him anymore.

Prince Jing had never had a pet before, so he had no way of knowing what a fish would want. Putting Li Yu in a bottle was intended as a kind gesture; all he had to do was somehow let Prince Jing know that he didn't like being in there. It wasn't like he had a grudge against the prince or anything, so he ought to find a better way than making him scared his fish had died.

Li Yu suppressed his curiosity toward the outside world and

floated peacefully at the bottom of the bottle. The little carp was usually lively and active, so when he became quiet and peaceful, it was a noticeable change. The moment Prince Jing glanced at Li Yu, he was immensely confused. His fish was in high spirits just now, so why had he become listless all of a sudden?

Worried that the hole at the top might be blocked, Prince Jing checked it not once, but twice. There was nothing wrong with the crystal bottle. But his fish was still lethargic, and he wasn't perking back up. Prince Jing ordered the servant who'd raised fish before to come over, afraid that the fish was sick again.

Every time this servant was called over to "diagnose" the fish, it was always a false alarm. This time was no different—he held the crystal bottle and looked him over several times, but he didn't see anything wrong with the fish.

Prince Jing's fish was fine, as usual.

However, the servant had kept many pets before and knew that they didn't like being cooped up, so he mustered his courage to tell Prince Jing, in tactful terms, that Master Fish wasn't used to being sealed in a bottle all the time. After all, the crystal tank the fish was originally kept in was quite large. Switching him to a smaller vessel meant his swimming range would become narrower, and eventually, he wouldn't want to move anymore.

The servant felt a little regretful after he spoke. It had been Prince Jing's idea to put his fish in the crystal bottle, but Prince Jing also insisted that he tell the truth, putting the servant in a tough spot.

But Prince Jing nodded, understanding what the servant meant. So that's what it was. The crystal bottle was convenient for taking his fish around, but he couldn't let him stay in there all the time or Xiaoyu would become unhappy. He had to consider what the fish wanted too.

But he couldn't leave his poor little fish alone in his room, helpless against thieves...

Prince Jing came up with a compromise quickly. He ordered fish tanks and larger tea bowls to be placed around his residence in the spots he often frequented—that way, the fish could still accompany him. Once he arrived at his destination, the fish would be taken out of the crystal bottle and placed inside a nearby fish tank or tea bowl. Problem solved.

Li Yu only had to pretend to be listless for about two hours before he found out he'd achieved his goal. He could spend more of his time in fish tanks now.

Prince Jing opened the lid of the bottle and placed the bottle in the fish tank himself. The little carp finally stopped wilting and jumped out of the crystal bottle like an arrow shot from a bow.

...It was better for fish to stay in fish tanks.

Li Yu sighed with emotion as he swam comfortably.

He looked back at the bottle, which was still in the tank. It wasn't that he didn't like staying with Prince Jing all the time; after all, that was part of his master's kindness. To show his gratitude, Li Yu danced a special seaweed dance around the crystal bottle, trying his hardest to show Prince Jing what he felt: the bottle was great, and he was happy to follow Prince Jing around as long as he wasn't constantly trapped inside it.

Prince Jing, of course, could tell that his fish liked it. He smiled and softly pinched the fish's slippery back. The human and the fish had reached a compromise.

...Hold on! Li Yu had spent a good while celebrating this turn of events, but the realization abruptly hit him that even if he got to be in a fish tank instead of the bottle, he was still with Prince Jing twenty-four-seven.

What was he going to do? He still had no way to transform! Had his once-a-day transformation skill functionally become a none-a-day transformation skill?

Li Yu's head hurt. Should he let Prince Jing know that the thief, the one Prince Jing thought was going to hurt his fish, was actually him?

No. Right now, his plan to save others was more important than the stress that came with not being able to transform.

Li Yu's plan to save Ye-shizi had already been implemented. Over the last couple of days he spent in the crystal bottle, he'd heard Wang Xi tell Prince Jing that the people of the House of Cheng'en had already started to keep an eye on the movements of the second and sixth princes.

Just as Ye Qinghuan had promised.

Li Yu's goal in sending the letter was to alert the House of Cheng'en. Without the romance storyline between Prince Jing and the little concubine, he wasn't actually sure if Ye-shizi's betrothal to the Jinjue princess would still end up happening. He tried his best to give a shortened version of events in the letter. It didn't matter if this plot didn't end up happening or if the letter was treated as fake, as long as the House of Cheng'en didn't fall into the trap the second and sixth princes set for them.

Though Prince Jing kept getting in his way, and his identity was constantly in danger of being exposed, Li Yu thought the rescue mission went pretty smoothly. But there was no notification of completion for the "Impenetrable Defense" mission to save Ye-shizi.

If there was no notification, then it meant that the mission wasn't complete. Li Yu's main goal was the saving people part; finishing the side quest and receiving the rewards was less important. But when he thought about it, did it mean that it wasn't enough to alert the

House of Cheng'en by sending them a letter? Was it possible that Ye-shizi might still suffer the same tragic fate as he did in the original book?

He'd made up his mind to save others, so he shouldn't half-ass it. But if sending a letter wasn't enough, what else could he do?

In the original book, Li Yu remembered that the trap that doomed Ye Qinghuan was sprung in the palace, just a couple of days after the Dragon Boat Festival. He'd mentioned it in the letter, but he wasn't sure how Ye Qinghuan would react—so he figured the most direct solution would be to stop Ye-shizi from entering the palace during this period of time. The farther he was from the trap, the better.

But stopping Ye-shizi from entering the palace was even harder than writing and sending him a letter. He might have been able to stop Prince Jing from going, but his fins were too short to reach Ye Qinghuan, who lived in Cheng'en Manor.

Li Yu worried so hard that his fish head hurt—would he suffer scale loss from thinking too hard? If you thought about it, he thought dizzily, hadn't he already gone bald?

Luckily, Prince Jing had the same thoughts he did. Wang Xi had only said that the House of Cheng'en had made preparations, but Prince Jing had no idea what Ye Qinghuan was planning to do, so he ordered someone to grab Ye-shizi and bring him over. Wang Xi gave him a good scolding on behalf of Prince Jing.

Ye-shizi was a little dejected. Just when he'd thought Prince Jing had finally started to care for him...

Prince Jing also wanted Ye Qinghuan to avoid the palace for those couple of days. *As expected from my master!* thought Li Yu, who was listening excitedly from the fish tank. They were truly kindred spirits! Ye-shizi would listen to Prince Jing, right?

But Ye Qinghuan shook his head and refused. "Tianchi, I can't just not enter the palace because of what was written in that letter."

Ye Qinghuan knew that Prince Jing was only suggesting this because he was worried about him, but he also knew that he couldn't refuse to enter the palace for no reason. For one thing, it was an imperial edict. Keeping his guard up on account of the letter was one thing, but if he deceived the emperor or refused to obey an edict because of a few words on an unproven letter from an anonymous source, his parents—and the entire House of Cheng'en, for that matter—would never forgive him.

"I will do as I always have," said Ye Qinghuan with an easy smile. "I'd like to see how those people plan to harm me."

Seriously...what a stubborn idiot.

Prince Jing judged Ye Qinghuan for his recklessness, but after a moment of thought, he gave Wang Xi a meaningful glance.

Wang Xi was almost moved to tears. "Ye-shizi, don't worry! His Highness has decided to enter the palace with you when the time comes! As long as His Highness is there, you'll be fine!"

"Tianchi, thanks so much!" Ye Qinghuan was momentarily touched. Prince Jing was normally so indifferent to others! He wanted to step forward and pat his older cousin on the shoulder, but Prince Jing waved him away, aggravated.

Li Yu felt like this was familiar somehow—the sparkly expression on Ye-shizi's face, and the way he looked like he was barely restraining himself from rushing to Prince Jing even though he'd just been rejected. He thought carefully for a moment... Wasn't he just like Xiongfeng? Xiongfeng always wanted to poke him with his nose. Li Yu would hide, afraid, but even through the crystal, Xiongfeng wouldn't give up on poking him.

He took another look at Ye-shizi. It was like he'd grown a tail just like Xiongfeng's. Li Yu could almost see it wagging happily behind him.

*Pfft. Dogs really do take after their masters.*

In the original book, Prince Jing didn't accompany Ye Qinghuan to the palace. Now that Prince Jing was going to go with him, they could take care of each other. Li Yu felt much more at ease. And since Prince Jing had been taking his fish wherever he went lately, Li Yu was definitely going to enter the palace too! He'd be able to keep an eye on Ye-shizi in person!

Ten days later, as the Dragon Boat Festival approached, the king of the country of Jinjue came to the imperial city to have an audience with the emperor. The emperor had the Ministry of Rites arrange a banquet with King Jinjue in the Taihe Hall.

Since it was an imperial banquet, Prince Jing and Ye Qinghuan had been invited as well. When they saw the sixteen-year-old girl next to King Jinjue greet the emperor, the two of them looked at each other in silent understanding. So this was the Princess of Jinjue... It was just as the anonymous informant had said! These people the letter had named, who they thought had nothing to do with them, were really starting to show up!

Prince Jing and Ye Qinghuan both tensed up.

The emperor had received a letter from King Jinjue recently, saying he wanted his youngest princess to marry into the imperial dynasty. Diplomatic relations between the two countries were good, so the emperor readily agreed. As for who the princess was to marry—the emperor mentally went through a list of men in the imperial city of the appropriate age.

The highest-ranking options were obviously his princes, but since Princess Jinjue was a foreigner, it wasn't proper for her to become a prince's consort. King Jinjue had mentioned in his letter that the princess did not want to become a concubine either.

The emperor thought of Prince Jing. Prince Jing was unmarried and couldn't inherit the throne, so it would be possible for him to marry Princess Jinjue... But he immediately dismissed the idea. Since Prince Jing was mute, the princess might not like him—what's more, since he hadn't chosen a crown prince yet, that meant Prince Jing held the de facto highest status as the di prince. If he let Prince Jing marry a foreigner, then how would he arrange the other princes' marriages?

The emperor decided to not choose from the princes and turned his sights toward other sons of noble families that matched Princess Jinjue.

It wasn't long at all before Ye-shizi from the House of Cheng'en came to his attention...

There in Taihe Hall, the emperor smiled and said, "Ye-shizi, I'm putting the safety of King Jinjue and the princess in the imperial city in your hands."

Ye Qinghuan felt his blood run cold. He gritted his teeth and knelt to accept the edict.

......

Once he sat down at the banquet, Prince Jing took out the crystal bottle from his sleeve. The etiquette at an imperial banquet was complicated, and he wasn't sure if his little fish had been stuck for too long.

He hadn't wanted to bring his fish into the palace at first, but the little carp swam into the crystal bottle and refused to come out, staring right at him with eyes like shining black jade. Prince Jing smiled. He had no choice but to shove the crystal bottle, with the fish inside, into his sleeve.

When he took the crystal bottle out, everyone around him was shocked. Did Prince Jing take a fish with him everywhere he went? Most of them had seen the large crystal tank Prince Jing had moved out with, and for a while they were rendered speechless.

The second prince, who was sitting among the other princes, chatting and laughing happily with others while looking very crown-princely, turned pale the moment he laid eyes on this fish.

*Second prince, we meet once more!* Li Yu flapped his tail casually at Mu Tianzhao. He was going to ruin the second prince's plans again!

# Can't Eat the Fish

WHEN PRINCE JING TOOK OUT the crystal bottle, Wang Xi, not far behind him, stepped forward and placed a small fish tank carved from coral on his table. Clear water had already been prepared in advance, so Prince Jing rolled up his sleeves and put the fish into the water himself, watching him swim about freely for a bit.

Prince Jing glanced at Wang Xi, wanting to feed the fish.

Wang Xi took out a bamboo box of fish food and handed it to Prince Jing. He then turned around and glanced at the servants who'd accompanied him. One by one, they brought over the pastries that they'd carried over from Prince Jing's residence and placed them neatly in front of the fish tank.

Prince Jing took two pieces of fish food and dropped them into the tank. Then he took a peach blossom pastry and split it in half, crushing one half for his little fish and eating the remaining half as if nothing out of the ordinary had happened.

With nothing to do but carefully watch Prince Jing feed his fish, the onlookers wondered if they were going blind, or perhaps mad. Was this the real Prince Jing?

After Prince Jing placed him in the fish tank, Li Yu docilely rubbed himself against Prince Jing's fingers. The fish food and peach blossom pastry floated toward the bottom. The little carp was

290 THE DISABLED TYRANT'S BELOVED PET FISH

getting tired of the same old thing lately—he guzzled the peach blossom pastry first, and when he was half-full, he started on the fish food.

Seeing how happily the little fish was eating, Prince Jing took another type of dessert, a yindan pastry, and broke it into pieces to feed him.

Li Yu was happy to try new food, so he gave it a taste. The new pastry tasted like peppermint, with a cooling sensation that rushed straight to his head—as a human, he would have liked it, but he couldn't stand it as a fish. Li Yu took a bite and tossed it away, then happily went back to the peach blossom pastry. Prince Jing watched. It was clear that his fish didn't like the yindan pastry.

"There's no need to prepare this pastry anymore," he said.

Wang-gonggong, known for understanding Prince Jing so well he might as well be a mind reader, immediately ordered the servants to note that down. The servants nodded repeatedly.

The people sitting around Prince Jing were astounded. Ye Qinghuan was the only one who didn't find it weird.

As music played around them, the second prince, Mu Tianzhao, stood. The Ministry of Rites had arranged for the oldest prince, the second prince, to lead the others in toasting King Jinjue at the imperial banquet. Mu Tianzhao was a natural conversationalist, and was graceful and dignified, so his conversation with King Jinjue was quite joyous. King Jinjue praised Mu Tianzhao and drank three cups in a row.

The emperor was satisfied with Mu Tianzhao's attitude; when King Jinjue praised the second prince, the emperor looked good too. Being capable and proper was another of the second prince's strong points.

Mu Tianzhao could tell that the emperor was in a good mood, and he gazed at the smaller figure beside King Jinjue with a smile.

He'd suffered several setbacks in succession recently, and the emperor wasn't really pleased with him. But the spy he'd placed in Qianqing Palace had recently sent him a message that King Jinjue planned to marry his princess off during his visit.

Mu Tianzhao had put in quite a lot of effort to restore the relationship between himself and Prince Jing, but Prince Jing ignored every one of his attempts. Mu Tianzhao wanted to win over the House of Cheng'en, but Prince Jing and the House of Cheng'en were clearly on the same side. He'd suffered defeat at Prince Jing's hands before, and the House of Cheng'en treated him coldly as well.

He'd heard that the third prince had successfully placed a concubine in Prince Jing's residence, and he was afraid that the third prince would get to Prince Jing first and gain the support of the House of Cheng'en. Mu Tianzhao knew he had no chance of winning over Prince Jing, and he had to find support elsewhere; however, the emperor was always keeping an eye on his sons, so he couldn't be too obvious about what he was doing.

That was when this marriage presented itself at his doorstep.

Mu Tianzhao had it all figured out. Jinjue was a small bordering country, but they had money and troops, so if he married the Princess of Jinjue, her kingdom wouldn't support the other princes over him. If this panned out, his position would be hard to shake even if the emperor ended up taking issue with him.

As for the Princess of Jinjue... Just becoming his side consort would be a huge honor for her. He could even promise her that she could become a noble consort once he ascended the throne. That would be more than enough for the king of Jinjue.

Originally, he'd been thinking that even if the little princess was ugly, he'd accept her in exchange for Jinjue's support. But when he got a look at her during the imperial banquet, he found she was stunningly beautiful. She had a different kind of beauty than the women of his own country. Mu Tianzhao was more willing than ever to go through with his plan.

"Princess." Mu Tianzhao gestured for someone to bring a plate of dessert and softly said, "This is our famous butterfly pastry. Please have a taste."

As its name suggested, butterfly pastries were made in the shape of a butterfly with its wings spread out, and the pastries came in pairs, symbolizing a century-long good marriage. Mu Tianzhao wanted to make a move first, to show others that the Princess of Jinjue was going to be his and ensure that any other suitor backed off.

The emperor noticed that the second prince seemed to have fallen in love with the foreign princess. He had wanted the Duke of Cheng'en's son and the Princess of Jinjue to marry but judging by Ye Qinghuan's solemn expression on receiving the decree, he wasn't very interested in the princess. The emperor wasn't going to make them marry right away, but he'd been thinking he'd test the waters again with Ye Qinghuan and discuss the matter with the House of Cheng'en too—but then the second prince popped up all of a sudden.

The emperor was a little irritated, but he decided not to blame the second prince. It wasn't as if his son could read his mind, after all. He'd already rejected the idea of marrying the princess to one of his princes—if the second prince had such intentions, he wouldn't get very far unless the Princess of Jinjue asked to be a side consort herself. That, he supposed, could be a possibility.

If the second prince wanted this marriage, then he'd need to have a few tricks up his sleeve. The emperor wanted to see how Mu Tianzhao would handle this, so he didn't try to stop him.

King Jinjue ordered the butterfly pastry to be served to the princess, but the little princess just smiled and didn't try reaching for the dessert.

Mu Tianzhao thought that the princess didn't know what the butterfly meant and was just about to take the opportunity to show off a little when he noticed that the princess wasn't looking at him at all—she was staring at something in the distance with that pretty face of hers.

*What...?*

Feeling humiliated, Mu Tianzhao didn't rush to speak again. His eyes couldn't help but follow the princess's gaze...only to see Prince Jing feeding his fish from the table full of desserts as the fish lay on the edge of the fish tank, wagging its tail.

So, the princess was looking at the fish—the fish that brought disaster whenever the second prince saw him. Every time the fish flapped its tail, the princess smiled.

Mu Tianzhao secretly hated this fish. He didn't want to be rude during the imperial banquet, so when he saw that Prince Jing had brought the wretched thing, he tried to pretend it didn't exist... But somehow, this fish of misfortune had entered his line of sight again.

The Princess of Jinjue smiled so hard she blushed, and whispered to King Jinjue occasionally. The second prince could only hear the word "fish" spoken softly and nothing else, but that was enough for him. He was certain that the stupid fish had stolen his stage again.

The Princess of Jinjue had no taste. How could a fish raised by a mute prince compare with him, a future crown prince?

Mu Tianzhao glanced at the emperor. The emperor had also noticed Prince Jing feeding his fish, due to the commotion around him, but instead of berating him, the emperor smiled as if he was happy to see Prince Jing busying himself with his pet. Mu Tianzhao felt the vine of jealousy taking root within his heart.

He was the respected second prince and the future crown prince, but he wasn't able to do anything about this fish. Mu Tianzhao sat back, frustrated, his expression turning dark. Even though he was silent for a while, nobody paid him any attention. Thus, the second prince gave a couple of orders to the servant in charge of his food.

The servant went to carry out his order and came back after a while, holding a bowl in his hand that contained a little soup.

The servant knelt down, trembling. "Your Highness, the kitchen didn't prepare carp soup today. They can start making it now, but it will take quite some time. For now, I brought White Jade Meatball Soup in case the wait is too long. Would Your Highness please at least have some..."

The servant spoke quietly, but there was no getting around the people nearby who were determined to pay attention to the second prince. Mu Tianming was seated close to the second prince, and he called out, "Second brother, are the dishes at the banquet not to your liking? Why do you want to drink carp soup all of a sudden?"

Mu Tianming deliberately raised his voice as he said the word "carp." Most people, after staring in surprise at the second prince, looked in Prince Jing's direction afterward—because Prince Jing was the only one with a carp right now.

Li Yu, in his fish tank, lifted his head and cocked it embarrassingly. *Ah, I'm so shy! Does the second prince want to make me into soup? But I'm still nibbling on the food my master has given me.*

Mu Tianzhao was silent. He could feel Prince Jing's ice-cold eyes look over, and for some reason, he felt panicked. But he didn't even do anything!

He gritted his teeth. "Third brother, you're overthinking it. I just wanted to drink some soup because I suddenly became thirsty." His heart felt like it was twisting in on itself. Why was everyone berating him just for wanting to drink some fish soup?

Prince Jing shot a cold look at Mu Tianzhao. Wang Xi was silent as he stood beside him, but he had already started cursing Mu Tianzhao in his heart on Prince Jing's behalf.

The emperor knit his brows. Wanting to drink fish soup wasn't a problem, but since Prince Jing was the only one who'd brought a fish, the target of that specific request was rather obvious. Perhaps the second prince just hadn't anticipated that the third prince would expose his little act of anger.

The emperor had an extremely good impression of the little carp. The way Prince Jing cared for his pet made the emperor fond of it too—he thought the second prince was being a little too emotional.

The Princess of Jinjue had been staring at Prince Jing's fish just now, and after watching it all this time, she had also come to like the fish. When she realized that the second prince wanted to drink fish soup, she immediately stood up and angrily said, "Your Highness, how could you drink fish soup in front of such a cute fish? I didn't think you were that type of person!"

To be honest, when the second prince had handed her that butterfly pastry, the Princess of Jinjue had actually been rather unimpressed. She was young, but she could tell that the second prince was trying to use her and Jinjue. She was also well aware that she'd be relegated to the position of a side consort if she married him—she wasn't stupid. A position like that, where she could be easily thrown away, wasn't worth the country of Jinjue's wholehearted support. What's more, there was no guarantee that the second prince could really ascend the throne, or when that would actually happen. Jinjue didn't necessarily want to get involved in the conflict between the princes.

So, she had ignored the second prince. And when she learned that he wanted to secretly drink fish soup, the bold little princess jumped out to give his ego a couple of stomps, even though no one else was willing to speak up—and at the same time, she used this opportunity to hint to the emperor that she wasn't willing to enter a marriage with the second prince. *Don't even think about it!*

"Princess, you've misunderstood. That's not what happened..." Mu Tianzhao was speechless. His heart filled with anger, and he didn't know how to explain himself anymore.

He didn't actually want to drink fish soup in front of the fish—he wanted to butcher the fish and make it into soup instead! Was he supposed to tell her that?

It was clear to the emperor that the Princess of Jinjue didn't have any intentions toward the second prince, so it would be better if the second prince refrained from using such dishonorable means. To put it nicely, he was trying to get into the princess's good graces, but to put it bluntly, he had failed to attract her. Earlier, the emperor had thought the second prince was earning him respect, but now he felt like the second prince's actions had slapped him in the face.

Ye Qinghuan was definitely more suitable.

The emperor looked over at Ye-shizi, who was sitting quietly a short distance from Prince Jing, and silently gave him a stamp of approval for being so mature and steady. He decided to keep the Duke of Cheng'en and Ye-shizi after the banquet to speak to them alone.

The second prince soon learned that the emperor planned to marry the princess to the Duke of Cheng'en's son and was already meeting with the Duke of Cheng'en to discuss it.

So, they were all in cahoots... Meanwhile, he was immensely humiliated at the imperial banquet and didn't gain anything from it. The princess rejected him, the Duke of Cheng'en refused to help him, and Prince Jing and his fish were laughing at him!

The second prince had endured too much for too long. It was time to make a move.

# A Courageous, Ambitious Fish

AN EXPRESSIONLESS YE QINGHUAN set down a stack of secret reports in front of Prince Jing.

Ye-shizi was normally very lively, and it was rare for him to look so solemn. When he put the reports down, Li Yu stopped swimming around his fish tank as well, afraid of missing a single piece of information.

The emperor had Ye Qinghuan and his father, the Duke of Cheng'en, stay behind after the banquet. Ye Qinghuan had acted guarded and restrained at the banquet, thinking he wouldn't stand out, but the emperor still chose him to marry the Princess of Jinjue. Those unbelievable words on the letter were slowly becoming reality.

The emperor did ask for the Duke of Cheng'en's opinion, but a marriage like this was a national affair, and Ye Qinghuan knew well that his father was loyal to the emperor and would not disagree. And thus, his marriage was decided upon—but it wasn't life after marriage Ye Qinghuan was worried about. The letter stated that the second prince would frame him for killing the Princess of Jinjue. Clearly, she was also a victim. Ye Qinghuan was determined to thwart the second prince's plans. After the second prince was dealt with, it would be the princess's decision whether or not she still wanted to go through with the marriage.

He'd kept an eye on the second prince and the sixth prince ever since he received the letter.

Since Ye-shizi's marriage was established, there'd been many more people coming in and out of Mu Tianzhao's manor.

The second prince was definitely plotting something.

With Prince Jing occasionally reminding him to be skeptical, Ye Qinghuan also didn't completely believe what was written in the letter. The more its contents came true, the more cautious he needed to be. His people soon uncovered the second prince's plot.

On the day Ye Qinghuan and the princess were to enter the palace and thank the emperor, the second prince planned to lure the Princess of Jinjue to Yanyu Pavilion and kill her there. He would then lure Ye Qinghuan there too, to take the blame. As long as Ye Qinghuan stepped into Yanyu Pavilion, he would find his fiancée's corpse with his own sword in her chest—the second prince planned to have someone steal it from Cheng'en Manor beforehand so he could plant it as proof that Ye-shizi had been the one to kill her.

The stage thus set, the second prince would lead a group of imperial guards to Yanyu Pavilion and capture Ye-shizi "red-handed." In the face of such concrete evidence, there was nothing Ye Qinghuan could say to save himself.

The second prince intended to frame Ye Qinghuan for sabotaging the marriage and killing the princess. It matched what most of the mysterious informant had written, but there were some parts of the letter that didn't match.

For example, the letter had warned them that the sixth prince had some part in this as well and asked Ye-shizi to not trust the sixth prince. Ye Qinghuan was only able to find out information about the second prince; the sixth prince hadn't made any moves. Compared to the second prince, who was used to putting on a mask around others, or the third prince, who jumped at any opportunity to compete with the second prince, the sixth prince was simply transparent. Even at an important event like the imperial banquet, he didn't even try to scoot closer to the emperor.

Ye Qinghuan wondered if the letter had been written incorrectly. After all, there were so many incorrect characters, it was a miracle that he'd had the patience to finish reading it.

But since the sixth prince hadn't done as the letter said he would, there was no way to tell who the sixth prince was going to harm. Prince Jing and Ye Qinghuan discussed it several times over, but in the end, they decided they should still have someone keep an eye on the sixth prince.

They also found out that the second prince had secretly prepared arsenic. It was clear that he meant to poison someone, but it was unclear who. At the very least, it couldn't be the Princess of Jinjue, because she had to die by Ye-shizi's sword so he could be framed. Poisoning would only complicate matters.

Ye Qinghuan made the necessary preparations on his end, and the imperial decree was issued shortly during the Dragon Boat Festival. Very soon, he would have to enter the palace to thank the emperor for his engagement.

Prince Jing, meanwhile, had agreed to enter the palace with Ye-shizi. On the day Ye-shizi was due to thank the emperor, Prince Jing changed into a lighter outfit, put on a black guan, and casually threw on a royal blue outer robe, made of cotton with a silver trim.

Ordinary people weren't allowed to carry swords into the palace, but since Prince Jing was a prince, not only did he have a sword hanging from his waist, he also calmly shoved a dagger into his cloud-patterned boots, as if he was going to fight the second prince to the death.

Li Yu swam around anxiously in his crystal fish tank. He wanted to go too. Since Prince Jing never got together with the little concubine, the House of Cheng'en had no reason to help the third prince. He didn't know whether the second or sixth prince would still follow the plot in the book, and besides, what if there were other details he'd missed when he last read it?

He couldn't for the life of him remember the name of the imperial princess that the sixth prince killed in the book. It was only mentioned in a single sentence, so she couldn't even be considered cannon fodder; thus, all he could do was remind Ye Qinghuan to keep an eye out for the sixth prince and trust that Ye-shizi and Prince Jing would work together. If the sixth prince was to make a move, he was certain that they could stop it.

All he wanted was to stay by Prince Jing and receive firsthand information, to prevent the worst-case scenario. He assumed Prince Jing would take him, but the crystal bottle was never brought out. That meant he wouldn't be taken along. It would be impossible for him to enter the palace on his own if Prince Jing didn't take him.

Li Yu flapped his tail and jumped into a tea bowl from the crystal fish tank. After a few consecutive jumps, he planned to jump onto the crystal bottle that was currently laying horizontally on the table—but since the bottle was smooth, the wet little carp slipped off the bottle before he could stabilize himself and almost landed on the table headfirst.

Prince Jing, with his sharp eyes and quick reflexes, scooped him up and put him into the petal-shaped tea bowl nearby.

*Sob sob sob!* Li Yu wailed internally. *Has Prince Jing made up his mind about not taking me, since he's not putting me in the bottle?*

Li Yu jumped again. This time, he bravely leaped onto Prince Jing's shoulder and used his fins to grab tightly onto his clothing.

He felt like he'd turned into a majestic eagle, shielding his master from the wind and rain from his position on his shoulder. In reality, his wet fins soon made Prince Jing's shoulder damp...

Li Yu started thumping on Prince Jing's shoulder. *Ahhh, that's not what I wanted to do!*

Prince Jing wiped away the water on his face and picked his fish up.

Li Yu knew Prince Jing wasn't happy—he'd been the prince's pet for so long, and he rarely lifted Li Yu by his head. He would only do this when something was wrong.

Was his master angry?

Knowing he'd made a mistake, the little carp tried to sweetly wrap around Prince Jing's finger, but since he was held up by his head, his tail couldn't reach that far and only rubbed against Prince Jing's palm instead.

Prince Jing thought the little fish just wanted to come out and play. Perhaps since he'd taken Li Yu everywhere with him lately, the fish assumed that he could play every day.

But not tonight. It was very likely he and Ye Qinghuan might have to fight against the second prince. Never mind whether or not it was convenient—the fish would probably be uncomfortable.

Prince Jing was originally planning to leave him with Wang Xi, but his fish even jumped onto his shoulder after failing to get into the crystal bottle.

*Hmph.* It seemed like he was spoiled too much and had become too bold...

Prince Jing silently criticized the fish, but now that he thought about it, if he left his fish in the residence, he might become victim to the thief again. Either way, going to the palace would result in getting his people in the palace involved, and he would definitely go to Jingtai Hall. Why didn't he just take the fish to Jingtai Hall for a few hours and ask Wang Xi to come along?

Prince Jing let out a silent sigh of resignation as he placed the fish carefully into the crystal bottle, then changed his outer robes.

Li Yu was thrilled. He was getting to enter the palace even though he had done something wrong. *Aaaahhh! My plan worked!*

Prince Jing brought his fish along and met Ye Qinghuan at the palace gate. Just as Prince Jing was holding on to the crystal bottle, Ye Qinghuan was holding Xiongfeng's leash.

Ye Qinghuan smiled. "I knew you'd bring your fish. I brought Xiongfeng too, so they can keep each other company while we're attending to business."

*...No way?!* Li Yu was floored. He had business to attend to as well! He wasn't here to keep a dog company!

No sooner than Ye Qinghuan had finished speaking, Xiongfeng excitedly reached his head over and poked the crystal bottle with his nose.

The crystal bottle was larger than the tea bowls, but it still felt like Xiongfeng could hold the entire thing in his mouth if he opened it wide enough. The crystal bottle was narrow and thin, so when Xiongfeng licked the bottle, Li Yu felt like the dog's teeth were suddenly much closer to him too. Even though he was already very familiar with Xiongfeng, it still made Li Yu a little nervous.

Prince Jing handed Wang Xi the crystal bottle. Wang Xi had already brought over the white-and-blue porcelain fish tank they used at Jingtai Hall before, and he put the little fish inside it.

Li Yu breathed a sigh of relief, finally feeling safe.

Before the day they entered the palace, Prince Jing and Ye Qinghuan had agreed to put the Princess of Jinjue's safety first, in case the second prince really did end up harming her. But since neither of them were close with her, it would be inconvenient to send someone directly to her. Inspired by the letter Ye Qinghuan received, Prince Jing decided to write an anonymous letter to the Princess of Jinjue stating that someone was plotting against her. Prince Jing had come up with the idea, and Ye Qinghuan was the one who delivered it. Since Ye-shizi oversaw the King and Princess of Jinjue's safety, nobody would suspect a thing if he delivered them a letter.

It was rumored that the King of Jinjue was furious when he received the letter and had summoned his trusted advisors to examine it for an entire night to try to determine the intent of the writer. For the safety of his daughter, the king ordered high-ranking guards to accompany her everywhere at all times, even when she entered the palace to give thanks to the emperor.

The emperor didn't know his reasons. He just thought the king was being too protective since the palace was quite safe. But it was a trivial matter, and he didn't want to limit the King of Jinjue over this.

So, the Princess of Jinjue was surrounded by sixteen high-ranking guards at every turn—and those were only the visible ones. There were probably many more hidden around her.

The second prince's plan would not succeed as long as the princess was safe.

A few days ago, the second prince's people had snuck into Cheng'en Manor under Ye Qinghuan's secret, watchful eye. To give the second prince a nice present, Ye Qinghuan had picked a special sword and let them steal it so the second prince would think everything was going according to plan.

After settling their pets down, Prince Jing and Ye Qinghuan started to wait.

Soon, an aide came to report that a stranger of unknown origin had tried to get close to the Princess of Jinjue, but her guards spotted the person and beat him up quite badly.

Prince Jing and Ye Qinghuan exchanged a look. They both guessed that the second prince must have sent that person to lure the Princess of Jinjue over.

"We should go," Ye Qinghuan said softly.

It was time to head to Yanyu Pavilion and say hello to the second prince.

Prince Jing nodded at Wang Xi, patted the little carp on the head, and headed into the night with Ye Qinghuan and his men.

Li Yu watched Prince Jing leave. He stopped in his fish tank, quietly analyzing the situation. Why hadn't the sixth prince made a move yet?

Most likely because Prince Jing wasn't with Chu Yanyu yet, and the third and sixth princes had not yet won the support of the House of Cheng'en—there was no need for them to take a risk now. The current situation was just the second prince's one-man show. But Li Yu didn't really understand why the second prince persisted with this plan even though the sixth prince had already retreated.

Perhaps narrow-minded and shortsighted people always made the same decisions.

The only thing Li Yu could do now was wait for information in Jingtai Hall...

Just then, he heard a light click. Xiongfeng, who'd seemed to be sleeping near the fish tank, raised his head, alert.

...It wasn't Wang Xi. Li Yu was familiar with Wang Xi's footsteps, and the sound had come from the window. Wang Xi was in Jingtai Hall, and he definitely wouldn't climb through the window.

Illuminated by the soft glow of a candle, a black shadow sprang into the room through the window. Who was it?

Li Yu immediately thought of the female assassin who'd tried to kill Prince Jing, and his fishy body started to tremble.

Xiongfeng, as expected of a dog who wanted to protect his fish friend, immediately started barking wildly. The black figure loitered in front of the table for a bit and was just about to walk over when Xiongfeng leaped toward the person and bit him on the hand, causing him immense pain.

"What's happening?" Wang Xi's voice rang out, and the surrounding guards were alerted as well. As the situation put him at a disadvantage, the black figure left the same way he came, holding his injured hand all the way.

Wang Xi was very frustrated that he hadn't caught the man, but thankfully both fish and dog were fine. Wang Xi, relieved, brought a box of fish food from the table to feed Master Fish and Master Dog.

Xiongfeng's tail wagged happily. Wang Xi put the fish food onto a jade plate, and Xiongfeng was just about to eat some when something occurred to Li Yu. He thought of how the black figure had rummaged around on the table for a bit, and a peculiar feeling rose in his chest.

Li Yu immediately flapped his tail and whacked a blue stone, one of the ones he used to play with, toward the jade plate. Since he used excessive force, the stone knocked the plate over, and the fish food ended up on the ground.

Wang Xi was surprised. The little carp rarely "lost his temper" like this. "Master Fish, what's wrong?"

Wang Xi's gaze landed on the fallen fish food, and he suddenly seemed to think of something. Could it be that...

Wang Xi quickly took out a silver needle from the inside of his robes. Nobody would think to test for poison in pet food. Wang Xi hoped he was just overthinking, but he feared the worst.

The silver needle poked into the fish food, and when he pulled it out a short while later, the tip was already black.

Li Yu's heart skipped a beat. *The fish food was really poisoned! Sob sob sob, I was almost poisoned, how scary!* Since he was basically the only one who ate that food, Li Yu was certain that someone wanted to harm him.

Soon enough, Wang Xi reached the same conclusion. With Prince Jing away, Wang-gonggong took charge and ordered someone to put Master Fish and Xiongfeng in a room without windows. He personally took up watch outside the room, determined to not let anyone slip by again.

# Fishy First Aid

As for Ye Qinghuan—he had also met the person the second prince had sent to lure him into Yanyu Pavilion.

Prince Jing glanced at him meaningfully, and Ye Qinghuan followed the person, pretending to be clueless. Prince Jing followed with his aides at some distance so that the second prince's agents wouldn't notice.

When they arrived at Yanyu Pavilion, they really did see a woman on the ground, pierced through by Ye Qinghuan's sword. And the second prince soon arrived on the scene with the imperial guards he'd prepared beforehand.

The second prince glanced at the corpse on the ground, who was dressed in Jinjue apparel. Mu Tianzhao, who was secretly pleased, acted surprised and said, "Ye-shizi, why are you here—what have you done to the princess?!"

Just as Ye Qinghuan opened his mouth to answer, the emperor's bright yellow dragon robe swept into the Yanyu Pavilion.

This was, of course, part of the second prince's plan. He'd privately told the emperor that he heard Ye-shizi and the Princess of Jinjue were meeting secretly in the Yanyu Pavilion. Though he had ordered the marriage, the emperor still thought the meeting was inappropriate, so he headed over to scold them a bit. He didn't expect to walk into a murder scene!

"What in the world is going on?" The emperor's questioning gaze moved from the woman on the ground to Ye Qinghuan.

"Your Imperial Majesty, I just arrived as well," Ye Qinghuan replied calmly. "I was just trying to figure out what had happened when the second prince appeared..."

Mu Tianzhao thought his tone was a little strange, but he was certain there were flaws in his plan. He gathered all the anger in his chest and shot back, "Anyone with eyes can see what happened. Ye-shizi, you're the one who killed the princess, yet you want to deny it?" He raised his hand and pointed at the sword in the woman's chest. "This is Ye-shizi's sword, is it not?"

The emperor realized how grave the situation currently was. Was it true that the Princess of Jinjue was dead? And that Ye Qinghuan had killed her?

With a single order, the imperial guards rushed forward to investigate. Everything the second prince had said seemed to make sense, but when the imperial guards flipped over the body, they realized that it wasn't the Princess of Jinjue—it was a woman dressed in Jinjue servant attire.

The emperor's sharp gaze swept over the scene. The imperial guards stepped aside, not daring to say a word.

The sword was also removed from the woman's chest and brought to the emperor.

The emperor was the one who'd given Ye Qinghuan his sword, so he had a good memory of it. This sword was extremely similar to Ye Qinghuan's, so much so that at first glance, the emperor thought it was his.

"Ye Qinghuan, is this not your sword? And you have no sword on you right now." The second prince was confident, and his words were forceful.

"Your Imperial Majesty, the second prince seems to have forgotten the rules of the palace," said Ye Qinghuan, his voice level. "As subjects like myself are not allowed to carry a sword in front of the emperor, I gave my sword to the guards at the palace gate for safekeeping."

The emperor nodded. Since Ye Qinghuan brought it up himself, the emperor immediately ordered someone to fetch the sword in question. Soon, a guard came over with Ye-shizi's sword.

Why were there suddenly two swords? The second prince started to lose his cool.

Ye Qinghuan solemnly asked the emperor to examine the swords.

The emperor carefully compared the two swords in front of him. Truthfully, the swords were nearly identical when viewed separately, but their differences were obvious when they were side by side. The sword the guards brought to him was shiny and silver, but the one taken from the woman was as dark as iron—it was just an ordinary sword.

It was clear which one was the real thing.

Meanwhile, the experienced imperial guards had come to the conclusion that this woman had been dead for several days already. Since she hadn't been killed just now, and the sword found in her wasn't even Ye Qinghuan's, there was nothing to support the claim that Ye Qinghuan was the murderer.

But why were the two swords so similar?

The emperor immediately deduced that someone had made the murder weapon almost identical to Ye-shizi's sword so they could frame him.

He recalled the second prince's earlier claims: "This is Ye-shizi's sword." "Ye-shizi killed the princess." But both were wrong—the sword was not Ye-shizi's, and the princess was not killed. The emperor himself had experienced many palace conflicts before. Now, even the way he looked at the second prince had changed.

"Tianzhao," he said lightly, "you hadn't even confirmed that this woman was the Princess of Jinjue when you arrived at Yanyu Pavilion, so why did you insist that Ye-shizi had killed the princess?"

Mu Tianzhao was still in shock. Why was the emperor suddenly doubting him? He was just questioning Ye Qinghuan a moment ago! The one who was supposed to die at Yanyu Pavilion was the princess—he'd arranged this long ago. Was there someone else?

But right now, the emperor was waiting for an explanation...

Mu Tianzhao replied with great difficulty, "I saw that the deceased woman was dressed in Jinjue attire, s-so, I thought she was the princess."

The emperor gave him an unreadable glance and ordered the imperial guards to carry the corpse to the second prince. Only then did Mu Tianzhao realize that it wasn't the Princess of Jinjue he knew, but...but...

Ye Qinghuan smiled. "This woman is dressed in Jinjue attire, but a servant's outfit is very different from what the princess wears. What good eyesight you have, second prince, to mistake a servant for the princess with a single glance."

Mu Tianzhao kept his mouth shut. Ye-shizi's ridicule was obvious. There was no way the emperor didn't know what the second prince was trying to do—why else would he have tried so hard to get Ye-shizi to come to Yanyu Pavilion?

Not only did the second prince fail to frame Ye-shizi, but he was the one caught red-handed instead.

The emperor was both angry and resentful toward the second prince, so much so that he wanted to kick him, but he still had to restrain himself. Since Ye-shizi and the princess were both fine, there was no need to take things any further. King Jinjue was still in the imperial city. He couldn't let the king know that the second prince had tried to harm his daughter.

"Tianzhao, you can't even tell people apart from each other," he said. "For the next few days, you should stay in your residence and reflect on your actions. You may not leave without our permission."

The emperor had never spoken so strictly to the second prince before.

He was simply put under house arrest; there was no other punishment. Ye Qinghuan knew that the emperor would most likely let the second prince get away with it. If he had fallen for the second prince's trap, it was certain his punishment would have been death. Now it was clear the second prince was the one trying to frame Ye-shizi, though, and the emperor refused to do anything to his son.

But they had plenty of time. The second prince's attempt to uproot the House of Cheng'en had failed, so when the House of Cheng'en started treating him as an enemy, he'd have no one but himself to blame.

There were many ways to ruin a person. Ye Qinghuan was upright and honest, but that didn't mean he didn't know how to retaliate. If someone hit him, he'd hit back. It was only right. He and Prince Jing had crafted the plan carried out today—they had used the body of an unknown female corpse from the dungeon to make the second prince think he had succeeded, so he'd let down his guard.

The emperor comforted Ye Qinghuan personally, and Ye Qinghuan didn't press the matter with the second prince any further. Internally, the emperor sighed. He'd already felt something was off with the second prince at the imperial banquet the other day, but he hadn't thought it was this bad—the second prince had come so close to landing himself in disaster.

He normally seemed pretty capable. Why had a marriage arrangement made him so impulsive? Did he have to destroy everything he couldn't have? The emperor didn't understand the second prince's frustration, but he was quite put off by the ruthlessness with which the second prince had plotted to ruin the House of Cheng'en.

Shortly after the emperor had finished speaking with Ye Qinghuan, Prince Jing slowly walked in.

Seeing his other son, the emperor smiled wearily. "Tianchi, you're here as well?"

Mu Tianchi came over and bowed to the emperor. Then, unexpectedly, he silently took out a memorial tablet from his robes.

The emperor's first reaction was to wonder why on earth Prince Jing would suddenly take out something like this, and he was a bit displeased. But after he read the words on the tablet, the emperor swallowed all his scolding. Because this was the memorial tablet of his first wife, Prince Jing's mother—Empress Xiaohui!

The emperor's original desire to smooth the situation over was shattered into pieces by the sight of this tablet.

He suddenly remembered whose family the House of Cheng'en was. They were Empress Xiaohui's maternal family and relatives—if the empress was still alive, would he let the second prince get away with it so easily?

Prince Jing was asking for justice on behalf of Empress Xiaohui and the House of Cheng'en. Ye Qinghuan wasn't able to ask for it, but Prince Jing could!

"Tianchi, I... understand what you mean." The emperor rubbed the spot between his brows. "You and Ye Qinghuan may go, for now. Let me give it some thought."

Ye Qinghuan dragged Prince Jing out of Yanyu Pavilion. What

a stroke of genius from Prince Jing! He hadn't expected something like that.

"How bold!" Ye Qinghuan laughed quietly, but he felt elated.

Some people thought the previous empress's maternal family had nobody to rely on. But Prince Jing was still protecting the House of Cheng'en... Well, the House of Cheng'en would return the favor. For Empress Xiaohui, as well as on their own behalf.

Prince Jing showed a rare little smile in front of his cousin. When Ye Qinghuan had headed to the Yanyu Pavilion, Prince Jing had followed at first, but he'd decided to take a risk and made a detour at Changchun Palace to retrieve his mother's tablet. It had ended up being quite useful.

In his opinion, if they were going to strike against the second prince, it was better to strike hard and fast, so he wouldn't have a chance to get up again.

Ye Qinghuan believed the same thing.

Someone ended up leaking the news to King Jinjue, who was furious that the second prince had plotted to harm his daughter. The emperor immediately summoned Ye Qinghuan, the future son-in-law, to deal with King Jinjue's wrath. Ye Qinghuan had been planning to return to Jingtai Hall with Prince Jing to reunite with Xiongfeng, but now he had no choice but to stay behind.

Prince Jing had no such obligations and set off for Jingtai Hall. He was halfway there when a black shadow suddenly jumped toward him and, seemingly without noticing, bumped into him.

*Who?* Prince Jing frowned and looked the person up and down.

The figure was masked, so he couldn't see his face. Prince Jing suspected this person might have been sent by the second prince for revenge, so his hand was already on the scabbard of his sword.

The person, startled, realized it was Prince Jing, and brandished his own sword, lunging toward him.

Their blades clashed.

The masked man and Prince Jing were matched in skill, but it seemed as if his sword hand was injured—his movements were always a beat too slow. It didn't take long for Prince Jing to knock the sword out of his hand, but the man took advantage of how unprepared he was to hurl a bag of white powder at his face.

Suddenly unable to see, Prince Jing dropped his sword. But he could sense that the man was coming closer; he sneered, calmly took out the dagger hidden in his boot, and stabbed him.

In less than a quarter of an hour, the fight was over.

The masked man, heavily injured, made his escape. Prince Jing was a little unsteady on his feet, and he couldn't make a sound, but he knew he must be close to Jingtai Hall.

Li Yu and Xiongfeng had been staring at each other all night. Of course, Xiongfeng had also occupied himself with gnawing on things, wagging his tail, and poking the fish tank with his nose.

Li Yu was about to fall asleep when Prince Jing finally appeared. Wang Xi, who was guarding the door, was overjoyed. "You're finally back, Your Highness! Did everything go well?"

Prince Jing waved his hand. Wang Xi noticed that there was something wrong—his eyes were red and there was powder on his face. Wang Xi tried again and again to ask what had happened, but Prince Jing's eyes still hurt, and he couldn't write anything. He kept waving his hands around, rather irritably.

It was clear that Prince Jing wasn't well. "This servant will help you into your room first and then summon an imperial physician for you!" Wang Xi assured him.

Since Master Fish was here and His Highness usually loved Master Fish the most, Wang Xi thought that His Highness might feel better if he stayed with his fish for a bit—so he helped Prince Jing to the room where the fish and the dog were currently waiting.

As soon as Prince Jing entered the room, Xiongfeng rushed over, wagging his tail and asking for praise. But Prince Jing couldn't see anything, so he accidentally stepped on Xiongfeng's tail, and Xiongfeng let out a couple of aggrieved barks.

"Quiet down, Xiongfeng. He doesn't seem well."

Li Yu started swimming anxiously in his tank. He was so happy that Prince Jing was back that he didn't want to sleep anymore, but Prince Jing seemed to be in bad shape. Where was Wang Xi?

Li Yu didn't know that Wang Xi was off summoning the imperial physician.

There was light in the room, but everything was still blurry for Prince Jing. He fumbled around and sat down—his eyes were still uncomfortable, so he wanted to find a handkerchief to wipe them with.

Li Yu glimpsed Prince Jing's red, swollen eyes, and the residual white powder. A thought crossed his mind: *Did someone throw lime powder at Prince Jing?*

He watched as Prince Jing took a towel from the edge of the washbasin and started to dip it in water. Li Yu hurriedly said, "No! You can't use water!"

If lime powder was washed with water, he could go blind. It was well-known in modern times!

But nobody could hear him, and the little carp swam anxiously up and down in his tank, hoping Prince Jing would see him and stop. However, Prince Jing was busy with his own problems and didn't notice. He wrang out the towel and was about to put it over his eyes.

Li Yu wanted Xiongfeng to do something, but Xiongfeng, a stupid doggo, was only reliable sometimes. Right now, he was staring at Prince Jing with his head cocked. He probably thought Prince Jing's stumbling movements were interesting.

What should he do?! Prince Jing was going to go blind! He was already mute, so he couldn't go blind too, right? It would be too devastating.

Li Yu stopped for a moment. He knew there was still another way to stop Prince Jing—

Even if it was dangerous for him, he had to try it!

The little carp gathered his courage and jumped out of the fish tank. He didn't mind that there were no tea bowls around or that it might hurt when he landed on the ground. Prince Jing's back was turned toward him, so Li Yu immediately used his transformation skill and turned into a human.

It didn't matter how he was going to explain this. He had to stop Prince Jing!

"Don't use water!" Li Yu yelled.

Prince Jing's hand stopped halfway to his face, and he turned around instinctively. This voice... He recognized it. This was the voice of the young man he'd been searching for all this time. Why did he suddenly appear in his room?

Prince Jing was about to turn around, but Li Yu said, "Don't turn around right now! Please wait!"

"..."

Having just transformed, Li Yu was still naked. He looked around frantically, but the remarkable thing was, the windowless room Wang Xi had chosen was one with no wardrobe, and no clothes.

Li Yu couldn't be any more embarrassed, but he couldn't just run around like this.

Although there was no wardrobe in this room, there were curtains hanging from the beams. There was no time, it'd have to do! Disregarding color or texture, Li Yu grabbed a random piece and wrapped it around himself. He didn't stop until he looked like a tube.

Prince Jing stood stiffly, not daring to make any sudden movements. He could hear the activity behind him, so the youth hadn't left yet, but it felt like if he turned around, he might just disappear into thin air again.

Right now his eyes weren't in a good state. He had to remain calm and not scare him away, Prince Jing thought silently.

Li Yu adjusted his curtain roll, then finally said, "Now you can..."

Prince Jing quickly turned around. But all he could see was a blurry tube...

Li Yu stood before him and explained quietly, "You... Your Highness, you cannot wash your eyes no matter what. Let me help you, okay?"

# Fishy Exposed

AFRAID THAT PRINCE JING wouldn't believe him, Li Yu put his hands up so the prince could see them. "Your Highness, don't worry. I mean no harm. Your eyes are uncomfortable, right? You should take care of them quickly..."

Prince Jing was a little hesitant. It was the first time he'd spoken to him, but for some reason, the young man seemed familiar somehow. Although he'd thought the young man was a thief at first, that assumption had faded over time. And the young man clearly didn't have any intention to harm him. If he was indeed the one who wrote and delivered the letter to Ye Qinghuan, then he had even helped them.

But why did he take away Xiaoyu the first time they met...?

Prince Jing automatically tried to look for his fish, and Li Yu was startled. He did have that pillow that was shaped just like him before, but it had disappeared, and he hadn't bothered looking for it—so now, there was nothing in the fish tank. Would he be exposed?

He looked at the fish tank too, worried. But Xiongfeng just so happened to be standing in front of it, and he was large enough to completely obstruct the tank.

*...Phew. Saved.*

Between the dog in the way and the discomfort in his eyes, Prince Jing probably only saw a swath of black. He realized he wouldn't be able to see his fish, so he turned back around.

Li Yu let out a sigh of relief, but Prince Jing still didn't move. Li Yu was afraid that Prince Jing still didn't trust him, so he latched onto his arm in desperation. "Please believe me. I'm not a bad person! I just want to help you get the powder out of your eyes."

When he was a fish, he often jumped into Prince Jing's palms, so he was used to touching him. At that moment, he still thought of Prince Jing as his tyrant owner, so he didn't think it was strange to hug his arm. He was more afraid that Prince Jing would think he was a bad person and kill him...

Li Yu's fishiness activated, and he hugged him even tighter.

Prince Jing was shocked. He'd never met someone with this little propriety—he couldn't push him away even though he was a bit uncomfortable.

"Let me try, please," Li Yu insisted. "If it doesn't work, you can do with me as you see fit."

...Either way, Prince Jing was sure this strange young man wouldn't be able to try anything funny when he was right in front of him like this, so he might as well give him a chance.                    :

He fumbled for the table and sat down. Li Yu wiped his hands clean carefully and found a dry handkerchief; once he'd made sure there was no water on it, he sat down next to Prince Jing and carefully pried open his eyelids, cleaning away the powder that had gotten into his eyes bit by bit.

Luckily, there wasn't that much. Li Yu worked quickly, and in no time he'd removed it all.

He could tell now that it was definitely lime powder. Li Yu had learned in the real world that lime powder released a lot of heat when it melted, so if someone tried to wash it out of their eyes with water, it would burn them. He'd turned into a human just in time to stop Prince Jing. The results would have been catastrophic otherwise.

Li Yu blew gently into Prince Jing's eyes, in case there were pieces he'd missed.

Prince Jing was much more relaxed now and could see the stranger in front of him clearly. He was so close that he could see the young man's lowered eyelashes, his slightly sweaty nose, and his rosy, pink lips, pursed in concentration. He felt his warm breath too and realized that he was blowing into his eyes for him. Prince Jing looked away, thinking it was inappropriate, and caught a glimpse of the young man's bare feet and the water droplets gleaming on his toes.

Prince Jing was becoming more and more intrigued by this youth by the minute. His curiosity was growing like a rolling snowball.

Meanwhile, after Li Yu had made absolutely sure, multiple times, that there was no lime powder left in Prince Jing's eyes, he wanted to wash them out with water. He recalled that there was a washbasin in this room, and the water the servants prepared had usually been boiled then cooled, so it was safe to use.

He got up to bring the washbasin over, but Prince Jing thought he was going to escape, so he grasped his arm tightly as soon as he stood up.

...!

Li Yu instantly understood the prince's intentions. He didn't know whether to laugh or cry. "I'm just going to get some water," he said. "The powder's been removed, so your eyes can be washed now."

But Prince Jing still refused to let go, even after Li Yu's explanation. The prince, whose eyes were almost back to normal, got up alongside Li Yu, still holding on to him, and they walked over to the washbasin together.

When Prince Jing stood up straight, Li Yu only came up to his shoulders. Li Yu was wondering how he was going to get Prince Jing back into his seat when the prince lowered his head, staring at Li Yu with his dark eyes.

...That meant he could wash his eyes, right?

Li Yu had finally experienced Prince Jing's stubbornness firsthand. In this awkward position, he didn't use a wet towel to wipe his eyes, and instead scooped up some water, poured it into Prince Jing's eyes, and rinsed them out.

After a couple of rinses, Prince Jing's eyes were still red and swollen, but he no longer felt any discomfort.

Just to be safe, Li Yu said, "Your Highness, please have the imperial physician take a look later. You may still need medicine."

Prince Jing nodded.

They stared at each other for a moment, and it finally sunk in for Li Yu that he'd completely exposed his human form to Prince Jing. There was nothing inherently wrong with that—it wasn't the first time he'd done it, after all—but Prince Jing was still holding on to him. He made a couple of attempts to pull his hand away, but he couldn't do it. He could only maintain his human form for an hour, so what would happen if he suddenly transformed into a fish?

He had to think of a way to either make Prince Jing go away or make himself go away!

As soon as Prince Jing's eyes recovered, Prince Jing didn't take them off the young man in front of him, whether he was looking at his face or his attire. This time, the young man's pale arms were exposed, and he was wrapped in strange cloth. It only just came down to his knees, so his calves were bare, and the movements of his delicate ankles were exposed. Prince Jing couldn't help but wonder why this young man always dressed so...peculiarly?

Prince Jing dipped his finger into the washbasin and wrote on the table: *Who are you?* He had a lot of questions, but this was the first and easiest one to ask.

*Ah...*

Li Yu shook his head, pretending he couldn't read it.

It wasn't that he didn't want to tell him, but he didn't exist in the book. He'd be in a lot of trouble if he lied about his identity and ended up needing to back up that lie in the future, so it was better to not say anything in the first place.

*Maybe,* Li Yu thought, *if I just don't say anything, Prince Jing will become impatient and leave?* He was very worried that the timer on his transformation skill would sneak up on him—that would be disastrous. Li Yu was quite a mess internally, but he still had to pretend to be calm.

Prince Jing, seeing that Li Yu didn't answer, kept writing questions.

*Why are you here?*

*Why did you save me?*

But Li Yu suppressed the urge to talk to Prince Jing and continued to shake his head.

Prince Jing frowned. He'd asked so many questions, but the young man didn't answer any of them. Perhaps he couldn't read?

Thinking back on it... Recalling the letter Ye Qinghuan received, the handwriting was terrible, and Prince Jing had wondered how there could be such horrible handwriting in the world. Was it because he...

...He couldn't read, so he couldn't write either?

Prince Jing glanced at Xiongfeng. Xiongfeng didn't react much to the young man's sudden appearance, so he was probably familiar with him—that was how he'd been able to use Xiongfeng to deliver the letter...

Prince Jing was comparing and analyzing the situation in his head. His questioning gaze made Li Yu's scalp go numb.

Just as he thought he wasn't going to be able to keep pretending anymore and was thinking of outright running away,

Wang Xi-gonggong, who'd left to summon the imperial physician, banged on the door.

"Your Highness! Your Highness, the imperial physician is here!"

The heavens always provided a way out! Hearing Wang Xi's shouting, Li Yu's eyes lit up. Prince Jing caught Li Yu's suddenly relaxed expression and immediately thought he was going to run away.

Prince Jing smiled. At this point, how could he let him escape again?

The imperial physician was right outside, but he didn't dare enter without Prince Jing's permission. Wang Xi walked inside to ask for further directions, only to see Prince Jing sitting casually in a chair with a strange young man wrapped in a tube-shaped cloth.

Since Li Yu was dressed so...freely, Wang-gonggong was so startled that he thought the tube was a blanket and almost didn't recognize him at first. He was screaming internally—he only went to summon the imperial physician, so why was some little minx trying to seduce His Highness again? But His Highness's expression... didn't seem very angry?

Not only was Prince Jing not angry, but he seemed to be in a strangely good mood for someone who was just plotted against. Wang-gonggong, who always made Prince Jing his top priority, thought things over quickly. Actually, as long as His Highness was happy, it was fine to have a little minx in here. He shouldn't ask too many questions.

Wang Xi pretended to not see Li Yu and said respectfully to Prince Jing, "The imperial physician is waiting outside right now. Would you like him to come in, Your Highness?"

Prince Jing didn't nod, but he stood up and straightened his clothes in preparation to go outside. Wang Xi followed quickly to take care of him.

Before Prince Jing went out, he took another look at Li Yu.

Li Yu didn't understand at first; he let out a sigh of relief, thinking he was free and could turn back into a fish.

He was still a little worried, though, and he walked to the entrance and looked through the crack in the door. The door wasn't closed all the way, so he could see that Wang Xi had set up a seat just a step away from the door. Prince Jing was seated squarely in place as the imperial physician leaned over him, checking his pulse and his eyes.

Argh, this guy was such an asshole! Li Yu turned into a human to save him, not to let him trap him in the room!

He'd taken a look at the room earlier, and he knew there were no windows and only one door. It should have been the safest place, but it'd turned into an inescapable prison!

Li Yu turned to Xiongfeng, blubbering. *Good boy, Xiongfeng. You're the only one who can help me now...*

Xiongfeng was completely removed from the situation and had no idea what his problem was.

After checking Prince Jing's pulse and eyes, the imperial physician praised, "Thankfully, Your Highness did well to take care of the situation. Your eyes are fine now, but I will prescribe medication later to improve your eyesight and detoxify your eyes. Your Highness will be completely fine after using it."

Prince Jing smiled slightly. He thought the young man had handled it well too.

Prince Jing ordered Wang Xi to reward the imperial physician. After the physician left, Prince Jing wanted to return to the room, but Wang Xi thought he was just in a hurry to return to the little minx inside, so he stopped him.

"Your Highness. After you left today, someone broke into Jingtai Hall to poison the food."

Wang Xi recounted the events in detail, including how the intruder broke into Jingtai Hall, how Xiongfeng bit his hand, how the fish food was poisoned, and how Master Fish knocked over the jade plate, saving both himself and the dog.

Wang Xi wanted to let Prince Jing know what had happened, but he also wanted to use this opportunity to remind Prince Jing to be on his guard, since that little minx's origins were unknown.

But perhaps it would have been better if he hadn't told him. As Wang Xi explained, Prince Jing's face turned as cold as frost. He was even more furious than when people had plotted against him. When Wang Xi mentioned that the silver needle had turned black, Prince Jing thought back to the arsenic that the second prince had been secretly keeping in his residence. Framing the House of Cheng'en wasn't enough for him—he even tried going after his fish!

Sooner or later, he'd make sure the second prince got what was coming to him.

Prince Jing remembered the masked assailant who had attacked him as he was returning to Jingtai Hall. That man's hand had been injured too; was it perhaps the same person that Xiongfeng bit?

...It was probably one of Mu Tianzhao's lackeys.

He still hadn't laid eyes on Xiaoyu since he got back, for a multitude of reasons. Xiaoyu and the young man should still be in the room...

Ever since the young man helped him wipe his eyes, he had the instinctive feeling that he would not harm the fish.

Wang Xi kept calling out "Your Highness," but Prince Jing gestured at him to wait and walked into the room on his own. Before he opened the door, he had a strange, indescribable feeling, even though he knew it was impossible for the young man to escape this time. But he didn't give it any more thought. He confidently opened the door, and saw—

The room was empty, cloth strewn about the floor, and the young man who was supposed to be waiting for him had disappeared again.

*That's not right.* Prince Jing's temples throbbed. He had left the room, yes, but he'd been guarding the door the entire time. There were no windows in the room, so where could he have gone? This had happened several times now. Prince Jing decided it was necessary to change his line of thinking, no matter how absurd...

The strange young man couldn't escape, so logically he still had to be here, but...most likely somewhere he hadn't thought of yet.

Prince Jing walked over to the cloth on the ground and thought back to all that had happened when he met the young man—and he abruptly realized some alarming details.

When the young man had appeared to help him, he didn't hear the door open, which meant the young man hadn't entered through the door. Did that mean the young man had already been in the room, and he just didn't realize it? Just as he couldn't find him now? The room hadn't been completely silent at the time, though. Prince Jing had excellent hearing, and what he'd heard then was...

The flapping of a fish's tail.

Xiaoyu often jumped in front of him, and he was certain he wouldn't mistake that sound for anything else.

Prince Jing looked over at the fish tank. The porcelain fish tank at Jingtai Hall wasn't as good as the crystal fish tank at his own residence, where he could see everything inside at a glance. But surprisingly, Xiaoyu, who should have been at the bottom of the tank, was instead lying on the edge with his back toward Prince Jing, so he could see his tail flicking back and forth.

Thinking about how his fish had almost died, Prince Jing's mood darkened further. He walked over, but right when he was about to touch him, his fish panicked and dove into the water.

Prince Jing blinked. He reached out again to touch his fish's back. Usually, Xiaoyu would circle his fingers with his tail, but now he only lifted his head and listlessly stared at him.

*Xiaoyu must have been scared,* he thought.

As he comforted his fish, Prince Jing kept thinking about where the young man could have gone. It was a small room and just a quick glance around the room was enough to see everything in it—there was nowhere to hide.

A thought suddenly came to Prince Jing as he recalled each place the young man had been seen. Why was it always...his room?

Only his aides and Ye Qinghuan had known that he was returning to Jingtai Hall today. Why...did the youth run into him here at Jingtai Hall? Besides, with the way he was dressed, it would have been impossible for him to enter through the palace gates.

Prince Jing stood up and accidentally stepped on the cloth on the ground with his cloud-patterned shoes. He picked up the cloth and moved it aside, revealing a puddle of water underneath it.

The young man's feet had been wet, he recalled, thinking to look around for wet footprints in his room. Through careful observation, he found some that led to the washbasin and to the desk, and some that stayed near the door, but a path was formed where the ground was wettest. He followed along this path and finally saw a large black-haired dog.

Ye Qinghuan's dog barked excitedly and wagged his tail at him. The wettest spot was right under where Xiongfeng was sitting.

Prince Jing was a bit startled. He thought he was losing it. Xiongfeng was the one who made these tracks.

Li Yu stared anxiously at Prince Jing until he left the room, feeling like he was about to break down at any moment. He had no other choice—he was afraid Prince Jing would figure everything out since he had no way to get rid of the water on the ground, so he'd had to resort to using Xiongfeng as a scapegoat.

*I'm sorry,* the little carp apologized silently to his owner. *I didn't mean to hide it from you on purpose...*

A stony-faced Prince Jing walked out of the room.

He'd taken the cloth on the ground. On the cloth, a few fish scales shone brightly. This wasn't the first time he found fish scales on the young man's clothes. And there was another detail he remembered: when he looked at the young man's ankle, he had also seen a silver light flash past.

He had an idea of what was happening now.

# Becoming a Carp Spirit

LI YU HAD SPENT the entire day in the grip of anxiety. Now that the excitement was over and he'd gotten away without Prince Jing noticing anything, the little carp slept peacefully at the bottom of his tank. Xiongfeng, who had been extremely helpful, leaned against the tank in blissful sleep as well.

Meanwhile, Prince Jing was pacing outside the room, and all of his weariness was blown away by the cool night breeze.

He lined up all the times he met the young man and connected the dots.

The fish scales that were on his clothes back then and the fish scales on the cloth now were undoubtedly both from Xiaoyu. If that was it, he probably would have assumed the young man had touched his fish, but how could the same fish scales appear on the youth's feet as well?

The young man was dripping wet and was always dressed strangely. Prince Jing didn't hear any footsteps when he appeared, but instead heard a fish's tail. He could never discern where he came from or where he was hiding, and was never able to find him—but he always appeared by his side. None of the people he sent from the manor to look for the young man were able to find so much as a trace of him.

When the young man escaped through the window, the guards who were lying in wait outside said they didn't see anything.

When looking for the person who delivered the letter, the guards posted there told him that only the dog had left the room.

None of the above could be simply explained by what he knew about the world.

He thought he was quite clearheaded, but he suddenly had a crazy idea. Once the idea formed, it refused to leave. Because it was the only way to explain everything. When you have eliminated the impossible, whatever remains, however improbable, must be the truth.

*Tianchi, is your house haunted?*

Ye Qinghuan had teased him about it before and he'd ignored it. But now...

Prince Jing swallowed. Ye Qinghuan...might be partially right.

The young man wasn't a "human."

As for what he was, the fish scales explained everything.

The young man was—probably—Xiaoyu.

Since the moon was already high in the sky, Wang Xi had already urged him to go to bed several times. With a complicated expression, Prince Jing glanced at the room where his fish was and waved him away.

He had to think things through. He couldn't just hold a person, or a fish, under suspicion because of his own wild speculation.

Ignoring how late it was, Prince Jing ordered Wang Xi to find servants from the imperial kitchen to bring him a couple of fish. Since Noble Consort Qiu's cat had picked up Xiaoyu from the kitchen, Prince Jing specifically asked for the same type of fish.

Wang Xi went off to complete his task, and the kitchen staff soon came over with a basket of fish, trembling because they didn't know what was going on. Prince Jing looked the fish over one by one—these fish looked almost identical to Xiaoyu, but their eyes were dull and lifeless. They didn't flap their tails or look up at him. Compared to Xiaoyu, they lacked the most important thing: spirit.

Prince Jing sighed in relief. He should have realized that Xiaoyu was special long ago.

Perhaps because he'd never had a pet before, he'd mistaken Xiaoyu's uniqueness as liveliness and intelligence. Even crows took care of their elderly, after all—he never thought it was anything out of the ordinary for his fish to be smart.

No wonder he always thought the young man looked familiar! It was his own fish. And no wonder the young man always appeared in his room and entered the palace at the same time he did—those were his own arrangements.

Prince Jing became more and more certain of this truth, but he wasn't sure about what to do next. He had raised Xiaoyu for so long, and he'd truly grown to care for him. Now that he knew Xiaoyu wasn't a normal fish... Prince Jing pursed his lips. He was the one who saved Xiaoyu from the cat's paws, but Xiaoyu had helped him several times as well, including saving his relatives, the House of Cheng'en.

Prince Jing smiled wryly. Who could say who was indebted to whom, in the end? How should he handle it?

As dawn rose, Ye Qinghuan was finally able to appease his future father-in-law, King Jinjue, and he rushed to the emperor to report to him. The emperor, however, was feeling irritated and didn't want to see Ye-shizi for too long, so he kicked him out after the requisite pleasantries had been exchanged. Ye Qinghuan was so tired that he decided to visit Prince Jing instead and beg for a bed to sleep in—with their relationship as it was, Prince Jing wouldn't just kick him out, right? But when he rushed into Jingtai Hall, instead of his normally composed, indifferent self, he found Prince Jing looking uncharacteristically worried.

Ye Qinghuan observed him for a bit and decided to ask him about it, even though he didn't know what had happened. He'd always been quite worried about this older cousin of his.

"Tianchi, what's wrong?"

Prince Jing looked up slowly, glanced at him, and passed over the cloth he was holding. Ye Qinghuan accepted it, unsure, and weighed it in his hands. The cloth was a bit rough and felt damp. There were even a couple of fish scales on it.

Ye Qinghuan giggled and said, "Did you wrap your fish in cloth?"

Prince Jing paused. Ye Qinghuan had also thought of his fish. He turned and ordered Wang Xi to bring a brush and paper, then ordered everyone out of the room.

Ye Qinghuan thought Prince Jing seemed more serious than usual, so he assumed there was a very important matter to attend to—he held his breath and waited. When he looked up, he saw Prince Jing concentrated for a bit, then raised his brush and wrote, *Have you ever raised a yao?*

Prince Jing thought that a fish who could turn into a human was probably not a ghost but a yao—a fish yao. That is to say, Xiaoyu was most likely a fish spirit.

Ye Qinghuan was dumbfounded. What kind of question was this? Ye Qinghuan, distressed, replied, "I can barely handle my own dog, so how could I have raised something like...like that?!"

He'd always thought Prince Jing didn't believe in ghosts and the like! Why did he suddenly start asking about them? This was so unlike the normal Prince Jing.

Prince Jing stared at him, looking annoyed. As if he was saying, *Of course I know you haven't raised one before.* After a pause, though, what he wrote was: *How does one raise a yao?*

Ye Qinghuan was at the end of his rope. "Why are you asking

these questions? Do you want to raise one? Stop that, and raise your fish properly! Don't mess with things like that, even if you're interested in them!"

Ye-shizi both feared and believed in ghosts and gods, including the yao Prince Jing was asking about.

Prince Jing kept asking. *Why can't I touch them?*

Ye Qinghuan stuttered, "I-It's a yao! A yao, you understand?"

Prince Jing had never met a yao before, so he didn't quite understand.

"I figured you wouldn't." Seeing as no one was around, Ye Qinghuan leaned closer to Prince Jing and whispered, "It's said that yao are powerful and can confuse the heart. If you meet one, they will suck away your essence. It's written in many novels."

Prince Jing considered this. He had never read a novel, because he thought they were rather pointless. But listening to how Ye-shizi was describing them now, perhaps he'd been too shallow.

Ye Qinghuan said, "If you want to know, I'll give you some another day! You can read the stories, but you can't dabble in yao."

Prince Jing frowned. *Why not? Do yao kill people?*

Ye Qinghuan thought carefully back to the stories he used to read—the yao in those books all tricked scholars into marrying them, sucked away their essence until all that was left was a bag of bones, and were ultimately dealt with by passing monks and Taoist priests.

Ye Qinghuan vaguely said, "They probably wouldn't kill you, but they'll make you wish you were dead."

Prince Jing was suddenly curious. If they weren't going to kill him, how would they make him wish he were dead?

Ye Qinghuan was incredibly stressed. Why did he and Prince Jing have to talk about yao? Was it a good thing to get involved with them? And why did Prince Jing actually seem interested?

Prince Jing seriously wrote: *How exactly do they suck away this "essence"?*

Ye Qinghuan stared at the note. He had just wanted a bed to sleep in. He had no answer to this, so he made the executive decision to kick himself out of Jingtai Hall instead.

"I'll bring some books for you tomorrow!"

Faced with Ye-shizi's quick escape, Prince Jing was still left with many questions, and much that he wanted to know. It seemed that despite being the one who'd accidentally enlightened him, Ye Qinghuan could not explain.

Wang Xi returned to ask him, "Your Highness, should we return to the manor?" The reason they'd come to the palace was to help the Duke of Cheng'en's son out. Since Ye-shizi was fine now, Wang Xi thought his master might want to return to his own residence.

Prince Jing nodded. He had to return as quickly as possible—there were a lot of eyes in the palace, so it wasn't a good place to have a carp spirit.

Wang Xi thus ordered servants to pack Prince Jing's things up, but there really wasn't much. The main thing was their little Master Fish, and this time, Ye-shizi's Xiongfeng as well.

Prince Jing ordered: Return Xiongfeng to Cheng'en Manor. As for Xiaoyu...

Wang Xi had already put the small carp into the crystal bottle and brought it to Prince Jing, just as Prince Jing preferred it.

Li Yu was extremely happy. He had a great night's sleep and was feeling awake and refreshed. He thought he'd heard Ye-shizi's voice that night. Did this mean the second prince's plot to frame Ye Qinghuan was successfully thwarted? He hadn't received a completion prompt from the system yet, but he couldn't think of anything else he had to do.

Prince Jing hesitated for a moment but didn't take the crystal bottle. Finding out that Xiaoyu was a carp spirit was one thing; figuring out how to deal with him was another. It felt a little weird for him to tease his fish the way he used to, but the thought of abandoning his fish or sending him away...

Prince Jing's expression cooled, and he took the crystal bottle from Wang Xi. He planned to observe Xiaoyu for a while after they returned to his manor—he'd been looking for the young man, who ended up being Xiaoyu, for a long time, but Xiaoyu had always tried to wipe away any clues that would lead to him. That meant Xiaoyu didn't want him to know his true identity.

If Xiaoyu didn't want him to know, he would just observe and wait. He still didn't know why Xiaoyu had come to him or what he planned to do in the future; he could wait to show his cards until he figured those things out.

But Ye Qinghuan said yao would make him wish he were dead... Would Xiaoyu do that to him too?

Prince Jing gazed at the little carp bobbing happily around in his crystal bottle. Xiaoyu sometimes turned around and spat bubbles at him mischievously. In spite of himself, Prince Jing found himself smiling from the depths of his heart. Ye Qinghuan must have been exaggerating. He could tell that this fish wouldn't harm him. He wouldn't have so easily accepted the fact that Xiaoyu was a carp spirit otherwise.

Li Yu spun around once inside the bottle and floated casually in the water. Ever since they started using the crystal bottle, he didn't have to worry about being stuck in one place, and he could even bask in the sun every now and then. Prince Jing always had a firm grasp on the crystal bottle, and when it swayed on occasion, it felt quite nice. Li Yu was drifting nicely with the motion of the water when a scale fell off him. At first, he thought his eyes were deceiving him, so he shook his head—but a scale had actually fallen off. He only realized recently that he'd been losing scales a lot over the past few days.

Perhaps he used his brain too much, or he'd been shocked? He wasn't really a proper fish, so he didn't know why his scales were falling off. He'd whined about the idea of losing his scales before, but he hadn't been serious. Now they were actually falling off! He didn't feel anything when he lost them or anything, and it was fine if it just happened once or twice—but would he lose all his scales if this kept going on?

If a person lost too much hair, they turned bald. Would a fish become a bald fish? But he wasn't even that old. Li Yu couldn't imagine what life would be like without his scales, and he didn't know if he could put them back on.

He anxiously picked up a scale. There was a pudgy, tender sort of... Li Yu poked at the spot where the scale just fell off. It seemed like it was his flesh. Li Yu pressed the scale into the flesh, and the neighboring scale also fell off.

...Ah! Sob! Was he suffering from descaling?!

Walking alongside them, Wang Xi saw the fish picking up his scale and almost laughed out loud. Prince Jing glanced at him, and Wang Xi immediately turned away as if he hadn't seen anything. However, Prince Jing also saw the scales fall off his fish and thought back to the ones he saw on the cloth. It did seem pretty severe. Even though he was a carp spirit, it made him seem quite pitiful.

Prince Jing frowned and gestured to Wang Xi: *Have the imperial physician come by and take a look at Xiaoyu.*

Wang-gonggong felt like with this trip into the palace, His Highness had changed from simply liking his fish to liking his fish an unusual amount. Even the "doctor" he requested had gone from a mere servant to an imperial physician.

# Fishy Suck

WANG XI WASN'T SURE if the imperial physician could cure Master Fish Xiaoyu's illness, but he couldn't go against Prince Jing's orders. As expected of a man who cared for His Highness Prince Jing the most, Wang-gonggong asked around and summoned an imperial physician who also had a fish at home. That was probably good enough.

Wang-gonggong brought the imperial physician to Prince Jing's residence. This imperial physician, who had the surname Xu, had dealt with many strange and mysterious diseases, so when he found out that Prince Jing had summoned him to look at his pet fish, he remained calm and unfazed.

To make it easier for Imperial Physician Xu, Prince Jing placed his fish in a shallow, petal-shaped tea bowl so that he could be examined more easily. Just now, Li Yu's fishy instincts had taken over as he fluttered a few times in the tea bowl, and he'd lost two more scales. He didn't dare move around too much anymore and gazed pitifully at Imperial Physician Xu with wet eyes. This physician should be able to cure him and prevent him from turning into a bald fish, right?

Without his gaze ever leaving the fish, Prince Jing coughed lightly and turned the teacup around, so Xiaoyu's face was pointed at him. He asked Imperial Physician Xu to look at the spine, and there were indeed some lost scales on Li Yu's spine as well.

The imperial physician looked over the fish carefully, then examined the teacup before coming to a rough idea of what was going on. He stepped forward and said, "Prince Jing, from what I know, most fish's scales grow along with them, so they don't shed or change the scales. There could only be two reasons for the scale loss: either some external reason or an illness."

When the little carp heard "illness," he trembled.

Prince Jing knew his own fish well, so he immediately looked at Wang Xi, who said, "If you need any medicine, please don't hesitate to let His Highness know. If we don't have it at the manor, then we'll find a way to get it." Wang Xi glanced at Prince Jing uncertainly, and Prince Jing nodded, so Wang Xi added: "But you must not hurt Master Fish Xiaoyu."

Imperial Physician Xu slightly smiled. "I understand. But please allow me to be frank: Your Highness's fish seems very healthy, so it shouldn't be an illness. Perhaps he accidentally bumped into something when he was swimming. It should get better after a few days of rest."

*Ah,* thought Li Yu. *What a beautiful misunderstanding.* Prince Jing put him in a tea bowl for the consultation, so Imperial Physician Xu thought he was normally kept in the tea bowl, and that bumps were inevitable since he only had a narrow space to swim in. The physician himself raised a group of koi at home, who often bumped into each other when competing for food and lost scales that way, so he naturally thought Xiaoyu was losing scales for the same reason.

But Li Yu himself was sure that wasn't it. The fish tank Prince Jing prepared for him was definitely large enough for him to swim around in, and he rarely bumped into anything. If his scales were falling off because of the impact from his jumping, they would fall from a specific area, but right now, it seemed like he was losing scales everywhere, no matter what he did—even if he just blew bubbles. Li Yu didn't really dare to move anymore. He was just thankful the scales didn't fall off in large patches, or his fish body would really be too ugly.

So Imperial Physician Xu's suggestion probably wasn't the real reason for his scale loss. Li Yu was a little disappointed, but it wasn't bad news as long as he wasn't sick. He comforted himself: perhaps a transmigrated fish body was different from a normal fish body. Even a dog as large as Xiongfeng would shed hair even though he was fine, so it was probably normal for him to lose some fish scales, right?

But would his tyrant master dislike him because of this? Probably not, right? He was just a black carp that was meant to be food. He got to where he was today not through his beauty but through his cuteness—would he not be cute anymore if he lost his scales?

Li Yu spent so long trying to comfort himself that he ended up almost completely inside his own head.

Prince Jing was influenced by the imperial physician's words— that keeping a fish in a tank that was too small would cause it to lose its scales. Since Prince Jing knew that Xiaoyu was a carp spirit now, it did seem wrong to keep him in an ordinary fish tank. Once he'd sent Imperial Physician Xu away, Prince Jing came to an immediate decision.

He gestured at Wang Xi to come closer. Since his orders were a little more complicated this time, Prince Jing wrote them out, and Wang Xi's eyebrows almost flew away from his face as he watched the brush move across the paper.

After Prince Jing finished writing, Wang Xi knelt and said in a trembling voice, "Your Highness, this..."

Was this okay?!

Wang Xi had guessed that Prince Jing wanted to switch out the fish tank for Master Fish, but he never imagined it'd be that kind of fish tank!

Prince Jing blew on the ink once he was finished writing and signaled with his eyes. *Go on. Hurry.*

Wang Xi had been with Prince Jing for many years, so he knew that once his master made a decision, nothing could change his mind. Wang-gonggong didn't bother saying anything else and scurried away to carry out his orders.

Li Yu watched him leave in confusion. What had Prince Jing just done?

After Prince Jing was finished with those arrangements, he habitually went to rub his poor fish's back, but he remembered at the last minute that Xiaoyu was losing scales. If he touched him, more scales might fall off. He had to listen to Imperial Physician Xu and take care of his fish, even more so because this was actually a carp spirit...

Prince Jing, who'd decided without blinking to commission a new fish tank for Xiaoyu, now hesitated. That same fish he always touched was actually a boy... He couldn't bring himself to do it anymore.

The little carp saw him reaching out with a finger and swam over and waited for Prince Jing to touch him, but Prince Jing stopped at the last moment.

*No way!* Did Prince Jing not like him anymore? Li Yu wrapped his tail around Prince Jing's finger, seeking a sense of security.

Prince Jing normally loved this kind of touch, but now he was starting to have wild thoughts. If this was a tail on the fish...what was it on the carp spirit? The fish head must be a person's face, so the tail should be his feet.

A pair of delicate ankles flashed across Prince Jing's mind. For a moment, he just sat there.

Then he stood up so abruptly that he startled the little carp, who swam aside and stared at him, confused. Prince Jing realized that he was a little too worked up. Afraid that Xiaoyu would realize he was acting strange, he stuck out his finger as usual.

Li Yu swam forward expectantly, but Prince Jing didn't touch his back or tail—instead, he tapped his head gently.

*This again?* thought Li Yu. *What exactly does it mean?*

Though Prince Jing had ordered the production of the new fish tank to be carried out as fast as possible, it would still take a few days for it to be finished, so he had to put Xiaoyu back in the crystal fish tank for now. He gave him the best food during this time. For his part, Li Yu was still losing his scales, and he no longer dared to move around too much. How was he going to finish his missions if he couldn't even move? He was very worried.

Right when the little carp thought he was truly going to turn into a bald fish, Qianqing Palace issued several imperial decrees. The emperor took away all of the second prince's positions and gave him the title of the Marquis of An; the Marquis of An was not given another residence and was instead confined to the residence he was currently in. Noble Consort Qiu was demoted to concubine, and as her house arrest from last time had not yet ended, it was set to continue. The emperor issued both punishments and rewards—the House of Cheng'en was promoted to a higher class, and Ye Qinghuan himself was promoted to a higher title as well. The emperor allowed the House of Cheng'en and King Jinjue to choose the date for the wedding themselves and built a residence for the Princess of Jinjue in the imperial city.

The changes he made showed that the emperor was quite determined.

The emperor had been thinking about how to punish the second prince for trying to frame Ye Qinghuan. When Noble Consort Qiu of Zhongcui Palace had heard the news, she knelt in front of Qianqing Palace and wouldn't get up; in the end, the servants had to carry her back. The emperor had refused to see her and instead went to Changchun Palace alone, where he remained seated in front of Empress Xiaohui's memorial tablet for the entire night.

The female corpse in Yanyu Pavilion turned out to be a death row prisoner from Heavenly Prison who had passed away from illness several days ago. The emperor knew that Ye-shizi had plotted against the second prince, but Ye Qinghuan had clearly been acting out of self-defense. In the end, the second prince had been the one who started it, and the one who acted like an idiot. If he had succeeded, how would he have explained it to King Jinjue? Had the second prince never considered the big picture, or did he think the big picture could be sacrificed for the sake of his own goals?

The emperor didn't mind if his sons used a few underhanded measures here and there, but the second prince had taken it too far. Just because of his future crown prince status, he'd impulsively lashed out at anyone he felt like. Even if he did ascend to the throne in the future, there was no way he would be able to command the people's respect.

The candidate he had previously favored was clearly not suited for the throne. The favor he'd showed the second prince had gone not only to Noble Consort Qiu's head but the second prince's as well. If he was unable to handle a little attention now, what would happen in the future?

Luckily, the emperor had told very few people about this possible choice and hadn't officially announced the second prince's candidacy for the crown prince position. As things currently stood, calamity had been averted, which meant this was the best outcome. If the second prince did not receive the punishment he deserved, however, it would forever disappoint the House of Cheng'en, Prince Jing, and most of all Empress Xiaohui.

After the emperor collected his thoughts, he issued another decree: Nobody was allowed to voice their opinion on this matter. These decrees nearly caused the court and back palace to explode.

There was an unwritten rule in this dynasty that if a prince was given a title early, he had no chance at the throne. Prince Jing was an example. Everyone knew that the emperor had given Prince Jing his title to appease him, as his di son, but the second prince's situation was different. The second prince was not given the title of prince but of marquis, and the emperor had decreed it in a hurry without discussing it with the Ministry of Rites. It was obvious that the second prince had completely lost favor.

When she received the decree, the former Noble Consort Qiu—the current Concubine Qiu—fainted on the spot. Hope started to blaze in the other concubines who had sons, especially the third prince's mother, Concubine Qian. If the second prince wasn't a viable option, then the next in line would naturally be her son, the third prince. Of the court councilors who had previously supported the second prince, believing that their high position and great wealth was guaranteed, not many would continue to help him. Most had begun making other plans.

In comparison to the palace, where some were happy and some were worried, Cheng'en Manor outside the palace was covered with festive decorations, auspicious and peaceful. Ye Qinghuan and the Princess of Jinjue had already exchanged their gengtie,[9] and the

---

9    Gengtie (庚帖) cards exchanged for betrothal, with information on it such as one's name, birth chart, ancestry, etc.

Duke of Cheng'en and King Jinjue were choosing a date for them already. As for Prince Jing—though he wasn't mentioned in the imperial decree, he was also rewarded. The emperor ordered Head Eunuch Luo to bring a set of suet jade boxes for Prince Jing to put fish food in. The emperor had seen the bamboo box Prince Jing was using at the imperial banquet and felt a bit sorry for him.

The emperor had rewarded Prince Jing, but Li Yu was happiest of all. The new fish food boxes were engraved with a fish design, and the emperor seemed to have had them made especially for him. He'd heard that suet jade was extremely valuable, so using it to make fish food boxes made Li Yu feel like his worth had doubled...

As soon as the imperial decree was issued, there was something else he could be happy about too. The "Impenetrable Defense" side quest was updated! The emperor's edicts laid out both punishments and rewards, and Li Yu realized that the side quest could only be considered complete once good was rewarded and evil was punished.

His scales falling off was one matter, but he still had to collect his mission rewards, so Li Yu entered the system. He'd never been too invested in the rewards for this side mission, but after patiently listening to the fish-scamming system introduce the rewards one by one, Li Yu's jaw nearly fell to the ground. The reward for the "Impenetrable Defense" side quest was a completely new type of fish scales. There were five colors to choose from—gold, red, green, silver, and purple.

Had he been losing scales recently because the mission would reward him with new ones?

*<You're overthinking, user,>* the system informed him immediately. *<Your scales keep falling off because normal fish scales can no longer handle the intensity of your behavior.>*

...Oh.

Since the fish-scamming system wasn't trying to hide anything, Li Yu had to believe he really had messed around too much, and his scales couldn't stand it anymore.

*But I haven't really been moving around that vigorously,* Li Yu thought, without any self-awareness, forgetting that he was constantly jumping up and down across Prince Jing's room.

The system informed him that the strength of the new fish scales would be better, and once they'd been replaced, they would not fall off. Li Yu was extremely happy to collect this reward, but his new scales were so different from his original scales. Only koi had flashy colors like that—if he had them, did it mean that he could actually become a koi fish?

H-h-he was just a little curious. He definitely wanted to turn into a human at the end!

The system only said: *‹There's no need to worry, user.›*

Li Yu became more alert. Usually, when the system told him not to worry, he was about to get scammed. He was used to it by now, but he was afraid that his tyrant master, who'd been a little colder to him recently, would suddenly grow suspicious of him. But since his original scales kept falling off, he might as well use the new ones that had just arrived at his doorstep.

*‹User, please choose a color and confirm your reward.›*

*Such bright colors—they're all about the same anyway, right?* Against his conscience, Li Yu picked the color closest to that of a koi: gold.

The system forced him out after he confirmed his selection.

How rude!

After returning to reality, Li Yu glanced at his body, but his scales were still as gray as before. Did the reward not take effect yet? When he raised his tail, a row of scales fell right off. Li Yu was incredibly embarrassed. *Since they're falling off like this, will my tail be bald first?*

He glanced at his tail and suddenly froze. There was a touch of gold peeking out of his originally gray-black fish tail.

Wang Xi brought some people over to change the water for Li Yu. He was chasing his tail in circles when he heard Wang-gonggong gasp.

"Your Highness! Your Highness! Look!" Wang-gonggong cried out in surprise.

Prince Jing rushed over at once. Li Yu, with his gray-black tail and its gleam of gold, swam around pretentiously.

"Your Highness, this servant has only seen koi with this shade of gold before..." Wang Xi had always thought that Master Fish was smart, definitely not an ordinary fish, but could it be that he was actually a koi carp? Even though his body wasn't really shaped like one?

Prince Jing himself had never seen such a thing before either. When he took a closer look at Xiaoyu's tail, he saw that there were new fish scales growing from where the old ones had fallen off, and some of those new fish scales were golden.

Prince Jing had already determined that Xiaoyu was a carp spirit. Since he could turn into a human, turning into a koi was nothing. After all, koi were a kind of fish. Prince Jing immediately accepted this new development and calmly ordered Wang Xi to take meticulous care of Xiaoyu.

Li Yu was surprised and happy that Prince Jing didn't seem to suspect anything. Was this what the system meant when it told him not to worry? It was rare for the fish-scamming system to do anything good.

With that, his new scales started to come in to replace the old. Imperial Physician Xu had said most fish didn't shed scales, but it wasn't an absolute statement, so Xiaoyu could just be a type of fish that did shed.

When he saw other scales falling off, Li Yu's entire mentality changed. They were probably falling because he was doing away with the old fish scales to make space for the new ones. He was excited to see what he would look like after all his new fish scales came in.

A day later, he had a whole new look. His overall body was still black, but there were many golden scales on his stomach and his tail. The system must have elected to just add to his original body color, he thought. Though it wasn't the whole-body gold refurbishing Li Yu had imagined, the black-gold coloring still looked quite distinguished. In any case, when the main quest "Tyrant's Priceless Pet Fish" was complete, there was a side quest called "Turn into a Koi" still waiting for him. Perhaps he'd still be able to change when that came around.

The little carp who was trying his hardest to turn into a koi hid in the leaf blanket and giggled to himself. He'd practically had a makeover. Since Prince Jing accepted it, the servants wouldn't gossip about it amongst themselves, and Li Yu was even less worried about the rest of the people in Prince Jing's residence. He was only growing golden scales on inconspicuous parts of his body like his tail and stomach, and most people didn't have the chance to approach his tank, so they may not have even seen his original appearance.

What he didn't know was that when Prince Jing saw his new coloring, in order to prevent gossip, he ordered Wang Xi to make everyone in the residence recount the same story: that Xiaoyu was descended from koi. He managed to cover up the whole situation for Xiaoyu impeccably.

Now that he completed the side quest, Li Yu started thinking about his main quest again. After his scales stopped changing, he didn't lose any more, but his tyrant master still treated him a little coldly. He wasn't keeping his distance; Li Yu could sense that his master still loved to spoil him. He would pat his head, watch him swim around, and often just silently gazed at him. But he wouldn't rub him anymore like he did in the past, even though Li Yu looked so much more distinguished now!

Did a distinguished fish not deserve to be rubbed?!

Yesterday, some books had been sent over from Cheng'en Manor, for some reason. Prince Jing seemed to be extremely interested in these books, immersing himself in them while he was in the room, and rubbed Li Yu even less. If Prince Jing didn't rub him, how was a fish to finish his missions...?

The little carp jumped out of the crystal fish tank. Ever since his scales had been replaced, he found that he could use his tail more smoothly. He jumped a few times, landing in the petal-shaped tea bowl on Prince Jing's desk and splashing a couple drops of water onto the books that were spread out there.

Aaahhh! He didn't mean to!

Li Yu only just remembered that when Prince Jing read books with him, Wang-gonggong would first put an absorbent towel on the table and Prince Jing would keep the tea bowl away from the book. But this time, since the fish had jumped out on his own, no protective measures had been put in place and he accidentally got Prince Jing's book wet.

Li Yu was agonizing over how he was going to salvage the situation when Prince Jing took out a dry towel and quickly wiped off the water droplets on the book. His dark eyes glanced at the little carp flapping around in the teacup. Li Yu immediately stopped moving, but the prince didn't chase him away. Prince Jing thought that Xiaoyu might want to read the book with him. Moving the tea bowl closer would be too obvious, so instead he imperceptibly moved the book toward his fish.

The little carp carefully raised his head. Prince Jing was so concentrated. What kind of book was he reading? His tyrant master usually liked reading books on the art of war or travel books. Last time, Li Yu had fallen asleep while reading a book on the art of war.

The little carp glanced at the black title written clearly on the white cover. This time, the book was... *The Tale of the White Snake*.

Huh. Li Yu recalled that his original world had *The Legend of the White Snake*, so what was *The Tale of the White Snake*? Li Yu started reading the book, curious. The general premise seemed to be that a white snake spirit fell in love with a passing scholar and transformed into a human so she could marry him. Li Yu guessed that this was a folk tale. When he started reading, the white snake and the scholar had already exchanged wedding vows; the white snake was confessing her true identity as a snake spirit, and she softly said to the scholar, "Husband, us yao all need to absorb essence..."

Li Yu was perplexed. It was difficult for him to read ancient books, but Prince Jing could read ten lines at a glance. Before Li Yu could read how the snake absorbed essence, Prince Jing had already hurriedly turned the page.

On the second night, the white snake spirit once again said gently, "Beloved, us yao need to absorb essence today as well." Prince Jing flipped the page quickly again—he flipped through over ten pages like this. Li Yu estimated that the white snake spirit had probably absorbed the scholar's essence at least ten times already, but he'd still read absolutely nothing.

In the end, with one more page in the book, a great monk came and denounced the white snake for disobeying the way of heaven.

He placed the white snake in a golden alms bowl, and the scholar came to his senses to become a monk alongside this passing monk.

*Huh, this is quite similar to* The Legend of the White Snake, *Li Yu thought. But why was there so much stuff about absorbing essence and pair cultivation instead of the other plotlines?*

Prince Jing closed the book. For some reason, Li Yu felt like his tyrant master's ears had turned a bit red.

Perhaps Prince Jing didn't like the ending of this book, because he immediately started another one. Li Yu glanced at the title—it was called *The Legend of the Fox Spirit*. It was probably about a fox spirit that fell in love with a scholar and asked to pair cultivate when she went to his room in the middle of the night.

The fox spirit was more powerful than the white snake spirit. The first night alone was a full twenty pages—Li Yu secretly counted as Prince Jing flipped the page twenty times. He only realized afterward what kind of book it was. It must be an ancient story about lovemaking. Li Yu was incredibly amused to learn that Prince Jing actually read that kind of thing! No wonder he flipped the pages so quickly—was his tyrant master shy?

But it wasn't a huge deal to read this stuff. When Li Yu was still a human, he had just turned eighteen. Who hadn't read a bit of porn at that age? Prince Jing was a young man in his twenties, so in ancient times, he should have had a courtyard full of children running around by now. What was wrong with seeing a bit of action in a book?

Li Yu tried to get closer. Master, I also want to see the indescribable things happening between a yao and a scholar!

Prince Jing had just closed the second book when he saw his carp spirit reaching his head out, trying to get closer. Prince Jing couldn't help but smile and flicked his fish's head lightly. The little carp fell back into the teacup with a splash.

Night had fallen. Li Yu wanted to secretly complete his main mission on this dark and windy night.

The main mission, "Tyrant's Priceless Pet Fish," was almost complete. All he had to do was rub his fish lips against Prince Jing's. He had put it off recently because he was either trying to save people or losing his scales, but now it was time to finish up the main quest.

Li Yu waited quietly in his crystal fish tank for Prince Jing to fall asleep. He waited a long time after there was no more movement from the sleeping prince, and then he jumped out of the fish tank toward Prince Jing's bed. He was already quite familiar with this route.

He arrived at Prince Jing's pillow without a problem. He remembered that Prince Jing didn't blame him for getting his book wet during the day, so he was for some reason equally confident that Prince Jing wouldn't blame him if he got the pillow wet this time...

The little carp jumped onto the jade pillow, aimed toward Prince Jing's face, and stuck his fishy lips out. He would never do this in human form because it was too shameless! But he could afford to be shameless when he was a fish.

Prince Jing was a little sleepy at first, but after he realized that Xiaoyu was a carp spirit, and especially after he started losing his scales, it was hard for him not to pay attention to the fish in the tank at night, aware of all his movements. He'd gotten into the habit of getting up to take a look at his fish after it fell asleep, and even though the scale loss issue had been resolved, this habit hadn't changed yet. When the little carp jumped onto the bed, Prince Jing was just about to fall asleep—but he suddenly heard a few flaps of a tail, quite clearly. Prince Jing was wide awake at once, and he continued to listen. What was Xiaoyu going to do? Would he turn into a human?

The sound of the fish tail was getting closer and closer, and Prince Jing was certain that Xiaoyu was coming toward his bed. When the fish jumped onto his jade pillow, a tiny droplet of water landed on Prince Jing's face, but, in his excitement, the little carp failed to notice. Prince Jing didn't move either. He'd been observing the carp spirit in secret for the past couple of days, but he hadn't learned anything yet. If he "woke up" right now, Xiaoyu would definitely be embarrassed. If he continued to pretend to sleep, he might be able to figure out the fish's goal.

He could feel that the other party, surrounded by an aura of water, was getting closer...

*Mwah.*

Something sharp touched his lips for just a moment. Prince Jing's breath caught in his throat as he realized what it was.

The lively, sweet scenes from the books he'd read about yao and scholars, especially the parts he'd flipped through quickly, popped into his mind one after another. The white snake spirit and the scholar, the fox spirit and the scholar, all became this vexing carp spirit and himself—

It wasn't hot in the room, but Prince Jing was covered with a thin layer of sweat. His body was stiff, and his chest was burning. He didn't know what he was doing, lying here half-helpless and half-expectant, waiting for the carp spirit to go further. But instead, the carp spirit blithely turned around and jumped back to his fish tank.

...What?

Was it so easy for the carp spirit to "suck essence" that it was over already?

# Drunk Fishy

HAVING SUCCESSFULLY STOLEN a lip rub from his tyrant master, Li Yu felt like there were fireworks going off inside his heart. He'd kissed his master's lips before, but perhaps because he was concentrating so hard this time, he felt like he'd gotten a bit lost in it. He jumped back into the fish tank in a silly, elated daze.

...Only to find that the last step of "Tyrant's Priceless Pet Fish," the "Intimate Contact with the Tyrant" mission that he was expecting to be done with, wasn't marked as complete.

Li Yu was stressed. Had he been wrong from the beginning? Did pressing his lips against Prince Jing's not count toward the mission?

At last, the system couldn't take it anymore and spoke up to give him a hint: *‹User, you've performed this action before. Repeated actions are not valid.›*

...Oh. So, since they'd touched lips before, it didn't count if they touched lips again.

Li Yu was very angry. He had done it by accident before, but this time he'd been really focused and deliberate. He meant it this time! If repeats weren't allowed, why didn't the system tell him so sooner?

*‹There was no repetition before you made your move, user,›* the system told him.

Li Yu couldn't be more disappointed. <...*Fine. You're the fish-scamming system, of course you're right.*>

He thought the last quest would go nice and smoothly—that he'd be able to collect his reward immediately and get right into the koi side quest. Instead, the fish-scamming system had given him an obstacle. If kissing didn't work, how else was he supposed to have intimate contact with the tyrant master?

<*User, please think for yourself.*>

...This system was way too annoying. He was so close too.

Li Yu was so pissed off at the fish-scamming system that he blew bubbles all night. When he woke up in the morning, his eyes felt a little sore. He saw that Prince Jing had dark circles as well, which meant he didn't sleep well either.

Ah...he and his master were in the same boat.

When a servant came to make the bed, he found the water stains that the little carp left behind on the pillow and that the mattress was slightly wet. The servant promptly reported it to Prince Jing, who just waved his hand at him and had the servant change the bed.

Li Yu had been confident about jumping onto the bed before he attempted his mission, but now he was even more so. Prince Jing had to be aware that he'd hopped over there at night, but he wasn't angry. This meant he could continue to visit at night from now on, right?

Unfortunately, he still hadn't figured out what entailed actual, proper "intimate contact," even after thinking all night. It wasn't that he couldn't think of anything at all, it was that there were so many places a fish could rub up against. With each option more shameless than the last, Li Yu had to pick one that was not too shameful but had also never been done before, which was the hard part.

For example, Prince Jing's face. Li Yu had rubbed against his face a lot in his time as a fish, so that definitely wouldn't count.

Li Yu was still thinking hard about areas other than the face when Wang-gonggong came to report that the Duke of Cheng'en's son had arrived. Prince Jing felt it was unfair to keep the carp spirit inside all the time, and besides, Ye-shizi was already familiar with Xiaoyu, so he decided to take his fish to see Ye-shizi and get some air.

Ye Qinghuan was still delighted with his recent successes. His marriage to the Princess of Jinjue had been set for after the second month, and of course, considering his relationship with the House of Cheng'en, Prince Jing was obviously invited. Ye-shizi was quite sincere—he came to give Prince Jing the invitation himself and even brought two jars of wine with him.

"Grandfather brewed these two jars of green plum wine himself. He insisted that I bring them to you."

Ye-shizi put the wine down. Li Yu recalled then that the book had mentioned the green plum wine from Cheng'en Manor before.

Ye Qinghuan's grandfather, the former Duke of Cheng'en and Prince Jing's grandfather, had once brewed a jar of green plum wine for each of his children. These jars of wine had been buried, to be dug up when his children were married. This was quite the elegant ritual. When Prince Jing's mother entered the palace, she did so as an empress, so her wedding was not held at home, and the wine stayed buried in the ground. In the past, he hadn't had the opportunity to give it to her, but after Empress Xiaohui passed away, he'd never be able to...

The former Duke of Cheng'en had now brewed wine for his grandchildren, so he asked Ye Qinghuan to take his own jar as well as Empress Xiaohui's. The former Duke of Cheng'en had been in poor health for some years now and usually stayed in Cheng'en Manor to rest and recuperate instead of venturing out. He quite missed his grandson, Prince Jing, who lived alone in his own residence.

As a prince, Prince Jing could understand things without needing to hear them said. Prince Jing understood why Ye Qinghuan had brought over two jars of wine. There was a faint glimmer in his eyes as he lightly stroked the jar that belonged to his mother.

He accepted the wedding invitation too and glanced at it. This time, instead of having someone kick his cousin out, he asked Wang Xi to grab Ye-shizi a seat.

Ye Qinghuan was overwhelmed with gratitude and sat down quickly. Ye-shizi recalled what he'd seen and heard on his way here, and he brought it up casually, without hesitation: "Oh, right. I saw a lot of workers around your residence on the way over. Are you remodeling?"

Ye Qinghuan had seen several areas of Prince Jing's residence surrounded by fences, and from the inside, there was the constant sound of digging. He and Prince Jing had known each other for many years, and he knew how indifferent he could be sometimes. Prince Jing had never put any thought into the layout and decor of his residence, and he hadn't changed anything since he moved in. This was the first time any sort of major construction project had taken place.

Was Prince Jing jealous that he was getting married and wanted to join in on the fun? If that really was the case, Ye Qinghuan was quite happy with himself.

Prince Jing shot a sideways glance at Wang Xi, who stepped forward and ruthlessly shattered Ye-shizi's daydream. "My lord, His Highness is building...a new fish tank for Master Fish."

What?? So it was because of the fish, not him? Ye-shizi had already struggled to believe his dog could lose to a fish, but now it turned out that he himself had lost to a fish as well. He couldn't help complaining, "Tianchi, isn't that too much?"

Li Yu was in his coral fish tank next to Prince Jing, still thinking about intimate contact, when he heard there was going to be a new fish tank. His tail started to flick in excitement, and as he flicked his tail, he contemplated Ye-shizi's words. He'd been holed up in Prince Jing's room lately—with him losing his scales, the prince hadn't wanted to take him out and about. Prince Jing was always keeping an eye on him, so he had almost no chance to transform into a human and was completely unaware that a new fish tank was being constructed at Prince Jing's residence.

If it'd been a new courtyard he was building, Li Yu wouldn't have been able to tell who it was for. But since it was a new fish tank, it must be for him. Prince Jing only had one fish!

Sob sob... Even though the tyrant master didn't pet him anymore, he still treated him so well...

Li Yu squeezed out a bit of water from his fish eyes and swam to Prince Jing's hand, using his mouth to bump against Prince Jing's finger.

Prince Jing was half-listening to Ye Qinghuan complain when, out of the corner of his eye, he glimpsed a dark shadow swimming over in the fish tank. The familiar touch on his fingertips made him put his hand out without even thinking about it. Before he realized what he was doing, Prince Jing had already grabbed the fish tail and tickled it. Without noticing, he actually...to the carp spirit...

Prince Jing immediately regretted it. It was one thing to have done it in the past, when he didn't know any better, but now that he did know, he shouldn't have touched the fish so casually.

But the fish was swimming in circles in his palm. Prince Jing had stopped moving, but the fish's silky tail was still gliding between his fingers. He'd been raising Xiaoyu for so long, he knew that this meant he was happy. It seemed like Xiaoyu...didn't mind it? In fact, he seemed to like it quite a lot. Slowly, a smile appeared on Prince Jing's face. Did that mean Xiaoyu had the same hopes that he did, that they could just continue like this?

He'd been feeling melancholy over the thought of never having met his mother, but now that sadness was swept away by Xiaoyu's tail. Prince Jing didn't take his hand back anymore.

Li Yu was thrilled. *Aaaahhh! He's petting me again!*

Ye-shizi was about to get married, so he was much bolder than before. Feeling like he was being neglected, he complained directly to the prince, but when he turned around, Prince Jing was focused on petting his fish and hadn't heard anything he said.

... Wasn't that enough? He'd lost completely, okay?

Ye-shizi sidled up to Prince Jing. "Tianchi, can I touch Xiaoyu too?" he said with a smile. "In exchange, you can pet Xiongfeng whenever you want." Even though Ye-shizi was always comparing Xiongfeng and the carp, he'd wanted to play with the slippery little carp for a while now.

Prince Jing narrowed his eyes, displeased. *Who wants to touch your dog?!* Wang Xi, who was standing in wait at the side, understood the situation and quickly ordered someone to keep Ye-shizi at a distance.

"My lord, how could you forget again?" he said, exasperated. "His Highness doesn't like it when people bargain with him."

Ye Qinghuan was surprised. "That was considered bargaining?"

"How is it not? He likes it even less when other people touch his fish."

*The only reason he didn't kick you out was because of the former Duke of Cheng'en,* Wang Xi silently thought.

Ye-shizi had no other choice but to stand pitifully in the distance, watching his older cousin touch his fish. He came to show off that he was getting married soon, but Prince Jing had turned the tables on him and now he was showing off instead!

Ye-shizi's eyes widened, though, as he noticed something extraordinary. There was gold on the belly and tail of the fish that Prince Jing was petting. It seemed different from the fish Ye-shizi had seen before. Ye-shizi stared at it for a long time, thinking that he was finally right for once. "Tianchi, did you get another fish?"

Prince Jing ignored him. Wang Xi, smiling, said, "My lord, what are you talking about? It's not a new fish—just that Master Fish has new scales."

"Fish can change scales?" Ye Qinghuan had a look of disbelief on his face. "How come I've never heard of such a thing?"

Prince Jing glanced at him mildly, and Wang Xi immediately said, "Just because my lord hasn't heard of it doesn't mean it doesn't happen. Besides, doesn't your Xiongfeng also shed his fur?"

Ye Qinghuan had to nod, since Xiongfeng did shed his fur. Every time he did, there would be piles of dog hair in Cheng'en Manor—but Xiongfeng wouldn't suddenly change the color of his fur, right?

But Prince Jing's fish was smarter than other fish, so he was probably just different, right? Ye Qinghuan blinked a couple of times and managed to convince himself. Prince Jing had no reason to lie to him. If he upset Prince Jing again, he'd probably be chased out of his manor.

"All right." Ye-shizi racked his brains, wanting to give Prince Jing a good impression, and managed, "Actually, a fish changing scales... is quite distinguished."

Prince Jing nodded coldly at Ye-shizi. Li Yu, who was enjoying his rubbing, shook his tail and thought, *Great minds think alike, Ye-shizi!*

Ye Qinghuan's hard work earned him a meal at Prince Jing's residence.

Of the two jars of green plum wine the old Duke of Cheng'en had brewed, Wang Xi had safely stored Empress Xiaohui's jar. Ye Qinghuan patted the other one. "Grandfather brewed this one for me, so let's try some together."

Prince Jing didn't say anything, of course, but Wang Xi guessed what his master was thinking and brought two glazed cups for Prince Jing and Ye Qinghuan to drink from.

The jar was opened, and the sweetness of green plums wafted out, followed by the mellow aroma of the alcohol. Wang Xi used a long-handled silver ladle to scoop out the green plums at the bottom of the jar and placed them onto a white ceramic plate. It was customary in this empire not to eat the green plums while drinking green plum wine, but there were people who liked them; Wang Xi took them out so Prince Jing and Ye-shizi could use them as they liked.

Li Yu's coral fish tank was also on the table. These days, he enjoyed the honor of dining with his tyrant master. While Wang Xi was preparing the green plum wine, Prince Jing had already given Xiaoyu a handful of red fish food and half a peach blossom pastry. Li Yu should have been satisfied with the fish food and peach blossom pastry, but when the green plum wine was opened, it was so fragrant that he could smell it from his tank. His ravenous stomach started crying out from yearning.

Li Yu held a piece of peach blossom pastry in his mouth and floated to the surface of the water, sniffing the aroma of the green plum wine. Sob, he really wanted to drink the green plum wine, but Prince Jing definitely wouldn't give wine to a fish. He could at least watch Prince Jing and Ye-shizi drink it, though, right?

After Prince Jing fed his fish, he ate the remaining half of his peach blossom pastry. Ye Qinghuan looked on enviously. It had been foolish of him in the extreme, he thought, to suggest that Prince Jing might raise another fish.

Wang Xi poured out the wine for the two of them. In the dainty, elegant glazed cups, the green plum wine looked like bejeweled nectar. Prince Jing looked down at the clear wine, his slender fingers fiddling with the cup lazily. He raised his cup and took a light sip; across the table from him, Ye Qinghuan downed his cup in one gulp.

"Good wine." Ye Qinghuan wiped his lips and smiled. He didn't need Wang Xi to pour more wine for him; he did it himself.

Secretly watching them drink, Li Yu thought, *Master is so handsome, so good-looking... Ye-shizi really gulped that down!* The scent of the green plum wine seemed to linger, tempting the fish immensely. Ye-shizi's unrestrained enjoyment made him want to drink it even more!

With the way Ye Qinghuan was drinking, Prince Jing had only finished one cup by the time Ye Qinghuan was downing his third. After the third cup, Ye-shizi's ears were a little red and his eyes unfocused.

"Tianchi," Ye Qinghuan said with a hiccup and a smile, "Grandfather brewed one for you too, so in the future..."

Prince Jing paused, put down his glass, and ordered Wang Xi to bring Ye Qinghuan some soup to sober up.

Some people would just fall asleep when drunk, while others would blab about anything. Ye-shizi was in the middle—when he was drunk, he liked to gather people and talk a lot of nonsense. Prince Jing noticed that Ye Qinghuan was about to keel over, so he had no choice but to reach out to steady him—only for Ye Qinghuan to grab on to him and start telling him about all the times his parents beat him for being a naughty child in the Cheng'en household.

Prince Jing listened in a daze for a long time.

Li Yu knew that Prince Jing might have thought of his own childhood, and was afraid that he might be sad, so he splashed the water a couple of times. Prince Jing heard the noise and turned around to look at him. His expression was reassuring.

It took Wang Xi a lot of effort to hold Ye-shizi down and make him drink the soup. Ye-shizi was still blabbering on, and then, out of nowhere, he said that he didn't want to get married anymore.

Li Yu was surprised. Even as lively and bold a person as Ye-shizi could get nervous, huh? One should never judge a book by its cover.

Well, it wasn't like Li Yu couldn't understand. After all, Ye Qinghuan and the Princess of Jinjue had barely exchanged any words with each other, yet they were expected to get married and live together for the rest of their lives. It was normal to be a little lost. Perhaps the alcohol was an excuse for Ye-shizi to blurt out what he was too afraid to say to outsiders.

Prince Jing couldn't understand Ye-shizi's feelings, and he wasn't good at taking care of drunks, so he had Wang Xi watch over Ye Qinghuan while he went back to his room with his fish.

He'd noticed that Xiaoyu's eyes had been glued to his glazed cup the whole time and thought maybe he wanted to try some, but green plum wine shouldn't be drunk so casually. Look at how intoxicated Ye Qinghuan was... But Prince Jing was still willing to satisfy the carp spirit's desires. He thought it over and took the plate of green plums that Wang Xi had taken out. If he just let him eat some green plums, rather than actually drink the alcohol, it should be fine.

As soon as Li Yu saw that Prince Jing had brought the green plums along with him, he started flapping his tail happily. Was Prince Jing going to give him the green plums?! He must be, he must be!

When Prince Jing returned to his room, he put down the green plums first and saw his fish staring intently at them. Prince Jing smiled and put his fish down too.

At that moment, Wang Xi caught up to them and said, "Your Highness, Ye-shizi doesn't seem to be feeling well... Do you want to take a look at him?"

In Prince Jing's residence, Wang Xi was usually the one in charge in Prince Jing's absence, but since Ye Qinghuan was the eldest son of the Duke of Cheng'en, it wasn't appropriate for Wang Xi to make too many decisions. So he'd rushed over to ask Prince Jing for directions instead. Prince Jing understood that something had happened that Wang Xi couldn't handle alone, so he decided to go back.

He was about to pat Xiaoyu's head when he realized that the carp spirit was staring so intently at the green plums that he hadn't even noticed his master was about to leave.

Prince Jing suddenly felt that the plate of green plums he brought in was somehow a nuisance.

A fish...couldn't eat green plums.

With that thought, Prince Jing suddenly remembered that he had been guarding Xiaoyu the entire time he was losing scales, for the past couple of days. Though Xiaoyu had finished changing scales now, he hadn't turned into a human since they got back from the palace. Could he only turn into a human when Prince Jing wasn't there?

At first, he was planning to mince the green plums and feed them to Xiaoyu, but he scrapped that idea. If he just left the plate of green plums there, would the carp spirit change into a human?

Prince Jing gave his fish a long, probing look before he rushed away to look after Ye-shizi.

Li Yu stayed in his fish tank for a bit, listening. After he was sure Prince Jing had left, he used his transformation skill.

Ever since he got back from the palace, he hadn't had any time to transform because Prince Jing was always watching over him. He was touched, but it wasn't very convenient. An hour, though short, was still enough for him to eat and play around.

There was nothing important to deal with right now, so he could transform into a human solely to eat the green plums and satisfy his craving.

There were a lot of green plums on the plate. He had watched Wang Xi scoop them out of the alcohol jar. Nobody would notice if he just ate one or two. It was safe!

Li Yu habitually picked a set of underclothes from the closet and put them on. He sat in front of the table and picked up a green plum. The green plum wine was amber, but the plums were still emerald green. The emerald color and sweet, fragrant scent were enough to make him drool.

Li Yu shoved the plum into his mouth and carefully bit down. The green plum was sour and sweet, and there seemed to be a lot of alcohol left in the fruit. The wine was sweet and fragrant, not too strong—he fell in love with the taste at once and immediately picked up another one.

Meanwhile, Prince Jing was learning that the soup hadn't helped Ye-shizi sober up at all. Ye-shizi was holding on to a pillar, crying and sobbing. Prince Jing listened to him wail for a while, blank-faced—this really wasn't something Wang Xi could handle. Prince Jing chopped straight down with his hand, and Ye Qinghuan fell silent.

Prince Jing ordered Wang Xi to find a carriage to shove Ye Qinghuan into and sent him back to Cheng'en Manor, where his people would take care of him.

Prince Jing had worked up a sweat handling Ye Qinghuan, but when he remembered that a carp spirit was in his room, he rushed back without wiping off his sweat, wondering if the spirit had really changed into a human or not. Would Xiaoyu have turned back into a fish already by the time he got back?

When he pushed open the barely closed door, he was met with the overwhelming scent of alcohol. The young man he'd met several times before was sitting on the ground in a daze, his face flushed and his eyes unfocused, holding a plate in one hand while he licked the other. There was only one green plum left on the plate.

What had happened here?

All of Prince Jing's questions turned into a single thought as he laid eyes on the young man: *He finally transformed.*

Prince Jing was a little delighted. He walked over slowly, thinking about what he should say to the human Xiaoyu... No, he couldn't speak. Even if Xiaoyu was human, it was still inconvenient. He had to find a brush and paper first.

Prince Jing paused for a bit and turned to look for the items, but Xiaoyu suddenly giggled, jumped up, and hugged him, nuzzling against him happily.

"Master, you're back?" The young man's voice was soft, even a little nasally.

The sudden hug made Prince Jing's heart swoop. At Jingtai Hall, the young man had called him "Your Highness," so why was he calling him "Master" now?

Xiaoyu's cheeks were red, his eyes bright; he carefully picked up the green plum with both hands and tried to shove it into Prince Jing's mouth. Prince Jing thought this wasn't quite appropriate, but Xiaoyu was so enthusiastic that he couldn't resist, and he ate it from his hand. The green plum in his mouth was saturated with wine that was much stronger than the wine he had drunk. Prince Jing was surprised; he glanced at the bare plate and the numerous plum pits scattered on the ground. Did Xiaoyu eat almost all of them?

He didn't realize the alcohol content in the green plums was so high. His fish was probably drunk off of them...

"Is it yummy? I left it for you!" Xiaoyu asked with a smile, lowering his head and nuzzling against Prince Jing's hand.

For some reason, Prince Jing nodded. His heart was strangely warmed by the fact that the fish had kept him in mind. Catching a whiff of the strong scent of alcohol on the young man, Prince Jing suddenly realized that this was a drunk fish who had transformed into a human but forgotten that he'd transformed. So that was why he called him "Master."

Such a large young man couldn't be held within the palm of his hand. Prince Jing didn't know how to deal with him, so he softly touched the drunk little fish's arm, hoping he would relax. Unexpectedly, the fish just lay down on top of him, as if he had no bones. Prince Jing was caught off guard. He thought his heart was going to jump out of his chest as he held this fragile young man.

"I'm so sleepy. Wanna sleep." The little drunken fish pouted and yawned, watery-eyed. He thought he was in his tyrant master's hands and that Prince Jing was going to pet him, but he was too tired and didn't want to be petted, so he nuzzled against his master's "hand" instead.

Prince Jing had been nuzzled several times by the drunken little fish already, but he still wasn't sure how to react. He felt like the sweat on his back hadn't had a chance to dry yet. After a moment's hesitation, he tentatively circled his arm around the drunken little fish. If he was drunk and wanted to sleep, Prince Jing thought, lying down might make him more comfortable.

The well-intentioned Prince Jing helped his fish to his bed. The drunken little fish's eyes were almost closed, but he suddenly jerked them open again.

"Not here. Where's my fish tank?" The drunken little fish put his hands on his hips and looked around, on guard.

Prince Jing obviously couldn't let a person sleep in a fish tank. Luckily, as the drunken little fish squinted and stared at the white sheets on the bed, he mistook it for his white stone bed. He walked over and lay down, kicking the jade pillow aside forcefully.

Prince Jing wanted to wait until the fish was asleep to grab a handkerchief to wipe Xiaoyu's face with, but the little drunken fish had barely closed his eyes before he immediately got up again, rubbing his eyes and demanding, "Where's my leaf blanket?"

Prince Jing was baffled. *What's...a leaf blanket?*

But he recalled the leaf that he often saw on the little carp's body. That was probably what he wanted, but Prince Jing obviously couldn't fish out a few pieces of wet seaweed for a human to use. After some thought, he scrounged around the room and found a grass-green brocade blanket instead.

Prince Jing was sweating profusely as he covered the drunken little fish with the blanket. As the familiar color swept across his vision, Xiaoyu wrapped himself in the blanket, satisfied, and murmured, "Thank you, ornamental mountain!"

Prince Jing wasn't sure how to react to that.

He wanted to wait until the fish fell asleep, but the drunken little fish got up yet again. Head wobbling, he stared at the tyrant master in front of him for a while before he remembered that he hadn't finished his mission yet.

"The system said repeated actions aren't valid," he said with a disgruntled frown.

Prince Jing didn't know what kind of thing a "system" was, so he was about to write it down, but the drunken little fish cupped the prince's in his hands and giggled. The little fish's teasing was making Prince Jing's heart beat thunderously in his chest. If the drunken carp spirit wanted to suck "essence" from him, he thought, he would definitely cooperate.

The carp spirit stuck his lips out, moved to either side, and plopped his lips lightly against Prince Jing's throat.

Taken completely by surprise, Prince Jing suddenly found himself being nibbled on.

# The Fish Nibbled Him

WHEN LI YU WOKE UP, he was sleeping in his fish tank on his white stone bed, covered by his leaf blanket. He rolled over comfortably...and suddenly remembered what happened before he lost consciousness.

He turned into a human to eat the green plums, and they were so tasty that he couldn't help himself and kept eating them. The plums were soaked in wine, and he unsuspectingly swallowed a lot of alcohol. Even though he didn't feel it at first, by the time his mind started feeling fuzzy...there was not much after that.

Li Yu shot up off his white stone bed with a start. Since he didn't remember anything after the dizziness, how did he get back into his fishy body?

Did someone else—did Prince Jing see him?

But he glanced at his leaf blanket and quickly rejected this idea. He was lying securely on his white stone bed and was covered in his leaf blanket. He must've done all that himself after he turned back into a fish; it couldn't have been anyone else. And besides, if Prince Jing saw him transform, he would definitely trap him. He wouldn't let him lie comfortably in his fish tank.

So he must have turned back into a fish before Prince Jing came back and jumped into his fish tank before falling asleep.

Li Yu swam around the tank for a bit. He was a little tired, probably because he'd been drunk, but he felt better after moving around.

Li Yu pressed up to the wall of the crystal tank to observe the room. The mess on the ground had been cleaned up, and Prince Jing was sleeping quietly on his bed. It was as if Li Yu had never gotten drunk off the green plums. He took a deep breath. Well, no news was good news. He probably hadn't caused any chaos, then.

He was so terribly anxious about the main mission that now that he was calming down, he wanted to enter the system first thing and check whether "Intimate Contact" had any new notifications. If not the face, maybe the ears or the throat? Considering how much Prince Jing spoiled him, he could just go for the nibble and deal with the consequences later. He just wasn't sure which one he should choose yet.

He didn't expect to be hit with the "quest complete" notification as soon as he entered the system!

What???

Wasn't the main quest the only thing in progress right now?

Li Yu clicked open "Tyrant's Priceless Pet Fish" and found that the main mission, the one that had tortured him for such a long time, had at last been completed.

He was just as shocked as he'd been when he first woke up. He immediately took a look at the details of the mission and confirmed that the last step of "Intimate Contact" had indeed been completed.

When and how? Li Yu was flabbergasted.

<*When you were drunk,*> the system helpfully informed him.

...Li Yu trembled a little. What did he do when he was drunk, and where did he end up biting Prince Jing? He must have nibbled him somewhere; otherwise, this step wouldn't be complete. He just didn't know whether it was the ears or the throat. He should at least find out that much before he died.

*‹You bit the tyrant's Adam's apple.›*

...Ah.

From now on, Li Yu thought, he had no respect to speak of.

As for whether or not he used his human or fish body to bite him, the system didn't tell him. Li Yu didn't question it either—he thought it must have been while he was a fish, or he wouldn't have lived long enough to even enter the system. That was at least a blessing in a mountain of misfortunes!

The system asked him if he wanted to collect his reward. Since "Intimate Contact" was the last step of the "Tyrant's Priceless Pet Fish" main mission, the reward was the final prize for the entire main quest.

Li Yu dragged himself out of his funk and got ready to collect his reward. The reward was...all of his stats were doubled.

At first glance, "all stats" sounded a little vague, but Li Yu's tail, healing ability, and other things that had been strengthened before all counted as stats for this transmigrating fish, so Li Yu figured that it was probably related to those.

Obviously, he clicked accept. He heard the system pause for a second before it mechanically droned on: *‹Congratulations, user. Your inventory space has increased to 4, your transformation time has doubled, the strength of your tail has doubled, your healing has doubled...›*

Li Yu was ecstatic. He didn't realize that his inventory space and the duration of his transformation could also double! The increase in inventory space meant he could carry a lot more things...and did the doubling of the transformation time mean that it had gone from one hour to two hours?

Li Yu checked the description of his inventory space and transformation skill and found this was indeed the case. He was so excited that he completely forgot all the distress he was in earlier.

"Priceless Pet Fish" was thus completed, but the next main quest hadn't been updated yet.

The system said: *<Now, the Moe Pet System will adjust the next main quest to the relationship between the user and the tyrant master. After the adjustments, the user will be notified of a new main quest.>*

Li Yu nodded in understanding. He had done another mission before that had also been adjusted according to his relationship with Prince Jing, so this wasn't new to him. He generously thought that if the system didn't give him a new main mission immediately, it was basically like taking a vacation. That wasn't bad at all.

*<You've met the conditions to start the side quest "Turn into a Koi,">* the system reminded him. *<Would the user like to begin?>*

Did that mean he could start on the side quests first?

Li Yu was cannier now. He asked, *<Does this mission have a time limit?>*

*<There is no time limit. The user only needs to complete the quest. Like other side quests, there is no penalty for failure.>*

The side quests were always so tempting that even though Li Yu had just been thinking about taking a vacation, he accepted it without a moment of thought. *<Let's do it, then! Please start the side quest for me!>*

Since he'd received his majestic black-and-gold fish scales, he'd been secretly looking forward to becoming a koi for a long time.

In the system, the "Turn into a Koi" side quest lit up for him to select.

This side quest was the same as the other fish-scamming quests he'd done—there weren't many details, and there was only a single line of explanation.

*To become a koi, one must have the characteristics of a koi.*

As mysterious as ever. Li Yu didn't immediately understand—but with all his experience, he knew that he could just accept the task and leave it for now. No need to rush; there would be time to figure it out and complete it later.

As he returned to reality, he was still suffused by the ecstasy of completing the main quest, so he took a leap in the water and swam around happily.

There were a lot of things in the crystal fish tank now other than the white stone bed, aquatic plants, and piles of various jewels. Prince Jing had also set up an ornamental mountain of rocks for him, as well as a rocking chair. Li Yu paddled over to the rocking chair and rocked in it forcefully for a bit; perhaps because he was too excited, the rocking chair couldn't contain him anymore, and it shook almost violently.

Then Li Yu slipped into the cave within the ornamental mountain. For some reason, the ornamental mountain was so beautiful today that he couldn't hold himself back, and he ducked into several caves one after another. The system had strengthened him so much that he didn't bother memorizing all of the stats that had been doubled—he knew he'd be able to discover any useful ones through firsthand experience. Right now, for example, it was clear to him that his swimming speed had increased significantly.

Li Yu played even more recklessly. He often swam around the caves and ornamental mountain in the fish tank. Usually, there was no danger, but for some reason, giddiness gave rise to sorrow—he darted through a narrow cave that he'd always easily swum through before and found himself stuck.

*What's going on? I used to be super agile when swimming through caves!*

He looked around carefully and was embarrassed to realize that the size of his body had doubled as well.

He used to be a small, palm-sized carp, small enough to easily fit into one hand, but now...he was the size of two hands. It was no wonder the rocking chair couldn't hold him anymore—the system had doubled his length and width too.

Li Yu wiggled fiercely, but he couldn't get out of the cave. It seemed that it wasn't just his length and width that had changed, but his height had as well.

Most of Li Yu's body was stuck in the cave, and he couldn't muster up any strength in his tail. Even if he could, knocking down the ornamental mountain was out of the question. The crystal fish tank was taller than a person, and the ornamental mountain inside was quite large. If it collapsed, not only would it crush him, it would also make a lot of noise and wake up Prince Jing.

The little carp didn't dare move. Someone would definitely find him once it was time to change the water, he thought, so the helpless little carp went back to sleep right in the hole he was stuck inside.

Soon after, Prince Jing woke up to look at his fish and realized Xiaoyu was gone. Shocked, he immediately looked all around the fish tank for him—and found him at last, sleeping soundly in the ornamental mountain. The corners of Prince Jing's mouth twitched, and he poked the fearless fish. Why was he sleeping in the cave instead of sleeping on his perfectly good white stone bed?

When the fish spirit had nibbled on Prince Jing's throat last night, Prince Jing had struggled to hold himself back from nibbling the drunk fish back, but the fish lay down on his chest after the deed was done and turned right back into a fish. The clothes he'd been wearing collapsed, suddenly empty.

No matter how much Prince Jing was mentally prepared for it, it was still a great shock. Xiaoyu had been thrashing about, uncomfortable out of water. Prince Jing thought the carp had only shown his true form due to being drunk, and he hurriedly put Xiaoyu back into the fish tank. He even remembered that Xiaoyu liked to lie on his bed, enveloped in the leaf blanket, so he carefully put the fish on the white stone bed and wrapped him with the leaf. If the fish woke up and remembered last night, it would be the perfect opportunity to come clean to him—but instead the fish had dashed straight for the ornamental mountain when he woke up.

Prince Jing recalled that the drunken little fish had confusedly called him an ornamental mountain last night—it was both infuriating and hilarious.

Once he was poked, Li Yu woke up. He flapped his tail happily when he saw it was his tyrant master; he struggled but still couldn't get free. He could only look at Prince Jing pitifully, trying to beg for help.

Prince Jing had been looking forward to the fish remembering what happened last night, but Xiaoyu's reactions were simply...fish reactions.

He sighed. Even Ye Qinghuan almost bumped into pillars when he was drunk. What could he expect a fish to remember? He would just have to keep an eye out for other opportunities in the future.

Xiaoyu flapped his fins, still unable to move—Prince Jing realized now that he was stuck. Torn between laughter and pity, he ordered someone to move the ornamental mountain aside.

It took the servants a full ten minutes to move the mountain, but the naughty little carp was finally out of danger, and he swam out and shook his tail. Prince Jing picked him up and carefully examined his body for injuries—the fish was fine, but Prince Jing realized that the reason he'd been stuck was that he'd become much bigger.

How...did that happen?

Prince Jing was able to accept the fact that Xiaoyu was a carp spirit, so growing bigger all of a sudden was hardly out of the question, but Xiaoyu had both grown bigger and started growing a new set of scales in such a short period of time... It put Prince Jing on his guard. Was it possible that the carp spirit had run into trouble? Could he be going through a tribulation of the sort the stories were always mentioning, and it required him to constantly change his form?

The books mentioned that snake spirits and fox yao were incredibly weak during their tribulation and needed to be taken care of at that vulnerable time. Prince Jing didn't know much about these trials and tribulations, but it was easy for him to take care of the carp spirit.

Prince Jing ordered a remodel for the ornamental mountain— the caves, rocking chair, and white stones were all changed to fit Xiaoyu's current shape and size.

The crystal fish tank was quite large, so Xiaoyu could still stay there a little longer. When the new fish tank was completed, he could move there instead. The crystal bottle and tea bowls, however, no longer fit him, so they needed to be replaced.

When he had organized his thoughts, Prince Jing called over Wang Xi. Wang Xi gasped when he laid eyes on the little carp that had grown so enormously.

"Your Highness, how... did he become so large?"

It was way too fast for a single day.

Prince Jing grabbed a handful of food for his fish and glanced at Wang-gonggong calmly. Wang Xi immediately understood what His Highness meant: *Because I feed him. You got a problem with that?*

If His Highness said so, then so be it; it was all fine as long as there was a reason. Wang Xi immediately shut up and followed Prince Jing's orders.

*Wait.* Prince Jing rang the jade bell again, asking him to come back, then handed him a list of items. Wang Xi glanced at it and was privately startled. It was a list of all kinds of robes, shoes, and socks… which wouldn't have been strange if not for the fact that the size wasn't His Highness's at all.

Wang Xi glanced up at His Highness, confused. Prince Jing's face looked normal—except, that is, for the faint red mark on his throat.

Wang Xi couldn't have been more shocked. As a servant, he knew very well what a mark like that meant. His Highness seemed to have someone he liked, and it was very possible that they'd been intimate already. But he, who took care of everything in the manor, wasn't aware of it at all, and Prince Jing never mentioned it himself. Was he in such a rush for these clothes because they were for the person he liked?

It wasn't impossible. It was so mysterious that it made Wang Xi think of someone.

Ever since they returned to the manor from the palace, there was one thing Wang-gonggong just couldn't figure out. When they'd last been at Jingtai Hall, he saw a disheveled little minx of a young man entangled with his Highness. Later on, when he quietly asked His Highness about him, Prince Jing told him that the person was the one who'd helped him clear his eyes. Wang Xi was incredibly grateful and only realized afterward that the little minx seemed to be the fish and clothing thief His Highness had been looking for—that male concubine of an unknown family.

The male concubine had disappeared later on, and Wang Xi never saw him again, but when they returned to the manor, His Highness withdrew all of the people he'd sent out to look for that male concubine.

Wang Xi thought it was the least Prince Jing could do, since that young man had helped His Highness.

Last night, after he sent the completely wasted Ye-shizi back to Cheng'en Manor and returned to Prince Jing's residence, he heard someone say that a disheveled young man seemed to be present in His Highness's room.

Wang Xi immediately sent the servants away, but the next day, there was this red mark on Prince Jing's throat—and he immediately thought of the male concubine. After all, he was the only one Wang Xi had seen entangled with the prince before. He was happy to run errands for Master Fish, but when His Highness asked him to order clothes... No matter how he thought about it, the clothes were probably for the male concubine.

His Highness was not only raising a fish but also hiding a lover—someone else's concubine at that, and he didn't seem to have any intention of revealing it. Wang Xi was conflicted. He felt both happy and worried, but his loyalty toward Prince Jing left him with no choice but to turn a blind eye to it. He sucked it up and ordered the clothes, then had them put in the designated wardrobe in Prince Jing's room.

As for where the male concubine lived... That remained a mystery to Wang Xi. He believed that His Highness would allow them to meet one day.

When Li Yu was eating his fish food, he also noticed the red mark on Prince Jing's throat and felt his face heat up immediately. If that wasn't a mark of being nibbled by a fish...

Any marks left on the tyrant master's body were always incredibly visible. It probably wasn't as bad as it looked, but Li Yu knew that he blacked out and had no sense of boundaries when he was drunk, so perhaps he had taken a pretty fierce bite.

He'd nibbled Prince Jing, but he couldn't let Prince Jing nibble him back.

Li Yu apologized silently, then turned around and grabbed a piece of peach blossom pastry to offer Prince Jing.

Prince Jing didn't touch the pastry; he just tapped on the fish's head with a smile. Li Yu's head felt itchy, but why wouldn't his master let him know what tapping on his head meant?

Li Yu's appetite had doubled along with the size of his fishy body. After he finished eating his fish food, he quietly dragged back the peach blossom pastry he had put out as an apology. He had no choice. Fish got hungry if they didn't eat.

Prince Jing also realized he ate more now. Not only was he not mad at Li Yu for eating the plate of green plums, he also started putting a lot of other delicious, beautiful snacks in his room, as if he was deliberately teasing the fish. Li Yu couldn't resist the temptation at all—he would end up craving whatever was left out. Prince Jing seemed to be busy recently, as he kept going out, only to return hurriedly at night, so whenever he saw something he wanted to eat, Li Yu would turn into a human and eat it.

He had enough time to turn into a human and turn back into a fish without worrying. It was fine, he thought as he munched away. He was on vacation.

Once, after transforming, he was flipping through the closet when he found several new sets of robes, shoes, and socks. These were very different from the ones Prince Jing usually wore, and there was a note inside that said the clothes from Prince Jing's younger days had been temporarily placed here because they were clearing out clothes.

These clothes certainly didn't look old to Li Yu, but he figured since Prince Jing was a prince in ancient times, several new sets of clothing were made for every season—there were a lot more unworn clothes than worn ones. It was possible these were robes the prince had simply never worn. They had been dried and were very clean. The size fit him well, so Li Yu chose a light-gold robe embroidered with green leaves and paired it with snow-white socks and shoes. He'd always been barefoot when he turned into a human before, and getting to wear shoes and socks was a rare novelty, so he happily put them on.

After he got dressed, Li Yu would sit down and choose his favorite snacks to eat. Sometimes, there would be a pot of tea at the perfect temperature on the table; Prince Jing wouldn't drink cold tea and would have the servants change the tea if it became cold. Li Yu thought it was going to be wasted if he didn't drink it, so he would secretly pour some out to eat with his snacks, to balance out the sweetness.

Someone had put a bronze mirror next to the closet for some reason too. The first thing Li Yu usually did after transforming was put clothes on, and things were much more complete with the mirror. He often strutted around in front of the mirror, grimacing or smiling. But he still remembered the auntie who was punished for helping him in the manor; those without an identity shouldn't go outside and wander around. He was satisfied with some tea and snacks.

Li Yu was merely relieving his boredom, and he didn't begin to suspect that the copper mirror was reflecting everything he did to the room next door.

In that room, only separated by a thin wall, Prince Jing was watching him.

He'd seen a human turn into fish, so he wanted to see a fish turning into a human. He knew that Xiaoyu would never transform in front of him, so he pretended to leave in order to give him space. But he found that once his gaze was glued to Xiaoyu, he couldn't take it off...

Whenever Xiaoyu put clothes on, Prince Jing had to look down. He wanted to see, but it didn't feel right.

Xiaoyu had nibbled him, and he wanted to nibble back.

# Fish Wants to Dual Cultivate

PRINCE JING DIDN'T KNOW WHY he felt such affection toward Xiaoyu. He'd only met him a few times in human form, and they'd barely exchanged words. In the beginning, he was a little curious about the young man who kept managing to escape from him, but he definitely shouldn't care this much. After he learned that the young man who saved him was his Xiaoyu who kept him company day and night, though, Prince Jing couldn't stop thinking about him.

Because regardless if he was fish or human, Xiaoyu was always the one who was willing to treat him with sincerity.

Over time, as he hid and spied on Xiaoyu like this, Prince Jing was able to learn many of his secrets.

Xiaoyu loved to eat. Prince Jing had known this ever since he discovered the fish's enthusiasm for peach blossom pastries, so in recent days, he spoiled the fish with plenty of tasty food. He would watch as Xiaoyu secretly transformed for just a bite—but Xiaoyu would only transform once a day, and no matter how much time the prince left for him, the little fish would turn back after about two hours. Once he changed back, he wouldn't turn into a human again, no matter how delicious the food was. Xiaoyu himself seemed reluctant to change back, however, so Prince Jing felt that it must not be because the little fish didn't want to change into a human again but because he couldn't.

Thus, Prince Jing theorized that the fish could only transform once a day for two hours.

After he came up with this theory, Prince Jing's mood took a hit. The carp spirit would transform to eat, but he never wanted to meet his owner. Prince Jing thought back to the first time he saw Xiaoyu's human form—it seemed he'd wanted to go to the kitchens to eat then too, and if his eyes hadn't been injured last time, Xiaoyu wouldn't have transformed to save him. Even the letter to Ye Qinghuan had come from Xiaoyu via Xiongfeng.

Prince Jing suddenly realized that he was no better than a snack or a bowl of rice to his fish.

However, this simpleminded fish had not yet realized that his identity was exposed and was currently diligently cleaning up to hide the fact.

Through the bronze mirror, Prince Jing watched as the fish rearranged the disorganized snacks, crumbling up the fruit peels and crumbs and then scattering them into inconspicuous corners. The carp spirit, whether as a fish or a human, was quite smart and vigilant. He never ate fresh fruits, which were hard to clean up—he mainly ate smaller snacks that could be stuffed into his stomach whole without leaving any debris behind.

Xiaoyu obviously wanted to hide it from him, but he remained at the prince's side. If he realized that Prince Jing had found him out, he might run away again. Thinking back to the fish's methods... There were always careless oversights, but if one wasn't attentive, it was easy to be fooled. Prince Jing had been tricked this way and could sympathize. He was glad, now, that Xiaoyu didn't remember anything after he passed out; if he had, then Prince Jing might not have been able to find him again.

After much thought, Prince Jing decided to suppress the urge to tell Xiaoyu what he knew and stay just as they were for the time being. He needed an opportunity first. It had to be an opportunity that would guarantee Xiaoyu would never leave, so until then, he couldn't do anything impulsive that might scare Xiaoyu away.

The books Ye Qinghuan gave him always mentioned that humans and yao were different. Prince Jing resented that sentiment. Even people were different from each other. He was no weak scholar, and Xiaoyu was a fish that he kept by his side at all times. He would never allow them to be separated.

But he still didn't know much about yao or carp spirits.

Prince Jing ordered servants to collect classic books on supernatural beings and Taoism. He wanted to know more about the carp spirit—for example, that "sis tome" Xiaoyu had mentioned when he was drunk. He didn't know what kind of "tome" this was, and as for trials and tribulations... He didn't know if Xiaoyu needed to go through one, but it was clear Ye Qinghuan's books weren't enough.

Soon, his confidant found some ancient books that were supposed to be very useful to Prince Jing. Prince Jing decided to get started immediately.

He was "very busy" these days, leaving early and returning late, and when he did return, he would bury his head in a book, making his pet fish quite dissatisfied. He felt like he hadn't seen his master in a long time.

Li Yu swam around in his crystal fish tank, suppressing his mischievous impulses and wondering what book Prince Jing was reading this time. If he was reading another scandalous book, he wanted to read it too! Masters should share good things! Why was he being left out?

After Li Yu got bigger, the tea bowls for him to jump around in the room also had to be larger. He always created a large splash when he jumped into one, and Prince Jing noticed him as soon as he jumped out. The prince smiled to himself when he saw the trail of splashes the carp spirit left as he jumped happily from bowl to bowl, knowing that Xiaoyu was interested. He set up the book properly and pretended to concentrate.

Li Yu quickly reached the table. The petal-shaped tea bowl he usually sat in had been swapped out as well, and the bowl he landed in now was a full lotus flower, over twice as large as the old one. Prince Jing had the lotus bowl carved specially out of red jade, so it looked vibrant and lifelike under the sun. While in the lotus bowl, the little carp looked like he was actually sitting on top of a lotus flower—and since Prince Jing had noticed that the fish was especially fond of green leaves, he'd had the craftsmen attach a ring of lotus leaves to the bottom of the bowl, made of jasper, to make it look even more lifelike. The little carp fell in love with it immediately.

It wasn't the first time they were reading together, and Li Yu confidently swam to the edge of the tea bowl and tried to stretch his head out to peer at the book Prince Jing was currently reading. The book looked extremely old, and several pages were about to fall off. Li Yu thought that the book was probably older than Prince Jing and must be telling the story of some thousand-year-old spirit.

Prince Jing noticed that his fish was trying to stretch his head out, so he picked up the lotus bowl and the fish together and placed them in front of him, facing the book. That way, his fish could read easily too.

And if Xiaoyu had transformed right then, he would have been encircled by Prince Jing's arms. Prince Jing couldn't help imagining it for a moment. With a faint joy that only he was privy to, he started reading with the fish again.

Li Yu was happy that Prince Jing was so willing this time, and he thought he could finally witness the elegance of ancient R-18 material—but he spent the longest time trying his hardest to read it, and he wasn't able to understand a single line! How awkward!

*I was tricked!* the little carp thought. This wasn't a novel at all; it wasn't even a book on the art of war or a travelogue. Th-th-this was a book on the cultivation of immortality!

Didn't the system say that the male lead's status as the protagonist wouldn't be affected, that Prince Jing could still become the emperor? Why had Prince Jing started reading books about cultivating immortality?! Did Prince Jing, a proper male lead in a historical political drama novel, want to cultivate instead of becoming the emperor?

That was way too hard! Li Yu never read cultivation stories!

This was making Li Yu pretty worried. He snuck a glance at Prince Jing, afraid that he was really changing paths and wanted to become an immortal. Prince Jing's expression was solemn and concentrated, unlike Li Yu, who couldn't understand a single line. Though Prince Jing was mute, he was talented—he read this book quickly and even seemed to understand it.

If he kept reading, he might ascend.

Li Yu quietly flicked a bit of water onto the book. He had to quickly chase away any ideas Prince Jing had of becoming immortal—cultivation was too difficult. It was exhausting and there was no good food to eat. If things went wrong, he might even lose his life. His tyrant master couldn't go off and cultivate no matter what!

Prince Jing watched as the old tome he'd spent an enormous amount of money to purchase was callously splashed with water. He glanced helplessly at his fish as Xiaoyu threw a tantrum. Perhaps the fish spirit had been alive for such a long time that he didn't care to read such simple books?

Prince Jing switched to an even more difficult book.

Li Yu was just about to flap his tail triumphantly for defeating the cultivation book, when he realized that Prince Jing had switched to a book about...concocting pills of immortality?!

*You can't eat pills willy-nilly! You can't read books willy-nilly either!*

Li Yu flapped about, getting Prince Jing's ancient book almost completely drenched.

Prince Jing pulled out the last book with a darkened expression. Li Yu glanced at it. Dual cultivation?!

*D-dual cultivation...?!* Li Yu's eyes widened. This was too much of a test—even though he didn't read cultivation books, he definitely knew what dual cultivation meant.

The edges of the book were almost worn away, so it must be a very deep topic... But dual cultivation? The little carp was quite conflicted. In the end, he raised his head. *Ah, you have this type of book too? I wanna see!*

Prince Jing's gaze changed slightly. Xiaoyu really did want to dual cultivate with him!

But...then why hadn't he started yet?

...

"Your Highness," Wang Xi softly called from outside the room.

The little carp had transformed the book into a wet book. Prince Jing gave up on fighting with the fish for the book, let go of it, and lightly jingled the jade bell. When Wang Xi entered, the little carp had slipped back into the lotus bowl. He didn't see anything.

Wang Xi's expression was serious. "Your Highness, there was a fire in Zhongcui Palace last night. Concubine Qiu was injured."

# Gold Fish Finger

ONCUBINE QIU?

Li Yu couldn't remember who that was at first. The original book didn't mention that many concubines of the emperor, and he only remembered a couple.

Prince Jing, however, knew who it was—Concubine Qiu, who had been demoted from noble consort just a short while ago. The second prince—the Marquis of An, now—had no chance of inheriting the throne. The only reason that Concubine Qiu was simply demoted rather than banished to the cold palace[10] was because the emperor wanted to preserve the dignity of the Marquis of An.

But it seemed like Concubine Qiu had still not given up. It had been a long time since there was a fire in the palace, and it wasn't the season for fires besides. If Zhongcui Palace caught fire and burned... it must have been for a reason.

Prince Jing noticed the fish's confusion and tapped his fingers on the table three times. Wang Xi was surprised—this meant that he was to explain in further detail. Since His Highness had grown up, he rarely made such a request. Normally, His Highness understood after just a few words, so today, why did he...?

---

10   The Cold Palace (冷宫) is a "prison" found in most modern back palace media that concubines were banished to after falling out of favor with the emperor, usually after committing some kind of crime or offense. This is not a place that existed in real history.

Though Wang Xi was confused, he still responded diligently, "Concubine Qiu is the mother of His Highness the second prince, as well as the former noble consort. She originally lived in Zhongcui Palace. At midnight last night, a fire broke out in Zhongcui Palace, and the night attendant found that she was injured. Luckily, though most of Zhongcui Palace was burned in the fire, it did not spread, and the emperor and other palaces are safe."

So the Qiu woman mentioned was the former Noble Consort Qiu? Li Yu's eyes brightened. He was growing so round recently from eating and resting well that he had almost forgotten about the Noble Consort! UwU

After Wang-gonggong's explanation, he was all caught up. The place Concubine Qiu lived in had caught fire, and she was injured. But how did it catch fire when the palace was so heavily guarded?

Li Yu recalled a scene from the original book. Concubine Qiu hadn't been rejected by the emperor so early but instead became a cannon fodder casualty in the fight between the second and third princes. In an attempt to help the second prince regain the emperor's favor after he'd lost power, she burned herself to earn the emperor's pity, but the third prince and his cohort exposed her. Concubine Qiu and the second prince ended up completely losing the emperor's trust.

The House of Cheng'en was well-protected, Concubine Qiu and the second prince had been imprisoned by the emperor, and the possibility of the second prince inheriting the throne was all but gone. Was Concubine Qiu still so ambitious that she'd resort to this brutal trick?

It wasn't impossible, but in the book, only a certain room was burned, and the fire was quickly extinguished—very different from what Wang Xi had said about most of Zhongcui Palace catching fire.

Had the previous plot been altered so much that Concubine Qiu was even more crazed than before?

While Li Yu ruminated in his bowl, Prince Jing grabbed the brush and ink on the table before him to ask Wang Xi, *Where is Concubine Qiu injured, and how are the others in Zhongcui Palace? How did the fire start?*

Wang Xi punched himself lightly. "My apologies for not being clearer. Concubine Qiu's injury was on her arm, and everyone else in Zhongcui Palace is fine, other than some minor injuries suffered by the ones who put the fire out. The emperor is already investigating the cause of the fire. No results yet, but there are rumors in the palace that a servant in Zhongcui Palace accidentally knocked over an oil lamp in the servants' quarters and burned a bed curtain."

Prince Jing gave a cold laugh. The servants' quarters were usually very far from the master's rooms, so how could Concubine Qiu be the sole casualty? And though Concubine Qiu had been demoted and her status was nowhere close to what it was before, she was still the master of the Zhongcui Palace. If the master was injured, why were her servants safe? What kind of logic was that?

"This old servant believes things are not as simple as they seem," said Wang Xi. "The servants are all fine, but they weren't able to protect their only master? That makes no sense. Could it be that the noble consort—ah, ah, that's not right. This old servant almost said the wrong thing. Could it be that Concubine Qiu inflicted the injury upon herself?"

Li Yu thumped his tail a bunch of times. What Wang-gonggong said made sense; he thought the same thing. At first, he hadn't been sure that Concubine Qiu herself was up to no good, but the details Wang Xi mentioned did indeed present a contradiction—and another was that, according to Wang-gonggong, the fire should have been quite large, so how could the injury be restricted to her arm? The more Li Yu thought about it, the more he found the situation suspicious.

"This matter has nothing to do with our manor," Wang-gonggong continued, "but since the palace caught fire, Your Highness should still visit the emperor. I received news that the third and sixth princes have already entered the palace, and the second...ah, the Marquis of An also sent a letter of well-wishes..."

Prince Jing understood what he meant. He nodded.

"I'll go make the preparations now. As for Master Fish..." Wang Xi glanced at the little carp, not sure what Prince Jing wanted to do.

Li Yu wanted to go too. He'd been stuck in the manor for a while and hadn't caused any trouble, always being a good pet.

Prince Jing noticed that the carp spirit's tail was lifted high behind him, almost creating a breeze with its flapping. He smiled at Wang Xi: *Let's do as we always have.*

That meant he would take his fish with him, wherever he went. Wang Xi rushed to grab the crystal bottle.

The bottle had been remade to be as large as a small birdcage, and a chain was still wrapped around the handle to prevent it from slipping. Prince Jing put his fish into the crystal bottle himself and added a lot of snacks in case the fish got hungry. If it wasn't for Wang Xi persuading him in a low voice, Prince Jing might have filled up the entire crystal bottle with snacks.

Wang-gonggong sighed. Why did it seem like Prince Jing's affection for his fish had doubled in size with the fish himself?

All the concubines and princes were at Qianqing Palace. The emperor had ordered an imperial physician to visit Concubine Qiu; the imperial physician reported that her arm was not in good condition, burnt to a bloody mess. He was afraid that she might not be able to fully recover.

The emperor froze. He had been extremely disappointed with Concubine Qiu before, but the imperial physician's description reminded him of the past. The first year Concubine Qiu entered the palace, she would often wear a dance outfit in private to try and please him; she was only sixteen then, and her jade-like arms were bright as the moon. So many years had passed in a flash.

The emperor couldn't help the waves of nostalgia as he reflected on how much time had passed. Later, he received a letter from the Marquis of An, which Mu Tianzhao had written with blood, acknowledging his mistakes. He said he dared not ask for forgiveness, but he was worried about Concubine Qiu's condition and asked the emperor to allow him to fulfill his filial duties before her sickbed.

Mu Tianzhao was very sincere, and his love for his mother was obvious. The emperor had originally hardened his heart against the Marquis of An, but he was a little moved now.

The concubines next to him were keen observers and realized the emperor was feeling pity for these two. Nobody dared say anything except to echo their agreement. The third prince didn't want to just watch as the Marquis of An came back to join the fun again, and he nearly spoke up several times, but the sixth prince managed to persuade him to sit back with a soft voice.

Right now, the sixth prince reminded his brother, the emperor was thinking about all the things he appreciated about Concubine Qiu and the Marquis of An. If anyone mentioned their faults, it would make the emperor unhappy.

The third prince was enraged. Was the Marquis of An still going to keep him down even though he was on house arrest?

The sixth prince gently nudged the third prince, urging him to wait and stay calm.

Head Eunuch Luo Ruisheng came to report that Prince Jing had arrived. The emperor put down the Marquis of An's letter and ordered Prince Jing to enter.

It wasn't news to the palace that Prince Jing was taking care of a fish. He'd brought his fish into the palace this time too. Prince Jing's fish had left a deep impression on the emperor. He'd even rewarded the fish several times; the emperor's mood improved a little when he thought about how Prince Jing took care of his pet.

Prince Jing performed a formal greeting first. The huge crystal bottle could no longer fit in his sleeve, so he held it in his hand. Seeing the bottle, which was clearly much larger than before, as well as the fish, who was also much larger than before, the emperor wasn't sure what to say...

Li Yu was a smart fish and swam in circles to show his respects to the emperor. As a result, the emperor caught a glimpse of the gold on the little carp's belly and tail and said in amazement, "Tianchi, your fish...?"

At a glance, like Ye-shizi, the emperor first thought Prince Jing had gotten another fish.

Wang Xi always followed Prince Jing—Prince Jing glanced at him, so Wang Xi immediately kowtowed and responded for him, "Your Imperial Majesty, the fish His Highness is raising has changed scales and grown larger."

Did fish change scales? The emperor had never heard of such a thing before. He was curious enough to be distracted from thinking about the pitiful Concubine Qiu and the Marquis of An and immediately ordered Prince Jing to bring the fish closer so he could take a look.

Prince Jing agreed. Upon closer inspection, the emperor realized that it was indeed the same fish, but a few of its scales had turned golden. The emperor stared at the golden scales on the little carp for a long time.

The emperor looked at Head Eunuch Luo. "Luo Ruisheng, what do you think?"

Head Eunuch Luo, who knew the emperor well, smiled and said, "This servant is uncultured and cannot say. But I believe a fish with golden scales is a good omen."

The emperor laughed brightly. "I think so too. It should be a sign of peace for our country and the people."

The emperor's bad mood wasn't only because of his concern for Concubine Qiu and the Marquis of An. If they couldn't find out the cause of the fire, it could be regarded as a warning from the heavens—he would have to take the blame himself. Now that he saw the golden scales, the emperor breathed a sigh of relief. If there was a good omen, who dared say otherwise?

Li Yu was dumbfounded. He just grew a few new scales on his belly, but the emperor somehow arrived at the conclusion that meant the country and people would be at peace? The emperor sure knew how to make up a bunch of crap.

As soon as Prince Jing arrived, the emperor remembered the foolish things the Marquis of An had done in the past. His heart did soften for a moment because of Concubine Qiu's injury, but if he pardoned the Marquis of An just because of this, then he'd be nothing more than a befuddled old man of an emperor. How would he explain himself to Empress Xiaohui when he met her again underground?

It was true that Concubine Qiu had accompanied him for many years, but didn't Empress Xiaohui give her life for him and their children?

He didn't have to spare much thought as to how he was going to deal with Concubine Qiu. Since she was injured, her relatives could visit her in the palace, but the Marquis of An's mistakes could not be written off so easily. If the Marquis of An wanted to fulfill his filial duty, he didn't have to come to the palace to take care of her while still bearing the burden of his crimes. He could convert to vegetarianism and commit to Buddhism, or he could ask his wife to take care of Concubine Qiu in his place. As long as he was sincere, there were lots of ways to show it. What's more, Concubine Qiu only injured her arm, but the Marquis of An was kicking up a fuss as if she were on her deathbed. Doing something as ominous as writing a letter in blood was like asking for her situation to get worse.

The emperor quashed his sympathy for Concubine Qiu and glanced back at the Marquis of An's letter, which now seemed to him like he was trying to use the opportunity to escape his punishment. The letter that he'd been about to immediately approve was now held back instead.

The guards entered to report the results of the investigation into the fire. It was rumored that a servant's room in Zhongcui Palace was most heavily burned, so they came to the conclusion that that was where the fire started. Huanhua, Concubine Qiu's personal servant, was one of the ones living in this room, but after the fire was put out, Huanhua had disappeared. Nobody had seen her, and the imperial guards were unable to find her.

The emperor sensed something off about that. Even if the fire started because of her, a servant shouldn't be able to hide so well that the imperial guards couldn't find her. If she was alive they ought to find her, and if she was dead they ought to find her body.

The emperor asked for the location of Huanhua's room. When

he learned that it was a fair distance away from the main courtyard where Concubine Qiu lived, his face immediately darkened.

The third prince finally saw his opportunity and gave his mother, Consort Qian, a look. Consort Qian promptly covered her mouth with a handkerchief and said, smiling, "Concubine Qiu is so unlucky. Nobody else was hurt, but she was burned that badly even though she was so far away."

The emperor glared at Consort Qian. She had taken the risk of speaking and privately glanced back at the third prince, angrily quieting herself. The emperor became even more upset. He knew what Consort Qian said was true, or he wouldn't have had such a cold expression.

Even the other concubines could tell that there was trickery behind Concubine Qiu's injury. She was injured by the fire even though she was so far away—and she might also have known that an arm injury would particularly upset the emperor. The emperor had spent his whole life believing he was wise, but he was almost played by a woman.

Since most of Zhongcui Palace had burned down, Concubine Qiu was moved to the nearby Yuxiu Palace. The emperor decided to pay her a visit in person and asked everyone to come with him.

Concubine Qiu lay on the bed, on her back, and couldn't stop crying out in pain. When she heard the announcement of the emperor's arrival, she was overjoyed. She draped a robe around her shoulders and was helped out of bed by her most trusted servants to greet the emperor formally. The emperor was a little suspicious of her and went straight to her room to take a closer look at her—only to see that she was still wearing elegant makeup and her hair was combed up into a delicate style, wearing a dress she had worn when she danced for him back in the day...

She had clearly been prepared and was waiting for him to come comfort her.

The emperor's heart turned cold. He ordered the imperial physician to examine Concubine Qiu's injuries in front of him.

What's more, although everyone had accompanied the emperor to Concubine Qiu's quarters, custom dictated that everyone except the emperor wait outside her room. So wait they did.

Prince Jing was afraid that Xiaoyu would feel suffocated, so he opened the bottle. Xiaoyu immediately swam to the mouth of the bottle!

Li Yu had been watching for a while and noticed that the plot had slightly changed—the small fire had somehow turned into a large fire, Prince Jing brought his fish into the palace, and for some reason, the third and sixth prince didn't expose Concubine Qiu. Overall, however, Concubine Qiu's plot was still similar to the one in the original book. Since she had hurt herself on purpose, checking her injury would change nothing, as her arm was truly injured.

He had the golden finger and knew the answer to the question, but how was he going to tell Prince Jing in a short amount of time?

Prince Jing could be harsh toward Ye-shizi, but it was only on the surface, and he truly saw him as a close relative at heart. He definitely wouldn't want the Marquis of An to come back—if the Marquis of An wasn't completely stamped out, it would be bad news for both the House of Cheng'en and Prince Jing...

Li Yu lay on the narrow mouth of the bottle, thinking so hard that he got lost in his thoughts and forgot that he had grown so much—and the crystal bottle flipped over.

After a moment of shock, Prince Jing scooped up the little carp. Wang Xi, without missing a beat, said to everyone, "My apologies. His Highness needs to change."

# My Name Is Li Yu

PRINCE JING CARRIED HIS FISH into the warm room of the side hall. Ever since Prince Jing started keeping a fish as a pet, Wang Xi had gotten into the habit of bringing a spare change of his clothes when they went out. So, as he was about to enter the room with Prince Jing, he readied the clothes. However, Prince Jing took the clothes from him first and asked Wang Xi to stand guard outside and not let anyone approach.

Wang Xi was perplexed, but he complied.

Luckily, Prince Jing's manor had made more than one crystal bottle. There were several identical ones in case of emergency; Prince Jing quickly put the little carp into another crystal bottle filled with clear water and looked around.

Fortunately, he and Xiaoyu were the only ones in the warmed chamber in the side hall. No one would interrupt them.

He remembered the first time he brought Xiaoyu to greet the emperor. His fish had drenched him in water, and he had no choice but to go change his clothes. When he returned, he saw the Noble Consort Qiu and her son freshly disheveled. Back then, he thought it was just a coincidence, but when he realized Xiaoyu was a carp spirit, it occurred to him that it was very likely that Xiaoyu had made him leave on purpose in order to punish those two.

Now, Xiaoyu had gotten his clothes wet again. Did he want to tell him something?

But how was a fish going to communicate?

Prince Jing secretly hoped that the carp spirit could transform and tell him in person.

He waited and waited, but Xiaoyu didn't transform. Prince Jing thought that he might have misunderstood and Xiaoyu didn't actually have anything to tell him. Prince Jing hadn't changed his clothes since he entered the room, so he decided to change first.

The little carp had been swimming in circles anxiously in the crystal bottle. He knew that Prince Jing had been staring at him, but it wasn't that he didn't want to say anything—the answer was too complicated for a fish to express. Knocking over the crystal bottle had just been an accident! He hadn't thought of anything yet, sob sob sob!

Li Yu continued to think hard, paddling the water irritably with his fins, when he suddenly realized that Prince Jing had turned his back to him.

Li Yu's attention was immediately diverted. *Hmm? What was the tyrant master going to do?*

The little carp immediately pressed himself against the side of the crystal wall.

The bottom of Prince Jing's robes had been splashed when the crystal bottle upended itself, so he was changing.

Since he thought of Xiaoyu as a human now, Prince Jing turned around out of habit and undid his jade buttons. He was changing, but he was paying attention to his fish out of the corner of his eyes when he noticed the formerly swimming figure had stopped moving.

Prince Jing immediately turned around. The little carp was pressed up against the crystal wall, staring at him with his dark fish eyes.

They stared at each other in silence.

Li Yu, now experienced, hurriedly swam to the other side of the crystal bottle, his tail pointed toward Prince Jing, pretending he was just passing by.

Was the fish watching…?

Prince Jing suddenly realized something, his lips quirking up into a mischievous smirk at the wildly swinging fish tail. What was wrong with him watching? There was nothing that couldn't be seen.

Prince Jing stepped forward and forcibly grabbed Li Yu's tail, turning him around so that the little carp, trying to escape, was now pointed toward him. The fish looked at his tyrant master in surprise, as he changed in front of him without any hesitation.

*Ah, don't do this!* thought the shocked little carp. *My fish eyes are going to go blind!*

It seemed like he was resisting, but he couldn't stop himself from watching, silently counting his master's abs.

Perhaps because he was stimulated by the delicious sight of Prince Jing changing, Li Yu's feverish brain came up with an idea that wasn't really an idea. Since the incident came so suddenly this time, it was impossible for him to make any preparations like a secret letter; since Prince Jing was right in front of him, the easiest way would be to transform into a human and expose Concubine Qiu directly. But how was he going to transform right under Prince Jing's nose?

Li Yu was still pondering when Prince Jing suddenly walked over and lightly touched his head.

What???

Touching his head seemed to be a signal of some kind. Afterward, Prince Jing left him behind and left the warm room alone.

Immediately afterward, Wang Xi loudly called from outside, "Your Highness wants tea? Please wait a moment. This old servant will go make it right away."

Prince Jing went out to drink tea?

Li Yu looked around the warm room. There was tea on the table already, but since this was the palace, Prince Jing wouldn't drink tea of unknown origins. When he wanted to drink tea, he would ask Wang Xi.

He knew that it was normal for Prince Jing to drink tea, but that wasn't the point! The point was that Prince Jing wasn't here anymore, so he could transform! This was a good opportunity, but... he had to be careful!

The first hurdle in transforming was clothing. There just so happened to be several sets of servant clothing hanging in the warm room, though, and some of them were about his size. Perhaps the servants changed here too... He could borrow one.

The next hurdle was that there were too many uncertain factors in the palace. As someone without an identity, he had to be careful at all times. Once he transformed, he had to find Prince Jing as soon as possible and say what he had to say; convincing Prince Jing to believe him in a short amount of time would also be a problem, but he still felt confident.

After Li Yu informed him, Prince Jing would go and expose Concubine Qiu himself, so all Li Yu needed to do was stick near the crystal bottle and hide. As long as he didn't run around the palace and waited out the two hours safely, everything would be fine.

When he transformed in Prince Jing's manor to go to the kitchens, he'd thought two hours was too short, but now it felt way too long. It was frustrating that he couldn't cancel the skill whenever he wanted, since it wasn't safe to hide in the palace. But he had no other way to communicate with Prince Jing. In a few days, the evidence that Concubine Qiu had injured herself on purpose might be gone—what if the emperor failed to gather evidence in time and believed her instead?

Once in a while, a fish had to transform for the sake of serious business!

His mind made up, Li Yu selected the skill. After he was transformed, his first order of business was to touch his stomach. It was humiliating that the crystal bottle had toppled over like that; he had to make sure that it was only his fish form that had increased in size and that his human form hadn't become fat. Only once he was reassured about his figure did he pick out a well-fitting servant's outfit and put it on.

After he changed, he gently pushed open the door of the warm room—only to see Prince Jing standing guard outside, waiting for Wang-gonggong's tea.

"You! I mean—Y-Your Highness!" Li Yu was startled. Luckily, he didn't make any loud noises inside, but why didn't Prince Jing sit down at the table to wait instead?

Prince Jing smiled down at the servant in front of him.

Li Yu quickly realized that he was wearing servant's clothing and was pretending to be a servant. A servant should always greet a prince, but how? And did he need to hold his hands the fancy way they did in the operas?

Wait. He might be wearing a different set of clothing, but his face had stayed the same. Prince Jing should recognize him, right?

"H-hello, Your Highness!"

Li Yu figured he would just kowtow to muddle his way through the greeting—when he was a fish, he often saw people kowtowing to Prince Jing! But Prince Jing stopped him before he could even bend his knees.

When that strong arm grabbed him, Li Yu knew that Prince Jing had recognized him.

Li Yu, for some reason, felt immediately reassured. He took a moment to arrange his thoughts before he spoke up.

"Your Highness, I need to tell you something," he said. "It's true that Concubine Qiu is injured, but it wasn't from the fire in Zhongcui Palace... Th-the injury on her arm smells of cypress because the wound was caused by a burning cypress branch."

That cypress branch was both Concubine Qiu's weapon and the evidence she had burned herself.

It was obvious the fire was Concubine Qiu's idea. How could she actually have fallen into the flames? If she ruined her appearance or if something went wrong, the loss would far outweigh the gains. In fact, long before Zhongcui Palace caught fire, she had already hidden far away with her closest servants. When the fire was almost extinguished, she had gritted her teeth and inflicted burns on her arms, before returning quietly. As long as she insisted that she was injured by the fire, nobody would doubt it!

The servant, Huanhua, was the confidant that Concubine Qiu had sent to start the fire in Zhongcui Palace. She had disappeared after the fire, so as long as Concubine Qiu herself kept her mouth shut, nobody would ever know.

That was how it was in the original book, but unfortunately, Concubine Qiu made several mistakes. One of those mistakes was her thoughtless decision to burn herself with a cypress branch. Cypress wood had a very particular fragrance, and the branch Concubine Qiu used was especially strong-smelling. Her wounds thus smelled of cypress, and it lingered for a long time—the sixth prince was the first one to notice it, originally.

Concubine Qiu had claimed she was injured by the fire in Zhongcui Palace, but there were no cypress trees in Zhongcui Palace. That meant she couldn't have been in Zhongcui Palace when she got injured, but rather somewhere else where cypress trees were planted.

In the book, the sixth prince was somewhat smart and helped the third prince find the place: Yaxin Terrace, not far from Zhongcui Palace. He even found a couple of guards who had seen her there, so they had witnesses. They also found the cypress branch that Concubine Qiu had carelessly dropped onto the ground; one end was burnt into charcoal, and the other end was wrapped in a thick handkerchief to make it easier to hold. The handkerchief was embroidered with Concubine Qiu's favorite crab apple blossoms, and, along with the cypress branch, ended up becoming evidence against her.

And a key person, Huanhua, was found later as well. As it turned out, since she knew the whole story, she was afraid that her mistress would try to silence her and ran away to hide in the imperial garden, where she was found by the third prince's agents. The third prince tortured Huanhua, forcing her to tell the truth to expose Concubine Qiu.

In the book, Concubine Qiu's entire role was basically to take one hit after another. But since the third and sixth princes were no longer doing anything, Li Yu was afraid that Concubine Qiu's wicked scheme would succeed. It was impossible for him to remind the third and sixth prince of such things, so he could only remind Prince Jing and let him make a decision.

Li Yu did his best to only mention the important points, especially Huanhua's hiding spot and the secret behind Concubine Qiu's injury.

Prince Jing stared at him.

Li Yu was afraid that he wouldn't believe him, so he anxiously said, "Your Highness, it's true. Please believe me. I can't explain how I know all this, but I can guarantee that I'm telling you the truth. I was the one who wrote the letter to Ye-shizi as well. You—"

This was the fastest way Li Yu could think of to make Prince Jing believe him and to prove himself—through the letter written to Ye Qinghuan. Since the letter had helped the House of Cheng'en escape disaster, Prince Jing had to believe the letter writer now.

Li Yu recited the contents of the letter without missing a single word. The letter was a secret only known to Prince Jing, Ye-shizi, and a few confidants; other than these people, the only other person who would know anything about it would be the letter writer himself. Since Prince Jing had chosen to believe the letter, then he should also trust Li Yu as the writer of the letter!

After Li Yu's fervent speech, Prince Jing nodded calmly, signaling that he'd understood. But he still didn't let go of Li Yu's arm.

Li Yu gulped. No way—why did Prince Jing react like this? He'd done the same thing the last time they met too.

Prince Jing took out the jade bell and rang it. Before Wang Xi went to make tea, Prince Jing had given him a note, asking him to pretend to make tea and stay away until he got permission to come back. Now, he rushed over and saw His Highness dragging a young servant whom he refused to let go of.

...This scene seemed somewhat familiar. Wang Xi's heart trembled, and he was startled to notice the servant did indeed look familiar. Wasn't this...another man's concubine? What was he doing in the palace?

Prince Jing glanced at Li Yu. Li Yu immediately understood and repeated everything he'd just said to Wang Xi.

Wang Xi understood how serious the situation was and asked for orders. "Your Highness, what will you do now?"

Li Yu thought, *His Highness is definitely going to do it himself.* But Prince Jing gave him an indecipherable glance and held up three of his fingers.

Wang Xi smiled. "This servant understands. I'll secretly pass the message along to the third prince's people. The third prince is still worried that the Marquis of An is somehow unbeatable—let's give him a chance to do it so His Highness doesn't have to do it himself."

What? That was an option?

Prince Jing signaled for Wang Xi to leave quickly with an impatient look. Wang Xi scurried away to carry out his orders, but Prince Jing was still holding on to Li Yu. They stared at each other.

Prince Jing took Li Yu to the table in the warmed chamber, made Li Yu sit down with him, and took out ink and paper from his robes.

...Was Prince Jing waiting for him? Li Yu had a bad feeling. He timidly said, "Your Highness, I have other things to do. I want to..."

Prince Jing quickly wrote, *Answer my questions.*

Li Yu peeked at him and pouted. "If I answer, will you let me go?" Li Yu had just finished saying this when he remembered something Wang Xi had said more than once: Prince Jing didn't like it when others tried to bargain with him. H-he actually dared to speak to Prince Jing this way. If Prince Jing got angry and threw him out, that would be... Wait, actually, that wouldn't be that bad, would it?

But the asshole Prince Jing raised his eyebrows and wrote, *I will let you go if you answer truthfully.*

No way. Prince Jing didn't get mad at him? He just agreed?

Prince Jing wrote, *What's your name? How old are you? Why are you here?*

If he wanted to leave as soon as possible, Li Yu had no choice but to answer him. If he resisted now, he'd only be dragging himself down.

With a bitter face and a low voice, Li Yu replied, "My name is Li Yu. I'm eighteen. I'm here because..." Li Yu remembered what the system had said about changing the tyrant's personality. He couldn't mention *that*. And as for why he transmigrated into this book...

"...I don't know either."

He had no idea why he'd suddenly turned into a fish, sob sob sob!

**THE STORY CONTINUES IN**
**The Disabled Tyrant's Beloved Pet Fish**
VOLUME 2

APPENDIX

# Characters, Names, and Pronunciations

# Characters

## MAIN CHARACTERS

**LI YU 李鱼:** A modern-day webnovel reader who has been transmigrated into a fish.

**MU TIANCHI 穆天池:** The mute fifth prince, also known as Prince Jing.

## THE ROYAL FAMILY

**THE EMPEROR:** Prince Jing's father.

**EMPRESS XIAOHUI:** Prince Jing's mother; deceased.

**NOBLE CONSORT QIU 仇贵妃:** Mother of the second prince, Mu Tianzhao.

**PIAOXUE 飘雪 ("FLOATING SNOW"):** Noble Consort Qiu's cat.

**SECOND PRINCE MU TIANZHAO 穆天昭:** The oldest prince, set to become crown prince.

**THIRD PRINCE MU TIANMING 慕天明:** The second prince's rival for the role of crown prince.

**SIXTH PRINCE MU TIANXIAO 穆天晓:** Supports the third prince.

**SEVENTH PRINCE:** Unnamed, yet to come of age.

**EIGHTH PRINCE:** Unnamed, yet to come of age.

## PRINCE JING'S MANOR

**WANG XI 王喜:** A eunuch; Prince Jing's personal servant.

**CHU YANYU 楚燕羽:** Prince Jing's love interest in the original webnovel, gifted to Prince Jing by the third prince.

## CHENG'EN MANOR

**THE DUKE OF CHENG'EN 承恩公:** Ye Qinghuan's father, and a relative of the late Empress Xiaohui.

**YE QINGHUAN 叶清欢:** Prince Jing's cousin, heir to the House of Cheng'en.

**XIONGFENG 叶清欢 ("FIERCE WIND"):** Ye Qinghuan's dog.

## JINJUE ROYAL FAMILY

**KING OF JINJUE 金绝王:** Ruler of the neighboring country of Jinjue.

**PRINCESS OF JINJUE 金绝公主:** The king's daughter, whom he seeks to marry into the emperor's family.

# Name Guide

## Diminutives, Nicknames, and Name Tags:

A-: Friendly diminutive. Always a prefix. Usually for monosyllabic names, or one syllable out of a two-syllable name.

DOUBLING: Doubling a syllable of a person's name can be a nickname, e.g., "Mangmang"; it has childish or cutesy connotations.

XIAO-: A diminutive meaning "little." Always a prefix.

-ER: An affectionate diminutive added to names, literally "son" or "child." Always a suffix.

## Family:

DI/DIDI: Younger brother or a younger male friend.

GE/GEGE/DAGE: Older brother or an older male friend.

JIE/JIEJIE/ZIZI: Older sister or an older female friend.

## Other:

GONGZI: Young man from an affluent household.

-GONGGONG: A respectful suffix for eunuchs.

-SHIZI: Denoting the heir to a title.

# Pronunciation Guide

Mandarin Chinese is the official state language of mainland China, and pinyin is the official system of romanization in which it is written. As Mandarin is a tonal language, pinyin uses diacritical marks (e.g., ā, á, ǎ, à) to indicate these tonal inflections. Most words use one of four tones, though some are a neutral tone. Furthermore, regional variance can change the way native Chinese speakers pronounce the same word. For those reasons and more, please consider the guide below a simplified introduction to pronunciation of select character names and sounds from the world of *The Disabled Tyrant's Beloved Pet Fish*.

More resources are available at sevenseasdanmei.com

## GENERAL CONSONANTS

Some Mandarin Chinese consonants sound very similar, such as z/c/s and zh/ch/sh. Audio samples will provide the best opportunity to learn the difference between them.

X: somewhere between the **sh** in **sh**eep and **s** in **s**ilk

Q: a very aspirated **ch** as in **ch**arm

C: **ts** as in pan**ts**

Z: **z** as in **z**oom

S: **s** as in **s**ilk

CH: **ch** as in **ch**arm

ZH: **dg** as in do**dg**e

SH: **sh** as in **sh**ave

G: hard **g** as in **g**raphic

## GENERAL VOWELS

The pronunciation of a vowel may depend on its preceding consonant. For example, the "i" in "shi" is distinct from the "i" in "di." Vowel pronunciation may also change depending on where the vowel appears in a word, for example the "i" in "shi" versus the "i" in "ting." Finally, compound vowels are often—though not always—pronounced as conjoined but separate vowels. You'll find a few of the trickier compounds below.

IU: as in **ewe**

IE: **ye** as in **ye**s

UO: **war** as in **war**m

## CHARACTER NAMES

**Lǐ Yú:** Li (as in *ly* from merri*ly*), yu (as in you)

**Mù Tiānchí:** Mu (as in moo), t (as in tea), ian (as in Ian), chi (as in *ch* from *ch*ange)
* *Note:* With chi, the i is not pronounced like ee, the way Li is pronounced. With chi, it is a sort of emphasized ch noise without any vowel sound. This applies to z, c, s, zh, ch, sh, and s.

**Yè Qīnghuán:** Ye (as in yesterday), qing (as in *ching* from tea*ching*), h (as in *h* from *h*ello), uan (as in one)
* *Note:* The difference between ch and q is that chi is a sound produced more with the front of the teeth with a puckered mouth, while q is a sound produced more at the back, with a wider mouth.

**Noble Consort Qiu:** Q (as in *ch* from *ch*eap), iu (as in yo)

**Piāoxuě:** P (as in *p* from *peas*), iao (as in *yow* from *yowl*), x (as in *sh* from *sheep*), u (as in oo), e as in (eh)

APPENDIX

# Glossary

# Glossary

**CONCUBINES 妻妾:** In ancient China, it was common practice for a wealthy man to possess women as concubines (妾) in addition to his wife (妻). They were expected to live with him and bear him children. Generally speaking, a greater number of concubines correlated to higher social status, hence a wealthy merchant might have two or three concubines, while an emperor might have tens or even a hundred.

**DI AND SHU HIERARCHY 嫡庶:** Upper-class men in ancient China often took multiple wives, though only one would be the official or "di" wife, and her sons would take precedence over the sons of the "shu" wives. "Di" sons were prioritized in matters of inheritance.

**ANCIENT CHINESE IMPERIAL HAREM 后宫:** Emperors would take multiple wives, and as a whole, they were referred to as the "back palace." This term can also be used to refer to the physical location where the concubines lived, which was the inner half of the palace. The concubines were separated into ranks, and their ranking directly correlated to how well they were treated, how much respect they were afforded, and how much money they were given. The ranks of the concubines changed throughout the dynasties, but these remain fairly consistent and are often used in modern media:

◇ Empress 皇后
◇ Imperial Noble Consort 皇贵妃
◇ Noble Consort 贵妃
◇ Consort 妃
◇ Concubine 嫔
◇ Noble Lady 贵人

**GOLDEN FINGER** 金手指: A protagonist-exclusive overpowered ability or weapon. This can also refer to them being generally OP ("overpowered") and not a specific ability or physical item.